Y0-DBW-270

MY MOTHER, THE MERMAID CHASER

ALSO BY JAMIE JO HOANG

My Father, the Panda Killer

MY MOTHER, THE MERMAID CHASER

JAMIE JO HOANG

CROWN BOOKS
NEW YORK

Crown Books for Young Readers
An imprint of Random House Children's Books
A division of Penguin Random House LLC
1745 Broadway, New York, NY 10019
penguinrandomhouse.com
rhcbooks.com

Library of Congress Cataloging-in-Publication Data is available upon request.
ISBN 978-0-593-64300-6 (trade)—ISBN 978-0-593-64301-3 (lib. bdg.)—
ISBN 978-0-593-64302-0 (ebook)

The text of this book is set in 10.75-point Adobe Caslon Pro and 11-point Whitney.

Vintage blank open notebook by daboost/stock.adobe.com, scribble by KPstudio/stock.adobe.com, and old user interface pop-up window by YummyBuum/shutterstock.com
Interior design by Megan Shortt

Manufactured in the United States of America
1st Printing

The authorized representative in the EU for product safety and compliance is Penguin Random House Ireland, Morrison Chambers, 32 Nassau Street, Dublin D02 YH68, Ireland, https://eu-contact.penguin.ie.

For the fierce women in my life:

Mệ Khuyen Hoang
Mẹ Nancy Ha Hoang
Dì Van Thi Hoang
Chị Kimberly Kay Hoang, PhD
Em Lillyan Thuy-Tien Hoang

CONTENT NOTE:

Certain passages in this book contain depictions of abuse, violence, assault, and death. Readers may notice honorifics like O instead of Cô or name spellings like Huong as opposed to Huóng that may not be familiar. Vietnam has many different dialects; from north to south, the way we speak and spell can deviate. My family is from Đà Nẵng and Vũng Tàu respectively, so I stayed true to our regional dialect and spellings. With regard to the names of places in Vietnam, I did not use the Vietnamese spellings (except in dialogue) because I grew up with the English spellings—I kept what was familiar.

For a list of resources for victims of abuse and trauma, see page 367.

THIS BOOK IS STILL NOT
A HISTORY LESSON.

BUT IT'S MORE TRUE
THAN JANE'S STORY.

LET'S CALL IT
HISTORY ADJACENT.

CHAPTER 1
PAUL

I've never loved my parents. My mother left when I was four—no chance for love. And my dad, well, he's not real lovable. To be clear, I don't *hate* him. But love? No. We're just not that kind of family. No one in my family says "I love you." Correction. No one in my family *used* to say "I love you."

Last week, my sister, Jane, and I were watching *Just Friends,* a rom-com about a successful guy who returns home to his small town and finds that all his awkward tendencies have returned with him. Because we own the DVD, we've seen this movie at least six times, yet my sister laughed just as hard this time as she did when we first saw it. Anyway, the film ended, and Jane turned to me, eyes watering with laughter, and said, "I love you, Paul. Thanks for watching this with me."

At first, I thought I'd heard her wrong, but then this silence hung in the air, confirming that those were indeed the words she'd used. For my part, I avoided eye contact while staring at the rolling credits as though I really cared about who Jock #1 and Jock #2 were. Jane got up, grabbed my popcorn bowl, and went to the kitchen. She appeared to be acting totally normal; she seemed not to be sick in any way; she simply went about cleaning up without acknowledging this major bomb she'd just dropped in my lap. Then, yesterday, before dinner, Jane walked into the house exclaiming, "Oh my god! I love you so much! Thanks for making bún riêu with Mợ Bích. You know it's my favorite." Yes, I do know it's her favorite. I also know that our aunt, Mợ Bích, makes this meal every time Jane comes home for dinner, so it's not that special. Once is a fluke; twice is deliberate.

Not that that kept me from ignoring it a second time. Now, though, Jane is making it impossible. We're at Walmart, preparing for our trip to Vietnam. Jane came with a list. I conquered said list while she spent thirty minutes getting her eyes examined for new prescription lenses. She's checking my work when out of her mouth comes "Damn, Paul, I love you for being so efficient. Let's hit up the toy aisle, though, I forgot to add some stuffed animals."

"Why do you keep saying that?" The words shoot at her far more aggressively than I intend, but I can't help it. "Are you dying?"

"What? No. Why would you think that?"

"You know why."

"Because I'm saying 'I love you'? Does it make you uncomfortable?"

I raise an eyebrow and wait. She knows it does.

"My therapist says we need to lean into the things that make us uncomfortable. It's only weird because Dad never says it."

Neither did you until now, I think, but I keep that to myself. Obvious things don't need to be said. Especially when she's now just dropped another casual bomb. "Your *therapist*?"

"Yeah. I've been talking to someone. Processing the trauma and stuff." I don't know what to say. We don't do therapy; we suffer, laugh about suffering, and suffer some more. Jane fills the silence without skipping a beat. "I can't believe these things are only five bucks. Bears or dinosaurs? Should we get all the same, so no one is fighting over them?"

Jane looks at me. I remember I still haven't spoken. "Yeah, probably. Get the bears. They're softer," I say. My sister and I are opposites. She's big-picture, and I'm all about the small things. Like my favorite sound is the fizzing noise water makes when it streams from a faucet. Jane, on the other hand, looks at water and wants to know how it fell from the sky, rolled down a mountain, got pushed through pipes, and ended up here.

When my dad was losing his mind and beating my sister, I used to sit in the bathroom with the faucet on and concentrate on the stream of water flowing down the sink. It became the white noise I needed to muffle what was happening in the house. Because of this, it's the only time I ever feel truly calm. At some point, I realized that silence eased the tension way faster than shouting or crying. When I was young, being quiet was my only power. I clung to it so hard that now I have to remind myself to speak aloud the thoughts inside my head.

When my dad was angry, any words that spilled from my mouth were wrong. "I'm sorry" made him hit me harder. "Stop" made him hit me longer. "Okay" was met with a question, "Okay, what?" that I never had an answer to, so the punishment would continue. Then I learned to stop answering. In science class, I discovered that fires require oxygen, so instead of speaking I held my breath. And it worked. My silence cut the beating time in half.

I look at Jane and it dawns on me that she's been unusually

quiet. Typically, she asks me all kinds of questions about school, my day, our dad, food, my friends, and whatever she can think of. While in law school, she would question me the way a prosecutor might cross-examine a criminal. What started as practice is now a habit. Except today, she hasn't asked anything. No *What did you eat? Why didn't you eat an apple? I better not find them rotting in the fridge later.* "What's up with you?" I ask.

"Huh?" She startles, looking at me like she's just remembering that I came along. "What?"

"Why are you all sulky and quiet?"

"Oh. I was just thinking about all the stuff I need to get. I don't want to forget anything essential."

Lies. "You can tell me now, or I can ask you the same question over a period of twenty-two hours while you're confined to an airplane seat beside me. Let me guess. You got dumped?"

Jane avoids eye contact, pretending to be interested in the bleach-free laundry detergent in her hands. After a moment, she says, "Who has time for a boyfriend? All I do is work and worry about you."

"Ah, so you dumped him," I try. Jane has had precisely one boyfriend (that I know of), and he ended up being a dud.

She ignores me. "I bet Bác Loan would love this stuff." She puts powdered detergent in the basket, grabs some stain-remover pens, and tosses those in the cart too. We continue on through the bedding and bathroom departments, and she adds a shower curtain. The candy aisle is where she loses all self-control. Any chocolate bag with a sale sticker on it ends up in our cart. We hit the jackpot. Peanut M&M's are on clearance. While she empties the bin, I walk around the corner.

I wander down an aisle bursting with furry colors. There's something about seeing so much fluff that makes me want to pile them all in a large heap and jump on top. I resist the impulse. Near the end of the aisle, a brown bear in a green Scout's vest stops me. His left paw holds a shovel while the other hangs at his side. Smokey Bear is a California icon. I pull him down and feel the soft fur. This forest ranger bear is on billboards throughout the national parks and highways. Next to the bear I remember the phrase "Only YOU can prevent forest fires."

A memory pops into my head.

Our family was together in the car. Dad and Mom were in the front, Jane and me in the rear. I kept sliding because the towel we had laid down to cover the giant tear in the seat was slick against the cracked and tattered leather. I had no idea where we were, but outside my window, lots and lots of giant red trees swooshed by. I remember the forest looking like it was on fire without any flames. And the trees were so tall that I couldn't see where their tops met the sky.

In the front, my parents argued. My dad yelled, and my mother disagreed. Tears fell down her cheeks, but her voice rarely cracked. Beside me, teen Jane cradled me in her arms. In a calm tone, she told me a story about three little bears living in this forest. Her voice was clear and steady, excited even as she whispered about this family whose biggest concern was their porridge's temperature. I was quiet. I didn't want to be in this car. I didn't want to be in this family, and my dad was driving so erratically that I was sure we were all going to die. The urge to speak tugged at my throat, but the sentences in my head were nothing but blank spaces.

Jane's voice contrasted with the yelling, but the two meld together as distinctly and clearly as if the car ride had been yesterday. My parents argued in Vietnamese. My sister told me the "Three Little Bears" story in English.

"If you don't know things, you should keep your mouth shut," my dad barked.

"That was not a good deal for us. If you had let me negotiate, I would've gotten a better deal. Now we're paying for a year at this high price. You listen to him because he's white, and he rips us off because he thinks we're stupid."

"Shut up. You know nothing, but you keep talking." *Shut up* is benign in English, but in Vietnamese, it's more akin to a booming *Silence!*

"Once upon a time, in a redwood forest full of trees as wide and tall as these . . ." Jane pointed to the outside as though seeing might override hearing what was happening in the front seat. "In this forest, there lived three bears. A momma bear, a papa bear, and a baby bear. The momma bear, being the momma, made their porridge, and then, for some reason, they had to leave the house." I knew this story pretty well, and even though Jane was butchering it, I didn't correct her. In hindsight, I think she hoped I might interject and start a fun debate that would keep my attention glued to our fantasy world. But I wanted to hear the fight. I wanted to know why my mother was about to leave us. Okay, I probably didn't think that because I couldn't have known she was going to, but I certainly think about it now. "This golden-haired girl broke into the house because people have no respect for bears. And she ate all three of their bowls of bear porridge!"

"I'm not dumb." My mother's voice was firm. I wonder if she meant to say this more to herself than to my dad. I've been told my whole life that my mother was a wallflower, but in this memory, I know that can't be true. In this memory, she is as hot as the trees outside. Her anger is as red as the burning leaves. Arguments in our family usually contain few words. Yet I remember their voices filling the air, making it thick with suffocating fumes.

Suddenly, the car shifted gears and sped up, weaving between and around slower vehicles. SUVs full of camping gear and perfect families honked at us.

No one spoke.

Vroom.

Jane's hand gripped my shoulder—too tight, scarily tight.

Finally, my mom broke the silence. Her tone was even, unafraid. Resolved, maybe? "Stop the car. Do you want to die? Die if you want to, but don't take us with you."

These back-to-back commands were sharp. My mother came to life, which was both exhilarating and utterly frightening. How could she not see that talking to my dad like this would only egg him on? Maybe she did. Maybe that was the point.

Somehow, all the other tourists abandoned us on the open road. Our car zoomed forward in a blur. I gripped my elbows, bracing myself for the pain of being mangled inside crunched metal.

Then a voice. Loud enough to be heard but low enough to be humble. "Ba, stop." It was my sister's gentle, even tone that caused the car to slow. The road ahead was curved with bendy twists meant to be taken at a speed far below what we were going. As the car slowed, I saw California's iconic mascot—Smokey Bear. The way the bear pointed, it was like he was singling out my dad and telling him to stop. When I was little, I believed Smokey Bear stopped my dad that day, but now I know it was Jane. She had a knack for calming situations fraught with tension; incidents sparked by anger that had nothing to do with us. My sister and I were nothing but collateral damage. The more our parents fought, the harder we clung to each other.

This is one of only a few memories I have of my mom, but my mom is not what tugs me back to this moment. My parents couldn't give two shits about me. Jane was the only person in the car who cared about me, the only one who loved me. This is how I know I don't love my parents. Because Jane is love and Jane is nothing like either of them.

I squeeze the paw between my fingers and listen as Smokey says, "Only YOU can prevent wildfires."

"Yo, what's the holdup?" Jane asks, disrupting the memory. She looks from me to the bear.

"Do you remember this bear?" I ask.

"Yeah, it's Smokey Bear. He's on like a million billboards everywhere. So what?"

I wait a beat to see if she'll connect it to that day in the forest. When she doesn't, I return the bear to the shelf and follow her around the corner. "No reason. It's a good slogan, though."

We park in the driveway to our town house and carry the haul inside. Jane and I pack everything we bought into boxes and weigh them. We make sure they're exactly fifty pounds—the maximum weight for checked luggage—and then fill the trunk of her Honda CR-V. I can't believe that in five hours, we're going to be on an airplane.

We're loading up the car when a maroon Toyota Camry pulls up. My best friends have arrived. Joe puts the car in park and Mai jumps out with a small blue gift bag that matches the tank top she's wearing under a V-neck T-shirt.

"Thank god we didn't miss you. Grandpa over there had to basically park the car at every stop sign on the way over even though we could see for miles that no one was around," Mai says.

"Rules are rules." Joe shrugs.

"I'm with Joe," Jane says before walking to the house.

Using her hand, Mai mimes blabbering behind Jane's head. "I had this dream last night that we went with you, and you were sitting in a tree but wouldn't come down. Joe gave me a lift, but when I finally reached the branch you were perched on, you dropped down from the tree like it was nothing. Then I was the one who couldn't get down!"

"What does that even mean?" I ask. I look at Joe, who appears equally perplexed.

"It means *Don't go climbing any trees because I'm not saving you*," Mai replies.

"Noted." I laugh. She hands me the gift and I open it. Inside is a roll of garlic in white mesh. Beside the garlic is a small laminated card with a picture of Mary on one side and the Hail Mary prayer on the other. "Seriously? You want me to put garlic in my suitcase?"

"Trust me, dude. Native spirits are strong. Plus, you're returning home, so they're really gonna be tryin' to grab at you." Joe's hands make two claws like he's a ghost grabbing hold of a soul. His wide eyes and serious expression say he isn't joking. Joe is Filipino, but I swear sometimes he's part Vietnamese. Vietnamese people use garlic for everything. Need a cure for a cough? There's garlic tea. Dislocate your shoulder? There's a garlic paste rub. Need an immune system boost? There's a garlic shot.

Putting up his hand to high-five me, Joe pulls me into a hug. His hugs are the very definition of a bear hug, and even though I'm used to it now, I'm not exactly comfortable, *which* is the reason he really emphasizes the embrace. "Just rub it on your clothes when you get off the plane, trust me. Have a safe trip, bro. Summer's gonna suck without you." I push away, and he squeezes me tighter before finally letting go.

I give Mai a quick "Vietnamese" hug—aka no lingering. "You thought this was a good idea too?" I ask, holding up the garlic.

"I'm all about preventive measures," Mai says before shoving her hands in her jean pockets. "All right, go inside before Jane flips a lid because you're forty-five seconds late."

I nod, feeling the love. They hop in Joe's car, and I wave as they drive away, realizing this is the first summer since I've known them that we're spending apart. *It's only a month,* I tell myself. *How much can change in a month?*

CHAPTER 2

NGỌC LAN

"Let's see. How to begin? I guess I'll start where you did."

Jane folds her legs up so they're crisscrossed on the couch. "You're not going to change my mind about her, Paul."

"I listened to you tell me Dad's story, a lot of which was inaccurate, by the way, and now you need to listen to me tell Mom's, er, Ngọc Lan's," I say.

"Why can't we just watch a movie?" Jane mocks.

"Because you're not seven. Plus, I embarrassed the crap out of myself speaking Englanese in Vietnam to get this info," I say.

Jane laughs knowingly. "I'm sure you did."

"Laugh it up, sister, and then get comfortable because we're going to set the record straight-er."

Spirits in Vietnam are bold. Two thousand years of occupation meant that heartache and pain were a normal part of life, and nothing tastes better to a lost shadow than despair.

This was why Ngọc Lan awoke every morning kicking her feet at the air like she was fighting off an attacker. Born feisty, twelve-year-old Ngọc Lan was determined not to be taken easily. At the foot of the bed, Chị Diễm's giggles turned to howls of laughter as she watched her younger sister's eyes burst open in fright.

"Isn't she Dì Diễm to us?"

"We're gonna be here for days if you keep this up. Just humor me with the titles. It's better this way."

"Go on," Jane huffs.

"Wake up, dead person," Chị Diễm said between fits of hiccups *she* now couldn't contain.

"If you're not careful I might kick you in the face," Ngọc Lan warned. She never understood why her sister taunted her when she herself was afraid of ghosts.

In 1975, the American War in Vietnam had been going on for nearly a decade. Before that, Vietnam fought off China, Cambodia, Laos, Japan, and most recently France. But the Hà sisters knew and cared little about politics. Life for them was a game, made fun by the joyous antics of their brother, Anh Hòa.

In the kitchen, a mud room with pots and pans dangling from the chicken-wire fence, seventeen-year-old Anh Hòa cut pieces of twig for the three of them to chew on. Unlike his sisters, Anh Hòa was militant about time, and they were late. "Đi,"[1] he said, trying to rush them. He wanted to reach the gas station before dawn.

While they biked, they brushed their teeth using these twigs that softened with saliva and frayed into thin pieces that slid between the cracks, like floss.

As the eldest, Anh Hòa took it upon himself to look after his sisters. His square face, when not smiling, was typically adrift in thought. He was always thinking ahead, always plotting. Chị Diễm, the middle sibling, was fifteen going on thirty. She was the most proper of the three. Never hurried, she always combed her hair and kept her chin perfectly straight when sitting, even while reading. Their mom, Mẹ, said Chị Diễm belonged in a different era. Then came the youngest, Ngọc Lan. She was the wild boar of the family; every morning, she left the house clean and returned filthier than a pig.

Different as they were, they got along extremely well. So well, in fact, that Ngọc Lan could tell something was wrong with Anh Hòa. She steered her too-big bike around a large puddle and raced to catch up to Chị Diễm.

"What's wrong with Anh Hòa?" Ngọc Lan whispered.

"He's probably just sad," Chị Diễm said.

Ngọc Lan nodded. She, too, had been feeling heavy with grief. Their most militant (and favorite) uncle, Bác Dạy, whose six gunshot wounds made everyone believe he was invincible, had succumbed to his seventh and final bullet. They'd buried him the year before.

---

1 *"Let's go."*

Their uncle's death was not the first time a family member had been killed; there were other uncles, cousins, cousins of cousins, siblings of friends, et cetera. But years later, when Ngọc Lan learned that Bác Dạy died on January 6, 1974—exactly one year before the northernmost province of South Vietnam fell to the Communists—she would mark his death as the beginning. A turning point, a bend, that would turn her life away from home. Away from everything she ever loved.

Anh Hòa abruptly halted. "Slow your pedaling," he said, while also motioning with his hand.

The girls coasted on lightly spinning wheels until the clunks and squeals of rusted metal tapping in rotation blended into the quiet terrain, and waited for him to explain. "Shhh," he said as they came to a complete stop. Anh Hòa stared at each girl with wide, slowly blinking eyes. "Feel that? Right beneath your rib cage?"

The sisters shook their heads. Each too afraid to check her stomach.

Anh Hòa nodded as if confirming that something was, in fact, among them. An animal scurried through the brush. Ngọc Lan's spine tingled. Then Anh Hòa peered at the sky, returned his gaze to the girls, and said, "It's Bác Dạy returning to grasp your meaty flesh!" Chị Diễm looked down, turning pale, and both girls cried out at the phantom fingers tickling their skin.

"Anh, tell him to stop!" Chị Diễm shrieked while brushing away at her shirt so vigorously that Ngọc Lan thought the fabric might rip.

Anh Hòa's stoic face broke into a laugh.

"Bác Dạy, ơi! Come over here. My little sisters don't want to play." Anh Hòa waved, staring at the space behind Chị Diễm. To lure their uncle's spirit, Anh Hòa lifted his shirt to tickle his own ribs. All three siblings followed the phantom as it slumped over to Anh Hòa. "Remember to thank me later for saving you," Anh Hòa sang as he hopped back on his bike and sped off.

Spirits were always lurking in Vietnam. They were most brazen, though, following a death. Given this, Anh Hòa saw it as his duty to toughen his sisters up—to prepare them for the horror that loomed with every rising sun. And not just from paranormal activity.

Oftentimes, Anh Hòa pretended that bombs were dropping from the clouds. He would point up to the sky, jump from his bike, and huddle with his sisters in the ditches that ran parallel to the dirt roads to prevent flooding. While they hid beneath clear skies, he made bombing noises—*boom, pow, shhpsh.* In this tiny sliver of space, where the three siblings formed a dash, they were invisible. "From up there, they cannot see such a thin line. This is why we duck like this."

The game was so effective that when actual bombs came dropping and explosions turned the land into clouds of dust that choked their lungs, the three siblings lay flat against the ditch, face down, while Anh Hòa coughed out, "Aha, see, they can't touch us!" And the girls believed him.

Ngọc Lan's siblings were the reason she loved biking twenty kilometers to collect gas—long before any of her classmates had stretched themselves awake. She would do anything to stay close to her brother and sister.

Once they had purchased the gas, daylight chased them back to the beach. On the shore, Anh Hòa scanned the horizon for the flicker of a flame sparked by a Zippo lighter. One, two, three, four times meant a fisherman needed fuel. Using the family's large basket boat, Anh Hòa then paddled out to sell his goods.

Then came time for the second part of their job: collecting mussels and clams. Ngọc Lan drew in a deep breath as she did every morning. Having tasted air filled with dust, she knew the value of pure, clean oxygen. She stared out at the blue-and-orange horizon, thinking about how normal certain pockets of time could feel—how peaceful.

"Ready?" Chị Diễm asked.

"Đi." Ngọc Lan nodded. The two sisters dove for the water, their feet sliding beneath the surface simultaneously. Both girls loved to swim. Part of growing up in a fishing village meant swimming was a skill as natural, and necessary, as breathing. Ngọc Lan chased Chị Diễm's beautiful fishtail braid as her sister glided around coral, pointing out two tiny pink shrimp scuttling across its membrane. Relaxing her arms, Ngọc Lan kicked as they swam toward the rocks, a dangerous endeavor for the best of swimmers.

The siblings were bold divers because in water they felt protected. "When you are lost, find water," their mother would say when any of them were distraught. Water, they were told, was a vital resource for life but also a conduit to their ancestors.

Carefully twisting the smooth shells anchored by byssal threads, they filled two large bags of clams by the time Anh Hòa had sold his last liter of gas.

Before school, they returned home to change, dropping off the clams so their mother could sell or trade them at the market. When they entered, they found their father sitting at the table. As an architect for the US Army, he came home only sporadically, and his presence sharpened the normally relaxed atmosphere.

Mẹ's words immediately raced through Ngọc Lan's mind: *He provides for us,* her mom would say; *Be respectful; Honor your father,* her mom would say. There were rules that existed only when he was home. Ngọc Lan did her best to comply. She smiled wide, speaking with enthusiasm despite feeling timid and anxious inside.

"Dear Ba, I have returned home." Ngọc Lan bowed.

At the door, Chị Diễm followed, bowing to their father, Ba, in greeting. She smiled brightly before adding, "Anh Hòa, Ba came home for your birthday."

"Is today your birthday? Happy birthday, son," Ba said. Ngọc Lan's heart swelled with joy and deflated just as quickly. Today was not Anh Hòa's birthday, his birthday was tomorrow. Their father didn't remember. Not that this should have been a surprise. Ba had never cared for birthdays.

"Chào Ba. Thank you," Anh Hòa greeted his father.

"Today we'll register you for the army," Ba said. He spoke these words as freely as one might say *Today, we'll pick up a loaf of bread.*

"Ba, are you hungry? Have you eaten yet?" Ngọc Lan asked. Her father waved her question away.

Like her siblings, Ngọc Lan carefully hid her true self when their father was home. She combed her hair, donned Chị Diễm's shirts (the ones with the stiff collars), and spoke only of things she knew would make him proud. The children never spoke of work. Their father provided for the family, end of story.

Mẹ emerged from her room just then, her eyes bloodred and puffy. Ngọc Lan's stomach dropped. In her mother's hands was a brown satchel filled with Anh Hòa's belongings. The kids all looked at their father.

"Đi" was all he said. Let's go.

"Where am I going?" Anh Hòa asked, the quiver in his voice unmistakable.

"I just told you. It's time to join the army."

No! Ngọc Lan cried, but the word never formed.

Mẹ draped the bag across Anh Hòa's shoulders. "Be safe."

Irritated, Ba huffed, "It's just registration. We'll be back for dinner."

"Wait!" Chị Diễm shouted. She ran inside and came back out with Anh Hòa's birthday present. For weeks, the girls had collected extra clams to pay for the miniature hand-carved elephant. Ngọc Lan's favorite part was the gleaming red apple curled in its trunk.

"Happy birthday, Anh Hòa," Chị Diễm said, cupping the elephant in her hands and gently placing it in her brother's palm.

"Whoa!" Anh Hòa beamed. "Thank you both, little sisters."

Ba turned on his heel and walked away. Anh Hòa followed.

Ngọc Lan's eyes moved from her brother to her father, wondering how two people who looked so much alike could be polar opposites in nature.

Unable to watch the father and son leave, Mẹ returned inside, where a feast of foods unlike anything Ngọc Lan had ever seen was being prepared.

"Mẹ, Anh Hòa is coming back, right?" Ngọc Lan asked.

"Mm," Mẹ said, but Ngọc Lan could tell she wasn't sure.

CHAPTER 3
PAUL

I got played. Man, I got played so hard. I knew Jane was acting weird for a reason. Now I know it was guilt. Jane was being nice because she knows ditching me on this trip is breaking the sibling code. Being the older one, she's supposed to be a buffer. Now, instead of us being a duo of misfits, I'm a hostage. Kidnapped at sixteen because I have no say in my own life. The handcuffs are invisible, but the shackles are real. With Jane I could sneak off to the beach or market or wherever. Without her, I'm stuck going wherever my dad goes, and he never does anything fun.

To make matters worse, I'm crammed in the middle seat between a random dude by the window and my dad in the aisle seat. Jane knows what she did is jacked up. That's why she waited until we were at the airport to tell me she wasn't coming. If I had been paying attention, I would've noticed that we only had four checked suitcases. No Vietnamese family travels back to Vietnam without maxing out the free baggage allowance. I know she thinks this tote of bribes she gave me makes up for her betrayal, but she is dead wrong. Inside, I found a leather-bound notebook, a Motorola Razr, and a brand-new Nintendo DS with my three favorite games: *Pokémon, Tetris,* and *The Legend of Zelda*. There is also a stack of converted money that I don't dare count in public. I'm surprised TSA didn't check me for drugs, the stack is *that* thick.

The phone vibrates in my hand. I flip it open. There are four unread text messages.

From: Jane

First: Don't be mad.

From: Jane

Second: Text as much as you want. I'll pay for it.

From: Jane

Third: Okay be mad, but also be open. Vietnam is an adventure.

From: Jane

Fourth: Answer me!

I was softening until that last message. I close the phone knowing it'll irritate her to not get a response. Yeah. I'm just going to let that one sit for a while.

The airplane door shuts. A gentle whirring and rumble hums beneath my seat. The plane pushes back. Emergency procedures are mimed by flight attendants who look bored as we pause on the runway. The crew takes their seats, the engine hisses to life, and we shoot forward. I feel a pressure on my chest as we defy gravity and leave the earth.

There are a bunch of different movies I could watch, most I haven't seen, because our family lives in a vortex of the past. New movies cost a lot of money, between gas to get to the theater and ticket prices, but a DVD can be as cheap as five bucks in the discount bins. Even still, Jane likes to watch the same four rom-coms over and over again. Old habits die hard.

When the drink cart comes around, I order a V8 juice. Selling soda at the liquor store we own and having access to it whenever I want means I've pretty much drunk a lifetime's worth of it. I tried to get Dad to stock juices, but they're like three times the price! Bottled juice is for rich people. But on this plane, it's free, so that's what I'm having.

I won't lie, the games are helpful, because the one thing I've got plenty of now is time. Getting to Vietnam takes twenty-two hours with all the layovers. That's right, *twenty-two hours*. After which, I will arrive in a country where I only passively speak the language and everyone I know is old.

My palms are sweaty and we've only been flying for an hour. I rub them on my jeans, feeling moisture cling to the hair in my armpits. I need more space. A person who is 5'10" should never ever be forced to sit in the middle seat. I shift a little, doing my best to stretch upward rather than sideways, and notice that virtually every other window shade on the plane is open. Every one *but* ours. Is it rude to lean over the guy next to me and lift the shade? I mean just because he's sitting next to the window doesn't mean he owns that window, right?

I reach over, just as the man takes a sharp intake of air and wakes himself up. His eyes open and he stares at me, glances at my arm, and leans back, shaking his head. I drop my arm.

Technically, having my dad on the other side should be an added comfort; it's not. For one, he snores. Two, he sleeps with his mouth agape. And three, he's been having some intense nightmares for the last month.

I know this is going to sound weird as shit, but I've started watching him "rest," knowing that as soon as he hits that deep dream state the terrors will begin. The first time it happened, he was asleep on the couch at three in the morning when I came down for some water.

"Uuuh, yauh, uh," he mumbled.

"What?" I asked. No answer.

"Uuuuh!"

I jumped away and then leaned over the couch half expecting to see my dad's face contort into a creepy smile—horror movie style. What I saw was so much worse. He looked like a petrified skeleton, both afraid and in pain as he struggled against an invisible demon that kept him pinned to the couch.

"Dad!" I said firmly, and he jerked awake.

"Huh?" he yelped. His eyes opened and I know for damn sure that he saw me, because we locked eyes, but then he just rolled over and fell back into the fever dream. It was almost as though he wanted to return to his demons, like he was determined to fight them off, and that really intrigued me. I couldn't look away! I've never been scared, because ghosts aren't real in *America*. Yes, that's what I've decided. My aunt, Mợ Bích, used to tell me stories of hauntings from her childhood in Vietnam. Mostly it was when she "bị ma đè"[2] and she couldn't move because the ghost pressed on her, causing paralysis. If I think too hard about what Mợ Bích is saying, I get chills, so I tell myself, *Terrors are just our brains misfiring and causing us to "see" things that aren't actually there*. Jane taught me that.

Anyway, Dad's room is two feet from my own, so I know these dreams have only started recently. I'd ask him about them, but then I'd have to admit I've been sleep snooping and I'm not about to do that. I'm thinking, though, I bet my dad has some guilt that's eating away at his brain and causing his imagination to go wild. He's done some bad shit. I should know, Jane and I were often on the other end of brutal beatings he used to give. I've never told Jane this, but I sometimes listened from the stairs when he hit her, and he'd repeat this phrase over and over. He'd say "Đứng yên," like it was a mantra. As I'm watching him struggle with the demons in his head, I wonder if they're telling him to "be still" also. It would explain why even though his body seems to be fighting, he never moves much.

My dad is not a large man, but he's an imposing one. Especially when I was young, the way he hit me made him feel like a ten-foot monster. He was the embodiment of all my fears. His strikes, when they landed, were painful, shocking, and emotionally numbing. Afterward, I'd be so angry. I still am when I think about it. What possesses a man to inflict that kind of hurt on his own children?

---

2 *was ghost pressed*

More than once, I've wondered if maybe we weren't biologically his. It would explain why he was so mean to us after our mom left. We are, though, I can see him when I look at myself in the mirror. Before Jane left, I mostly witnessed her absorbing the lashings, but then came my turn—until I put a stop to it.

I remember it was late winter because the tile floors felt cold against my bare feet. That day, instead of kneeling on the floor as I was told, I handed him the stick (this is how jacked up Vietnamese parents are, they make you go get the object they plan to beat you with and give it to them, *with deference*) and spun around to face him.

"Kneel down," he said.

"No."

The rod swung back and came flying toward me way faster than I had anticipated, but I blocked it nonetheless. After the wood hit my forearm, adrenaline kicked in. Instead of retreating, I lunged at him, taking the stick and throwing it on the floor.

He stepped back, pointed a finger at me, and said, "You just wait."

I knew a shitstorm was brewing but I didn't care. This abuse for no legitimate reason was bullshit, and at fourteen I was already a few inches taller than him. Like how pathetic was I to be looking down at the person hitting me and not be able to stand up for myself? I didn't think about the consequences; I legit felt stupid letting a man three-quarters my size beat me up—it was humiliating even if no one else ever saw it.

That night, while I was sleeping, he came into my room and struck my thigh so hard I swore thunder had just clapped down beside me; then the burning sensation kicked in. I clutched my leg as he yanked the blanket off my body.

Thigh, thigh,

calf,

ankle,

thigh, calf.

He left welts all along my left side. My bedroom window faced the backyard, and I remember staring out at the trees and wondering what it would be like to bite into a lemon. That's how bad the beating was. I don't know the psychology behind why absurd thoughts kept the pain at bay, but they did. I later learned that acid can actually ignite a fire, which to me was all kinds of hilarious. Without humor there is no surviving abuse. A knocking on the wall made him stop. Mợ Bích.

"Don't wake up the neighbors," she hissed through the wall. He got in a few more wallops for good measure, or maybe to show me that he stopped when he wanted to and not when anyone told him to. Then my dad dropped the stick on the floor and left. Wild, right? He actually left it on the floor. That's how confident he was that I would never hit him back. And he was right.

That was by far the worst beating he's ever given me. My left arm and leg felt like appendages attached to me for the mere purpose of causing me pain. But I didn't care. I stood up for myself and the dynamic in our house shifted.

He hasn't hit me since. When I was a kid his anger was suffocating. His presence had this amazing ability to wordlessly fill the air with inescapable heat and rage. After he beat me lying down, it was like he'd excised all his demons in one big manic blowout and didn't need to hit me anymore. Would I still flinch if he raised a hand? Probably. But am I mad proud of myself for standing up to him? Hell yeah.

This is why it's strange to see him looking petrified and small. I don't know how I feel about it.

The plane lurches. I hate turbulence. To distract myself, I open up the Nintendo DS and pop in the *Tetris* cartridge. This game may be old, but I love it. I like seeing the completed rows fall away.

Zzz, inhale, *zzzz,* breathing, *zzzzz.*

How can someone snore so loudly and not wake themselves up?

"Huh!"

Spoke too soon. My dad's head jerks upward, and he registers that he's on a plane before closing his eyes to drift off once again.

As his breath returns to a normal slumber, my eyes meander toward the open window across the aisle. The night sky is black, with the occasional red blinking from a light on the plane's wing. I return to *Tetris*. This is going to be a looooong flight.

I'm killing it on level 57 when the guy next to me aggressively places his arm on the armrest between us. I nudge his arm off, figuring he's asleep anyway, and the bastard puts it back up, *with* his eyes still closed. As I stretch upward, the only space that's fully mine, I see a dark gray face pop up on the screen of the person sitting across the aisle in front of us. There's a girl with long black hair coming forward, a scene from *The Grudge*. I'm so engrossed in the film that I don't notice the passenger who is now looking directly at me. *When did she turn around?* Her face is so startling that I jump a little, because she has the same blank stare and long jet-black hair as the chick on the screen. I blink. When I open my eyes again the screen is dark and the girl is no longer facing me. And *yet* I swear I can feel her eyes still on me. The weight of my DS drops forward, knocking my cup over and spilling V8 across my table. Crap.

The juice drips everywhere off the sides, eerily resembling blood. Shaken, I lean forward to grab napkins, except my body doesn't comply. I'm stuck, frozen in place as the liquid stains everything around me. *What is happening right now?* My mind focuses on lifting my arms, but they remain limp. It's like I'm in an invisible straitjacket, except I also can't speak. This pressure on me, it doesn't feel cold—quite the opposite, it feels warm. I can't believe I'm saying this, but it feels a lot like Joe's bear hug.

Suddenly, the pressure releases and cold air spills across my torso.

My body jolts inward, my knees hit the table, and my Nintendo drops to the floor. I suck in a deep breath, then look around for a person, or some sign that I'm conscious and this is reality. No one meets my gaze. A plane full of passengers and I'm the only one not sleeping. The chick across the way has blond hair. Wasn't it black a minute ago? Hang on, what happened to my juice? My cup is tucked neatly into the seat pocket in front of me. There's no mess.

My mind is spinning. I lean fully over my dad, check the aisle, and see two attendants working in the back. I pinch my forearm as hard as I can. My voice confirms that I'm awake with an "Ow."

Mợ Bích's and Joe's stories about ghosts poke at the edge of my thoughts, and before common sense has a chance to intervene, I'm thinking, *Holy shit, was that a ghost pressing?*

I push my head into the headrest as my leg bounces with anxiety and try to focus on other things. I'm supposed to be hanging out with my friends this summer; I got my license this past November when I turned sixteen. My free time is supposed to be filled with mini golf and giant overpriced turkey legs at the county fair. Not paranormal experiences or whatever this is. *Stop.* I kick the thought away, but Joe's voice rings loud in my ears: *Dude, I gave you the garlic.*

I reach for my wallet to prove to myself that his other talisman didn't work anyway, only to find it's not there. I stupidly packed the Hail Mary prayer card into the zipper lining of my checked suitcase. Well, shit.

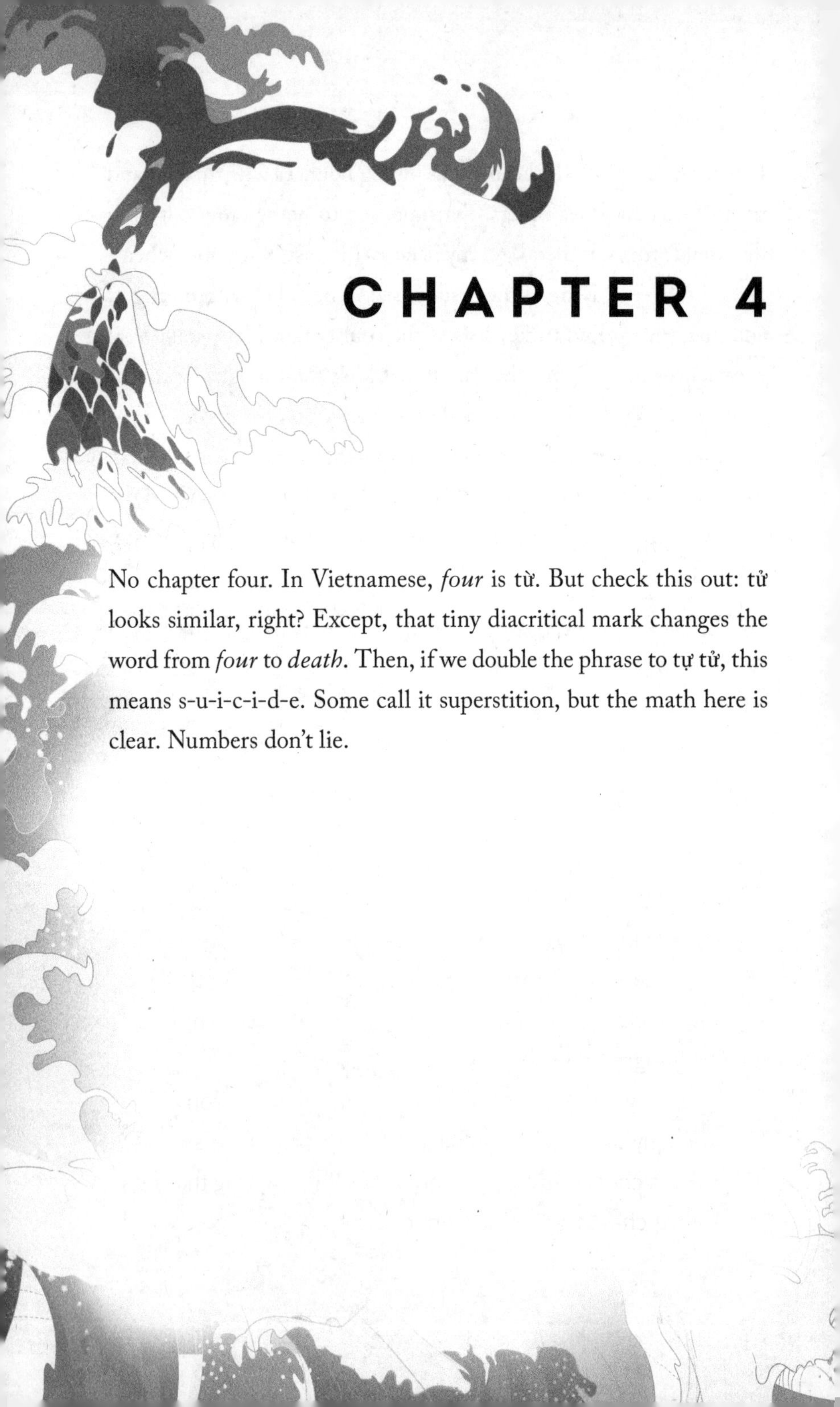

CHAPTER 4

No chapter four. In Vietnamese, *four* is tứ. But check this out: tử looks similar, right? Except, that tiny diacritical mark changes the word from *four* to *death*. Then, if we double the phrase to tự tử, this means s-u-i-c-i-d-e. Some call it superstition, but the math here is clear. Numbers don't lie.

CHAPTER 5

NGỌC LAN

Anh Hòa returned that evening with their dad, Ba. The relief Ngọc Lan saw on her mother's face confirmed what she'd suspected earlier—her mother had prepared a feast in the hope that Anh Hòa would return. But she didn't know. Her mother's helplessness angered Ngọc Lan. Why didn't she stand up to their father? Why didn't she protect her children? How was it that her mother could haggle with strangers to find the best deals, but she could not convince her husband not to enlist her son in the war? Ngọc Lan wanted to ask these questions, but she was afraid of being punished. She too was a coward. Following her mother's example, Ngọc Lan said nothing.

That night the three siblings lay on the floor listening to their parents' angry whispers.

"You're gone three, four months, and then you come home and take my son to war?" their mother hissed. Hope swelled in Ngọc Lan's chest. Perhaps her mother was preserving their dad's ego by not chastising him in front of them.

"Each family has to make sacrifices. If every father kept their sons at home, who would fight?"

"Anh already took himself to battle. This family has offered the war enough," Mẹ retorted.

"Em cannot be this selfish."

"Anh is not a true father."

CRACK.

Silence.

Footsteps. Their father left the house.

Ngọc Lan curled herself more tightly into Anh Hòa's shoulder. She sobbed quietly into his shirt because in this moment she knew her mother had lost. In the morning, Anh Hòa would leave and that was that.

"Don't cry more," Anh Hòa whispered. "There's nothing to worry about. It's okay." Anh Hòa wanted to shield the girls from their father's violence. This wasn't the first time their father had hit their mother. In fact, it had become so typical during his visits that they knew exactly what would happen next. First, tempers roared, a palm met a face, and their mother fell silent. Then their father would leave the house. In the morning, he would appear beside them on the sleeping mat that the family shared. There would be no further discussion.

Ngọc Lan grew more and more anxious. She knew what happened to brothers sent off to fight—if they returned, they never came back whole. One classmate's brother had to have his leg amputated. A friend's brother was blinded by shrapnel. Another classmate's sister, a medic, was killed en route to gather more supplies. In war, no one was safe.

After breakfast, Mẹ handed Anh Hòa a cross-body satchel filled with his favorite foods. While the family ate, she collected all the best food preserves, like chả and xôi.[3] The small tubes of boiled pork sausage wrapped in banana leaves would give him energy. The sweet sticky rice cooked in coconut milk would remind him that he was loved. Mẹ had heard of men being captured by the North and forced to work without food until their bodies, slimmed to skeletons, crumbled into a pile of bones. She knew she could never pack enough food to keep him healthy if that happened, but if every ounce consumed meant another day of survival, she would give him everything they had.

As Anh Hòa hugged each of his sisters, he slipped some of the rations into their pockets. When Chị Diễm started to protest, he said, "Don't," with a curtness neither had heard from him before. Then they stood helplessly as their father and brother began the three-kilometer trek to the bus stop.

By this time, so many people had died that it was hard to feel patriotic. Anh Hòa's departure was heavy with fear and uncertainty. No one dared to say farewell.

"Bring back a sister-in-law!" Chị Diễm shouted, angry that her last images of Anh Hòa were blurred through tears.

"And candy," Ngọc Lan added in the happiest tone she could muster. Anh Hòa laughed, waving both arms joyously.

---

3 *pork roll and sweet rice*

"Be careful," Mẹ whispered to herself.

Dressed in long pants, his usual button-down shirt, and sandals, Anh Hòa looked more like someone going to the beach than a soldier about to face gunfire. Ngọc Lan tried to imagine him with a weapon strapped across his chest and ammo on his belt. Her mind couldn't picture it.

The moment their father and Anh Hòa turned a bend, disappearing from sight, Ngọc Lan's whole world changed. Ba's absence was routine. He left for months, then returned for less time than he was gone. But Anh Hòa's departure made every room cold, every street desolate, and every bike ride solemn.

Chị Diễm and Ngọc Lan worked tirelessly to maintain the business. They wanted to prove they were just as capable as Anh Hòa. They wanted to make him proud. But the sellers, not knowing the girls, didn't trust them. They didn't think the girls, being female, could handle the physical labor and secure the transport of cargo as precious as gasoline. Within the week, the girls had not only lost the ability to buy gas, they'd also lost the last of their supplies to boat owners who took the gas, promised to pay, and then pretended they had paid already.

At the end of the month, when school tuition fees were due, Mẹ was unable to make up for Anh Hòa's lost income. Their father believed the money he sent was enough—it wasn't. If the kids wanted to go, they needed to pay for it themselves. However, trade was inconsistent, ebbing and flowing depending on US military aid and the health of crops. And in the months before the end of the war, Mẹ felt a downward economic shift, though she didn't yet know that it meant the war was nearing its end. What she did know was that the family could only afford to send one girl. Chị Diễm would have to go alone.

"No," Chị Diễm said, when Mẹ broke the news.

"Did Mẹ ask you?" her mother scolded. "Tomorrow you will return to school and thank the heavens and the earth for your good fortune."

Ngọc Lan did her best not to cry. She didn't much care for school and was happy not to go, but she'd already lost her brother—she didn't want to lose Chị Diễm too.

"For what? This month you scrape together enough and then what about next month? What's the point of school if we're going to starve to death anyway?" This was the most forceful Ngọc Lan had ever seen her sister be with their mom. The sisters didn't want to be separated. They didn't want to risk losing the last and closest connection they had—each other.

"You want to be dumb? You want to go out into the street not knowing how to read or write and let people make fun of you?" Mẹ shouted. Her roar was loud, but her trembling shoulders belied the confidence in her voice. She was scared too.

Chị Diễm softened her demeanor but leveled her gaze and said, "I'm not dumb. I don't need a teacher to teach me. I will teach myself."

Both Mẹ and Ngọc Lan were shocked by this—Mẹ because

Chị Diễm rarely disobeyed, and Ngọc Lan because in this moment her sister had transformed from a bird into a phoenix, fierce and steadfast. When Chị Diễm spread her wings, Ngọc Lan felt protected. Without Anh Hòa to stand behind, Chị Diễm stepped into her role as eldest sibling, which apparently meant she was done with school.

No one offered to send Ngọc Lan in place of her sister. School was never her passion. Delighted in the hours they could now spend in the water, Ngọc Lan pushed the frightful thoughts of her brother's demise out of her head and, determined to prove that she was useful, dove deeper and deeper to forage for seaweed and shellfish. Bold and unafraid, Ngọc Lan pushed the limits of her lungs daily. She held her breath for so long, in fact, that when bombs rained down around her, Ngọc Lan didn't notice. She had been gliding underwater for three blissful minutes, weaving through schools of parrotfish, while collecting clam after clam. A force pushed her forward with a jolt, and the impact kicked the air from her lungs. Her eyes peered upward. Ngọc Lan accidentally sipped salt water and knew immediately she was in trouble.

Pushing for the surface, which was still impossibly far, she stretched toward the light.

Air.

Gone.

Lungs.

Collapsing.

Water.

Rising.

Breath.

Impossible.

Sinking.

Blackout.

"Breathe!"

Blink.

Light.

Blinding.

Expulsion.

Sand.

Conscious.

Hhhhhh. Inhale. Ngọc Lan pulled air into her lungs to inflate them. Spicy pepper granules scratched her insides as she gulped life into her limp body. Chị Diễm panted as she frantically sat her sister up, relieved to see her eyes open. With tears choking her words, Chị Diễm whispered, "You scared me half to death."

"Why'd you have to press so hard? I think you broke my ribs," Ngọc Lan said.

"Serves you right. When I pulled you from the water, your face was so pale I thought you were dead already."

"Our ancestors were watching out for me." Ngọc Lan looked inland. She hoped they were doing the same for her brother. Smoke billowed toward the sky. Ash rained down on the city in a flutter of gray snowflakes.

In a different world, under other circumstances, it might have been scenic, magical even—like those snowy mountaintops tourists liked to pose in front of. She put out her hand and watched a flaky crumb of gray fall into her palm. Was this ash from a tree or ash from a corpse? She didn't know. But her siblings had roasted many flat fish and crisp crackling squid over a fire, and none smelled as rancid and pungent as this. Neither spoke. What was there to say? Both sisters knew that while the bombs had missed them, somewhere on the mountains their brother might not have been so lucky.

Ngọc Lan followed Chị Diễm away from the water, her clothes clinging to her body, the large bag of clams still roped around her wrist. Tears fell from her face. She looked up at the mountainside with its singed leaves and broken plants, which mirrored her broken country. Ngọc Lan knew she wasn't supposed to think bad thoughts about her brother, she wasn't supposed to imagine him burning in the mountain fires being set all across the land, but the images came to her like nightmares she couldn't escape. Her wish was selfish. She wished it anyway. Ngọc Lan begged God to please just end the war. She even went so far as to tell him that he could let the northern army win if he wanted, but please just stop the fighting.

CHAPTER 6
PAUL

"Good evening, ladies and gentlemen. The captain has turned the seat belt sign on. Please remain in your seats until the fasten seat belt sign is turned off."

My stomach lurches as Mother Nature plays Hacky Sack with the aircraft. This is where I'm gonna die, I'm sure of it. My dad brought an evil spirit onto this airplane and it's wreaking havoc on my dreams while causing engine failure because he did some bad shit in his life and as his only son I have to suffer the consequences of his mistakes. *Terrors are just our brains misfiring*, I remind myself. In truth, I'm feeling weird, and by weird I mean concerned. My grip on reality is slipping.

Stop. Mợ Bích and Joe are getting in my head. My aunt's a devout Catholic; she says exorcisms are absolutely real, and God is our only protection. Joe, also a devout Catholic, claims his family has ghosts and spirits around all the time. To them, hauntings are an unquestionable norm. Whereas I, the fallen, barely Catholic-adjacent heathen, should know better.

When we moved into neighboring town houses, Mợ Bích had a priest come to bless each home. I didn't think much of it. A blessing might not be real, but I figured it couldn't hurt. The man came in his regular black dress shirt with the white Roman collar. He had a bottle in the shape of Mary that contained holy water. With a prayer and a sprinkling of said holy water, he blessed each room. We followed, first through every room in our house, then in Mợ Bích's. I felt the urge to chuckle most of the time (a sign that the devil was prodding me, according to Joe), but honest to God, it did not feel like the house was any different post-blessing.

The plane dips. My stomach drops. I glare at my dad, the source of all my problems. He's snoring. How the hell is he sleeping through this? We're bouncing all over the place while he snoozes with his mouth agape. It's as though his body thinks he's sitting on a beach, enjoying fresh coconut juice.

That's the ghosts holding him down, I hear Joe say in the back of my mind. I shake the thought away—Joe and I have been friends for way too damn long. I can't believe he's all up in my head now with this shit.

I clasp my hands beneath my blanket, then try to meditate like that Buddhist monk I saw on YouTube who maintained his praying pose while on fire. It doesn't work. My clenched fists ache from the stress. I force them open, rubbing my clammy palms across my jeans. *Tetris* is calling me, but I refuse to be lulled unconscious. There will be no more rest for me on this aircraft. My dad's mouth closes. His lips twitch into a grimacing smile. It's almost as though he enjoys hanging out with the demon that's haunting him. I don't want to think about my ghost pressing, but I can't *not* think about it. This spirit is obviously affecting my dad, and now it's trying to hop on over to me, but why? Maybe it's bored of the same old thing every night. Maybe Mợ Bích was right and ghosts believe that sons should have to atone for their fathers' sins. Maybe there's no such thing as ghost pressings and I should stop thinking about this. Maybe it's a woman scorned. Oh shit.

No . . .

But who else?

No.

Someone would've told me.

Oh my god . . .

She's the only person who makes sense. What other person would haunt both me and Dad? I bet Jane knows it too. It's all coming together now. The rush to get to Vietnam, the nightmares plaguing my dad, my own ghost pressing just now, *and* Jane not being here. It's gotta be my mother.

Jane hates our mother.

I've brought her up a handful of times in my life and I've regretted it every time. Jane's hatred has somehow grown exponentially despite no contact with our mother in nearly thirteen years.

Even still. How could she keep this from me? I'm old enough to know. I *deserve* to know.

God, how messed up are we as a family that the adults would legit keep me in the dark about my mother's death? *About as messed up as it is that I would be zero percent surprised,* I guess.

Anyone who doesn't know my family might wonder how I could be flown across the world and be told nothing of the itinerary or purpose of the trip. The answer is simple. No one is obligated to tell me shit because I'm the youngest.

This is bullshit. This is wrong.

Obviously, I have nothing concrete to base this on. But the more I consider it, the more I start to believe. In all my imagined scenarios of meeting my mother, I never considered it would be at her funeral. I don't know how I feel about this. Will I be sad? I shouldn't be, considering I don't know her. I'm definitely not feeling nothing. In my mind, it was never a question of *would* I meet her, it was always a matter of *when*. Or, I guess I always thought *not* meeting her would be a choice I made, not one made for me (like everything else in my life).

Thinking about my mother as a ghost is an unnatural kind of torture. The ride stays bumpy clear through to landing, but we do land.

The moment the wheels bounce against the asphalt, I am delirious with joy. Then I remember we're only in Seoul, South Korea. My dad and I have another five-hour flight to Vietnam after a two-hour layover. Kill me now.

Passengers deplane and I stand up to stretch my legs. As the row in front of us exits, the blond girl turns and looks me dead in the eye. My brain is playing tricks on me. She is the girl in my nightmare—her hair is bleached blond but it's her. The edge of her lip curls into a smile before she turns to exit. I'm stunned.

As we roam the airport, I keep an eye out for her while trying to remember if Mợ Bích ever mentioned ghosts looking like real people. I must have seen her face at some point when we boarded. How else would I have known what she looked like? I can't explain the twitch of her lip. Who smiles like that at a stranger?

"Can ghosts look like real people?" I ask my dad.

"What do you mean?"

"When you see ghosts, do they look like people you know?"

"People you know that are dead are ghosts," my dad says. He's not getting what I'm asking. I know I'm not explaining it well, but his response frustrates me. Maybe I imagined it. *Terrors are just our brains misfiring,* I repeat to myself. I board the next leg of our journey in a daze.

I sit down, blink, and suddenly we've begun our descent. My seat belt is locked. I don't recall buckling it.

Small

world.

Tranquil.

Water,

deep,

dark,

blue.

Land,

skyscrapers,

lights.

Runway,
tarmac.
Red Flag,
yellow Star;
Vietnam.

The first and only other time we visited was nine years ago in 1999. Being seven, I was overwhelmed by how different and uncomfortable everything was. Like the heat—the heat is something else. The moment we step outside, it hits me like a roiling wave. Summer in Vietnam is melt-your-skin-off hot. My grandma's driver meets us outside. He's an older guy, maybe fifty-something? He wears a short-sleeved shirt with brown linen pants and black floppy sandals. Grandma isn't with him.

Even with the windows down my clothes cling to me. I feel like I tripped and landed in a swamp. Inhaling a lungful of exhaust, I check out my surroundings. Vietnam is busy. The streets are filled with people on scooters, on bicycles, and in compact cars. A few tourists take photos from the back seat of a rickshaw. Without windows and steel frames to separate them, I wonder whether people make friends on their commute.

My grandparents' house is exactly as I remember it. They added some planters in the courtyard, but the walls and building haven't changed. We help the driver unload our stuff at the entrance, then he nods to my dad and leaves. As soon as I step inside the house, the chain around my neck feels hot—not sweaty and warm; rather, like it was baked in an oven and then placed around my throat. My skin tingles like it's burning. I swipe at the necklace, ready to yank it away from me, only to find that in my fingers it's actually cool. What the hell?

A year ago, as I was reorganizing the register area inside my family's liquor store, I noticed an open pipe that was glued to the floor. No doubt some old remnant of a hack repair that no one had bothered clearing out. I had no idea what the pipe belonged to, but I stuck my fingers in and found this gold chain. I asked my dad if he put it there—Vietnamese people have a tendency to stash gold in odd places for safekeeping—but he said no. So I put it on my neck and forgot about it. I consider taking it off now, but I don't want to lose it.

"Mẹ!" my dad shouts as we head toward the kitchen.

"You've arrived!" My grandmother, Bà Nội, rushes through the doorway. She greets us with big hugs and inhaling kisses. For a newly widowed woman, she looks—happy?

My grandfather, Ông Nội, died this past March. He was seventy-eight. No one expected him to live this long because his health had been declining for a decade, but I guess he wasn't going to leave on anyone's terms but his own. Dad and Jane flew back to Vietnam for the funeral, but I couldn't go because my passport had expired and I was still in school. I remember him being a real mellow man, happy to do the most mundane things like go up and down the escalator at the newly built mall in Saigon or bike aimlessly around the neighborhood.

In Vietnamese, we don't call our parents or grandparents by name. That's straight-up rude. It's Ông (person of grandparent age) + Nội (father's father) or Ngoại (mother's father). I've never needed to use Ông Ngoại.

I didn't cry when I heard Ông Nội died. I was sad, I really liked my grandpa, but it felt disingenuous or something to be dramatic because he wasn't a big part of my life. I only met him once and talked to him on the phone a handful of times before he died. Because he lived so far, we weren't that tight.

The closest I came to shedding tears was when I watched the videos of the funeral. My grandpa didn't look like himself at all. My dad said that was normal because of the embalming process or whatever. When he described holding my grandpa's cold hand, I thought he was messing with me. But then I saw him do it in the video Jane recorded for me. My dad has never been afraid of dead bodies. I'm not saying this makes me proud, but I couldn't do it. Ghosts are one thing, zombies are a whole other, and I've seen too many zombies return to life in movies to trust a corpse, family or not.

Bà Nội's wail, though, is something I'll never forget for a million years. I could hear it in the background. I'm surprised I didn't hear it clear across the ocean; it was *that* loud and piercing. Not like a shriek that breaks glass and hurts your ears, but one that explodes in emotion and breaks your heart. I teared up then.

I guess that's why I'm so surprised to see her standing before me, looking . . . normal?

"Chào Bà Nội," I say, greeting her sheepishly.

She smiles wide and hugs me firmly, like really firm, almost as though she's trying to suck the life out of me. Then she presses her face to my cheek and inhales deeply. My grandma is weird. I smirk because it tickles and because it's hilarious to have someone's lips on your cheek while they breathe in. She appears to be taking in the scent of freshly cut flowers. But her nose must not be working. After traveling for a full day, I know I do *not* smell like flowers. I probably smell like durian.

CHAPTER 7
NGỌC LAN

There was no news of Anh Hòa's survival, no information at all, though the girls checked the mail daily. Sometimes, if families were lucky, a loved one might show up, albeit badly wounded, in a nearby hospital. Wounded bodies were a blessing, broken limbs a prayer answered, because at least it meant your kin were still alive. Before Anh Hòa left, the three siblings lived under a cloud of protection that kept danger at bay. Once their brother was taken away, though, it was like the sky opened up and suddenly catastrophe lurked in every shadow. To get through the days, they did the only thing they knew how to do. They kept moving. Fear was not a shield, fear would not protect them from injury, fear only served to keep them still. And according to Chị Diễm, "Stillness is just a slower way of dying."

Several months after Anh Hòa's departure, their father came home. Based on radio reports, many central provinces had fallen to the North Vietnamese Army. Ngọc Lan couldn't be sure, but she had a feeling in her gut that her wish for the war to end was about to come true.

The kids never knew how their father felt about the conflict. When he was asked to join the Army of the Republic as an architect, he took the job warily. But by the time he returned home six months later, he had become a staunch believer in the cause. Then as months turned into years, fatigue set in. It sank deeper and deeper into him until his cheeks wrinkled with worry. His eyes sagged with sadness. His once-shiny black hair was now completely gray. They saw the physical effects, the stress, and the anger. But each of them interpreted these changes differently.

Anh Hòa thought their father allowed himself to believe the propaganda and became political as a result. Chị Diễm was most sympathetic, though he was the cruelest to her. She thought that maybe the conditions he had to work in were so harrowing that it caused him great stress. Ngọc Lan honestly didn't know what to think. Of the three siblings, Ngọc Lan's view of her father was most idealistic. Perhaps this was because she spent the least amount of time with him. When she was a toddler, she would cry when he left. To comfort her, Anh Hòa told her of all the fun games their father would play with them when he returned. As such, in her memory, Ba liked to swing her around in circles at the beach. In her memory, he would find her the largest crab to eat. In her memory, her father was a hero who fought to keep the bombs away. In reality, when her father squeezed her shoulders or patted her head—he rarely hugged her—the image in her mind felt disconnected from the person.

As a child, Ngọc Lan assumed that this strangeness was normal because, well, it was. But Anh Hòa would tell her later that it was because everything he told her was a lie. Those memories she had were of Anh Hòa and her—not their absentee father.

"Where is Hòa?" their mother asked, expecting to see her son return with her husband. Mẹ naively believed that when Ba signed Anh Hòa up, her husband might protect him or that they would be stationed together, at the very least.

"I asked, but no one seemed to know where he was placed," her husband responded. His tone was dismissive, but that wasn't what got Mẹ's attention. What sent a piercing pain down her spine was an unwavering rumble—an understanding that she had been wrong. Her husband had not protected their son.

"Go back and ask again," she insisted.

But he just shook his head. "Tonight, pack everything valuable we own. Tomorrow we sell it."

"How can you just abandon your child? If the fighting is over, we need to find him."

"Ay. Don't worry so much. We're going to the market. Hòa will return home soon," her husband scolded. But Mẹ didn't believe him. He wasn't sharing what he knew.

Ngọc Lan watched her father get up from the table and stand at their door. Goose bumps raced up her arms. Something was wrong. He didn't seem possessed or demonic; more like someone whose body was alive despite his soul having wandered off. She worried that, without a soul to protect him, a spirit would enter.

As the youngest, Ngọc Lan was privy to all the stories circulating among the older kids. In hushed groups, they whispered about ghost pressings, ghost entries, and ghost appearances. Ngọc Lan had seen with her own eyes the scars and markings across the bodies of those who had encountered someone possessed. So it wasn't just that she believed in ghosts, she knew for a fact that they were real.

When pestered about the existence of evil spirits, Anh Hòa told the girls, "Vietnam is a small but mighty country that has had to fend off invasion for more than two thousand years. Each time war came to our doorstep, blood, both foreign and native, spilled onto the Vietnamese soil." Because of Vietnam's history of occupation and subsequent war, it was no surprise to anyone that many lost souls wandered the land.

Watching her father move zealously about, Ngọc Lan knew his body had been taken over. She wondered whether the ghost inside him was ancestral or random. "Make sure we collect anything we can sell. Anything spare," their father said. He gathered clothing, brushes, cups, plates, even an old tea set that had cracks so deep water dripped through—nothing was of immense value, but they were things the girls loved nonetheless.

"Not my brush," Chị Diễm whimpered, reaching for it. Chị Diễm had given up ice cream for weeks to buy this wooden brush, which had on the back a hand-painted girl wearing a sea-blue áo dài,[4] with her long, beautiful hair blowing in the wind.

Ba glared at her cruelly. "What do you need these for? A girl who is shallow on the inside needn't be shallow on the outside," he jeered.

---

4 *traditional Vietnamese dress*

Chị Diễm's hands, which had been braiding her long black hair into a halo, dropped into her lap. She peered down, letting tiny droplets of tears wet her purple pants. Chị Diễm was a phoenix whose tail was being trampled by a giant.

Mẹ said nothing as she witnessed her husband's insult washing over their elder daughter. She stared at her husband and saw someone else. That was when she knew for sure. The war had cost her husband his soul. The person she married, the man who once picked longan,[5] lychee, and coconut from his neighbor's trees to make her a fruit bowl, was bound and trapped by a sinister spirit who had taken over his being.

That night while her husband slept, Mẹ lit three incense candles and burned votive offerings of paper boats, fish, fruits, clothing, money, and gold—all of which she had hand-drawn. She desperately needed ancestral protection.

In the hour before dawn, the family headed to Chợ Bà Rịa.[6] They rode bikes carrying baskets of clams, dried fish, and a few jars of homemade fish sauce. But as they passed the Cỏ May Bridge, instead of continuing straight, Ba took a detour.

"Where are you taking us?" Mẹ asked.

"Just say we're going to the market. If anyone stops us, we're going to the market. That's all you need to know, don't ask more questions," her husband whispered. Mẹ biked in silence, knowing

5 *traditional fruit of Vietnam*

6 *Bá Rịa Market*

it was not her place to question her husband. Then, turning down a small dirt path marked by two parallel lines made of tires, they reached a clearing. A small crowd had already formed around two large military helicopters.

"What is this place?" Ngọc Lan asked. She received no answer. The atmosphere was thick with panic as the crowd pressed forward for a spot. Foreign soldiers huddled around their families.

"Ba!" Chị Diễm cried. "Why are we here?"

Hopping off his bike, which he abandoned at the side of the road, their father moved toward the crowd. He gestured for the girls to do the same. Not wanting their bikes to be stolen, Mẹ quickly pushed them deeper into the brush off the main path. She unlatched her basket of goods, but her husband stopped her.

"Leave it," he scolded. She reluctantly obeyed.

Gripping both of their hands tight, Ba rushed the girls toward the crowd, searching for a familiar face, any familiar face. He spotted an American soldier. "Take us with you. I'm an engineer. I can help you fix the helicopter if it crashes," he offered.

The soldier scoffed. "If the chopper crashes, we're all dead. Step back."

Undeterred, Ba tried another soldier and another until he happened upon Jacob, a sizable Filipino soldier he had worked with when he designed a hidden airplane hangar in Bình Thủy, Cần Thơ.[7]

"Help my family," Ba begged. The urgency and pathetic

---

7 *Bình Thủy is a district in Cần Thơ province, located in South Vietnam.*

pleading in her husband's voice was frighteningly humbling. Suddenly, Mẹ understood how dire their situation was. Jacob looked at his friend despairingly.

"I'm sorry."

But Ba pressed on. "Please, I help you. They kill me." Their father was a known architect for the Army of the Republic. His punishment under the new regime would be severe—if he survived.

The blades of Jacob's chopper whirred to life as he leaned over the pilot's shoulder. The two men argued back and forth until finally, Jacob reached for Ba's hand and pulled him up. Seeing this, the crowd clamored to be let on. Before Ba could grab his wife and daughters, the pilot pivoted and began his ascent.

"Stop!" their father yelled. In a moment, the aircraft was skybound with Jacob's arm stretched across Ba's chest like a seat belt preventing him from jumping off.

"Another helicopter will be back! Another helicopter is on its way!" a soldier shouted.

Anh is sorry. Ngọc Lan read the words on her father's lips as the sounds blew away in the wind. For the first time in Ngọc Lan's life, she saw her father cry. Beside her, Mẹ stood stoic, watching the aircraft disappear from view. The moment of abandonment was so quick it hardly registered even after the wind and sound of the helicopter blades were long gone.

"Ba!" Ngọc Lan screamed, reaching for the sky.

SMACK. Mẹ slapped Ngọc Lan hard across the face. "Be

quiet." Her mother wasn't telling her to shut up because of her tears. She was telling her to shut up because there were people around. In the chaos, a sinking feeling told Mẹ not to draw attention to their abandonment.

"They'll return," someone murmured. "They have to return."

The stricken looks on the faces of the Vietnamese people left behind held the truth. They would not be coming back. The helicopter had come to extract its foreign nationals, and they were gone.

"Ba! Ba! Ba!" Ngọc Lan whimpered in a quiet, heart-shattering cry that only a twelve-year-old could muster. But he was gone. The sky was clear, and her dad was absent. Beside her, Chị Diễm stood emotionless as Ngọc Lan remembered their father's harsh words toward her sister the night before—the last thing Chị Diễm's father ever called her was "shallow."

Mẹ didn't always trust her instincts, but her intuition was never wrong. This was why, even though their mom had no idea why she felt the need to hide her bikes, her impulse to do so was what saved her and her daughters.

Ever the practical woman, their mom returned to their hidden bikes. She stepped beside the front wheel, and her foot sunk into soft mud. A tiny stream wove just beneath them. She led the girls home. As they moved among people, rumors about what was to come spread in hushed tones like gossip, except it was news—except it was important.

"Remember what your father told you before we left?"

The girls nodded. If anyone asked, they were returning from

the market. Later they would say they had been deserted by their husband and father. The best lies were the ones closest to the truth.

Several days after that, on April 29, 1975, when the North Vietnamese Army circled Saigon, and without much resistance, the capital fell, most of the country already knew the South had lost. If the propaganda was to be believed, the North Vietnamese government was about to unify Vietnam. They were going to make the country whole again.

Home again, their mother searched the house for what she already knew would be missing. Her husband had taken their entire life savings with him. In her pack, he put the items they planned to "sell." In his, he carried every valuable item they owned. Their total net worth consisted of two thin gold wedding bands, both broken—crushed under the weight of congratulatory handshakes on their wedding day—plus a long gold chain with a delicate cross attached. The family's valuables fit in a pouch the size of a rubber bounce ball. Still, it was more than some. Gold was hard to come by when the currency for life was food. Excess or abundance of food was the stuff of fairy tales. During the war, survival had already been a day-to-day effort. They were lucky that Mẹ made the best nước mắm[8] in the South.

---

8 *fish sauce*

Frantic, their mother went into the courtyard, moved the stove and the logs beneath it, and began digging. Two feet below the surface was a rusted circular tin with the words *Les Fraises* in cursive and the remnants of bright red strawberries on the lid. Inside lay an antique necklace: an heirloom passed down from Mẹ's mother. The perfect green-and-white jade circle dangled from a simple clasp that glided along a thin gold chain. Bà Cố, Great-grandmother, had given Ngọc Lan's mom this jewelry on her wedding day in secret. All day, Mẹ wore it hidden beneath the thick collar of her áo dài. It was meant for her daughters. Now, she might have to sell it. But to whom? She knew it was just as likely to be stolen from her than actually traded in this tumultuous time. No one could be trusted, not even her own husband.

Ba and Mẹ had not discussed an escape plan. Ngọc Lan's father had detailed the route. He alone knew what avenues might be available once the Communists took over. Now he was somewhere in the sky, and her mother needed to make dinner.

"Mẹ," Ngọc Lan called, but she had no idea what to ask. Her mother didn't answer.

That night Chị Diễm sat beside Ngọc Lan as she silently cried. She sang Ngọc Lan the song their mother normally sang when any of them needed comfort.

Tình mẹ bao la như biển khơi xa
Như dòng nước ngọt chảy mãi trong ta
Mẹ bước trên con đường gập ghềnh, sáng ngời
Để bảo vệ bước chân con trong đêm tối.[9]

When she ran out of tears, Ngọc Lan hummed along.

Hm, hm, hm, hm, hm, hm-hmmmmm, hm…
Hm, hm, hm hm, hm hm, hm-hmmmm…

---

9 *A mother's love stretches ocean wide*
Like sweet water flowing endlessly inside
She walks a broken path, calm and bright
To protect her child's steps in the night.

CHAPTER 8
PAUL

I'm upstairs pretending to "rest," when in fact my eyes are wide open and I'm trying to catch a stubborn Charmander for the third time. Downstairs I can hear the arrival of family. A sense of dread fills my whole body. It's not that I don't like my relatives, it's the sheer number of them that show up at once that's overwhelming. Plus, there's this whole system for properly greeting people that is based on age + extra variables like parents' age or grandparents' age depending on how far back your family's relationship with theirs goes. Basically, the naming conventions add a level of confusion that make me never want to open my mouth. This is why Jane is supposed to be here. She's supposed to fumble through the greetings while I simply follow behind and repeat the correct one. Now I have to do it myself.

"Paul!" my dad shouts from the stairwell. Time's up. I stand and lumber down the stairs as he waves me over. "Come say hi to everyone."

I peek my head around the corner. It's worse than I thought. There are maybe twenty adults all sitting around an array of rice, fish, sour soups, and sautéed vegetables. I start on one side of the room. While bowing, I say, "Chào Cô." I pause because I do not know her name, and she fills the silence with "Dì Dô." My aunts and uncles rescue me by saying their own names. After my pathetic greetings, they scoot aside, making room for me to sit next to my dad. I'm handed a warm bowl of rice and begin eating.

One aunt squeezes my face and says, "These cheeks are so plump I could bite them!" My eyes widen and she laughs.

"Can Quốc speak Vietnamese?" another aunt, whose name I've already forgotten, asks.

"He can speak with a stutter," my dad says. I don't actually stutter, but I guess it does sort of sound like stuttering because I'm stammering so much.

"Do you understand Vietnamese?" an uncle asks.

"Dạ,"[10] I answer. A collective cheer erupts. I laugh. "I can speak a little. I understand more than I can speak," I say in Vietnamese. This short response gets big smiles from everyone.

"Good!" I hear a few different people say. I'm pretty sure it's genuine too. This isn't as bad as I thought it would be. It's actually kind of embarrassing how *little* they expect of me. I must not have made a great impression last time I was here. My relatives ask my dad about the shop and America. They, in turn, tell him about their children, new marriages, and how one uncle (or cousin?) became a priest recently. I slurp my canh rau má với tôm[11] and take in my surroundings. There isn't much on the green walls, no artwork or decorations, just an ancestral altar with a wooden crucifix up top.

There are several black-and-white portraits on the wall. None of

10 *Deferential "Yes." In this case, it would be accompanied with a bow, but I forgot.*

11 *pennywort soup*

whom I recognize. My grandfather Ông Nội is one of only two photos in color. The other is a young woman—could that be my mom?

"Who is that?" I ask.

"My cousin," my dad says.

So *not* my mom. Makes sense, I guess, that my mom wouldn't be here since these are all relatives on my dad's side of the family. "What happened to her?"

"She drowned."

"Oh." I'm not sure what I was expecting, but it wasn't that. I want to ask how, but he's already returned to his conversation with an aunt. As I watch him, I wonder how he can slide into this home so easily. My dad left Vietnam in 1976; when we came in 1999, it was his first return. Now, nearly a decade later, it's like no time has passed with people he's barely had contact with in more than thirty years. The stories are endless. Maybe because they've been waiting so long to tell them. What I'm diggin' is how they mostly recount blunders. I swear a comedy show doesn't have a laugh track this consistent.

"I wash the boat of all the algae. Sand it for three days. Repaint. Then we put the boat back in the ocean and not twenty minutes later it's sinking. Fuck me, I forgot to plug the drain." My uncle laughs. I don't know his name or true relationship, I just know everyone in this room is related to me. His face is red after two Heinekens. His forehead sweats from the humidity and he's laughing so hard his torso is rolling backward like a Weebles wobble toy that self-rights when pushed down. His story is horrifyingly hilarious. I'm legit laughing so hard my shoulders are bouncing.

My grandparents' house is one of the newest buildings in the neighborhood. Made of stucco, it's plain but feels sturdy, which

I'm grateful for when a plinking sound catches my ear. I turn to the kitchen to see a full-on torrential downpour slapping the aluminum roof. For a minute I can't hear anything except raindrops—it's *that* loud—but as suddenly as it began, it stops.

Vietnamese people have mad respect for nature. There's a tree in my grandma's kitchen that I'm pretty sure was there before the house was built. It's rooted in the ground and springs up through a hole cut in the tin roof. When I asked my grandma why they didn't cut it down, she looked at me strangely and said, "For what?" The idea had never occurred to her.

Rooms in my grandparents' house are constantly converting to fit whatever function is needed. The "living room" was also the "wake" room when my grandpa died, and it'll turn into a festive dining area more than a few times while we're here.

An aunt I'm sure I met last time I was here puts some fish into my bowl. "Eat until you're full," she says, encouraging me to continue.

I bow slightly, say "Dạ," and bring my bowl to my lips.

When I'm done eating, I take my bowl to the kitchen. A wooden fence surrounding the perimeter is covered in pots, pans, and cooking tools that hang from nails and hooks. There's a low wooden shelf along the bottom for bowls and serving plates, and one corner is constantly wet with soapy water. Dishes are done not in a sink but in a basin full of dirty water, then transferred to a basin of soapy water and another basin of clean rinsing water. If Californians could learn to use water like my family in Vietnam, we'd never be in a drought. Only that first bucket of dirty water is poured out at the end of a washing. In lieu of pipes, dirty water drains into a moat that runs along the house's perimeter.

Because our American stomachs are weak, they have to boil water to rinse our dishes. Even my dad can't drink well water here without getting sick.

I awkwardly greet the two maids whose names I can't remember with a bow. "Chào hai bác," I say. They're about Jane's age, so I should've called them chị instead of bác, which is meant for a person older than my dad, but I dunno, that felt somehow disrespectful or something. Neither of them corrects me. They just smile at me and say "Giỏi," which means "Good." I'm sure they think I'm stupid. Honestly, I feel stupid, so I guess we're all on the same page.

My uncle, a member of the Communist Party, is not home. He's a stern dude who scares the bejeezus out of me, not because he's ever been mean to me, but because he doesn't talk much. Plus, I dunno, the uniform he wears sometimes is just kind of scary-looking. I'm not used to being around military people. It's like living with a cop you don't know that well.

Bà Nội and my dad appear behind me.

"Have you organized your things?" my dad asks her.

"What do I have to organize? This is still my house," Bà Nội says.

"If you forget things here it won't be easy to return."

"I know already." Bà Nội's response is biting. I think she might be mad.

Whatever is going on, it's tense. I want no part of it.

"I'm gonna go unpack," I say to my grandma in Vietnamese.

"Ừ." She nods. I head upstairs. The first thing I need to do is charge my game.

Our bedroom is nearly as bare as the living room, with just a queen-sized bed frame with a box spring. No mattress. At the foot of the bed are sheets, no blankets because it's too damn hot here to need them. From the ceiling, white mesh drapes over the bed with an opening on one side, a mosquito net, which, if I remember correctly, does nothing. To unpack, I unzip my suitcase and . . . that's it. I unzip it and leave everything inside because there are no closets, chests, or drawers to put the items in.

On top of my clothes is the bag of things from Jane. I count the Vietnamese bills and shove it all in my wallet. I can hear Jane's nagging voice telling me to spread it out in the pockets of my clothes and in my suitcase, so I won't lose it all if I get pickpocketed. I'll do it later. Right now, the more pressing matter is charging my devices. There are two converted plugs, one for the game and the other for the cell phone I haven't even turned on yet. I flip open the phone and power it up. There's only one number in it: Jane.

I text her:

From: Paul

Thanks for the money.

A couple of seconds later, she responds:

From: Jane

Don't be dumb, spread it out.

It's amazing how I extend an olive branch and the first thing she thinks to do is to insult me. I don't respond.

After ten minutes the phone lights up.

From: Jane

I don't mean that you're dumb, it would just be a dumb thing to do. Have fun!

I ignore that too and instead open the notebook she also put in the bag. It's made of leather and feels precious in a way my school spiral-bounds don't. I open the cover and begin to scrawl:

- *This notebook is nice. I don't know why I'm writing in it.*
- *Vietnam smells like I remember.*
- *Ba Noi doesn't seem as depressed as a widow should be.*
- *At the airport I saw a Black woman speaking perfect Vietnamese.*
- *Grandpa's dog, Cho, is dead. I don't know why I thought he'd still be alive nine years later, but I did.*
- *Everyone here is Jane's height. My neck kinda hurts from looking down—best part of Vietnam so far.*

I close the journal.

CHAPTER 9
NGỌC LAN

"Despicable. Good riddance. I'm glad Ông was never in our lives. We have enough BS to deal with," Jane says, kicking her feet up on the couch. "No wonder Cậu Hòa never told us about him."

It's not lost on me that she leaves off Grandpa's proper designation, Ngoại. Not that I disagree. "You're ruining the story, Jane."

"What?"

"Can you please just not *talk? You're messing with my focus."*

Jane looks annoyed but doesn't say anything else. I continue.

People who had a lot lost the most. In the South, anything of value that could be taken was taken. Our family, luckily, had very little. The shack Ba and Mẹ owned was oceanside in an undeveloped area. It was made of mortar with a tin roof—a strong monsoon would've blown it over. Besides the view, they had none of the luxuries the Communists could find in Saigon, which was only a few hours away. So, in some ways, poverty meant that many Vung Tau residents were not kicked out of their homes.

The end of the war in 1975 left Vietnam in a state of destitution. The lush land had been cracked open and covered in dust by bombs. Farmers either fled or had their land repatriated to party loyalists who lacked the skills needed to properly tend to the soil. Cut off from outside trade by global superpowers like America, the Communist government officials accepted bribes for things like traffic violations, licenses, business taxes, and safe passage for escaping refugees. As things worsened, families in the community started to disappear.

Chị Diễm's best friend, Quyên, was one of the disappeared, and Chị Diễm longed to know what happened to her. Ngọc Lan tried not to appear bothered by the missing people. Her siblings were her best friends. What she wanted most was for the vacant stare in Chị Diễm's eyes to go away. She wanted her sister not to worry.

"When do you think Quyên will return?" Chị Diễm asked one afternoon as they were getting ready to go diving. Ngọc Lan didn't answer. Her sister had been the one to teach Ngọc Lan how to explore while diving. Chị Diễm was technically the better swimmer, but recently she didn't want to swim because her mind was elsewhere. Everyone knew that when people left, they didn't come back. Sometimes because they were dead. As more and more horror stories began circulating, Chị Diễm's worry turned into unrealistic hope.

"Idle brains think too much," Ngọc Lan said, mimicking their mom. "Come, let's swim." Ngọc Lan didn't like these conversations. She wanted to be optimistic, but mostly, what she felt was fear.

Chị Diễm ignored Ngọc Lan. "What bothers me, what I can't get out of my head, was Quyên never told me she was planning to leave. One day Quyên wasn't at school, then the next and the next, and after two weeks passed, I knew. How could she not tell me?"

"Come on, Chị Diễm, let's not think about things that makes us sad. She probably didn't know. She's probably really sorry," Ngọc Lan offered.

"Do you think if we saw each other on the street ten years from now, Quyên would remember me?" Chị Diễm asked.

"Of course. But it won't be ten years before you see each other again. The fighting is over, the government will set itself up, and Chị Quyên's family will return." Ngọc Lan wasn't placating her sister. Despite what she saw and heard, she had faith. Just as she had faith that their brother would return home any day now. Ngọc Lan tried to cheer Chị Diễm up by offering her lost treasures she found at the bottom of the ocean: forks, glasses without lenses, hair ties, goggles, and even a rubber duck. But her sister wasn't interested.

"Stop sulking. Come on, let's explore. Aren't you curious about what's out there?" Ngọc Lan asked.

"No," Chị Diễm said flatly.

"Ba is out there."

"Don't wait for Ba to live your life," Chị Diễm replied icily.

"What are you saying, Chị Diễm?"

Chị Diễm looked at Ngọc Lan's innocent, shocked face and softened. "Nothing. I'm tired today. Go get the clams and let's head to the market before noon."

The Vũng Tàu Market bustled with people selling anything they could. Fresh produce was difficult to come by, so clothing, toys, accessories, furniture, even fence lines could be found at discounted rates in the market. Ngọc Lan's ability to clam meant they didn't feel the hunger pangs that she knew the orphans did, but she missed the taste of rice, potatoes, and herbs. She never allowed herself to dwell on her desires, though, because whatever she was feeling, she was sure Anh Hòa was suffering something worse. *Where is he?* she wondered. Ngọc Lan's father was gone, her brother was still missing, and the burnt rice wrapped in banana leaves she had been saving for one of their returns was beginning to rot.

In the market, everything was negotiable. And no one was better at bargaining than Mẹ. She was so precise in her calculations that the sellers were rarely happy to be making the sale, and that was how she knew she'd obtained the rock-bottom price. The family's stall was a sliver of space inside the Lê family's sprawling squid and fish stall. Bác Nga, a family matriarch, ruled her house with admirable efficiency. Like a hawk, she noticed the smallest of details. Her husband, Bác Hiếu, was the opposite; he never sweated the small things. "Don't worry, the universe always finds a way to right itself," he'd say when Bác Nga worried about what the Communists might confiscate next.

Bác Nga wasn't wrong to worry, though. Their shelves, like everyone's, were meager. All they had were a few freshly caught gobi, several packages of dried squid products, and two bottles of yogurt.

"Chào Bác Hiếu. Chào Bác Nga," Chị Diễm and Ngọc Lan said in unison while bowing to the older couple, who nodded back in acknowledgment.

Chị Diễm left Ngọc Lan at the stall and walked to a seamstress shop at the other end of the plaza. There, she was paid to hand-sew sparkling sequins onto delicate silk fabrics.

"Point the mouth down," Bác Nga instructed her husband.

"Relax, my wife. Have some squid," Bác Hiếu said, not bothering to fix the display.

Ngọc Lan wondered how Bác Hiếu could remain unchanged. Since the Communist takeover, much had been seized. Still, the couple showed up at the market every day to work. This wasn't the first time tragedy had struck his family, though. Ngọc Lan remembered when a messenger delivered news of Bác Hiếu's parents' killings in 1968. They lived in the My Lai hamlet of Quang Ngai province, in the South. For reasons no one understood, the Americans massacred the citizens even though nobody had any military affiliations. The Americans. The ones her brother fought with. The ones who abandoned them.

What she did remember was seeing Bác Hiếu's knees buckle under the weight of the news. Until that moment, she hadn't known words could break a man.

"Keep talking," Bác Hiếu said, over and over again. He said nothing else, just "Keep talking." He wanted to know everything, every detail. After that, Bác Hiếu disappeared for a while. When he returned, no one mentioned what had happened. This was the first time Ngọc Lan realized that pain could be ignored.

Behind the counter, hidden from the customers' eyes, Ngọc Lan watched Bác Nga peel back cellophane, cut off mold, and reseal the food. Bác Nga took pride in her display, but Ngọc Lan didn't see the point. She would have traded every clam she had for a bite of that stale rice.

Ngọc Lan studied her mother as she sold their two hundred clams. With every customer, she bartered a different deal.

Curious, Ngọc Lan asked, "Why don't you just mark it all the same price?"

"Because some days you don't have enough to be selling so cheap."

"Then raise the price," Ngọc Lan concluded.

"And lose the sale to another stall?" Mẹ huffed.

At the end of the day, using their profits, Mẹ bought one small bag of rice noodles, two potatoes, one sweet yam, an onion, and a bag of beef bones to flavor the broth. Seeing this was enough to make Ngọc Lan want to master the art of selling.

Just as they were closing up, a man in a North Vietnamese uniform approached. His arrival changed the market atmosphere as people shrank away. No one wanted to be singled out by a new authority. "Chào em Hang," the man said to Ngọc Lan's mother.

Mẹ looked up in astonishment. "Chào Anh . . . Anh is—?" she asked, unsure of what to call him. His calm and relaxed face had, before, reminded her of a monk or philosopher, someone noble who thought deeply about life. Now that same face sitting atop a green army uniform with the bright red Communist flag on the arm made her feel tense and afraid. It was hard to believe, even as she looked right at him, that he was the same person. He had been buying nước mắm from her stall for years. In fact, she had on occasion suspected he was a Communist, but seeing him in uniform frightened her.

"Đại Tá Duy Thái," the man said proudly. "But em Hang should call me Anh Duy as before."

"Chào Đại Tá Duy Thái," Mẹ said, using his formal title. Flustered, she wondered how he knew her name. Had she given it to him before? She couldn't remember. Fear gripped her as every prior interaction they'd had flashed through her mind. The Communists had been known to say one thing and then punish a person for doing exactly as they asked.

He seemed to be taken aback. Surprised and a bit amused by Mẹ's fear of him, he asked, "Aren't we friends?"

Mẹ was afraid to answer. Was she supposed to just accept him as a friend? Was he using her to try to convince the community that the Communists were good people? She nodded in agreement because he had all the power and she had none.

He looked around. "Where is em's husband?" he asked. His tone was gentle, but the question felt menacing.

"Anh Vinh has not returned yet," Mẹ lied. Her husband would not be returning.

"Em shouldn't worry. Your husband will be home soon enough. It's night, em is probably going home. Do you have any bottles of nước mắm left? My wife has been craving your fish sauce."

Mẹ pulled a bottle out from beneath the counter. "So lucky I have one bottle left. It has been difficult to get sardines lately." She hoped it would deter him from returning.

But he smiled and said, "That's an easy fix."

Ngọc Lan popped up behind her mom and said, "Chào Chú!"

"Chào Đại Tá Duy Thái," her mother corrected while pushing the back of Ngọc Lan's head down into a low bow. Confused, Ngọc Lan did as she was told. She looked up at the man for clues as to what had changed. He was in uniform. Lots of men in uniform had come through here. Some were even foreigners. Uncle Duy was a regular. He smiled at her as he normally did and handed her a bag of taffy, which he also normally did.

"Cảm ơn, Đại Tá Duy Thái," she said, thanking him with the proper title this time.

"Ey! Uncle told your mother already. Call me Chú Duy like normal. Are you well?"

Ngọc Lan nodded, but before she could say more, her mom interrupted her: "Go call your sister so we can go home."

"Chào Chú Duy." Ngọc Lan bowed before running off to get her sister.

The next day, two large baskets of sardines were dropped off at their stall. No note accompanied the fish, and the delivery person had no message, but everyone knew who'd sent it.

"Someone has an admirer," Bác Hiếu teased. For a man, Bác Hiếu was a rare romantic.

"Bác Hiếu knows he's a Communist, right?"

"The Americans killed my family. In this war who really are the bad guys?"

"Are you turning Communist?" Mẹ joked.

But Bác Hiếu remained serious. "If it wasn't my family, it would be someone else's, and I do not wish that kind of pain and longing on another person."

"Not even the Americans then?" Bác Nga asked, prodding her husband.

"Not even the Americans. People are people. When we study the history of this time, we'll see that both sides will have bled."

"Don't speak ridiculously." Mẹ shushed him, returning the conversation to the fish sauce. "It's probably just that Anh Duy's wife really likes our nước mắm."

"This is Vietnam. Fish sauce is nothing special. But you watch out, don't let him see you casually," Bác Hiếu said.

Mẹ looked at the couple curiously. "What are you two saying?"

"Anh Duy has been coming here for years. His heart is not ugly," Bác Nga said.

As Ngọc Lan walked to get Chị Diễm, she wondered if Bác Hiếu's family being murdered by the Americans made him sympathetic to the Communists. Maybe he thought Bác Duy was a decent person because he felt like the Americans were no better. These were not conversations adults had with children. Ngọc Lan didn't know what her mom thought of Chú Duy, because she simply stacked the fish onto her bike and together they rode home. There she began the fermenting process.

Inside her small home near the water's edge, Mẹ focused her attention on providing for her daughters. If Anh Duy wanted nước mắm, she would make nước mắm, and for every bottle she made for him, she would siphon a little to trade.

CHAPTER 10
PAUL

I jerk awake. The sky outside is dark. Shit. I was supposed to force myself to stay up until nighttime to avoid jet lag. I let myself fall asleep anyway. The clock on the wall says 8:15 p.m.

My dad's snoring is no doubt contributing to my insomnia. He's in the bug net beside me but didn't bother to actually close the net so mosquitoes have needled their suckers into my legs and arms. I reach up to feel an itch on my cheek and yup, got bit there too. I kick my feet in the air, crawl over my dad, and get out.

In the living room Bà Nội is asleep on a reed mat with no pillow. Grandma is immune to mosquitoes, so she sleeps freely wherever she is. Her face twitches in the dark, but she looks serene.

The house is quiet aside from the squeaking gate hinge that beckons me. I grab my shoes and head outside. The alleyway is dark, lit only by moonlight. Before I venture off, I turn to make sure I know which gate is ours. We live just off a busy street. Once I hit the main road, scattered lampposts dimly light the way. There aren't paved sidewalks, but paths have been created by other pedestrians, bicyclists, and motorists. I don't see any strip malls or actual malls, just houses in between fluorescently lit restaurants that are probably both. In Vietnam it's common for people to live above the shops they keep. Customers sit on stools at tables that spill onto the sidewalk, and everyone appears to be . . . uniform? Not the same or identical, but like everyone fits together. Everyone belongs. Everyone but me, that is.

I'm not used to being around so many Vietnamese, and even though I look Viet, I don't feel it. I don't know what I feel. White? Not exactly. I feel like a knockoff. Like I'm a fake Lego trying to fit into the scene, but my foot-pegs are the wrong size, so I don't stick to the board. In public, I'm used to being surrounded by non-Vietnamese. I'm used to being a minority.

The damp air smells of exhaust mixed into an ocean breeze. Call me weird, but I love the aroma of gasoline and motor oil. Put them together? Even better. I'm diggin' all these idling vehicles beside me. Most of the shops are closed, but a few restaurants still have their lights on. I peek my head inside one. I smell lemongrass. I keep walking. Four motorbikes pass with two or three people on each bike. The riders don't look much older than me, and whatever they're up to, it looks fun. Maybe I'll borrow one of Grandma's bicycles in the morning.

A cold breeze moves across my back even though it's hot as hell. This sticky heat makes me want to strip down and do nothing but sit in front of a fan with a piece of ice pressed against my neck. Searching for the source of the breeze, I turn around expecting to see a door swing shut, but then I remember that stores here don't have doors. Like in Chinatown back home, most storefronts have roll-up covers.

There's just a few pedestrians and bicyclists, no one within ten feet of me. And *yet* I feel eyes on me. It's the same feeling I get when I'm purposely avoiding eye contact with a teacher, and somehow they know it, because three seconds later they're calling my name. Yeah. That's the vibe I'm getting, like someone's about to confront me.

I turn around again to scan the area. Am I imagining things, or did I see a couple of heads duck behind a wall? Two more mopeds pass me going in the other direction.

Shi-et, I think to myself. I remember the money in my wallet. I should've spread it throughout my belongings. Some in my shoe, a little in my actual wallet, some in the zipper sewn into my boxers, and the bulk of it was supposed to stay in my suitcase. *Calm down, it's fine.* No one but me knows it's even there. I'll just head back now, separate it out, and everything will be fine. I step up my pace.

"Ey, Việt Kiều, where are you going?" *Việt Kiều* is me. In America, we call the newly arrived immigrants from Vietnam FOBS. Fobby kids, or FOBS, talk or dress like they're "fresh off the boat," meaning they wear pants that are too short and shirts that are too long. Here in Vietnam, I'm a Việt Kiều, which means "overseas Vietnamese." It essentially makes me the FOB in reverse. In either instance, it's not a good thing.

I pretend not to hear the question. The hairs on my neck rise as I contemplate which direction to run in. I know not every country operates the same, but back home, almost nothing good happens when a stranger hollers at you.

I walk on, doing my best not to look afraid or move in such a manner that it might look like I'm running.

"You don't hear us?" someone else demands.

I don't look to see who. I turn right, instantly regretting my choice when I see that it's a tiny alleyway. Footsteps follow me down the turn. I have no choice but to run now. I take off sprinting. The pitter-patter sounds move closer, too close. I reach the end and turn back toward our block. My eyes dart quickly down each row of identical lanes. Crap. Is that my alleyway? Or is it the next one? The mud-brick walls all look the same. There are no signs anywhere. I look for the rounded gate top of my grandparents' house. It's the most distinct thing I can remember. Heat travels up my spine as they near me. I'm pretty sure I'm about to get the beatdown when a hand slaps me on my shoulder.

"Hey, stop. Why are you running? We're all brothers here."

They don't feel like brothers. They feel like gangsters.

"I'm sorry. I don't understand," I lie in English.

The guy with a vise grip on my shoulder is maybe 5'5", but he's all muscle. Dude isn't buying my bullshit either.

"If you don't understand, why are you running?"

Damn. I have no good answer.

"I understand a little," I admit in Vietnamese.

His eyes widen like an alligator realizing he just bit into a fawn. "Việt Kiều knows Vietnamese." His tone sounds complimentary, but I doubt he means for it to. "Where are you going?" he asks.

"I'm walking," I say. It's the truth.

"What's your name?" he asks. His crew of guys vary in age. Their expressions range from amused to sinister.

"Paul," I say, opting for my non-Vietnamese name.

The guy pinches my shoulder and gestures to a noodle shop. "Surely, our Việt Kiều cousin wants to treat us to a dinner?"

"Dạ," I agree. If they wanna eat, I guess we're gonna eat. A part of me is hoping maybe my uncle or grandma will show up and rescue me.

We sit down at a restaurant that has no menus. A few torn posters of Tiger beer advertisements hang above the smattering of tables.

The ringleader shouts an order for five bowls of miến gà[12] to a stout lady whose floral shirt with misaligned buttons matches how I'm feeling.

"Can I also get a Coke?" I ask.

"Ooooo, Việt Kiều has money." One of the boys, who looks like the child version of my dad, smiles. He puts a finger up and says, "Four more please, *with ice*." Ice is not common in Vietnam, so it's expensive here. I see what he's doing.

The woman nods, goes to the kitchen. She returns with a tray of glass-bottle Cokes next to cups of ice. As she places the drinks on our table, I notice the guy holding my wallet.

He meets my gaze. "I had to make sure you had enough money to pay for this meal." He shoves my wallet into his pocket. I guess I should've seen that coming. Who knows when he jacked it from me, he's obviously a pro.

Each of the guys grabs a bottle, then angles the cap against the table. With a slam the metal caps pop off. I try twisting mine off—it won't budge. They all watch me as I tip the cap against the edge of the table. I lift my palm but before I can slam it down, I'm blocked by the leader's forearm.

"Anh Sáu should let the Việt Kiều try it," a beefy guy with high dimples says. So that's my captor's name: Anh Sáu, Brother Six.

---

12 *glass noodles with chicken*

"For sure. Lucky for him, I don't like to eat with blood at the table." Anh Sáu pops the lid off my soda.

The beefy guy pushes the ice away. "Uh-uh. No ice for Việt Kiều's weak stomach."

I don't know if he's saving me or taunting me. I swig. "Ulch!" Warm Coke on a hot, humid night is a form of punishment I didn't know existed until now.

A mosquito bites my calf. I slap it, smearing blood across my leg. Too late, my skin swells. I scratch the itch knowing I shouldn't.

Thankfully a large, and I mean large, silver tray emerges from the kitchen. On it, five bowls of steaming hot glass noodle soup with chicken. On the top are chopped green onions, some cilantro, and whole kernels of black pepper. I take a bite. It's delicious. Without stopping, I down the entire bowl, knowing this will be the most expensive meal I've ever had.

When I'm done, I stand to leave. I figure there's nothing left for them to shake me down for, so I start my walk home.

"Don't you need this?" Anh Sáu says, holding out my wallet. I reach for it. He yanks it back. I mentally slap myself for being such an idiot. "Việt Kiều is rather careless, maybe Anh will hold it for safekeeping."

It's humiliating to be punked like this. Especially by guys way shorter than me. But what am I gonna do, pick a fight that's six against one, then go to my grandma's house all bruised and bloody? No thanks. I slink away with their laughter ringing in my ears the whole way home.

Honestly, you'd think by now that I'd be immune to shame, given the crap I've endured as a child of refugees. One time, in the middle of a school day, my shoe split. At first, I tried to ignore the toe breeze and kept walking. My shoe had other plans. Every step stripped the glue more until the bottom half flapped so big, it looked like my shoe was a puppet. Also, my sock had a hole.

"You want me to find you some duct tape?" Mai asked, when I met up with her and Joe for lunch. The slapping noise my shoe made when it hit the pavement was kind of hard to miss.

"Umm, no. I'd rather walk around with no shoes," I said. Duct tape calls attention to itself, and I prefer invisibility.

"Remember when I cut my foot on that glass at the park? Let's not repeat that," Joe said, shaking his head. I remembered. Blood everywhere, stitches and crutches for a week. All because of a freaking cut.

"I'll be all right. The bottom is still there," I say.

"It's not a big deal. Just fix it, then ignore it. Like you taped it on purpose. It'll be like a new style," Mai suggested.

"The fact that you're telling me to ignore it instead of saying it's not embarrassing means it is embarrassing," I said.

"It's only embarrassing if you act like it's embarrassing. Like those guys with the sagging pants. Do they look embarrassed when they fall down? No, they just pull their pants over their asses and keep walking," she argued. Mai is always like this, very matter-of-fact in her answers. Easy for her to say, though. Mai always has new shoes. Homegirl probably has like forty pairs of sneakers. I'm talking high-tops, low-tops, Velcro, and even some identical ones, just in different colors. She denies being rich, but sneakers don't lie.

Returning from the memory, I look down at my own formerly white sneakers. They're scuffed, stained, and creased all over. *At least I still have my shoes,* I tell myself as I continue home. Sweat makes my neck itch. I reach up to scratch my collarbone. Dammit to hell. Those jackasses took my necklace too. I knew I should've left it at home. I press my palms against my temples. My return to the homeland is going super fucking well. *Thanks a lot, Jane.* None of this would've happened if she hadn't abandoned me.

I walk for a few minutes before I realize I have no idea where I'm going. One thing is for damn sure, I'm not turning around. I take a right and look for the yogurt stand I remember passing earlier. It's not there. I have no choice but to zigzag through the neighborhood. Panic creeps in when I realize I don't know my grandma's address. I loop two more blocks until I see the iron gate that I'm pretty sure is ours. "Thank god," I mutter, pushing through the gate into the familiar courtyard.

The house is as quiet as I left it. I climb the stairs and see a swiveling fan. I pull the tab to keep it from oscillating and climb into bed. At this point I don't even care if the mosquitoes bite me. It's not like this trip can get any worse.

Thankfully, I hadn't thought of taking the cell phone Jane gave me for emergencies. I flip open the silver Motorola Razr to text her. Halfway through a plea for help, I stop myself. What's the point? My plight is ripe for a lecture and that's the last thing I need right now. I delete the message.

Rolling my face into my pillow, I force myself to sleep. Tomorrow will mark one less day in hell.

CHAPTER 11
NGỌC LAN

"There's no way Grandma was chummy with the Communists," Jane says. "South Vietnamese hate them."

"I'm sorry, were you in Vietnam this past summer? I'm not saying this is how it for sure went down, but Grandma definitely does not hate the Communists. Maybe it's not about loving or hating them. Maybe it's just about survival."

"I mean, okay, but how does she go from selling fish sauce to being, like, rich?"

"Unclear, but this story isn't about Bà Ngoại, it's about Mom."

Jane looks out the window. I take that as my cue to continue.

While their mother sat in her home with a mortar and pestle, crushing sardines into a paste for fermentation, Vietnam was changing. The government organized itself, and life for South Vietnamese citizens became dire. Rations were meager. Uncertainty was high. Multiple neighbors stopped by to check on Mẹ and her daughters. They hinted, sometimes not so subtly, at their departure. They asked her to consider joining them. Their mother couldn't do it. She couldn't abandon her home knowing that her son could be fighting his way through jungle and fire to find her.

Chị Diễm worked longer hours as more and more people fled. Surrounded by bolts of fabric and spools of thread, she sat hunched on a wooden stool while customers bargained with the seamstress. Instead of sequins, though, her job now consisted of adding secret linings and inner pockets to plain clothing. There was decent money in helping people hide their valuables. Patrols placed along the beaches to monitor and stop escapees meant that Ngọc Lan was no longer allowed to swim. To pass the time, she lay on the floor in different parts of the house while looking for shapes in the rusted tin roof.

Mẹ hissed in the other room. With a click of her tongue she said, "Ngọc Lan, Mẹ needs a piece of cheese cloth from Cô Văn. Go ask for it and pick up your sister."

Ngọc Lan sprang up. "Dạ." She bowed. Then she ran for the door before her mom could change her mind.

Free to roam for the first time in months, Ngọc Lan took the long way to the market by biking up the coast along the beach. When she was a few kilometers away, the smell of smoke wafted around her. She looked skyward to see plumes of black. Pedaling as fast as she could, she raced for the market as people were fleeing and found several stalls crackling under bright orange flames.

"Trời ơi,"[13] Ngọc Lan whispered. Panicked, she biked to Cô Văn's stall. Heart pounding, knuckles white with fear, she arrived to find the fabrics ablaze. Spools of thread lay beneath the heat. The chair Chị Diễm normally sat in was a heap of melted plastic. "Chị Diễm!" she screamed.

"Don't stand there, go home," a voice said calmly. Ngọc Lan to turned see Chị Tuyết, a budding journalist whom Ngọc Lan had sometimes seen taking photos. White dust covered her neck and hands. She didn't have a camera now. People were leaving in the opposite direction from Ngọc Lan—where had Chị Tuyết come from?

"Have you seen my sister?" Ngọc Lan asked.

"She left."

"Which direction?"

Chị Tuyết looked around and pointed behind Ngọc Lan. She was calm. Not at all hurried. Ngọc Lan didn't know why, but it felt like Chị Tuyết was lying.

Despite her gut telling her to continue searching for her sister, Ngọc Lan went home.

"Mẹ! Cô Văn's stall burned. There's nothing left!" Ngọc Lan shouted.

Mẹ's eyes went wide. "Where is your sister?"

"She isn't home? I ran into Chị Tuyết, who told me Chị Diễm ran home." Stupid, stupid girl. Of course she should've looked for her sister! Why did she listen to Chị Tuyết?

---

13 *"Oh heavens."*

Both mother and daughter ran to the street, looking left and right for any sign of Chị Diễm. Terror gripped Ngọc Lan. Her body began to shake. "Chiị Dieễem . . ." Her lips quivered.

"Mẹ!" came a voice. Chị Diễm ran toward them. "Mẹ! The soldiers came. They told Cô Văn to pile her fabrics onto their wagon. Cô Văn tried to negotiate with them. She told them she would tailor whatever they wanted for free. A soldier slapped her."

Gripping Chị Diễm's shoulders firmly, Mẹ spun her around, looking for injuries. One pant leg was singed, along with the bottom quarter of her plain blouse. "How did your shirt burn?"

"I'm telling you. Cô Văn didn't want to give them her fabrics, but she couldn't argue with them. When they started carrying armloads away, she pulled out a can of gasoline, threw it on the fabrics, and lit it on fire."

"Huh?" their mom gasped. "Is that lady crazy? She let you stand there while she lit the world on fire?"

"No. She didn't know how big the flames would get. The fire jumped to me and Cô Văn put it out with her own two hands," Chị Diễm corrected.

Seeing the burnt fabric hang pathetically down her sister's back sent a surge of guilt flying through Ngọc Lan. "I saw the flames and ran to find you, but Chị Tuyết told me you left."

"Who?" Mẹ asked, as though hearing this name for the first time.

"Chị Tuyết, Bác Cào's daughter."

Mẹ shook her head. "No. Ngọc Lan probably mistook her

for someone else. Tuyết is dead. She died trying to pull her friend from the rubble of a bombed building."

"Impossible. I talked to her," Ngọc Lan said. She stopped. The white dust on her hands and neck. Was it rubble? This wasn't a stranger; Ngọc Lan had grown up buying friendship bracelets from Chị Tuyết. Her pennies had helped Chị Tuyết pay for her camera.

That night Ngọc Lan couldn't sleep. Images of the flames flashed through her memory. The sensation of heat all over made her afraid. Footsteps shuffled in the main room, then fell silent. She nudged Chị Diễm, who was also awake. Together they quietly chased after their mom.

Not particularly stealthy, the girls made it less than three blocks before Mẹ turned around abruptly to confront them. "Oh heavens, why did you two children follow Mẹ? For what?"

"We didn't want to be left by ourselves. What if someone lit our house on fire and we burned alive?" Ngọc Lan asked.

Their mother relented and the three of them continued on.

What had been roaring fires earlier in the day were dim embers by the time the mother and daughters arrived. Fire showed no mercy. Black smoke that had risen earlier returned to blanket the city center in ash. How something could go up black and return to earth white was something Ngọc Lan would think about for the rest of her life.

"Do you need any help?" their mom asked Cô Văn. Cô Văn appeared to be pulling unusable fragments of cloth from the piles of ash.

"Tell your boyfriend to leave us alone. I worked my whole life for this store and now I don't even have a piece of fabric to cover my crotch." When Cô Văn stood up, Ngọc Lan could see that her clothes had several burn holes. The patches of fabric in her hand were perhaps just big enough to lay over the gaps. "What's so special about *you*? You need fish and it arrives in a vat. We beg to make things for them and *look*." Cô Văn thrust scraps of blackened fabric at their mother.

"There is nothing special about me. If they want fish sauce, I will make fish sauce. A mother needs to feed her children."

"Remember this: a plain woman with beautiful morals is better than a beautiful woman with no morals. And *my* children don't need food? Without fabric to sell, clothes to sew, what are they supposed to do? Scoop dirt and eat it?"

"You chose to burn your own things. You should have let them take what they wanted," Mẹ responded. She regretted the words as soon as they came out of her mouth, but their mother didn't like how the woman blamed her for something she had no control over.

"And let the blood of my hands adorn the bodies of Việt Cộng wives? Kill me first," Cô Văn retorted.

"Wise people bite their tongue," a voice said from behind. The girls turned to see Bác Nga and several onlookers gawking at the verbal confrontation. Bác Nga wasn't chastising Cô Văn, though. This was her way of saying *Be careful what you say too loudly.* Bác Nga then turned to their mother and finished the proverb, "And strong people keep their arms folded."

Both women stopped arguing.

As the months wore on, curfews were put in place. Fear transformed into suspicion and paranoia. Communities broke apart, each family retreating inward as they strategized their survival. When the weekly rations distributed by the government were watered down to the point of nothing, the girls' bodies became weak with hunger.

Then rumors of labor and torture camps spread across the South. And not long after, those rumors arrived home. Men returned in the form of walking skeletons, many surviving the trip only to die in the arms of their loved ones. What was once talked about was now undeniable. More people fled.

Mẹ considered selling the fish sauce she had prepared for Bác Duy. Fear kept her from caving in to the gaunt stares of her daughters. Instead, she diluted the sauce more and more. If he or his wife noticed, they never said.

Desperation led people back to the beach. Unfortunately, too many untrained hands in the water scared away the catches. Then the dead body of Bé Bình Cao washed ashore. He was alone. His arms, legs, and torso had large gashes, probably made by the sharp rocks scattered across the shallow edge of the sea. And though his face was bloated, there was no mistaking the boy's centipede-like scar. A toddler with no fear, he had climbed a tree, then slid down it too fast, dragging his chin behind him. Bé Bình's family hadn't been seen in many months. Ngọc Lan would never learn what had happened to them. As with many of the lost people at sea, there was no recordkeeping, no book of answers.

The boy's death tainted the water. No one wanted to go

diving or fishing. No one but Ngọc Lan. She channeled her brother's bravado. Then she held her breath, stretched out her arms, and plunged in. When Ngọc Lan didn't feel any ghosts tugging at her body or hair, as others had warned her would happen, she went about collecting clams. Her courage was rewarded with a full bag and two beautiful blue crabs.

Upon her ascent, a thick, solid shadow swam beside her. *There's nothing to fear. Ghosts only haunt evil humans,* she told herself.

Be brave. She forced a gaze in its direction. Clear open water filled her peripheral vision. *Just your mind playing tricks on you.* Her lungs tightened. What if she was wrong? If a ghost pushed the air from her lungs this deep down, she'd drown. Everyone would assume that her death was an accident, a careless error. Ngọc Lan kicked for the surface. *I will not go without a fight.* Bursting through the top, she gasped. She hadn't felt this desperate for oxygen in years.

She locked eyes with Chị Diễm, who dutifully sat on the sand waiting for her stubborn sister. Normally, when Chị Diễm saw Ngọc Lan emerge, she met her at the water's edge. Today, though, Chị Diễm's vacant stare was somewhere far beyond Ngọc Lan. A strand of seaweed caught on Ngọc Lan's foot. She shook her leg, but the leaves clung tighter. Frustrated, she dipped under to pull herself free, and came face to face with a figure draped in red, with skin covering only half her face.

Thrashing upward, Ngọc Lan closed her eyes and moved in the direction of the shore. For every stroke forward, she fell two strokes back. The beach shrank farther and farther into the distance. Fatigue stretched her muscles. She considered giving in. Then her palm slammed into sand and she found herself ashore. Ngọc Lan stood up, her legs shaking as she stared at the bruised purple finger imprint on her left ankle. A yellow shimmer, the color of jaundice, fell away with the receding water, but the imprint remained.

"Whoa! You collected so much!" Chị Diễm exclaimed. Ngọc Lan had no idea when her sister had appeared beside her, but she was grateful not to be alone. "Wait until we sell the clams. Today we're going to eat until our stomachs are full."

Ngọc Lan forced herself to smile. Even though Chị Diễm was older, she had always been more cautious. Ngọc Lan knew that if she confided in her sister about the ghost pulling, Chị Diễm wouldn't let her return to the water. She had heard of mothers seeing spirits more vividly after losing their children in bombings and explosions. Perhaps the same thing happened when dads and brothers deserted their daughters and sisters.

At home, the girls boiled water and cooked fifteen clams, five for each of them, in anticipation of their mother's return.

"Should we cook a crab too?" Chị Diễm asked.

Ngọc Lan's mouth immediately began watering, but she pushed her hunger aside and said, "No, we need rice." Crabs were far more valuable than clams, and rice kept them full longer.

Mẹ walked in the door as the girls pulled the clams out. "Mẹ, come eat," Ngọc Lan said.

"Mẹ isn't hungry. You two go ahead," their mother said. Without looking at the girls, she entered the bedroom, gathered her nightgown, and went to the bath. Worried, they followed. Within seconds water splashed onto the ground. Soon, with each bucketful a sob fell with it. Through the curtain they could see their mother, still fully clothed, pouring water over herself as she scrubbed viciously at her legs.

Ngọc Lan stood frozen. Even with Chị Diễm's arm wrapped firmly across her shoulders, she felt like a statue.

"Don't stand here anymore," Chị Diễm whispered. "Đi."

Together, the two returned to eat their dinner.

"Do you think Mẹ was—"

Chị Diễm cut her off: "Shh." They each knew what the other was wondering. Had their mother been raped?

After thirty minutes—an eternity, compared to their mother's normal five-minute baths—Mẹ emerged humming the tune she used to sing to lull the girls to sleep at night.

Hm, hm, hm, hm, hm, hm, hm-hmmmm…
Hm, hm, hm, hm, hm, hm, hm-hmmmm…

Chị Diễm offered her mother food a second time. Again, she refused. "I ate already. My stomach is very full." The sisters didn't know what to do, so they accepted their mother's lie. And they ate her portion though neither of them were hungry any longer. As she chewed, Ngọc Lan bit down on sand. Instead of spitting it out, she opened her throat, swallowing both sand and clam whole.

The walk to the beach the next morning was solemn and quiet until Chị Diễm blurted, "Do you think Mom is being raped by Bác Duy?"

Ngọc Lan looked at her sister wide-eyed. She had not expected her to say this. "No. No. That's not right. Mẹ wouldn't let that happen. And Bác Duy is a gentleman."

"You saw Mẹ yesterday. If not Bác Duy, then who?"

Ngọc Lan was silent. Everything she knew about Bác Duy contradicted this, but she knew that women without husbands were not treated with respect. And there was no denying that something had happened. Seeing her mom broken and vulnerable infuriated her. She ached for her mom, but selfishly, she also wondered how a mother who couldn't protect herself could possibly protect them.

This was why, when they reached the water, Ngọc Lan left her sister sitting in the sand. She dove in before her mind had time to think. Deeper and deeper she went, silently telling the ghosts to grab her if they wanted. She was afraid but refused to let her thoughts betray those fears. Her mind was strong. If they came, she would fight them. If they won, well, she'd be dead anyway. Fury propelled her forward. She collected abalone, clams, and urchin before realizing she was deeper than she'd ever gone before and no spirits had touched her. Ghosts prey on the weak, and Ngọc Lan wasn't weak.

CHAPTER 12
PAUL

When I come downstairs after an oddly restful sleep, I notice that the sun is just barely lighting up the early morning.

"Did you sleep to your heart's content?" Bà Nội asks, startling me. As my eyes adjust, I see my grandma sitting a few feet away from me. In her lap is a garment she's sewing by hand. How can she even see what she's doing? I squint and still can't make out the needle and thread, even though I can see her hands moving.

"Dạ. Did Bà Nội sleep well?" I ask.

"Bà Nội is old. I'll sleep when I'm dead."

I laugh. I forgot how funny my grandma is.

I rub my eyes. The sky is a speckled navy blue. My grandparents always keep their front door open. I guess it's protected by the high-walled perimeter. Also, there isn't much to steal. I'm not surprised because our house is the same. Everything is functional. Decorations are a waste of money.

I take a seat beside her as she straightens out the garment. "Today, what will we do?" I ask. My language skills aren't great, but they're way better than they were nine years ago.

I am a native English speaker first. I learned Vietnamese because my aunt Mợ Bích forced me to. It began during inventory day. I said, "We need more chips."

She replied, "Quốc Bảo cần thêm chip."

So I nodded, saying "Dạ," as in "Yes."

Mợ Bích was having none of that. "Quốc Bảo cần thêm chip," she said over and over.

I relented, saying, "Paul cần thêm chip." Nobody called me by my Vietnamese name, so I wasn't about to let this strange lady, family or not, rename me.

She conceded with a simple nod and "Giỏi," which was one of the few words I knew—it meant "Good."

We volleyed words and phrases like this for more than a year. Then one day, I made it through an eight-hour shift at the shop without using a single English word. After that, the rest kind of came naturally.

"Today we go hit fish," Bà Nội says.

"Hit fish?" I imagine my grandma standing in the water and slapping fish into submission. Straight up, the image checks; Bà Nội is definitely badass enough to do it.

"Hit fish," she repeats while pretending to reel with her hands. We're going fishing. It never ceases to amaze me how hilarious a lot of the literal translations are. The more I speak Vietnamese, though, the more I see how the language reflects the culture. It's not just what the words mean but how they're used to construct sentences that really highlight the Vietnamese spirit. Of course a Vietnamese person would hit a fish to catch it; we're big on slapping things into submission.

"Where is my dad?" I ask.

"Your dad went to Sài Gòn to turn in paperwork."

My dad left for another city in the middle of the night without saying anything to me—how *not* surprising.

I wait for her to elaborate. She doesn't. As far as I know, my parents never actually got a divorce. Mợ Bích says that's why my dad can't remarry. God, I hadn't ever considered what a stepmom would be like. I always thought owning a business with your ex-(not actually divorced)wife's brother would be enough to deter a woman. I mean, if I walked into our situation, I'd turn around and walk right out too. Then a thought hits me: if they brought my mother's body to Vietnam to bury her, it makes sense that my dad would have to turn in paperwork or whatever. I wonder if they'll have a funeral. I wonder if I'll be attending.

"Đi," Bà Nội says, getting up. "Let's eat quickly before the sun rises too high."

No offense, Grandma, it's already too hot, I want to say, but don't.

When my grandmother is up to no good, her eyes twitch as she smiles. She has prominent wrinkles at her temples that are so deep they look like scars; they betray her devious nature because they wiggle when she thinks she's cleverly hiding a secret. After breakfast we return to the courtyard, where she deftly hops on a motorbike, kicks up the stand, steps down on the starter, and steadies herself before gesturing for me to hop on.

"Which instance do I get to drive?" I ask.

"When do you get to drive?" she corrects. "When I'm ready to see God." She's still laughing as she gases the engine. We speed off.

Vietnam is noisy even in the early hours, with motorbikes

crisscrossing this way and that. Every time I think I understand the traffic patterns, we move counter to what I believe. No wonder she won't let me drive. Unlike the paved roads we took coming in from the airport, we're now bumping along on dirt pathways full of mini-craters. She weaves around or through the holes with ease despite the 155-pound person on her rear. I really hope the tire beneath me doesn't pop. My only job is to use my legs to steady us when she stops—something she tries to do as infrequently as possible.

When we reach the beach, Bà Nội unloads the foam cooler strapped down by a bungee cord behind me. I offer to carry it, but she swats my hand away. "I may look old, but I'm stronger than you."

I laugh. I'm as scrawny as I am tall. None of this matters, though, because the box is empty. I don't argue. I'll carry it when it's full of fish. As we approach the water, a boy my age greets us. I do a double take. *What in the actual hell?* My eyes must be lying to me.

"Chào Bà Tâm," Anh Sáu says, bowing to my grandmother. Tâm is my grandmother's name. I rarely hear it used in our house, but it was scrawled all over our luggage boxes. He winks at me. I want to punch him in the face.

"Today, you will teach em Quốc to hit fish," Bà Nội says to Anh Sáu.

"Oh no," I say, backing away. Uh-uh, no way I'm doing anything with this asshole.

"Dạ." He nods in deference to my grandma. Then to me, "Let's go, Paul." Grandma doesn't catch his use of my American name, but I hear it loud and clear.

"I don't want to," I say to my grandma. The words sound petulant, and make me feel like a child. This guy is obviously a two-faced lying sack of shit. I wonder if he's still holding my wallet. What if he tries to feed me to the sharks or something?

"Go, go," Bà Nội says, flicking her wrist the way one might shoo away a dog.

The guy smirks at me. "Don't worry. I watch after you, Việt Kiều," he says in English. When people call me this, I never know if they're being friendly or making fun of me. Also, the way he says he'll watch over me implies that he'll keep me alive but doesn't guarantee I'll retain my limbs.

"You stole my wallet," I say in English.

"Anh really hates Việt Kiều that can't speak the Vietnamese language," he replies.

"Anh robbed me," I say in Vietnamese.

He laughs. "Calm down, the neighborhood just wanted to welcome Việt Kiều home."

"That's a weird freaking welcome," I mutter.

He pulls my wallet from his pocket and hands it to me. I tear it open to check for my missing bills. It's all there. He doesn't look at me. Relief washes over me as I stuff it deep into my pocket.

"What about my necklace?"

"What necklace?" he asks.

"My gold necklace. I was wearing it the same night you stole my wallet."

"I don't know about any necklace, but seeing how careless you are, I'm not surprised someone stole it from you."

"I just barely stepped out of my house when you robbed me. Who else could have taken it?"

Anh Sáu glares at me like I'm stupid. "And you held on to it tight on the airplane, through the airport, baggage claim, customs, and through the mob of people outside the airport?"

He's got me there. I touched it at some point, didn't I? Yes, it was cold. There were lots of people around after that, though.

I think he's waiting for me to apologize. Not happening. C'mon, dude, you literally stole all my money yesterday. Why wouldn't I accuse you of taking my necklace?

He hands me a cone-shaped straw hat. I think he must be joking. I'm already wearing a baseball cap. Also, just being honest here, his hat looks ridiculous. He looks like a human spin top. "No thanks," I say, pointing to mine.

He shrugs, then tosses the hat into a large basket we've stopped in front of. When I say it's a large basket, I mean exactly that. Take a round basket from Michaels, remove the handle, and make it a hundred times bigger. That is what this guy is planning to use as a boat out in the open ocean. "Are you sure this will float?"

He doesn't answer me. I'm confused. Yesterday when he was stealing from me, he was all bright and fun. Now he's being all emo and moody.

"Jump in," he says.

"I don't want to drown," I say, holding my throat and trying to mime drowning. Anh Sáu appears perplexed. I start waving my hands, pretending to gulp for air.

The corner of his mouth twitches. He tries to turn away from me, but not before I catch the biggest shit-eating grin on his face. He full-on bursts out laughing. "You think I'd let a precious Việt Kiều drown? Bà Tâm would whup me into infinity."

Truth. Grandma is squatting under a large umbrella with the two large foam containers from our motorbike next to her. She's a thin woman, but she's muscular and vibrant. The first time I met her, I was a little kid, so she seemed like a giant, especially because Jane is a shorty. Now she barely reaches my chin, but that's pretty tall by Vietnamese standards, even in America. According to what Jane told me, my grandma is a total warrior woman who built and rebuilt her home during the war.

With Anh Sáu on one side and me on the other, we shake the basket loose of the sand divot it's sitting in. He pulls while I push until we're knee-deep in calmly lapping water. I can see forty or fifty of these baskets dotting the horizon amid motorized wooden boats. Once we're in the basket, he hands me a plastic jug. Upon closer inspection, I see that it is a milk gallon container with the top third carefully cut off. The milk jug is now a pitcher.

"Scoop the water out, so we don't drown," he says.

The bottom of the basket pools with water every few minutes. I get the sense that this job is some sort of penance. Honestly, I'm about ready to jump my ass out of this boat and swim back to shore. Only thing stopping me is having to explain why I hate this punk to my grandma.

I bend down to do my job. The boat immediately tips toward Anh Sáu's side. Without a word, he steps a foot toward me, balancing us—all while still paddling. I scoop the water as quickly as possible, stopping when there's about an inch left because no matter how much I scoop, the basket is never entirely dry.

When I look up, he's brought us beyond where any of the other baskets or boats have stopped. "Are you sure this thing can handle being this far from shore?"

"Can you swim?" he asks, feigning concern.

"Yes." *I'm a state champion, in fact,* I think but don't say. It's probably best not to encourage him to push me over.

"Then don't worry about it. Worst thing that happens is the boat sinks and you swim home." Anh Sáu obviously takes pleasure in my discomfort. Just when I think I should cut and bail and swim for the shore, he stops. He pulls the paddle in, then picks up a net he had carefully draped on one side of the boat. "Watch it," he says, before flinging it over my head, into the water.

The clear net shimmers like a giant spiderweb hovering over the surface before sinking. He lets the mesh fall for a bit before he starts tugging in intervals. As the snare is pulled carefully into the boat, fish drop into the basket. Surprised by the flopping, I step back, nearly falling overboard. My high center of gravity is not meant for these boats.

"Now what?" I ask.

"Now we wait for the water to calm." He sits on the rim, triumphant. Every time he moves, it feels like the boat is going to capsize. I don't ask him to stop.

Out of nowhere Anh Sáu says, "You know, just because you live in America doesn't make you better than me."

I'm confused. "When did I say I was better than Anh?"

"You Việt Kiều are all the same. Uppity Vietnamese who think your money makes you kings here. You're not shit."

I've heard enough. Get me the hell away from this guy. I shake my head and glance down at the water. It's not that deep. The shore looks like it's maybe six pool laps away. I'm out.

I stand abruptly, causing the boat to tilt. As I lean into a dive, my stomach scrapes against the basket's edge. I belly flop overboard. Not exactly the "screw you" leap I was going for. Note to self: It's really hard to dive from a basket boat. Surfacing, I take a breath. Then I swim for shore.

I haven't spent much time in the ocean. All my swimming happens in pools, so I'm surprised by how much the water moves. I'm a solid swimmer, but this is different—it takes twice as much effort to move half the distance. About halfway to shore I stop to rest, letting my body float in the water. The sky is bright and serene, calm even, until I feel something wiggle beneath me. Then I remember that there are living creatures in the ocean.

Cool water passes under me. I shiver. Time to keep swimming. I beeline it toward the beach with steady strokes. The salt water stings. After a while, I'm forced to swim with my eyes closed. I open them only every ten strokes or so to make sure there's nothing in front of me or that I haven't drifted. I'm exhausted by the time my feet find water shallow enough for me to stand in. I catch my breath. Looking around, I notice that there's not a single other person in the water. Odd.

Waves push me forward as a pelvic pressure pulls me back. I stumble, losing my balance, and have to catch myself. It takes serious effort to keep my body upright. My shoes feel like twenty-pound weights wrapped around my ankles. The shore somehow keeps stretching farther away. I look down. My reflection wobbles in front of me before another figure appears beside it.

A familiar tune begins to play.

Tình mẹ bao la như biển khơi xa[14]

Hm, hm, hm, hm, hm, hm, hm-hmmmm . . .

Where have I heard this song before?

The sallow and sunken face of a girl about my age peers up at me. She kind of looks like me, but more than how she looks, she feels connected to me. It's like how in my dreams I know people are my friends but when I wake up, I have no idea who they are. She is mesmerizing, like a siren from that book *The Odyssey*. I'm drawn to the girl in a way that feels controlled, by *her*. What's wild is I know following her will cause me to drown; yet I'm pulled to follow anyway. My body is leaning in to dive toward her when something hits my back.

"Ey! Mày nghĩ mày ngon, eh?" Anh Sáu says. He's glaring at me. The literal translation to his jeering is "Hey, you think you're so tasty?" What it means is "Oh, you think you're hot shit?" "Next time I'll let you drown," he adds, paddling past me to the shore. First, what he's saying is hilarious considering I swam the whole way myself. Second, I'd rather drown than be rescued by him.

"Next time I'll let the ghost pull you all the way, so you learn your lesson," he mutters. This catches my attention. "This crazy asshole, jumping in water he doesn't know." He's talking about me, to himself.

"Hey," I say, chasing after him. I grab onto the basket, pretending to help. Really, though, I don't want to let go. I'm caught between my hatred for him and my curiosity about what I just experienced.

---

14 *A mother's love stretches ocean wide*

He looks at me, amused. For a moment I wonder if she was an elaborate prank he set up. But how could he have known I'd jump? The basket hits sand. He leaps out. I follow, still thinking about the girl. "I only need to look at your face to know."

"Know what?"

"Việt Kiều was pulled by a ghost." His smile is sinister now; he's enjoying the shit out of this. "Do you know how many people have drowned in that water?"

The photo of my dad's cousin on the family altar flashes before me. I'm suddenly very aware of my feet, which are still in said ocean of death.

"More than one hundred thousand. Think about it, more than one hundred thousand lost souls looking for a replacement."

Anh Sáu's taunting me. I shouldn't listen, but shit if I don't feel a light brushing of fingertips across my ankles. On instinct, I sort of run/trip until the water is several feet behind me.

"What's going on?" Bà Nội asks, approaching us.

"Anh chàng nay[15] wanted to go swimming. He had a ghost pull him. Look at his pale face," Anh Sáu says.

"Mmm, a lot of wandering souls in the ocean," Bà Nội laments. Then she knuckles Anh Sáu's temple. "Let Quốc drown and he'll come drag your spirit with him."

"For sure," I say without much energy. Honestly, I'm feeling gross all over. Like I've been groped by something I didn't consent to. It doesn't help that I'm dripping wet. My clothes cling to me like they too are afraid of getting pulled back into the water by a restless spirit.

---

15 · *This guy*

CHAPTER 13

No thirteen either. It's bad luck in the US *and* Vietnam!

CHAPTER 14

Four is bad. *Fourteen* includes *four.* Fourteen be gone.

CHAPTER 15
NGỌC LAN

"Did Grandma confirm the rape?" Jane asks.

I stare at her. "What do you think?"

"I think you didn't ask her."

"Bingo. Why does it matter anyway? I mean, do you really need to know? I don't."

"No, I guess not," Jane says. "Has anyone ever told you you're wiser than you look?"

I smile. Not only because Jane rarely gives compliments unless they're dripping in sarcasm, but because I can see her softening.

After months of eating nothing but seafood with a few radishes and carrots, the girls started having digestive issues. Chị Diễm's weakened immune system developed into a persistent cough. When her wheeze turned shallow, a sign of Chị Diễm's waning energy, their mother and Ngọc Lan went to Bác Nga's house to beg for medicine. Bác Nga welcomed them into the courtyard.

Since the market burned, Bác Nga and the other merchants traded from their homes.

"What has happened with Diễm?" Bác Nga asked.

"She has been sweating and shaking for three days. This morning she threw up blood." Ngọc Lan's eyes went wide—she didn't know what this meant, but she knew blood coming out of someone's mouth was bad.

"Chest pain, trouble breathing?" Bác Nga asked.

"Yes. She's so weak that I can barely get her to open her mouth to eat."

Bác Nga was highly regarded in the community for her homeopathic remedies. She boiled herbal teas, grew gingerroot, and pounded turmeric leaves into medicines used by everyone. She had a cure for almost everything. Hope sprang forth.

"Persistent cough?"

"Dạ." Mẹ nodded eagerly, hoping this meant she had the remedy.

"Tuberculosis."

"I don't know," Mẹ said.

Bác Nga ignored her; it wasn't a question. She brought out green medicated oil, dầu xanh. "Every day, dip her body in the ocean for at least ten minutes. Rub this under her nose and on her chest. Coin her. Make sure it soaks in. After two weeks, she should get better." In a tattered plastic bag, she collected: clothing, overripe bananas, a slightly molding papaya, and a single clove of garlic.

Holding the garlic clove in her palm, the same way one might hold a diamond, Bác Nga said, "Make sure she eats this raw."

Ngọc Lan had come along in case Bác Nga needed her to fetch ingredients, but Bác Nga had everything.

"Bác Nga is planning on crossing over?" Mẹ asked after noticing that the courtyard, typically lined with motorbikes, was empty.

"Don't talk nonsense," Bác Nga said, reluctantly pushing Ngọc Lan's mother inside the house before any of the neighbors overheard. Inside, the emptied-out home confirmed what Mẹ suspected. They were preparing to flee the country.

"Can you take Ngọc Lan with you?" Mẹ whispered pleadingly. She did not want her family to separate, but her inability to provide was becoming undeniable.

Bác Nga's posture stiffened. "Take Ngọc Lan where? I don't know what you're saying."

"Bác Nga knows what a good girl Ngọc Lan is. Don't leave her here to rot."

Bác Nga's tone softened. "Every person has their time of bad luck. Don't worry. It will turn."

"My children are starving. Diễm is gravely ill. I can't be sure I will survive my next bout of sickness. If I die, what will become of them? Please, bring Ngọc Lan with you."

"Go, go quickly. Take care of your daughters." Bác Nga's hug told Mẹ everything; it was long and tight. A promise that she would try. In a low voice, Bác Nga added, "There is no guarantee that we won't all drown at sea." Then, in her normal voice, she said, "I have lived here my whole life. I don't want to go anywhere else."

That last part Mẹ knew was true. No one wanted to leave.

Not like this. Bác Nga and Bác Hiếu had a thriving business. Her sons had avoided being drafted into labor camps by providing the new government with bountiful amounts of daily fish. But rebuilding after a war was no easy task. They would be called eventually. Bác Nga's face carried the weight of her worries. Her normally assured feet toddled unsteadily. Bác Hiếu had always been generous. That goodwill earned the family loyalty. If anyone could secure safe passage, Mẹ believed it was Bác Hiếu.

"All these years, Bác Nga has helped my family. Thank you for the medicine. If not in this lifetime, then the next one, I will repay my gratitude."

"Ay! Don't say more. Go, go!" Bác Nga said firmly. She waved them off the way she might shoo away a fly. Compliments made her uncomfortable. But before Ngọc Lan turned to follow her mom, she caught a twitch of a smile.

On the street, her mother walked with her head down as small rocks and pebbles were thrown at her. With her arms wrapped tightly around Ngọc Lan's head, she hoped her daughter would close her ears to the harassment. By this point it was clear to everyone that Mẹ's husband had abandoned them. Women without husbands were not looked upon kindly. What made Mẹ's situation worse were the rumors that spread after the fish arrived.

"You're like a cockroach that won't die."

"Just wait, God will strike you from the sky."

"No wonder your husband left you. Tell your daughters to steer clear of mine."

"My family is starving because of you."

"Women like you bring shame on all of us," someone spat. At this Mẹ's bristled. Whether they were true or not, her mother swallowed the insults the way one might gulp water while drowning.

Deep down, Ngọc Lan knew that whatever they were talking about had something to do with her mother crying in the shower. And she too looked down in shame. Ngọc Lan didn't want to hate Bác Duy. Her stomach twisted at the thought of all the candy he'd given her over the years. If they were right, her belly was full of rotten sugar.

Before they reached the door, Ngọc Lan tugged at her mom's arm. "Mẹ, did Bác Duy rape you?"

Her mother stopped. Without hesitation she said, "No. Bác Duy is a good person."

"Was it someone else? Because the other day. In the bathroom. Chị Diễm and I . . ." Ngọc Lan tried to say the words, but she couldn't bring herself to speak the rest.

Clutching her shoulders in a firm grip, Mẹ explained, "There's a lot that you can't possibly understand. Sometimes Mẹ's feelings hurt. I cry to let go of the pain." Looking Ngọc Lan in the eye, she added, "Look at Mẹ. Mẹ is tough. Not like you and your sister. A little ache and you're out for days." Her mother smiled, trying to make light of the situation, but the situation didn't feel light.

Despite the medicine, Chị Diễm's fever continued to ripple through her body. Her moans and delirium rose to frightening new levels.

"Mẹ, Chị Diễm is dying," Ngọc Lan worried aloud.

"Be quiet," her mother scolded. "Don't speak nonsense. Come help Mẹ." Mẹ picked up Chị Diễm's thin frame. They walked to the beach.

As her mother entered the water, Ngọc Lan grew anxious. The current was strong. Others looked on. No one moved to stop them. "Mẹ? Mẹ, what are you doing?" Ngọc Lan heard Bác Nga's instructions, *ten minutes in the ocean every day,* but Chị Diễm was shivering. "Stop, please, Mẹ. Come back. Chị Diễm is so cold. She's too cold," Ngọc Lan begged.

Mẹ shuddered despite the humid heat. "My daughter," she said, "you need to gather your strength. You need to toughen up. Mẹ needs you. Ngọc Lan needs you." Chị Diễm's body relaxed and she stopped shaking. After a few minutes, her mother draped Chị Diễm over her shoulder like one might hold a toddler. They returned to the house.

They changed her clothes, wrapping her in a blanket. When her sister's quivering reached new heights, they moved her to a mat in the kitchen. There she was kept close to a small stove fire.

Every hour, Ngọc Lan rubbed more dầu xanh[16] over her sister's temples, under her nose, then down her torso.

Night turned into day with no change. Again, Mẹ carried Chị Diễm's now yellowing body to the ocean. This time, with Ngọc Lan's help, she cradled her daughter's head while Ngọc Lan kept Chị Diễm fully immersed. Ten minutes later, they went home.

---

16 *Herbal medicine. It's Advil, Tylenol, Sudafed, Robitussin—all the remedies—wrapped in one.*

At the door, several food bags sat on the stoop. One contained a bowl of warm rice congee with several rare pieces of chicken and a generous amount of scallion. Mẹ pulled Chị Diễm upright, using her body as a seat back so that Ngọc Lan could spoon-feed her sister.

The soup dribbled out of Chị Diễm's mouth. "Keep going," her mother urged.

Ngọc Lan's stomach grumbled. She hadn't had rice of any kind in months, and cháo was one of her favorite dishes.

"Eat a little of it yourself while it's still hot." Her mother nodded.

Ngọc Lan took a bite, telling herself to only have three spoonfuls. Far from satiated, though, she felt an angry hunger take over and she couldn't stop herself from stealing a fourth.

"Feed your sister more," Mẹ said gently. Ngọc Lan could tell that it pained her mom not to be able to offer her a full meal.

"Is Chị Diễm even able to digest?" Ngọc Lan asked. Hunger made her selfish.

Mẹ didn't chastise her. Instead, she pointed to Chị Diễm's throat. "Watch here as she swallows."

She saw an ever-so-slight wiggle. Encouraged, she added chicken. Chị Diễm immediately began choking. Mẹ thumped her back with a force generally meant for punishment, until the stringy meat spilled onto the floor. Ngọc Lan couldn't help but think of the waste.

Chị Diễm groaned.

"More," Mẹ coaxed. "Try harder, my daughter."

Chị Diễm swallowed two more spoonfuls.

"Good! Good, eat more," Mẹ encouraged.

Two hours later, having consumed only half the bowl of congee, Chị Diễm fell asleep.

Once her sister was beside the cozy fire, Ngọc Lan asked, "Mẹ, does the food mean no one hates us anymore?"

Her mother sighed. "It's hard to understand, but Mẹ thinks many people don't want to be mean. They are scared to be ostracized too. Daughter, try not to bear a grudge against them for what they say."

Ngọc Lan sat silent, unable to find comfort in her mother's words. Instead, she lay down beside her sister, listening to the steady inhale and exhale of her shallow breathing. Her sister was the only thing that mattered. If the food helped her sister heal, she could forgive anything.

They stayed like this for a long time before her mother asked, "My daughter, are you asleep?"

Ngọc Lan considered saying nothing. The way her mother asked the question scared her. "Not yet," Ngọc Lan answered, staring into the flickering flame.

"Mẹ needs you to listen carefully," her mother began. "Mẹ doesn't know when, but there will be a time when you need to leave us. Bác Hiếu and Bác Nga are preparing to cross over. They will take you with them."

Tears immediately fell from Ngọc Lan's cheeks. "I don't want to go."

"Bác Hiếu and Bác Nga see you as their niece. You'll be safe."

"But I don't want to live in a different place than Mẹ and Chị Diễm."

"Mẹ needs you to be brave. Can't you see? Mẹ cannot take care of both of you. But don't worry, Mẹ and your sister will follow close behind you."

"And what about Anh Hòa?"

"It's possible . . . it's possible that Anh Hòa has left already."

Left Vietnam or left this earth? Ngọc Lan wanted to ask. She choked down her sob. Ngọc Lan knew the words would only cause her mother more sadness.

"When you get there, find your father. He will help you. Your father probably misses you very much. Mẹ has heard that in America, food is in abundance. The portions are so generous that you can eat until your stomach hurts, and still, there is more food. If you lose your way, return to water. Mẹ wants you to have a bright future . . ." Her voice trailed off.

Ngọc Lan understood. She was a burden, an extra mouth to feed when her mom already had one daughter requiring medical attention. They needed her to go. "Dạ," Ngọc Lan whispered.

"Good girl," Mẹ said. Kissing her daughter's forehead, she let her lips linger for as long as a goodbye.

CHAPTER 16
PAUL

When Anh Sáu said he'd pick me up at 7 a.m. I figured he meant 8 a.m. because Asian Pacific Time runs an hour late. But no. I have somehow met the one punctual Vietnamese person on the planet. When I hear his motorbike pull up, I'm having my usual breakfast in the dark with Bà Nội (thank you, jet lag).

"Have you eaten yet?" Grandma asks him.

"Dạ I've eaten already," he says. With that, she leaves us alone.

"Who taught you how to ride a motorbike?" I ask, gesturing to the bike in case he doesn't fully understand me.

He laughs. "As soon as I could get my leg over the top, I stole the key, revved the engine, and crashed into the courtyard wall. I taught myself."

"Is that legal?" He looks at me, confused. "The police don't care?" I rephrase.

"You must be eighteen to get a license, but sixteen-year-olds can drive bikes under 50cc."

"So, I can ride one?" Vietnam is about to get a whole lot more interesting if this is true.

"You can if you can find someone to loan you their bike," he says. "You see this?" He shows me a scar on his calf. "Stopped at a light. This lady pulls up next to me, squeezing in where she doesn't fit, so I, of course, don't move, and she burns me with her exhaust pipe. Đụ mẹ,"[17] he laments. "Anyway, we wouldn't want Việt Kiều to go home with ugly scars."

"You're sixteen, the same age as me?"

He nods. "But you have to call me Anh because my grandmother is older than yours."

This is what I hate about the Vietnamese language. Anh Sáu could be twelve, and I'd still have to call him Anh, meaning "older," because his grandmother's higher status automatically trumps any age gain I might have over him. And what would the world be if everyone didn't know their place? Instead of finagling over who is upper and lower, we could all just use names OR *gasp* the simple catch-all-word *you*. In Vietnamese, *you* is like *asshole;* it can be both endearing and used to start a fight.

"So, you want to learn to ride?" he asks. He's taunting me.

"Yes." I say this like I'm daring him to teach me.

"No! You want your grandma to kill me?" he says loudly, looking behind me. Then he whispers, "We have to leave this place first." I hesitate for a second. He lifts his chin to me. "What, you scared?"

Scared of riding the motorbike? No. Scared of getting the living crap beat out of me if my dad sees me, yes. "Đi," I say because as scared as I am of my dad, I'm not about to step down from a challenge from Anh Sáu.

---

17 *Vietnamese curse word roughly translated as "motherfucker."*

"Việt Kiều has some balls!"

I can't tell if he's starting to like me or if he's found the perfect way to have me killed without getting his hands dirty. As soon as he says that, though, I know it's on because it's obvious Anh Sáu is not one to play by the rules. Jane would kill me with a capital *K* if she knew what I was about to do.

But Jane isn't here. And it's not like I met Anh Sáu on the street. He's family.

My phone dings. Jane.

From: Jane

Checking for a pulse.

It's like she has ESP. Creepy.

From: Paul

Alive. Only 30 mosquito bites so far.

From: Jane

Must be all that Vietnamese food Mo Bich makes for you. Confuses the skeeters.

I tuck the phone into my pocket.

"You crash my bike, I take your phone. Deal?" Anh Sáu says.

"My phone?" I should've known there was an ulterior motive.

"Yeah. Phones are costly here. I could sell it for a lot of money."

I think about it: a cell phone for a motorcycle? Seems like a pretty good deal. "Okay, but I have to keep it until I leave."

"Okay." He puts out his hand and we shake. "Đi."

He takes me to a secluded stretch of the beachside road and parks.

Anh Sáu shows me how to turn the throttle and pull on the handle for the front and back brakes. The lesson lasts about forty-five seconds before he's handing me the keys. It occurs to me suddenly that we have no helmets. Only half the people wear helmets here. Maybe because it's not as dangerous? Yeah, let's go with that.

I throw my leg over the bike, standing easily above it. Sit. Turn the key, step on the starter, and . . . nothing.

"Step harder," he says.

I step down again, but still, it doesn't turn over.

Anh Sáu comes over. He puts his full weight on the starter. It roars to life. "The motorbike is not a girl. You don't have to be gentle."

I don't respond, but in my head, I can hear Jane schooling him on how women are actually stronger than men. If she were here, she'd take the keys and show us how she can not only do whatever we do, but she'll do it better. Jane's competitive like that. A lifetime spent correcting our dad's sexist remarks will do that to a person.

I brace myself and turn the throttle slowly. The bike lurches forward just as I realize I don't know how to slow down.

"Ahh!" I screech.

"Release your hand!" Anh Sáu shouts. I don't know which hand to release, so I let go of both.

Oh shit, oh shit, oh shit . . .

Suddenly, he's on the seat behind me. Anh Sáu takes hold of the handlebars and slows us down to a safe stop.

"Việt Kiều drives wonky!" Anh Sáu laughs. "More." He gestures for me to retake the handlebars. Putting his hand next to mine, he very gently revs the engine. We glide forward.

I try again. Not great, but better. Anh Sáu slaps my shoulders. "What are you stopping for? Go, go."

He points to the road. I shake my head.

He pats me harder. "No problem, just go. You have to learn on the road."

Two more openings pass us before I awkwardly merge.

Anh Sáu grips my shoulders and screams, "Whoo! Việt Kiều knows how to ride now!"

His encouragement makes me go faster. I turn the throttle more, picking up speed. It's exhilarating.

After a while, he points to a parking lot, and I pull in. "Turn around," he says, directing me to head back. "We're almost out of gas."

I need to cross traffic and make a U-turn.

Taking the next opening I see, I pull the throttle too hard. We jerk forward, nearly hitting someone who swerves out of the way. I make a sharp turn. Too sharp. This motion kills the engine. We're stalled in the middle of the road with other bikes coming up on us from behind. Everyone is honking.

"Go, go!" Anh Sáu shouts.

I jump on the starter with no luck.

"Turn the engine off, then back on," Anh Sáu instructs. He's oddly calm for a man who is about to be pummeled by ten thousand motorbikes.

I cut the engine, switch it back on, then stand up off the bike. I slam my foot down as hard as possible on the starter. The sound of the motor kicking to life feels like a hard-fought victory. Amped with new energy, I rev the engine, nearly hitting two more riders as I finally complete the turn.

"Don't you know how to drive a car? How are you so bad at riding a motorbike?" Anh Sáu says.

I start laughing. "It's not the same." Talk about a shit show of a lesson. But this is how my dad teaches me everything too. Like swimming: there was no lesson or discussion—he just put me in the pool and said, "Swim." When I gulped water and started drowning, he picked me up and told me to stop screaming. Then he dropped me back in. This is the Vietnamese equivalent of "trial-and-error" learning.

Before we reach the pump Anh Sáu shuts off the bike. He opens the gas cap.

"Fill it full," he instructs the attendant.

I gaze at the beachside road. It's not unlike the California coastline, but it feels altogether different. I'm not sure why. I look down and notice that Anh Sáu is wearing sandals.

"Who rides a motorbike in sandals?" I ask.

"Sandals are shoes, so what?" he says.

I laugh. "Look, bro, if you want me to buy you shoes, just say so."

Anh Sáu whips a look in my direction and I know I've said the wrong thing. "Rich guy. Do you want to buy me a new motorbike too? And a house? What about an airplane?"

"No," I say lamely. That's not what I meant. When we were here last, Jane or my dad always paid for everything. We'd go shopping or out to eat and they *always* paid. Jane even told me before I left that it was my job to pay for stuff, like, not to be weird about it or anything, that it was just an unspoken rule. I guess that's the part where I messed up, *unspoken*.

"I just meant shopping could be fun." I'm backpedaling so hard, I can actually feel myself trippin'.

"You know, for a guy whose Bà Ngoại is a working girl, you sure think highly of yourself."

That is the weirdest insult I've ever heard. Even translated. Maybe especially translated. It's like a "yo momma" joke but about my grandma and goes so far overboard it's more gross than funny. I laugh along, though. Go along to get along, right?

"She's my Bà Nội," I correct, she's my grandma on my dad's side.

"Not Bà Tam, your Bà Ngoại," he repeats. I get it, he wants to insult my maternal grandmother because he actually likes and respects my dad's mom. Sure, whatever floats your boat, dude. "Wait. Do you not know your Bà Ngoại?"

This is getting weird so fast. "No. Do *you* know my Bà Ngoại?" I mean for it to sound sarcastic, but he doesn't catch my drift.

"I've heard rumors."

"Okay," I say, because I really just want to get off this topic that has somehow spiraled out of control.

"Give me a hundred thousand," Anh Sáu says. I retrieve my wallet. He yanks it from me. When he opens it, he sees that most of the bills are gone. He smirks, then hands it back sans the hundred thousand bill, which he gives to the attendant. I've learned my lesson and spread the cash throughout my stuff.

We have a full house for dinner. Bà Nội, Bác Long, my dad, Anh Sáu, and I sit around an array of dishes spread out on the living room floor. It's a feast of rice, egg pancake with scallions, caramelized pork belly with mini duck eggs, stir-fried broccolini, and the fish we caught yesterday. The slimy catfish sits staring at me with its mouth agape. I shove my chopsticks into its side and peel away the skin before putting it in my bowl. I love this fish.

"Are you watching your figure?" Bà Nội laughs.

What? Oh, because I pulled off the fatty part of the fish. "No. I don't like it," I say.

"The fat is where all the flavor is," Anh Sáu says, shoveling a large bite into his mouth.

"Correct," Bà Nội says. She drills her knuckles into the left side of my skull, giving me a shove that nearly knocks me over. Because Vietnamese people aren't very affectionate, this is equivalent to an American side hug. I thought it was mean the first time she did it, but I've grown to like it—it's basically a mini knuckle massage on my temple.

On the other side of the table my dad and uncle talk about ashes. I keep listening for my mom's name to confirm what I think is true. She never comes up. I'm hella mad at my mom, but I want to know if something happened to her.

"The paperwork has to be stamped, approved, and submitted to the office in Hồ Chí Minh City," Bác Long says. My uncle is a

Communist. He fought in the war on the other side. Somehow after the war was over, he returned, and our family reconciled. I don't know how much is true, but supposedly he beat my grandfather upon his arrival home. The beating enabled them to get past being on opposite sides. Seems unbelievable, but I guess it's kind of like when Joe and I got pissed at each other. It escalated until we were throwing punches. He legit gave me a black eye. At some point, he shouted, "What are you doing, Paul?" and I yelled back, "I'm kicking your ass!"

Something about saying it out loud was just so hilarious that I started laughing. He joined me, and we ended up catching our breath through fits of laughter. We've been best bros ever since. Throwing down made us tighter. So it makes sense to me that my dad and his brother are chill.

"Tomorrow," my dad confirms.

"If Chú Phúc wants, I can show Quốc around the city. I've been many times. I know my way," Anh Sáu offers.

"What? Do you have itchy feet? Learn to sit still," my dad says to me. He softens his tone for Anh Sáu. "Paul needs to stay home."

"Stay home for what?" Bà Nội says, surprising me. "Let him go. Sáu knows the way. Let the two of them explore. This house is boring him to death."

Now my dad is in a predicament because on the one hand he has always been the decision-maker, but on the other hand, Grandma has final say. I glue my mouth shut.

"It's going to be two weeks," Dad says to me in English.

"Okay," I say in a neutral tone, while avoiding eye contact with

Anh Sáu. He's up to something. Even though I know I probably shouldn't go along with it, I'm too curious to stop it.

Later, Anh Sáu and I swing side by side in a wide hammock, which hangs from two large trees covered in wild bunches of bright red flowers. On a clear day like today, the contrast of deep red against the blue sky makes the leaves shine like rubies in the sky.

"You have a girlfriend in Sài Gòn or something?" I ask.

"We're going to go find your Bà Ngoại," Anh Sáu says.

"For what?"

"Because she's rich."

I open my mouth to say she's not richer than us but remember how arrogant that came off last time. "I don't need her money."

"Okay, then don't take it."

Anh Sáu is acting nonchalant, but I can tell there's an endgame at play here. "What do you get out of it?"

"I told you. She's rich. I bring her her grandson; she will thank me." Ah, now I get it. He wants a reward for my return.

"Let me get this straight. I offer to buy you shoes and you're offended, but taking money from my grandmother is fine?"

"I'm not taking money from her. I'm earning it. Besides, don't you want to know your Bà Ngoại?"

Yes is my first thought. "No" comes out as a reflex. My mother has always been off-limits in my house. By extension, I assume my grandma is too. "No. Yes," I say, changing my mind.

"No? Or yes?" Anh Sáu asks. He looks amused.

"Yes." The word burns in my throat. I know this is wrong. In my bones I know it's a betrayal of some sort, but of who? Jane? My dad? What about me?

I'm doing it, I'm gonna find her. I mean, who needs to know?

"You got a plan?" I ask.

"There's nothing I can't figure out." He smirks.

CHAPTER 17
NGỌC LAN

When Chị Diễm awakened at home for the first time, she was not the same. She spoke slowly, her naturally round face looked gaunt, her bloodshot eyes were dry, and her thick wavy hair was flat—still, she looked beautiful.

"Chị Diễm is up!" Ngọc Lan exclaimed, rushing over to her sister's side.

"Umm." Her sister nodded.

"Chị Diễm slept for so long, em was scared you would never rise," Ngọc Lan half joked.

"Ha," Chị Diễm said. The word was a laugh, but her voice held no happiness. Typically, her sister would have said something snide, like *Why would I die and leave Mom to deal with only you?*

Ngọc Lan carried over a bowl of warm soup, but Chị Diễm shook her head. Instead, she stared at the doorway. Ngọc Lan followed her gaze. Nothing appeared out of the ordinary. What was her sister looking at? "Mẹ will be home tonight. But look, the villagers brought food here for Chị Diễm. They don't hate us anymore."

"Later," Chị Diễm said.

Ngọc Lan watched her sister, wondering if a different spirit had inhabited her body. She had heard of this happening with patients who were in a coma for too long. Their weakened mental state allowed a wandering soul to take over.

"Help me stand," Chị Diễm said after a while.

"It's been many days since you've stood. It might make you dizzy. How about Chị Diễm sits a little while longer. Let your body gather its strength."

Chị Diễm ignored Ngọc Lan. She got to her knees. Her thighs trembled, but she persisted, placing one foot flat on the ground. Ngọc Lan rushed to her sister's side to help.

Together, they took painstakingly slow steps toward the ocean.

"Do you hear that?" Chị Diễm asked.

"Hear what?" Ngọc Lan asked.

Chị Diễm didn't answer. Perhaps she'd lost the energy to speak. Ngọc Lan wondered if the ocean had healed her like Bác Nga said it would. About halfway to the water, Chị Diễm collapsed into the sand. Ngọc Lan tried to lift her, but Chị Diễm pushed her away. With her ear to the ground, she said, "Do you hear that? The dead. They're calling us home."

Ngọc Lan stood above her sister, not knowing what to say.

A few moments passed. Then Chị Diễm laughed. "Your face is pale. Like you've seen a ghost."

"Can you say something that makes sense?" Ngọc Lan

pleaded. She really couldn't tell if her sister was joking, possessed, delirious, or what.

"Get out of my light." There it was again, that steely coldness her sister had never had before. Ngọc Lan didn't move. "I beg of you to please sit down. Looking up at you is killing my neck, and if you'll remember, I already nearly just died."

Ngọc Lan slumped until she sat cross-legged. Her shadow followed.

"Stop looking so worried. All I wanted was a little sunlight." Chị Diễm reached over to tickle Ngọc Lan's toes. Ngọc Lan swatted her sister, who flinched in real pain.

"Ey!" Chị Diễm smiled. Then both sisters began giggling.

"You scared me to death," Ngọc Lan said.

"Were you scared that I was going to die or that I'd come back and haunt you?"

"Both!"

Chị Diễm smiled as she closed her eyes. She vacillated between energy and exhaustion. "Let me rest a minute," she said, seemingly unaware that she was already lying flat. Ngọc Lan didn't mind, though. She dug her feet into the sand and stroked her sister's back the way their mother did when they were sick. She thanked the heavens for Chị Diễm's return.

A half hour later, the sun reached its highest point in the sky. Chị Diễm opened her eyes. "How long have I been sick?"

"Seventeen days."

Chị Diễm's breathing turned shallow before she said, "I don't want to scare Ngọc Lan, but I had many fever dreams. I saw em and Mẹ taking care of me. I remember my body was so tired. I thought I might cross over. As I was lying there, our great-grandparents, aunts, and uncles appeared."

"How did you know they were our family?"

"I just knew."

"Were you scared?"

"The opposite. I felt fully at peace. I wanted to follow them."

Horrified, Ngọc Lan looked at her sister. "Why would you leave me behind?" How could her sister be so willing to abandon them, to just die?

"I wasn't thinking about it," Chị Diễm admits. "I've never experienced a calm like that before. It was bewitching. But our family wasn't there to take me home. We were meant only to meet each other."

Hot tears ran down Ngọc Lan's face. She quickly wiped them away.

"C'mon, don't cry. Tears do nothing but wrinkle your face," Chị Diễm said, nudging her sister lightly in jest.

Ngọc Lan didn't answer. She wanted to say: *I worried you wouldn't wake up. Every day I turned away from you and cried silently into my pillow. I even warned you that if you died, I would follow.* But no words emerged, only more tears.

"Chị didn't tell you this story to make you sad. I wanted you to know that death is peaceful, and our family is waiting on the other side. When we go, we won't be alone. There's nothing to be sad about."

How could her sister say that? Since Anh Hòa had left, Ngọc Lan clung to her sister harder. She never wanted to leave her.

"I saw other people too. Not just family," Chị Diễm said. "Do you remember that girl we used to see walking into church after school every day?"

"Chị Oanh," Ngọc Lan said, nodding. The girl was two years older than Anh Hòa, and everyone suspected her fiancé had died, because no one in the family had heard from him in more than a year. Some speculated that he was a deserter, but no one really knew.

"Every day her fiancé follows behind her, desperate for her to understand that he did not abandon her. He repeats over and over that he is sorry that they killed him because he wasn't a better fighter."

"That is so sad."

"Difficult for real," Chị Diễm said.

"Wait, wait. STOP. Our aunt did not say 'For real,'" Jane says, rudely interrupting me.

"Khổ thật, aka difficult for real," I say, challenging her.

"Actually, khổ means suffering, so suffering for real, I guess," she says.

I look at Jane, surprised. I can't believe she actually let me win that argument. Jane never lets me win debates, especially logic ones, and if I'm being honest, I'm pretty sure I'm bullshitting even myself because my aunt wouldn't talk like that. "Can I continue with my story then?"

"Yes."

I consider the phrase and decide to change it. Jane's right (knowledge I will keep to myself). This is my mom's story, and I was interjecting myself.

"That is real suffering," Chị Diễm said. Ngọc Lan considered how many people like Chị Oanh spent years wondering what happened to their loved ones. She thought about how, without answers, the suffering continued.

That evening Ngọc Lan's mother pulled her aside. She unfolded newly sewn black trousers. "In the seam of these is a jade pendant. If something happens to me and you need money, sell it. Don't let anyone know it's there."

"I thought Ba took all our money with him," Ngọc Lan said. She couldn't believe something so valuable existed in their home.

"Your dad never knew I had it. There are things a woman doesn't need to tell her husband."

Ngọc Lan nodded. Her mother had been hiding small things, like taffy from Bác Duy or gifts from Bác Nga, from their father for as long as she could remember. Ngọc Lan put on the pants. She ran her fingers along the threads. It took her a minute to find the pendant neatly placed inside the cinched ankle of the pants' hem. No matter what, she would protect her mother's gem.

After Chị Diễm fell asleep, Ngọc Lan told her mom about the things Chị Diễm saw while she was sick. She left out the part about her sister wanting to leave them—partly because she couldn't bring herself to repeat the words and partly because she thought it might break her mother's heart.

Her mother nodded. "Sometimes, when a person is close to death, they are lucky enough to meet our ancestors. Tomorrow, Mẹ will go tell Oanh's family about her fiancé."

"You believe her?" Ngọc Lan asked.

"Of course I believe her. Why wouldn't I?"

Ngọc Lan supposed her mother was right. Chị Diễm barely knew this girl, what reason would she have for making this up?

As the weeks passed, Chị Diễm grew healthier and healthier. Then one morning, Chị Diễm unexpectedly said, "I'll race you to the water!" In a flash, she took off. The two sisters sprinted with speed reminiscent of the time before the war ended—before food was truly scarce. Both doubled over at the shore as they caught their breath.

"I'll race you to the clams," Ngọc Lan said, diving into the water. Driven by her intense desire to win, she held her breath, then went straight for the largest grouping of shells.

When her bag was full, she turned around to find her sister's body flailing at the surface. In a panic, she dropped the clams and rushed to Chị Diễm. Dragging her by the arms as her sister choked on seawater, Ngọc Lan kicked hard. Her muscles bulged with fatigue as they reached shallow water. Chị Diễm gasped for air, grabbing at the sand as though clutching for life.

"What happened?" Ngọc Lan asked.

Chị Diễm didn't answer. Instead, her whole body shook with fear as she curled into Ngọc Lan's arms. How could this be? Ngọc Lan was the one who loved to collect things, but Chị Diễm was the graceful one. Her sister was the mermaid. She was the one who'd taught Ngọc Lan to swim, who instructed her on how to move with the waves rather than against them. "Were you pulled under?" Ngọc Lan asked.

Chị Diễm shook her head. "I panicked." The admission seemed to stun even her.

"I don't understand," Ngọc Lan said.

"I don't understand it either. When I put my foot in the water it felt different. Like an idiot, I persisted. I waded in. At first, I was still standing in shallow water, so everything was fine. Then a current pulled me out. I couldn't find the floor."

Did Chị Diễm forget how to swim? Was that even possible?

"Promise me you won't tell Mẹ," Chị Diễm begged as they approached their door a little while later. "I don't want her to worry."

This didn't sit well with Ngọc Lan, but she agreed. Inside their home, Bác Nga smiled as they entered. "Diễm, you look healthy," she commented.

"Cảm ơn, Bác Nga," Chị Diễm said, bowing to her in thanks. "I surely would have died without your medicine."

Bác Nga reached for Chị Diễm's hand and squeezed it. Then she turned to Ngọc Lan. "Go pack your things, okay? Your mom has agreed for you to come help me for a month."

Ngọc Lan nodded. The two sisters went into the bedroom to pack as Mẹ brought lettuce soup in from the kitchen. Being sent to live with someone else wasn't uncommon in those days. Kids were sent to live with relatives all the time, either because the parents couldn't take care of them or because the relatives needed help with the sick or elderly.

"While I'm gone, don't go in the water by yourself," Ngọc Lan whispered to Chị Diễm. Her sister nodded, not looking Ngọc Lan in the eye.

At dinner, Ngọc Lan's mother was unusually affectionate with her. She gave her two helpings of rice, adding more meat and greens to her bowl. She even commented on how helpful Ngọc Lan had been while Chị Diễm was ill. Buoyed with pride, Ngọc Lan soaked up the praise. She promised to be a dedicated helper to Bác Nga. Ngọc Lan was so grateful to Bác Nga for saving Chị Diễm's life that she would've done anything to repay the kindness.

They finished eating. Ngọc Lan hugged her mom and sister goodbye. "See you in a month." She waved, following Bác Nga home.

CHAPTER 18
PAUL

After landing in Ho Chi Minh City, we're shuttled to a hotel. A colossal rotunda made of marble and glass engulfs us as we enter. The floors are so clean I can see my reflection as we walk past tall vases full of purple orchids.

"Whoa, you Việt Kiều really know how to travel," Anh Sáu says. We both crane our necks to take in our surroundings.

"I think we're at the wrong place," I reply. My dad approaches one of the desks. I'm sure he's asking for directions to our actual hotel. Which is probably around the corner or across the street, hidden in some dark alley with crumbling walls.

He returns with a key card and says, "Let's go." We follow him to a suite that's the size of an apartment. We've never stayed in a place this nice. Jane would be jealous.

Our room on the tenth floor (which is actually the ninth floor because there's no fourth floor due to superstition) has a large window that faces the city center. Ho Chi Minh City is a strange mixture of old and new. A few skyscrapers stick out above a sea of shorter commercial and residential buildings. Bumper-to-bumper (or, more accurately, wheel-to-wheel) motorbike traffic with a scattering of luxury cars covers the roads. I see older, run-down stores with tattered signage and densely displayed merchandise for sale. There are more helmets being worn here than in Da Nang, but they're not like motorcycle helmets I've seen in the States; they look more like old military bucket helmets that fit loosely on people's heads.

"I need to go submit some documents. You two can stay in this room," my dad says.

"Bà Tâm asked me to pick up a few things from Chợ Bến Thành.[18] I know Sài Gòn well. Let me show Quốc around," Anh Sáu suggests casually.

"Okay," my dad says.

Where has this guy been all my life? Both Grandma and Anh Sáu have gotten my dad to agree to things he'd never allow at home. I say nothing. If I act excited, he'll turn around and force us back home. In my dad's eyes, Paul happy = Paul is up to no good.

"What time should we return? I know a great place to eat close by," Anh Sáu says.

"I don't know. You two go eat."

"We'll bring food back," Anh Sáu says.

With that, my dad opens up his wallet. He hands Anh Sáu a bill for 500,000, which is about thirty US dollars. "Is that enough?"

"Dạ," Anh Sáu says, nodding.

My dad leaves. Anh Sáu clicks the TV on. "This Thee Ve is so large," he muses. It actually isn't that big, maybe a thirty-two-inch. For a room this decked out, I would've expected a giant flat-screen

18 *Bến Thành Market*

to appear behind a magic wall or something. I'm watching a commercial for Nestlé chocolate milk when Anh Sáu abruptly shuts off the TV. "Đi," he says, getting up. I follow.

Outside our hotel, Anh Sáu breezes past the taxis.

"Are we walking?"

"These cars charge Việt Kiều prices. Your American legs don't work?"

"They do . . . just asking," I say lamely.

I have no idea what street we're on, but the traffic is dense. I smell exhaust, petrol, and lemongrass. Storefronts displaying fruit, nuts, and flowers are located next to restaurants with basic plastic furnishings. There are no doors. Every place springs at me with an overwhelming force that makes me instinctively need to jump away. Personal space is not a thing in the city.

Outside what looks like a sports bar, Anh Sáu stops. "How much for two bikes for two hours?"

The men look at him. They look at me. "Two hundred."

"Dead mother," Anh Sáu curses, though it sounds jovial. "Em (meaning me) is a Việt Kiều, but I'm Vietnamese. Forty." I half expect the guy to spit at us. Instead, he puts on his helmet and starts the engine of his motorbike. The driver next to him does the same. He hands me a helmet. I guess we have a deal.

They introduce themselves as Anh Hiệp and Anh Chim.

Once I get on the motorbike and place my feet, my driver, Anh Chim, follows Anh Hiệp and Anh Sáu with assured maneuvering. I relax, finally able to take in the city. When I was a kid, I remember noticing all the things Vietnam didn't have: aboveground toilets, showers, paved roads, sidewalks, cars, things I had taken for granted. Now, so much reminds me of my dad and my aunt and uncle. I always thought they reused plastic jugs because we were poor. As we move about the city, I'm thinking maybe this is just what Vietnamese people do.

After about ten minutes of weaving through traffic, we end up at a place called Chợ Bến Thành, a huge outdoor market. Here, aromas of broth, rotisserie meats, and homeopathic Asian medicines mix with the general fragrance of exhaust. The deeper we venture into the abyss of shops, the more the fumes fade; that's how big this market is. Anh Sáu buys fish sauces, dried squid, raw sesame rice paper, and bags of seasonings.

"What's the plan?" I ask.

"Let's start with her address."

"Okay."

Anh Sáu looks at me and I look right back at him. "What?"

"Where does your Bà Ngoại live?" He says this slowly, like he's talking to a child learning to speak.

"How should I know? I thought *you* knew."

Anh Sáu looks at me, confused. "How would I have her address? She's your Bà Ngoại, not mine."

I'm dumbfounded. "You're the one who said you could find her. Did you not say, 'Leave it to me'?"

"I meant logistically. I know how to get around. Ay." Exasperated, he tilts his head to the sky like her address might fall from the clouds. Unbelievable, this guy.

"Forget it. Let's just get something to eat and sightsee. What's there to do around here?"

"Wait. I think I know. First, we go to Vũng Tàu."

"What's there? A person who will look into a Magic 8 Ball and tell us where she is?"

Anh Sáu ignores my sarcasm. "That's where she lives."

"So you do know something?"

"That's all I know."

"Oh man, forget it. Let's just go to the hotel and watch TV. This is dumb," I tell him. My brain is exhausted from the ups and downs of this conversation.

"I'm done. Let's go," Anh Sáu says.

I don't realize Anh Sáu has disregarded my request to return to the hotel until we've exited the city and are passing through rural areas. Two and a half hours later, I'm told that we've arrived in Vung Tau. Anh Sáu's plan is the dumbest thing I've ever heard, so I doubt we'll actually find her. However, being so close, knowing that she lives somewhere in this city, makes it real.

I've never met my grandma. I don't know anything about her. What if she's cruel and dismissive? What if she wants nothing to do with me? What if Anh Sáu is wrong and she's not rich, but extremely poor? What if she asks for my help but I can't assist her? What if I hate her? What if I really like her? What do I do if she tells me my mother really *is* dead?

When I think about my mom, it's like she's a sad story I heard about on the news. Aside from that car ride in the forest, I don't remember much about her. Plus, what I remember contrasts so starkly with how my family gossips about her that I sometimes wonder if I made it up. Maybe I wanted to believe my mom was strong. Mợ Bích actually knew my mom when they were kids. They were on the same ship that traveled from Hong Kong to Guam. When they knew each other, my aunt had not yet met my uncle, my mom's brother, Cậu Hòa. That's just one of those "it's a small-world" coincidences they discovered years after being in America.

The thing about Vietnamese people is that what is *not* said is often more telling than what is said—at least according to Jane. Jane says, "Silence is passive-aggressive judgment." I disagree, I think Vietnamese people are pretty explicit and direct when they're criticizing how I look, act, and speak. Our family loves to judge each other, and pretty overtly in my opinion. I've heard Mợ Bích scold her husband, Cậu Hòa, for saying things like "A son without a mother acts like that." He would be talking about me, because when kids act poorly in our culture the parents are to blame—our wrongdoings are the cause of all their shame. Which is why my dad feels the need to beat us into submission. He refuses to be shamed for our misbehaviors—says Jane. I say his shame has nothing to do with me and he should leave me out of it. One time, when I was feeling particularly frustrated, I snapped at my aunt. "Cậu Hòa's right, if I didn't have a rotten mother, I'd probably be a better kid."

"Whether you're good or bad is your decision. You don't know what your mom's life has been like. Have some compassion."

I'm pretty sure I scoffed. *Have compassion? For the person who abandoned me? No thanks.*

And then randomly, while we were rinsing some green mung

beans to make my favorite kind of chè,[19] she said, "Back then everyone suffered a lot, but women suffered the most. The life of a woman is really hard. People say bad things about your mom, but they don't know." It was like she was continuing the conversation months later, like she'd been playing what to say over and over again in her head and finally just let it out.

"What do you mean?"

"During the war there was a lot of pain. Afterward it didn't stop. We left behind a lot of people, you know." I didn't know. Even still, if family mattered so much to my mother, why would she *choose* to leave us?

My driver abruptly veers right. He parks. We've arrived.

Raised on wood pillars, the open-space restaurant has barstools with standing tables scattered throughout. The hostess wears a traditional áo dài, the waitresses are all in tight dresses. I am confused. What is this place and what are we doing here?

Anh Sáu and I get off our bikes. I'm awkwardly following my cousin inside when his driver, Anh Hiệp, stops us. "You made us drive you all the way to the coast for this? We could've saved you some money and taken you to places in the city."

"Come back in one hour," Anh Sáu says with more authority than he should possess given their age difference.

"One hour? Forget it. I'll be napping here." Anh Hiệp sprawls out across his motorbike, his torso on the seat, his legs dangling over the handlebars, and a cap over his face to block the sun.

We approach an older lady with big curls, fierce eyebrows, a

19 *Vietnamese dessert. It's the best. If you haven't tried it, get some.*

possible nose job, and too many layers of makeup. "Hello, Cô. Is there anyone who works here named Hang Ngô?" Anh Sáu asks.

"How many years is em? Sixteen?" she smiles. "This is no place for children."

"Dạ." Anh Sáu nods in deference. "We are simply trying to locate a family member."

"And if your family member doesn't want to be found?"

"This is her grandson."

The woman looks up and suddenly straightens. "I don't know a person by that name. This place is not for children, go." Her tone is harsh and loud, the jovial smile from moments ago gone. We turn around. Two officers stand in the doorway. The woman's tone goes up two octaves in excitement. Her smile broadens as she ushers us out the door and moves to greet the men. We stand outside on the deck peering in. I'm surprised to find that the officers are, like . . . legit. They check her paperwork, nod toward us, accept an envelope from her, and exit the building.

"Đi," Anh Sáu says. We return to the bikes.

"Not even five minutes, and you already got kicked out," Anh Hiệp says without lifting his hat. He sits up, appearing bored. "What are you two kids searching for? Let me help you. Watching you get rejected from this brothel is hurting my heart." He's mocking us. I don't blame him. I'd mock me too, if I were him. *Wait, did he say brothel?*

"That's a place where men go to . . . ," I whisper to Anh Sáu. I don't exactly know how to say "have sex." I sense he gets the point.

"It's just a bar. If you want to sleep with them you have to take them out," Anh Hiệp supplies.

"Why would my Bà Ngoại be there?"

"She's a prostitute," Anh Sáu says.

"Your Bà Ngoại? No. She's too old. Unless she's a madame," Anh Hiệp says.

I let out a laugh until I realize he's not joking. "Yeah, right," I say, but something twists in my stomach.

Anh Sáu watches me, amused. He's been quiet this whole time. "Paul really knows nothing about your Bà Ngoại?"

I shake my head. "After the fighting, we lost contact," I say. This is super vague, but I don't want to explain why I have no idea who my own grandmother is.

We hit up a few more places. I leave my number with hostesses who stare at us with such skepticism that I'm sure the contact info is going straight into the trash. When it gets too late to stay out, we grab food, then return to the hotel.

In our suite, Anh Sáu and I mill about restlessly. Today was a dud. But I'm glad. I can tell Anh Sáu is giddy to meet my grandmother, and that makes me angry. At her for being who she is, at him for making fun of her, at myself for agreeing to go along with this stupid plan.

"Searching like this is a waste of time," I say. "Let's just call it quits."

"Are you scared of your Bà Ngoại?" Anh Sáu mocks.

"No. I don't want to spend all my time going into these weird places," I say. It's mostly true.

I've set something in motion. Opening the door to my grandma is opening the door to my mom. I'm not supposed to do this. Jane will kill me if she finds out. I know most teens don't care what their sisters think. But their sisters didn't raise them when their mother abandoned them, or take the harsher beatings when their dad couldn't control his temper. Jane's neurotic and bossy, but I love her. And a betrayal this big isn't something I'm sure she'll get over.

A key card slides into the door. We both turn. I expect to see my dad, but a gloved hand opens it and in walks a woman. Anh Sáu stands up immediately, and I awkwardly follow. A chill wafts past her and around me. I shiver. When our eyes lock, my universe shifts. Bà Ngoại looks exactly like how I remember my mother—if my mother was a member of the British royal family. Dressed in a cobalt-blue pantsuit with a jeweled peacock pendant above her right breast, she is regal. I have the urge to take a knee but don't.

"Chào Bà Ngoại." I stumble over the words.

"Chào Bà Hang," Anh Sáu adds. I suddenly remember he's there.

"Mmm." She nods. "Giỏi, sit down." We both take a seat on the sofa bed, which, thankfully, Anh Sáu hadn't pulled out yet. She sits in one of the chairs opposite. I notice that she doesn't lean against the chair; she has perfect posture with her legs crossed at the ankle, exactly like the queen teaches her granddaughter in that princess movie with Anne Hathaway.

"Con is who?" Bà Ngoại asks Anh Sáu.

"Dạ, I am Sáu, son of Mỹ Khánh, who is the daughter of Bà Kính, the oldest sister of Bà Tâm." I mean, really, are we even cousins at that point?

"Is your mother well?"

"Dạ, she is well, thank you." Anh Sáu nods. He's smiling like someone who has just met their celebrity idol. I want to smack him on the head.

"Where is your father?" Bà Ngoại asks me.

"I don't know," I say, realizing how late it is by the darkness outside.

"What kind of father lets their kid run around alone?" Bà Ngoại comments. *What kind of mother abandons her kids on a refugee boat?* I think. Every story I heard about refugees was that they were poor. This lady clearly is not poor. *But also, why am I defending my dad?*

"Dạ, I'm here," Anh Sáu says. "I've come to the city many times. I know the way."

"How many years are you?"

"Sixteen, almost seventeen."

"Same age," she says, referring to me and nodding. Apparently, in Vietnam, sixteen-year-olds going to another part of the country alone is not strange. It'd be like me saying, *I'm going to San Diego for the day. Bye, Dad!*

We sit in silence for what feels like thirty years but is probably only forty-five seconds before the mechanical lock turns. My dad enters the room. His entrance makes me realize I did not open the door for my grandma. Somehow, she got the front desk to let her in? Without speaking to my dad. Shiiiiet.

My dad must think the same because his mouth drops open before he says, "Chào Mẹ."

Err, what? I know he hasn't seen her in, like—actually, have they *ever* met? There's no way she could've come to the US for the wedding. As far as I know, our trip to Vietnam nine years ago was the first time my dad returned since fleeing as a refugee. So why is he calling her Mom? My dad tries to act unaffected by her presence, but I can tell he's rattled.

"Who comes to the city and leaves their kid in a hotel room? If you couldn't watch him, you should have called his Bà Ngoại."

"I didn't know how to contact you." My dad's tone is even, like he suddenly remembers that he's the man in the room and he's not about to be bossed around.

"Sé!"[20] Grandma scoffs. "This child found me in half a day, but you couldn't reach me in twenty years. What were you waiting for? My funeral?" So it's like that, huh—Grandma just threw me under the bus. So much for grandma-grandson solidarity.

My eyes dart back and forth between the two. The tension in the room is making me hot. This is the most direct conversation I've ever witnessed between two Vietnamese people. Usually, heated discussions like this begin at opposite ends of a maze, with each side yelling while running through the labyrinth. If they're lucky, they might run into each other, but usually, by the end of the conversation, they're merely exiting at the opposite ends.

Sweat drips down the back of my neck. I should say something, but my mouth is glued shut. I mean, Grandma's not wrong. But I'm not sure it's my dad's fault since she is my *mom's* mom. *Then again*, he did just call her Mom, so . . .

"Already, Mẹ is here. What would Mẹ like to do?" There's an edge to my dad's tone like it's killing him to be deferential to my grandma.

If she senses it, she doesn't seem to care. "Leave him here with me."

My ears go up at that. Ummm, what? I hope I get a say in this.

---

20 *"Oh, please!"*

I mean, she's kinda scary, and I only just met her. What if she has me flogged or something?

"Not possible. We leave for Đà Nẵng tomorrow." *Oh, thank god.* Wait, did my dad just lie? I'm pretty sure he said yesterday we'd be here for two weeks.

"Change your flight." *Oh no.* I wanted to meet the woman, not be trapped with her. "Grandmother and grandchild need time to know each other." This is not a request; it's a command. No one gives my dad commands. My body feels like lead.

"How long?" my dad finally says.

"Three days."

"Two."

"Three." The woman doesn't bargain, apparently.

"I'm not staying here for three days. When Mẹ is bored of him, send him back to Đà Nẵng."

"Don't test me or I'll keep him a month," my grandma says.

Oh, holy hell, did he just tell her to take me and send me back by myself when she's done? Is he out of his mind?

"I can't read Vietnamese. How am I supposed to figure out the airport?" I say. My dad shoots me a look that says: *Stop in your tracks. You're in enough trouble.*

I shut my mouth.

"I'll stay and help him," Anh Sáu says. I turn to face the corner he's in and glare. *You asshole.* He ignores me.

CHAPTER 19
NGỌC LAN

The moment Ngọc Lan entered Bác Nga's house, she knew she'd been lied to. It was true that Bác Hiếu, who was still recovering from his six months in a reeducation camp, did not look well, but both of Bác Nga's sons had returned home. Her two adult daughters, Ngọc Lan would later learn, did not join them because their husbands refused to leave. Three toddlers, a boy and two sisters, ran unabashedly throughout the house.

They reminded her of herself and her siblings at that age. The Lê house felt full in the way hers had when Anh Hòa still lived with them. Seeing how they cared for one another made her miss her siblings. She didn't understand why they had yet to reunite. One thing was clear, though: Bác Nga didn't need Ngọc Lan's help. There were more than enough people to help care for her husband.

"Put your things here. Keep it packed so it stays organized," Bác Nga said. Despite her growing unease, Ngọc Lan did as she was told.

When the family sat down to dinner, a knot formed in Ngọc

Lan's stomach. There was an abundance of rice, potatoes, soups, and fried fish. No one ate extravagant meals like this anymore. Something was happening. Though she knew deep down what it might be, she was afraid to think it.

"Tonight, we will cross over," Bác Nga said. Ngọc Lan's heart sank.

"Why didn't my mother tell me?" Ngọc Lan whispered. Tears fell from her cheeks, splashing onto the heels of her cracked and ugly feet.

A tissue appeared in her hand and she wiped her eyes. "You are family," a voice beside her said. "Don't worry, we'll take care of you."

Ngọc Lan looked up. Anh Luân, Bác Nga's second son, was looking at her. He was her brother's age. Once, he and Anh Hòa had been good friends. Ngọc Lan didn't want to appear ungrateful, but she had a family and they weren't here. "My sister is going to wonder why I didn't come back."

"Diễm is still weak. Your mom didn't want to burden her with knowing that you were leaving. You surely understand that, right? Bác Nga promises that I will raise you as my own."

Ngọc Lan understood. She understood that she didn't do enough to help her sister; that her pathetic skills couldn't make up for Anh Hòa being gone; that she was a burden to her family.

Hours before dawn, the family walked to their boat, then quickly trawled along the coast, collecting more escaping passengers.

When the boat was at capacity, Ngọc Lan sat with the Lê family and seventy other passengers. Quietly they maneuvered out to sea. They passed two checkpoints where Anh Minh spoke to officials. Documents, money, and jewels were exchanged. Everything in Vietnam at the time depended on trusted relationships. Whatever hushed deals, sleight-of-hand bribes, or favors transpired were done with only the most trusted of confidants. Bác Hiếu had these connections because in his many years of doing business he'd always been fair and generous.

With water lapping hard against the wooden hull of the boat, they set off toward the horizon. Ngọc Lan watched Vietnam grow smaller and smaller. She looked at the shape of its earth, the mounds of rolling green hills and thin ribbon-like strips of brown sand. She wondered how different they would be when she returned. Boards creaked and wobbled as Anh Minh and Anh Luân maneuvered the ship. At a distance, the loud engine rattled to life. Gray smoke billowed into the air. Everyone on the boat waited for what would happen next.

Anh Minh was a strategist. He had scheduled their departure during the monsoon season, knowing that Thai pirates were less likely to roam the seas. And they met no Thai pirates. About a day into the journey, they came across a Thai fisherman who supplied them with gas in exchange for a few pieces of gold and two diamonds. Thai pirates and Thai fishermen were two very different types of people. Like all pirates of the sea, the Thai pirates were lawless men who stole with impunity and beat all people—men, women, and children—without mercy. The Thai fishermen were businesspeople who price-gouged refugees who had no choice but to pay exorbitant prices. The former were murderous, the latter capitalist, and boat people understood the difference. They thanked their lucky stars when encountering Thai fishermen.

After five days at sea, they spotted land. Ngọc Lan was excited to see Malaysians waiting for them. When something hard hit her shoulder, her eyes darted all around, hoping to see where it had come from. Another hard object hit her head. Then suddenly a shower of rocks rained down on them. Wrapping her arms around her head, she waited, confused.

"Stop, don't throw rocks anymore!" several women shouted. They waved their arms in protest.

Bác Hiếu and a few other men flew their shirts in an arc above their heads. They were a civilian boat. They had no weapons. The barrage of stones continued. Anh Luân, who had been ripping at the engine's starter cord, finally pulled the engine to life and they retreated. The Malaysians cheered, shooing them away like they were starving stray dogs who didn't belong on their island.

Several other boats approached. Bác Hiếu warned them to stay away from the island. One skipper didn't heed the advice. Everyone watched as they were subjected to the same stony greeting.

A few hours passed before a navy boat appeared. In accented Vietnamese, a Malaysian soldier shouted at them to tie their vessels in a line. Soon nine boats were linked together, each filled to the brim with fellow refugees. A buoy was tossed to them. Up above, along the ship's deck, rows of gunmen stood at the ready. *How ridiculous to gear up with no enemy present,* Ngọc Lan thought.

The battleship's engine roared as it gained speed, slowly towing them out to sea. They reached deeper waters, then kept on going. A full day passed. Then another. The vessels headed away from Malaysia toward Indonesia. On the evening of the second day, moonlight danced across the warm waters. Stars flickered, basking in their own reflection. Ngọc Lan swallowed, feeling the dry ache of thirst. She was just about to drift off to sleep when a loud whirring sound startled everyone. Thick, roiling water began spewing from the battleship. Slowly at first and then with stunning intensity, they shot forward. Ngọc Lan's boat bounced against the water so hard she felt her body lift into the air.

Screams from behind rang out in shrill bursts.

"Stop!"

"Stop!"

Immediately, Bác Hiếu and Anh Minh leaped for the rope tied to the bow of the vessel. They began sawing. Loud whooshing sounds ripped through the night air—bullets—and then came shocked screams as one of the middle boats flipped over.

Whoosh. Refugees scrambled out from underneath. Women's arms, which moments before had clutched their children, turned up empty. Bobbing heads in the water begged in agony for someone to find their loved ones. They searched, but they couldn't see. When something sinks in the ocean, it's hard to find, especially in the dark.

Wailing.

Every other captain followed suit, sawing desperately at the line that tugged them.

Chaos.

The ship's unrelenting momentum ripped at their tethered shackles. More boats flipped.

Sorrow.

Desperate splashing in the water met with frantic rescues as the remaining boats pulled in who they could from the wreckage.

Loss.

Less than a minute, maybe two, was all it took to kill ninety-seven people. For no reason.

Finally, the rope tore loose. No longer bound, the military ship continued on while the refugees scrambled backward.

Ngọc Lan's heart pounded from fear long after the Malaysian ship had disappeared. Her whole body shook with anxiety, despite her telling herself that she was fine. *I'm alive, I'm not hurt, I'm alive.* Her body knew what her mind could not process. She trembled.

"Ba, Ba, Ba!" a male voice bellowed.

"Đạo?" Anh Minh asked, calling at the voice in the water.

"Minh!" the voice called back. "Minh, can you see my dad?"

As the boat closest to the Malaysian ship, they were pulled farthest away from the boats that flipped. By the time they reached the other ships, only a few bodies still swam in the water. Anh Minh looked in every direction, but he didn't see the man. "He's probably on another boat. Give me your hand." Anh Minh pulled his friend aboard.

Đạo's father wasn't on another boat. He had been shot by a Malaysian sniper while struggling to cut their boat free. Đạo was told this not once, not twice, but three times before the words rang true.

"Why does no one want to help us? Are we so ugly that we don't deserve to live?" Đạo asked.

No one answered.

Above, thick, fluffy cotton-ball clouds began to form. Apparently, humans weren't the only ones against them. God was about to spite them too—the monsoon was coming.

"Land!" someone shouted.

Behind Ngọc Lan was the dark outline of an island. The military ship had tugged them all the way to Indonesia, only to murder them a kilometer from shore. Ngọc Lan could not fathom why the world had no empathy for their plight. Why were refugees met with resistance rather than welcomed everywhere they turned?

Afraid of what might await them on the island, the six remaining boats anchored near one another. Together, they debated about what do next.

"These boats will sink in a monsoon," Anh Minh said quietly. He wanted only his dad to hear.

"The eye of the storm could still pass over us. Let's observe," Bác Hiếu said. He looked at the clusters of gray clouds, gauging their intensity. Rain dampened everything. Then the winds picked up. Ngọc Lan cupped her hands together, waited for a pool to form, and drank. Quenching a thirst she'd forgotten she had, she started to collect more, but Bác Nga stopped her.

"Slowly. You're dehydrated—if you drink too fast, you'll throw up." So Ngọc Lan turned her hand over and licked the droplets instead. Chị Diễm would've slapped her hand away. She would have told her she looked like a stray cat. Her sister was always concerned with looking proper. Ngọc Lan didn't care, though, because that was exactly how she felt—like a stray cat.

Ngọc Lan gazed up at the fast-moving clouds. For as ominous as the sky appeared, the ocean was calm. She longed for a swim.

Eight days since leaving Vietnam, the refugees sat crammed together on vessels filled beyond capacity. Of the nine towed boats, three had flipped, spilling hundreds of refugees into the water. All three turned boats eventually sank. Those who didn't drown ended up crowding onto the remaining vessels. This was why, despite sitting on an open-air deck, Ngọc Lan felt like she couldn't breathe.

The shore was close, less than a hundred meters. She peered at it, confident she could make it.

"Want to race?" Anh Luân asked.

Ngọc Lan beamed. Finally, someone who understood her. "Đi," she said, standing on wobbly legs.

"Don't," Anh Minh warned. "The water is dangerous."

Anh Luân looked at his brother, then back at Ngọc Lan. He raised his eyebrows. "Are you scared?"

"No!" Ngọc Lan shouted as she leaped off the bow. Ngọc

Lan was not afraid of the ocean. The ocean was her safe place and it was calling her.

"Me either!" she heard Anh Luân shout after her.

The moment her foot hit the water, Ngọc Lan knew she'd made a mistake. Another set of feet sliced through the water beside her. Anh Luân's eyes went wide; he too felt the pull, the deep tug of an undercurrent that could easily drown them. Together they swam for the top.

One moment they were side by side. The next, Ngọc Lan was yanked sideways by an invisible force—a tornado beneath the surface. Disoriented, she had no choice but to wait for the pull to stop. When it did, she was far away, too far for how much air she knew she had reserved in her lungs.

An arm grabbed her by the waist. And together, they kicked upward. She fought to breathe as soon as air became available. The water was surging now. Rain pelted the surface. Large waves launched them up and dropped them down. In seconds, they had drifted far from safety. Ngọc Lan looked up to see Anh Minh holding on to her. Where was Anh Luân? Had he drowned?

"I'm going to need you to swim with strength," Anh Minh said.

"Dạ." She nodded, feeling for the first time in her life how violent the mighty ocean could be. The boat was not an option. They had to swim for shore. The more they kicked against the waves, the farther out to sea they seemed to go.

"Hold on," he said. "Stop for a minute." He was thinking. Fighting against the water was futile, but swimming with the current could set them adrift with nothing to keep them afloat. "The surface is too turbulent; we need to dive. Can you do that?"

"Dạ." She nodded, though she was afraid, the last plunge still fresh in her mind.

"Don't go too deep, just a few feet below the surface, and kick toward shore." Beneath them, the once-clear water was a murky gray, its sandy bottom having been churned up in the storm. Together they propelled themselves forward, taking breaths as infrequently as possible because each inhale pushed them back a few feet. Soon Ngọc Lan's arms ached; her legs grew stiff and heavy.

"Don't stop. Kick harder!" Anh Minh shouted.

Closing her eyes, Ngọc Lan dove back down. Pushing herself beyond her known limits, she forged on. Doubt crept in. She slowed. From behind, two hands pushed against her back. The forceful nudge encouraged her, which in turn allowed her to persevere. She closed her eyes, then imagined green scales washing over her legs. Using the fin she and Chị Diễm had always dreamed of having, Ngọc Lan glided toward land.

Her body crashed against the shore; the fin vanished. On her back, she lay staring at the sky as water pooled around her before washing away. Beside her, Anh Minh caught his breath. His three children rushed to hug him. Ngọc Lan pressed herself up on shaking arms. Her eyes darted left, then right, scanning the crowd of people descending from the beached boats. Where was Anh Luân?

"Anh Luân!" she yelled, eyes darting across the stormy horizon.

"He's over there," Anh Minh said, nodding toward Anh Luân, who lay farther across the way. His gaze met hers. Ngọc Lan could tell that he was sorry, but it wasn't his fault. She had been the one who wanted to jump.

"There is nothing wrong with con?" Bác Nga asked Ngọc Lan, checking her body for abrasions or bruises.

"There is nothing," Ngọc Lan said, embarrassed. Had she really almost drowned?

"A truly idiotic kid," Chị Mậu said, shooting Ngọc Lan a hateful scowl.

Ngọc Lan dropped her head in shame. Chị Mậu had every right to be angry with her. Her recklessness had nearly cost the woman her husband and brother-in-law. "I'm sorry," Ngọc Lan said.

"We've left our home behind, Bác needs you to be more careful. It's not just you that I need to care for," Bác Nga said. This was as close to a scolding as Bác Nga had ever given her.

"I'm sorry," Ngọc Lan repeated.

"Sorry, sorry. Stupid girl." Chị Mậu scowled. Chị Mậu was the type of woman who could have been a beauty queen if that type of pageantry existed for refugees.

"Let it go. She's just a kid," Anh Minh scolded his wife. Chị Mậu kept her mouth closed, but the distaste in her eyes told Ngọc Lan she'd made an enemy with the queen.

Thirsty, Ngọc Lan turned toward the forest. A deluge of rain spilled from hundreds of shiny green coconut tree leaves, creating the illusion of a thousand floating waterfalls spread across the landscape. The water sparkled and danced as it splattered against the island's many surfaces. Ngọc Lan reached out to touch the cool, fresh liquid, then brought her lips to the closest cascading waterfall to drink.

More and more refugees poured onto the island. Rain continued to pound the earth. Darkness made it impossible to see into the wilderness. But there were no bullets, rocks, or yelling in an unfamiliar language. Anyone on the island had to shelter from the monsoon as well. Come morning, though, whoever lived there was sure to find them, which meant the refugees needed to come together to protect and defend themselves.

CHAPTER 20

PAUL

From: Paul
Mayday, mayday. I need help!

From: Jane
What happened?

From: Paul
Dad left me with Ba Ngoai.

From: Jane
What's the big deal? You've been hanging out with her this whole time, anyway. She's not gonna eat you.

From: Paul
NOT Ba Noi, BA NGOAI.

From: Jane
Why would he do that?

From: Paul

Because he's cruel.

From: Jane

But why would she even come up?

From: Paul

Because Anh Sau thought it would be funny to try and find our grandmother. And she showed up at our hotel, somehow got the key, argued with Dad, then convinced him to let her take me.

From: Jane

Who is Anh Sau? And why did you listen to him?

Busted. Jane does this, she asks seemingly stupid questions that make it seem like she's an idiot who doesn't understand English, and somehow, I end up admitting guilt to everything.

From: Paul

Not helping.

I start typing: *Because I found out she exists. Because I heard she was a madame. Because no one talks about Mom and I think she might be dead.* But the text looks ridiculous when typed out.

From: Paul

Did you know she was alive? Don't you think that's weird that even Cau Hoa doesn't mention her?

From: Jane

Maybe they didn't tell us because it's none of our business.

I huff. I should've seen that coming.

From: Paul

Maybe you're just scared to find out.

I shut the phone. My ears burn with anger. Jane can be real condescending when she's angry. It's like a reflex she can't control. She always has to be the one to punch first. I didn't text her to get a lecture. I reached out because her ass should be here too.

Anh Sáu and I sit in the back seat of a black car on the way to wherever my grandma is. She was supposed to get us at 9 a.m. Chú Phương, her driver, showed up instead. He's a serious guy who looks like his focus never strays from his job. He walks with a military gait. Maybe he's a veteran. I wonder if he carries a gun. I should've known Jane would be more snarky than helpful. I wish I could text Mai and Joe, but neither of them can access international texts without getting charged.

We're outside a high-rise building somewhere in the city. Chú Phương gets out to open the door for us, but I quickly open it myself. He might be driving me, but he's definitely not my servant. Anh Sáu closes the door behind him. Before we make it three steps, a lady wearing a fitted black suit-dress and church lady heels moves quickly toward us.

"Quốc, is that right?" she says to me.

"Dạ." I nod.

"Anh's Bà Ngoại is upstairs," she says. She doesn't wait for me to say anything, which is good because I wouldn't have known what to say. She walks inside. I take that as my cue to follow. Strange that she called me Anh when she's older than me.

I turn to Anh Sáu to give him a *what the hell* eyebrow raise. He's not there. He's leaning against the car with the driver. The two appear quite chummy. So Chú Phương can relax after all. "Ey!" I shout, waving for Anh Sáu to come. He shakes his head. "Come on," I urge, not wanting to call attention to myself. He gazes past me to the lady.

She glances from me to Anh Sáu. In a singular motion, she waves him forward. It's the most passive-aggressive small gesture I've ever seen. "What is your problem?" I mutter to Anh Sáu in English.

He shakes his head at me. This only confuses me more. At the elevator bank a door opens. The woman pushes the button for the top floor. She doesn't join us.

I slap Anh Sáu's arm. "What was that?"

"You idiot, you don't know anything. These types of places don't let people like me in."

"People like what?" I ask, genuinely confused. He shrugs, but I get the feeling he knows exactly why she didn't invite him. "Well, I don't care. Wherever I go, you go. You can't leave me alone with these people. What if they try and sell my kidneys?"

He stares at me strangely. I point to where I think my kidneys are, beneath my ribs. "Sell—" I point again. A smirk crosses his face. Jackass.

The doors open on the nineteenth floor. As soon as we step inside, I understand why she tried to ditch Anh Sáu. We're standing in a restaurant with floor-to-ceiling windows that showcase a 180-degree view of the city. It could be that the elevator ride made me dizzy, but I think it's rotating. I see two types of people: swanky-looking locals and tourists. The tourists are frumpy in their cargo pants and dorky travel clothes full of pockets, compared to the locals in business attire. I peer down at my jeans and T-shirt. I fit in more with the tourists than the Vietnamese. A quick once-over at Anh Sáu's cracked and dusty sandals explains why he wanted to stay with Chú Phương.

Despite our raggedy appearance, we're seated at a two-top table by the window. My grandmother approaches in an emerald-green suit-dress with sequins over the left shoulder. Her signature peacock brooch adorns the right breast pocket. The sparkling jewels match the stones on her pink heels. "Bà Ngoại has some work to see to. Order what you like."

"Dạ," Anh Sáu and I reply in unison.

She seats herself at a large table full of men. Each of them has a young lady next to them. No matter the age of the man, the woman appears to be in her twenties—Jane's age.

"Are they prostitutes?" I ask.

Anh Sáu hisses at me to shut up. There's my answer. He waves a hand across my face. "Rude. Don't stare."

Why not? Everyone else in the room is. The group of men is boisterous. Several bottles of liquor litter the table. It's only ten in the morning, but I know all too well that liquor has no time constraints. I notice that the girls who dutifully pour for the men also serve my grandmother. Bà Ngoại politely sips her drink until she's addressed in a salute. At that point, she lifts her chin and downs the shot. As soon as her glass hits the table, it's refilled.

I force myself to look away because Anh Sáu is becoming increasingly agitated with me.

"Order some food," Anh Sáu says. We don't have any menus. I'm about to call a waiter over when a tray of hot hand towels is placed on our table.

"Sorry, can I see a . . ." I fumble at the word for *menu*.

"Thực đơn," Anh Sáu supplies.

"Cô Hang has chosen some dishes for you. I can add anything additional you'd like," the waiter says. He doesn't supply a menu.

"Do you have fried potatoes?" Anh Sáu asks.

"We don't normally serve that, but I will have the chef make it for you." I can't help but think the waiter is being a bit rude to Anh Sáu. What is it with these people?

"Cảm ơn." I thank him. I don't want anyone spitting in my food.

We wipe our hands with the warm towels, which he immediately retrieves with a pair of wooden tongs. I can't decide if he usually does this as part of his exceptional service or if he does it because he thinks Anh Sáu might steal the cloth. The waiter glances down at Anh Sáu's sandals; it's the latter. Now I get why Anh Sáu gave me the cold shoulder when we first met, but this dude is Vietnamese, he's his, uh, our (?) people. Plus, the waiter and I are *not* the same. I don't think like him.

The first dish arrives. It's a plate with four cured salmon rolls stuffed with chive cream cheese. On top are tiny black pearls that look like boba but are super salty, and a green sprig of fresh thyme. We each eat one. Our eyes pop in surprise. That's delicious.

I poke at the pearls and ask, "What is this?"

"Fish eggs."

I make a face, *Ew*.

He straightens his posture. "Now who's the unrefined country boy?" I laugh because, I mean, he ain't wrong.

We eat plates of broken rice, admiring the tall cucumber cut into the shape of a pagoda—a freaking PAGODA! I never eat the vegetables in this dish, but today that changes. Neither of us touches the plate of fries.

"Damn, that's good," I muse. The men at my grandma's table stand. They shake hands with one another, then disperse.

Bà Ngoại approaches. "Are you done eating? Đi." She doesn't wait for an answer.

Anh Sáu and I stand. I'm about to tell her we haven't paid, but she's far enough away now that I'd have to shout. I avoid eye contact while exiting in case dining and ditching is a thing she does. Bà Ngoại walks like she owns the place, though. She nods and the staff bows to *her* as we leave. Not one but two people show us out. One holds the door. The other calls the elevator. Strange.

Downstairs the car door is already open for us. Bà Ngoại tells the driver where to go, but I don't catch it.

As we move through the city, people on motorbikes peer into the window. We're sitting in the only luxury car around. They must be wondering if someone important is inside. Is my grandma someone of importance? I can't reconcile how anyone in my family could be part of this elite world when all I ever heard about is how poor Vietnam is. How poor our families here are. When compared to Western retail shops, even store owners seem poor. What we would probably call the slums in the US seem like just everyday living here. I'm not sure what expression I have on my face, but Anh Sáu stares at me like he can read my thoughts. Damn. I guess I *am* just as judgmental as the server.

Chú Phương pulls over on a busy street. I'm confused because I don't see any stores, shops, or food stalls. We walk for half a block before an entryway to a Buddhist temple appears. Our family back home is Catholic, so this is new and feels a bit sacrilegious.

We enter through bright orange gates with red-and-orange detailing. Prayer flags fly every which way above the temple. Bustling city noises contrast with the quiet, reflective space. The courtyard somehow expands the deeper we go, causing the noise from outside to grow distant. A few people stroll in meditative contemplation along dirt pathways. Buildings housing deities fill the rest of the space. Toward the back sits a seven-tiered pagoda in the same bright orange as the entrance gates.

Bà Ngoại stops in front of the pagoda. She bows three times but doesn't go inside. Instead, she takes a left toward a woman sitting at a small table. Surrounded by red plastic chairs, she appears to be drawing calligraphy on large square pieces of fabric.

"Chào em Hang," the woman says, greeting my grandmother warmly. "Who is this?"

"Chào Chị Kim. This is my grandson."

Even though I've been calling her Grandma, hearing her call me her grandson shocks my ears. Finding her was a fluke, a joke that turned real, but that doesn't make her related—it doesn't make her *family*.

"Come." The woman gestures. "Let me hold your hands."

I extend my palms. She scoops them face up into a gentle grasp. Then Bác Kim (she's chị to my grandma and bác to me, it's an age thing) begins scanning my face. "Umm" is the only sound she makes. Bác Kim releases me. My arms fall heavily at my sides. When I feel them brush against my thighs, I realize she had me in a trance. I try to hide my discomfort, but I think it shows. "Your mother left you when you were a little boy. You have a longing to find her. I see it here," she says, pointing at my eyebrows. "And standing beside you is a ghost."

CHAPTER 21
NGỌC LAN

"Did that really happen? The Malaysians flipped those boats on purpose?" Jane asks. She looks as horrified as I felt when my mom told me this story.

"Yes."

I wait for Jane to say something. Whatever she's thinking, though, she doesn't want to share. I press her anyway. "What are you thinking?"

"People suck," Jane says, deflecting. My disappointment must show because she adds, "To be honest, I'm not sure. I have mixed feelings."

"Okay," I say. In my head, though, I'm thinking, Mixed feelings are great! *Mixed means she's on the fence, on the fence means she is swaying, and swaying of any kind is progress.*

In the morning, it became clear why their arrival was met without resistance—the island was uninhabited. After they'd slept in shifts, or rather, hardly slept, the clouds cleared, and a few people ventured in and around the area. Anh Minh and Bác Hiếu walked as far as they could go in each direction. They found no humans, no fishing poles, no docks, no boats, no shoes, no tents, and no burned-out remnants of fire pits.

Ngọc Lan sat up, shaking off the tiny pebbles clinging to her skin. This wasn't the first time she had fallen asleep in the sand. It was, however, the first time she'd woken up shivering. Getting to her feet, she moved to a fire pit Bác Nga had built to boil water and cook food. The flames danced beneath her hands as she warmed her fingers above the crackling sounds.

"You need to eat something," Bác Nga said. She handed Ngọc Lan a plantain. "Now that you're awake, why don't you go see if you can find some clams." Bác Nga wasn't being mean—she was busy cooking several different pots that smelled of stew and herbal remedies. She needed Ngọc Lan to make herself useful.

"Dạ." Ngọc Lan nodded. Taking the plantain with her, she strolled down to the water.

Along the shoreline, wood from the masts of sunken boats jutted up from the water. Not a single vessel that had docked at the island remained afloat.

A gentle wave crashed against her ankles—she froze. Her spine stiffened. Her legs turned to lead. Fear took over. Ngọc Lan wasn't ready to return to the water, not after what had happened the day before. She thought about the day Chị Diễm nearly drowned. Had she experienced the same panic that had almost caused her sister to drown?

"Why are you standing here alone?" Anh Luân asked.

"I . . . ," Ngọc Lan started, but stopped herself. She nodded toward the boats. "I guess we're stuck here."

"We had no choice. My brother sank the boat on purpose to prevent them from kicking us off the island. And to keep our supplies near. When the tide is low, we'll be able to gather what's left."

Ngọc Lan looked down at the empty pots lined up around the fire. She hadn't thought to take anything with her, but while she'd slept, the others had brought what they could ashore. Wet clothes draped across low-hanging branches made Ngọc Lan think of the market, the lingering heat beneath her fingers reminding her that it was gone. Along with her family and everything she knew. "But why would we want to stay?" she asked. Was this place what they'd left Vietnam for? This uninhabited, empty island? No. She did not want to stay here.

"We can't return home. We need to look forward," Anh Luân said.

"Come eat," Anh Minh called from across the sand.

"Come," Anh Luân said.

Ngọc Lan hesitated. "Chị Mậu is mad at me."

"Chị Mậu's personality is such that she is mad at the world. Don't read too much into it. Come," he urged again. Unease settled onto Ngọc Lan's shoulders. Casting her eyes downward, she dug her heels deeper into the sand.

Anh Luân stepped in front of her. "Hide behind me. She'll never see you."

Ngọc Lan laughed. When she was younger, Anh Luân and

her brother would race shopping carts, with Ngọc Lan in one and Chị Diễm in the other. Chị Diễm was heavier but Anh Hòa usually won. Ngọc Lan always suspected that Anh Luân held back a bit for her safety. A few years ago, Anh Luân had left to work on his brother's fishing boat. Then Anh Hòa started selling gasoline and the girls didn't see much of Anh Luân. He was older in appearance now, his personality more subdued. But he had the same protective nature she remembered. Ngọc Lan followed.

When the two brothers were standing side by side, Ngọc Lan could see that even though Anh Luân was younger than Anh Minh, at eighteen, he was already taller than his older brother.

"Your things are over there," Anh Minh said, pointing to a tree where Ngọc Lan's clothes had been hung to dry. She flushed at the sight of her pink underwear dangling from a branch, though everyone else's clothes were also hanging from low branches.

"Thank you." Ngọc Lan was unable to look him in the eye.

The family was splitting a can of sardines. When Bác Nga put three fish into Ngọc Lan's palms, she shoved the salty creatures into her mouth, savoring the flavors. By now the food rations had dipped dangerously low. She knew this was all she'd get, but she couldn't help staring at the can in hopes of having another bite.

Anh Minh's youngest daughter giggled as she held the flopping sardine in her tiny fist before taking a bite. Ngọc Lan's stomach rumbled.

Noticing, Bác Nga handed Ngọc Lan the container with one

remaining fish. The soft bones tickled her throat as she swallowed. She scraped every last bit from the can, longing for a piece of bread to go with it.

As granules of sand slipped between her toes, she thought about home. *The earth is similar everywhere we go,* she thought. This beach had the same sand and ocean, but it wasn't home. Here she had no mother, no father, no brother, and no sister. A girl without a family was an orphan. Ngọc Lan had been orphaned by both her family and her country.

An older man Ngọc Lan didn't know—an herbalist named Ông Sơn—began ordering men and boys to help him gather large sticks and rocks as well as cut down palm leaves. It didn't matter what occupation anyone had held back in Vietnam: while stranded, every single person who wasn't finding or preparing food helped build shelter.

Survival on the island was laborious. Scavenging for food, finding cover, fishing from the shore with tattered nets, climbing trees for fruit; everything had to be made from raw materials. They might have been the first to arrive, but they were not the last. Every few days more boats docked. This meant more people to feed, more shelter to build, and more wounds or illnesses that needed tending to.

When a cough erupted and spread throughout the camp, Bác Nga sat hunched for hours at a time, pressing remedies from the plants. Ngọc Lan dug for clams on the beach but found none. The tide wasn't low enough. She needed to dive for rock clams, but she couldn't bring herself to enter the water.

Bác Hiếu thought they'd only be stranded for a few days because the Malaysians knew where they were. But instead of rescue came more refugees. To help, Ngọc Lan followed the herbalist into the forest. She listened to Ông Sơn explain what plants to eat and which to avoid. They foraged seaweed, cut down coconuts, pulled kale, and gathered berries.

Over time, she became quick at spotting different fruits. When she discovered a yellow berry wrapped in a thin paper coating, she picked a shirt-full, twisted it into a knot, and ran back to camp. She wanted to know, was it edible?

Leaves crunched beneath her feet; insects skittered away. For a brief moment, she remembered what it was like to feel free. And she flew

until she began to fall

in an uncontrollable tumble.

Tripped by a root, she braced herself for the landing by letting go of her berry-filled shirt. Dirt streaked her pants, but she was not hurt. Squatting down, she retrieved what fruits she could.

Suddenly, she felt the urge to laugh.

Then she was laughing.

Huge, belly-aching, stomach-knotting howls of laughter fell from her lips.

She didn't know why she was laughing. Perhaps it was because she'd tripped, or because this deserted island was ten times worse than starving in Vietnam. Maybe it was simply that she couldn't remember the last time she'd laughed. When she stopped, tears replaced the momentary joy. Ngọc Lan wanted to go home. She missed her mother and sister. She wanted to find Anh Hòa and her dad. Alone, she cried until the blue sky turned orange and fatigue took the place of her longing. Dazed and exhausted, she slumped back to camp empty-handed.

The following day, Ngọc Lan returned to the forest. She picked lettuce and root vegetables in a bucket Bác Nga gave her, muttering to herself along the way. At first, she spoke under her breath: "Don't be lazy. Flatten the leaves so you can fit more." Then her words grew louder: "Work faster. Be more careful. Open your eyes. Reach deeper. That's too firm, it's not ripe." Before she knew it, she was full-on arguing with herself. "Don't step in the mud. It will ruin your pants," Ngọc Lan said, mimicking the way Chị Diễm always nagged her about sitting upright and being tidy.

Ngọc Lan clomped around in the mud giggling to herself. "There is no one out here, Chị Diễm. Why should I take care to look decent?"

For a split second, Ngọc Lan looked up, expecting an answer. Chị Diễm wasn't there. There was, however, a faint whistle passing through the trees. *If I caught just the right breeze, could I send a message to my sister?* she wondered.

On the off chance that it was possible, Ngọc Lan continued her conversation. "You look sophisticated and bright for yourself. Not for others. We have value. Stand like you know it," imaginary

Chị Diễm said. Ngọc Lan straightened her back, lifting her chin to Chị Diễm's imaginary approval.

For her part, Ngọc Lan huffed at no one and continued on, all the while sidestepping mud puddles. She wandered up an embankment, thinking about how Chị Diễm's hair was always braided in a beautiful fishtail, whereas her hair was usually a tangled mess covered in sand or seaweed. Gathering her hair in one hand, she stroked the many knots.

"Water flows everywhere. If you can't hear it moving, look for where it has traveled," Chị Diễm said.

Ngọc Lan followed the moist mud tributaries farther and farther upland until she heard the sound of trickling water. Through a narrow pathway covered by long, thin leaves, she found a small pool. Fully clothed, Ngọc Lan dipped herself in, scrubbing her legs and arms.

Above her, birds chirped. Their silhouettes fluttered from one branch to another in a mating dance. Then the water suddenly grew warm. Ngọc Lan sank into the comfort of it.

"How can you clean your body with all that fabric in the way?" Chị Diễm asked.

"I'm not looking for a husband. Who cares if I'm dirty?"

"Just wait. Your time will come," Chị Diễm warned.

Ngọc Lan closed her eyes. "Where have you been, Chị Diễm?" she asked. "Why couldn't you find me sooner?"

"Find little sister for what? So you could steal my food?" Chị Diễm said. Ngọc Lan didn't laugh. That wasn't something Chị Diễm would have thought. Her sister would have been the one to share her meal while pretending to be full. Being the youngest,

Ngọc Lan often took Chị Diễm's offerings. As the saying goes, "Chị phải hy sinh cho em." Older siblings had an obligation to sacrifice for their younger ones. Hot tears blurred her vision. This was the closest she had felt to her family since leaving.

The warmth faded. But in her left hand was a burning sensation, like hot tea spilled over clumsy fingers. The heat folded her palm in a firm grip, squeezed tight, then disappeared, taking the connection with it.

A large group had gathered on the beach when Ngọc Lan returned. More boats had washed ashore. Chị Quyên, Chị Diễm's best friend, the one whose disappearance had caused Chị Diễm's depression, stared at Ngọc Lan in disbelief. Her eyes, large and intense, were altogether frightening. She appeared afraid. Of Ngọc Lan, though? Why? Ngọc Lan's stomach twisted. Why was Chị Quyên looking at her like that?

Chị Quyên stepped aside. Behind her was a body dressed in Chị Diễm's favorite brown-and-pink floral shirt. Chị Diễm's... *Chị Diễm?!*

No. No. No!

Chị Diễm! Ngọc Lan screamed, but no words came out.

In a flash, Chị Quyên was beside her, holding her up on legs that were failing. "Xin lỗi em."[21] Chị Quyên's voice, cracking and faint, was far away.

---

21 *"I'm so sorry."*

Disbelief and realization bounced back and forth in her mind. Ngọc Lan's heart pounded.

Crawling.

Ngọc Lan couldn't get to her sister fast enough.

Tripping.

Legs trembling in shock.

Sand.

Gnashed between her teeth.

Screaming.

Without sound.

Face. Hands. Feet.

Every part of Chị Diễm's body clutched in shaking hands. Tears spilling. Vision blurred. Salt on her tongue. She swallowed. Hands tugged at her shoulders. "Don't weep over the body," someone said.

Denial.

"Let me go. My sister isn't dead. Wake up. Wake up. Wake up!" Ngọc Lan pleaded.

Bác Nga's arm moved across her torso. She gripped Ngọc Lan tight. "Let her go," she whispered gently. Her voice was firm, but Ngọc Lan heard the wetness of a sob in her throat.

"Chị xin lỗi em," Chị Quyên repeated. "Chị apologizes to em. We were swimming together for shore. I don't know what happened."

Questions raced through Ngọc Lan's mind. Was Chị Diễm's body weak? Were her muscles fatigued? Did she underestimate the distance? Was she lulled by a ghost? Did she *choose* to let go?

Ngọc Lan pushed Bác Nga away, running to her sister's feet. She needed to touch her, to feel the weight of her sister's body in her bare hands.

"Chị xin lỗi em," Chị Quyên said again.

"Leave me alone. Everyone leave me!" Ngọc Lan cried.

Chị Quyên left and Ngọc Lan buried her head in Chị Diễm's stomach.

Chị Diễm had been heartbroken by Chị Quyên's abandonment. Then Ngọc Lan had done the same thing. Now her sister was gone. The punishment of a thousand knives wouldn't come close to assuaging the guilt Ngọc Lan felt.

"Chị Diễm has to know that I would never leave Chị." But she did leave.

"Chị Diễm has to know that I would have told you if I knew." But she didn't.

"Chị Diễm has to forgive me." But how does one forgive the unforgivable?

Ngọc Lan hugged her sister's feet, her fingers brushing against the seam of her pants. The necklace. Beneath the thin fabric, she felt the rough bumps of tiny links clasped together.

Ngọc Lan sobbed at her sister's feet. She didn't want to carry the burden of life for both of them.

"Why did we have to leave Việt Nam? Why did we abandon our homes to wander the ocean and die without family? Why did my sister, who did nothing wrong, have to lose her life fleeing?" Ngọc Lan asked. No one answered.

Ngọc Lan was left to grieve alone. Tearing open the threads

of her sister's pants, Ngọc Lan pulled out the gold chain. She clutched it in her palm. Nothing felt more like a betrayal than this moment, but she had promised her mother. Later she would reunite it with the jade pendant. Afterward, she sat Chị Diễm up, folded herself around her sister, and braided her hair.

Hm, hm, hm hm, hm, hm, hm-hmmmmm, hm...
Hm, hm, hm hm, hm hm, hm-hmmmmm...

Ngọc Lan rocked forward and backward, softly humming the melody of the song their mom used to sing to comfort them.

CHAPTER 22
PAUL

I jump, not really in any direction, just—away. For such a tranquil space, this temple has given me a jolt. I'm feeling kicked off-balance. On the one hand I'm thinking, *This has got to be a joke*. Are hidden cameras about to pop out? Surprise, you're on a Vietnamese prank show. I notice Bác Kim takes no offense to my reaction. She barely registers it. Anh Sáu, on the other hand, looks ready to ditch me.

"Your daughter walks beside him," the woman says. "A young woman who is regal but gentle." My knees go weak. She's confirming what I thought. My dead mother is haunting me. I'm too freaked out to move. "There's no need to worry. The girl is serene and nearly content. All she needs is to be brought home."

Bà Ngoại's eyes are glassy. "I knew this already. But Ngọc Lan wants to keep her near, in America."

"When did my mom die?" I ask. I'm feeling a strange mixture of anger and nausea.

"A?" Bà Ngoại looks at me, confused. "No. Your mother isn't dead. The ghost beside you is your aunt, Dì Diễm."

Oh. Somehow this knowledge is *less* comforting. Though I am surprised at the relief that washes over me, knowing that my mother *isn't* dead. I have so many questions. Like why my uncle never mentioned another sister? Usually, when family members die, there are photos of them on an ancestral altar of some sort. Is Cậu Hòa holding a grudge? Or maybe he feels so guilty about her dying that he can't bear to look at her every day? That's more likely. I make a mental note to ask Mợ Bích about it later. Why is my mom holding her sister's ashes hostage? Don't *her* mom's wishes take precedence over her own? Of course not. My mother is selfish. How is it that with each new thing I discover, I have less clarity than I did before? The more I learn, the more confused I become.

I decide confirmation is needed. "My mother is *not* dead?"

"Correct, your mother is still alive. After the war, Bà Ngoại was too poor to travel. My daughter was just across the ocean, yet I couldn't retrieve her body. But your mother returned to Indonesia and brought Dì Diễm's ashes to America. The right thing is to return her home, to where she lived," Bà Ngoại laments.

"I knew it," Anh Sáu says, pressing my gold chain back into my palm. "I was going to hang on to this until you left so someone else didn't steal it, but it's hot like a ghost."

My palm opens, nearly releasing it. Then I quickly clamp my fist shut. I drop it in my pocket. "Thanks a lot," I say, not at all grateful.

"Do you have a special garlic or something to get her to leave me?" I ask. Damn if I'm not regretting abandoning that garlic from Joe and Mai now. Not that his Mary picture is helping me much. Maybe Filipino blessings don't work on Vietnamese ghosts.

"No," Grandma says sharply.

Crap, I messed up. I'm just not sure how. I barely know my aunt. Also, I have zero power to help her. I'm the guy who five minutes ago thought *she* was my mother.

The soothsayer speaks to me but locks eyes with my grandmother. "I could give you a talisman that would ward her off from coming near you. In this case, I think it might be best to just go ahead and bring her home?"

Easy for you to say. She's not creeping around your personal space, I think. I don't say it because there's a look on my grandma's face like she's talking to her dead daughter. I shift my eyes from the empty space beside me to Bà Ngoại. Her eyes smile, narrow, and weep in succession.

Hold up. *Do I believe in ghosts now?* Before, I could convince myself that my mind was playing tricks on me. Now, this woman is telling me she sees the ghost. Plus, my dad is having obvious nightmares. Also, there was the creepy girl from the plane, the siren in the ocean, and all the spiritual energy I've been feeling . . . Basically, the evidence is pretty damning at this point. Shiiiiiet. I do, I really freaking do. "Why me, though? Jane is older. Why not haunt her? Or my mother, she's the one holding on to my aunt's ashes—"

Anh Sáu cuts me off: "I need one." Jackass, of course, he'd protect himself and leave me hanging.

"Five hundred đồng," the woman says. She hands him a small scroll tied with red silk string. Then, to answer my question, she says, "Spirits can tell which souls will be receptive to them." That's real. Between me and Jane, I'd haunt me too.

Anh Sáu pays while muttering about how Việt Kiều came to stir the spirits. Me, he's talking about me, I'm the Việt Kiều, but he's too chickenshit to say my name for fear that my dead aunt will affect him in some way.

I must wear a worried expression on my face because Bác Kim clasps her soft hands over mine. "Don't be afraid. In Việt Nam, there are many ghosts, but only one can inhabit your space at a time. By your side is a gentle ghost. Consider yourself lucky. Your Dì Diễm won't let other spirits abuse you."

Oh good, I think while feeling not at all good. I nod anyway.

"Cảm ơn, Chị Kim," Grandma says, apparently grateful. She leaves a stack of bills in the woman's basket. Before we exit the grounds, we stop at a Lady Buddha statue. Bà Ngoại lights incense. While she prays with her eyes closed, her hand reaches into her bag. Out comes a tiny crane. She drops it in the fountain at the deity's base. The discreet way in which she does this makes me think she's not supposed to. My aunt's ghost leans into me in the form of a warm wind. Is *she* becoming more brazen or am *I* more attuned to her?

The crane floats for a moment, then dissolves into a blue-and-gold streak. "Whoa," I say, mesmerized by the vanishing effect. "What is *that*?"

"In water, we connect to our ancestors. This bird sends my veneration and love."

I would've laughed if Joe or Mai had said this. I don't know how, but Bà Ngoại just made something hokey sound legit. I want to say something profound—to show that I appreciate where I come from—but all I manage is "Cool." Lame.

On the ride to Bà Ngoại's house, Anh Sáu—who used to be all up in my space—sits pressed so far into his door that he might as well be hugging it. As for me, I'm wondering if I'll soon regret this spontaneous search for my grandmother.

I open up my phone and text Jane. Vietnam is fourteen hours ahead of California, so it's six in the morning over there.

From: Paul
Yo. Wake up.

From: Jane
I never sleep.

From: Paul
Grandma's fortune teller thinks there's a ghost following me.

From: Jane
Oh lord. Lol. She's just trying to freak you out. Ghosts aren't real.

I debate whether or not to tell her about my ghost pressings. Screw it, if I suffer, she should suffer.

From: Paul
I've felt ghost pressings! I thought maybe Mom died and was haunting me.

From: Jane

Mom's not dead.

How can she know that? Has Jane been talking to our mom behind my back? Is that why she isn't pissed that I found Bà Ngoại? Because she's known this whole time? As if reading my mind, Jane texts.

From: Jane

Cau Hoa would've said something. Death trumps all grudges.

From: Paul

Maybe he didn't know either.

From: Jane

Our family is like water. There's no place on earth they can't reach.

I look at her text again and nearly drop the phone. First Grandma dissolves a crane in water. Now Jane is talking about water connecting all of us? That siren nearly lulled me to death *in water* too. A shiver shoots down my spine.

From: Jane

Dude. Stop freaking out. There are no such things as ghosts. Think about it, if he didn't tell you there was a ghost, who would keep paying him? The guy's gotta eat.

I laugh. Who knew her snark could be so steadying? Not me. Jane is ultralogical. I bet if I told her about each of my encounters, she'd find proof that it happened because of some basic scientific reason. The problem is I *felt* it. I can't deny my own experience. It *happened* to me. More than once.

From: Paul

The person was a she. Why would you think it was a man?

From: Jane

Humm. I dunno, must be the patriarchy seared into my psyche.

Yup, that's Jane for sure.

We arrive in Vung Tau just after dusk. Bà Ngoại's house sits facing the ocean. It's not visible, but I can hear waves and smell salt. White walls enclose a small compound with slatted wooden doors, which the driver opens manually. The modest two-story home is magazine clean. There's no clutter—at all. Not even mail or random papers.

In the center of the room is a wooden staircase. Beyond that is an open-plan kitchen with a breakfast table, matching chairs, and a love seat facing a small TV. Our room has a bed (no headboard) and a nightstand/mini-dresser, and that's it.

"Both of you will sleep here, huh?" Grandma says. It's framed as a question, but it's not really a question.

"Two people and a ghost," Anh Sáu mutters. I don't know why he's so bent out of shape when *I'm* the one she's haunting.

"Con is lucky it's Diễm and not me. If it were me, I would've bitten you by now." Bà Ngoại smiles. What is it with Vietnamese people and biting? Also, dang, she's wicked.

Joe and Mai would love my grandma. Mai would be fascinated by what a boss she is. Joe would want to know about all things supernatural. He's a ghost hunter in the making. I may be a believer now, but that doesn't mean I want a spirit following me, family or not. So unlike Anh Sáu, I'm relieved to be sharing a room. We follow her upstairs, where I catch the view from her balcony. Grandma has beachfront property with a killer view, even at night.

"Towels for bathing are here. Whatever you two need, just take it," she continues, flipping the lights on so we can see and then off again as we move back downstairs. We get ready for bed.

Bà Ngoại retreats to her room to change. Once she's out of earshot, Anh Sáu plops down on the love seat and says, "If I knew madames lived this well, I'd put on a dress and become one too." I slap him, but I'm laughing along.

"What the hell is happening right now?" I muse aloud.

Someone clears their throat. Both Anh Sáu and I jump. In the kitchen, tending to the large pot of bún riêu, is a woman. When did she come in? I wait for her to say something. She doesn't. She simply continues cooking by the stove. I can't believe I'm asking myself this, but *Is she real?*

Bà Ngoại appears in a silk robe and matching house slippers. "Are you two hungry yet?"

"Dạ," we reply.

To the cook she says, "If the food is done, you can head home." The woman bows quickly before exiting. This is when I notice that the table has been set with three bowls, a plate of raw bean sprouts, mint leaves, Vietnamese balm leaves, purple perilla leaves, and sliced limes in the middle. How did Anh Sáu and I walk past without noticing her or the food? Anh Sáu's pasty face tells me he's wondering the same thing.

We sit down to eat.

"What school subjects are you good at?" Bà Ngoại asks me. I guess this is the part where we "get to know" each other.

The question irks me. I feel like she's going to judge me when I tell her that I don't like physics and hate chemistry. Besides, I'm not here to tell her about me. She never wanted to know me before now. I'm here for *her* to tell *me* stuff.

"Where is my mom?" I ask, ignoring her.

"Your mom lives in Las Vegas."

So the rumors are true. Her directness surprises me. I expected her to equivocate.

"When your mom was little, she was adorable. Adorable and filthy. She loved to swim. Like you." I look up. How does she know that?

From a drawer, she produces photos of me at swim meets. Anh

Sáu nearly spits out his food from laughing. "Is that *you*?" Any notion I had that I was over being embarrassed about my uniform (a red-and-gold Speedo) is wiped away. My cheeks burn.

"Every week Cậu Hòa calls Bà Ngoại. He tells me about you," she explains.

I can't tell if this is a violation of privacy, an invasion of my space, or if it means something else. Not love exactly, but care? I'm shocked Cậu Hòa has anything to report. He rarely talks to me. It's not that he ignores me or does anything mean. He's an adult, whereas I'm a "kid." The unspoken bylaws of Vietnamese culture dictate that adults and kids do not deep-dive into each other's lives. Some chastising, maybe. A "Congratulations" if I bring home a medal or award. Never anything unprovoked, like *Hey, Paul, what's life like these days?* How, then, could he pass on anything useful when he knows nothing about me?

"Bà Ngoại knows you have a lot of questions. Today has been a long day already. Finish eating and tomorrow Bà will tell you more."

Part of me wants to say no—to demand that she stay up and answer all my questions—but I'm so overwhelmed that I have no idea what questions to start with. I'm not prepared, how could I be? A week ago, I didn't even know my grandmother was alive.

I brush my teeth, but before I crawl into bed, I open up my neglected journal and add:

- *Grandma is a badass. I think she might be famous.*
- *She was a prostitute. Could be a madame, but it's unconfirmed. She's rich.*
- *Mom is not dead. Aunt Diem is haunting me. The soothsayer lady says she's nice.*
- *If my mom isn't haunting my dad, who is? Can a ghost haunt two people at once?*
- *I still can't believe Dad just let Ba Ngoai take me. He must think she's going to teach me some kind of life lesson. No way he thinks this will be fun for me.*
- *Cau Hoa doesn't say much, but apparently, he listens.*
- *Mo Bich's bun rieu is better than the one Grandma's cook made. Maybe she should sell it.*
- *Anh Sau snores. I'm glad I'm not alone.*
- *Ba Ngoai reminds me of Jane, which must mean ~~Jane is not like our mom~~.*

I scribble out the words as best I can. Jane would hate me if she saw that. I'm a bit surprised she hasn't written me off already for finding Bà Ngoại. If my sister could step past her anger for a moment I think she would enjoy hanging out with grandma. Bà Ngoại defies the stereotype of a demure Vietnamese woman. As does Jane. Somehow Jane knew *not* to become subservient despite growing up with our Dad. I mean, she chose a profession where she argues with people all day. Add in the fact that I stood up to him too, and I'm thinking maybe defiance is genetic.

CHAPTER 23
NGỌC LAN

"I'm confused. Are you saying that Mom's sister visited her before Mom found out she was actually dead?" Jane asks.

"Kind of. More like: Mom missed her sister so much she was talking to her, but Dì Diễm was also really there."

"So was Dì Diễm a ghost or a figment of Mom's imagination?" Jane asks me.

"How are those two things different?"

"You know I hate it when you answer a question with a question." She glares.

"Well, unless you believe in ghosts . . . ," I say, already knowing the answer. Jane doesn't believe in ghosts because Jane is afraid of ghosts. If she believes in them, they become real. I call that denial.

Jane pauses for a moment and then says, "Continue."

One day I will get her to admit that I'm right.

Ngọc Lan buried her sister on the windy, cold day of April 17, 1977. But Chị Diễm was not the only person they laid to rest here; she was one of more than forty people who had washed ashore. Markers for those whose bodies were never recovered brought the total to over a hundred.

In a clearing to the left of camp, the refugees found an area they preserved for burials. The opening was surrounded by bamboo, which when knocked together by only the slightest of breezes drummed a message to the heavens: *Take care of our loved ones.* Though it was covered in patches of overgrown grass and weeds, Ngọc Lan noted the area's shape: a perfectly round bottom that narrowed into a pointed tip to the north—a giant teardrop.

Anh Minh and Anh Luân dug Chị Diễm's grave using the cracked pieces of a broken plastic bucket. Ngọc Lan searched for the largest, most distinctive rock to mark her sister's resting place. She picked a stone with red and orange hues. The colors reminded Ngọc Lan of the Fairy Stream not far from their Vung Tau house. Cutting through the rock's surface were several blue veins reminiscent of tributaries. In the corner, the outline of a pink butterfly. Chị Diễm would have loved this rock.

There was no ceremony, no burning of incense, or whatever people did at funerals. Just refugees standing around another body being buried on land far from home.

"Do you see the butterfly?" Ngọc Lan asked Chị Diễm. Fresh tears pooled in her eyes. "Fly with the butterfly across the world, but don't forget to come back to visit." After that, Ngọc Lan stood up and walked away.

Checking behind her to ensure that no one was following, Ngọc Lan sprinted for the bathing pool.

As she reentered the crisp, cold lake, her arms shivered. She splashed her face. Holding her breath, she submerged herself. She loved how the sounds above fell away when she dropped beneath the surface. After a few minutes, she stood up. The tips of her fingers pressed against her swollen lids. When she opened her eyes, she froze.

Before her, Chị Diễm floated just beneath the surface. Her eyes peered directly at Ngọc Lan but held no meaningful expression. Her plaited hair wrapped across her chest like a vine. Ngọc Lan reached for her sister with a shaky hand. Chị Diễm's long hair touched back. The thin, silky strands rested like corn hair on her palm.

Afraid that any wrong movement might make her sister disappear, Ngọc Lan stood cautiously beside her. Of course Chị Diễm would be here. Where Ngọc Lan loved the ocean, Chị Diễm gravitated to rivers and streams. Both girls loved water, just in different forms. "I didn't mean to abandon you," Ngọc Lan said.

Chị Diễm frowned. She didn't believe her. Worse yet, where Ngọc Lan expected anger she found only sadness. Chị Diễm's soul was not at rest.

"Stay with em. Chị Diễm stays by my side, okay?" Ngọc Lan selfishly pleaded. Traditionally, she knew this was not the way. She was supposed to urge her sister's spirit onward to press her to cross over, but Ngọc Lan didn't want to.

Plop.

Ngọc Lan looked up, expecting to see a fish scurry away. A girl stood smiling at her from across the pool. "Sorry, I didn't see you there," the girl said. When Ngọc Lan didn't say anything, the girl asked, "Can you see me?" The girl must have been wondering if her mind was playing tricks on her.

Still not answering, Ngọc Lan returned her gaze to the water. Chị Diễm was gone. Her silhouette now blended with the features of the rock and moss below. Ngọc Lan thought about all the times her mother had told her: water remembers. Dropping her hand beneath the surface, she felt relief wash over her; it was still warm. Her sister's presence lingered because *water always connects back to itself. Whether in a cup, pool, or bowl, water springs from only one source—the earth itself.* To show the girls how cohesive water was, their mother took two cups, spread her hands wide, and dumped the water on the ground. The two splashes landed far apart, but as the streams traveled outward, the water rolled forward until it connected again.

"There, you blend into the scenery when you stand like that. Your legs are like two baby tree trunks, and your dirty shirt kind of disappears against the sunlight," the girl tried again.

"Are you sure I'm here? Maybe I'm not," Ngọc Lan said, more to herself than the girl.

"What?"

Ngọc Lan peered down at her stained shirt, which had once been beige but was now a splattering of natural stains. "I'm lucky this shirt doesn't have holes in it. If it did, you might be able to see right through me."

At this, the girl, who was about Ngọc Lan's age, laughed. Quiet at first, then louder, she laughed until tears appeared in her eyes. Her cackle, bright and untethered, was contagious. Ngọc Lan hadn't meant to tell a joke, but she joined in. This was the sort of thing only two girls who had left their homeland by boat to sleep in the mud on a strange island could find funny.

When she caught her breath, the girl introduced herself. "I'm Thảo."

"Ngọc Lan."

"Was that your older sister?"

Ngọc Lan looked up at her, mouth agape. Had she also seen Chị Diễm?

"My adopted mother said she drowned in one of the boats that flipped," Thảo said. Her frankness astonished Ngọc Lan. Especially because no one had told *her* this. She hadn't thought to ask. "You chose the prettiest rock of all the headstones."

"Chị Diễm liked multicolored rocks with lots of veins. She could stare at the same one for hours, searching for all the hidden shapes, like stars, jellyfish, clouds, trees, or faces—all sorts of things."

Thảo clapped her hands like she'd gotten an answer right on an oral exam. "I told my mom I saw a bear playing with a little girl." Chị Diễm would have liked this girl.

With milky dark skin and curly hair so thick that it sprang

out like beams of sunlight from her head, Thảo was a rare gem in Vietnam. The family she traveled with had bought her from her mother because she appeared biracial. Children of US soldiers, claimed or not, were given priority admittance into the United States. Thảo was purchased to help the family cut through the bureaucratic red tape of immigration. Ngọc Lan hadn't known any mixed-raced kids her age back home. She did know they were generally made fun of for being unwanted bastard children. Ngọc Lan thought about her own mother and wondered if she too was considered the child of a prostitute now?

The water turned cool. Chị Diễm was gone. Ngọc Lan got out. She shivered as she twisted water from her shirt and shorts.

"You're still soaking wet," Thảo said, stating the obvious.

"It's okay. I used to get drenched by rainwater all the time. It will dry."

Thảo seemed skeptical. "You need a comb," she said, gesturing at Ngọc Lan's tangled mane.

"Are you sure my dead sister hasn't taken over your body?" Ngọc Lan asked. It was uncanny how similar they were.

Thảo laughed. "How would I know?"

"True," Ngọc Lan lamented. "Come, let's go find a comb."

At camp, Thảo pointed to a wooden comb sitting on top of a neat pile of clothes.

Ngọc Lan's heart sank. "Not that one. That belongs to Chị Mậu. She hates me."

"Oh, Chị Mậu is so pretty," Thảo said longingly. "Why doesn't she like you?"

"Because I'm not as pretty as she is," Ngọc Lan lied. She

wasn't ready to admit that she'd nearly drowned at sea and taken the two brothers with her.

"Yeah." Thảo understood. Unlike Ngọc Lan, Thảo probably *was* bullied for her appearance. Realizing this, Ngọc Lan immediately felt guilty.

Giving up on the search for a comb, the girls took turns detangling portions of each other's hair with their fingers. Four hours later, their arms had tired despite making little progress.

"You need oils and a comb to fix the mess you've made." A male voice chuckled from behind them. The girls turned around. "Come. I'll teach you how to make one."

Ông Sơn's cloudy gray eyes twinkled in the sunlight.

"Make a comb from what, Ông Sơn?" Thảo was skeptical.

"From nature." Then he started into the forest.

Ngọc Lan and Thảo jumped to their feet to follow.

"Ông Sơn is crossing over alone?" Ngọc Lan asked. Every time she saw him, he was by himself—something they had in common.

"My family is buried next to your sister," he said. There was no sharpness in his tone, no sorrow either, just distance like he was reading a book out loud about someone else's life. "This way."

Off the main path, Ông Sơn led them to a tree with giant paper fan leaves. Pulling the branches aside, he revealed a small floral oasis. Together they pulled brittle and aromatic twigs from the base of the plant.

"This smells so good, like perfume," Thảo said, breathing in deeply. "A-choo!" she sneezed. Ngọc Lan giggled.

The old man shook his head, smiling. "If you want to smell it, then smell it. You don't need to shove it up your nose."

He sounded so much like Ngọc Lan's grandmother that she wondered if her mom's mom was here. She had heard of ghosts dropping into the bodies of the living to deliver messages. Maybe her ancestors sensed her loneliness. Bác Nga did her best to look after Ngọc Lan, but Chị Mậu's dislike for her made being around the family hostile and awkward. She ate as little as possible, filling her stomach with diluted broth. Under Chị Mậu's watchful eye, she relied on Bác Nga to offer extra helpings—she was a beggar sitting beside them at every meal.

"Is this enough?" Thảo asked, holding up two fistfuls of rosemary.

"Not even close. Count one leaf for every strand on your head. Then double it for all the knots," Ông Sơn chided. He shook open an old shirt that he'd made into a sack. Thảo dropped in what she'd collected. *How can he be so jovial?* Ngọc Lan wondered.

Ngọc Lan pretended to gather more shrubs as tears cascaded down her face. She admired Ông Sơn's resilience, but Ngọc Lan didn't want to be resilient. She missed her sister.

They returned to camp. Grabbing an unused pot, Ông Sơn boiled the bamboo until nearly all the water had evaporated. He did the same with the dried rosemary leaves. Then he split the pieces by hand. The boiled bamboo stripped apart as smoothly as a banana peel. Once he began carving, seemingly by magic, a comb appeared.

He dipped his hands into the rosemary pot, then pressed the

hot oil into Ngọc Lan's hair. He did the same for Thảo. "Everything you need can be found in nature. You just have to know what to look for," he said. Ngọc Lan pressed the comb into her hair. It slid through with ease. Thảo's beautiful curls danced. When the comb hit a snag, Ngọc Lan pulled it out, expecting to find a splinter. She blinked. Were her eyes playing tricks on her?

"Do you see this?" Ngọc Lan asked Thảo.

"See what?" Thảo peered at the comb until her eyes went wide too. "Wow, is that a girl?"

Within the veins of the wood was the silhouette of a girl in an áo dài, her long, billowing hair blowing in the wind behind her. Ngọc Lan ran her fingers across the shape of her sister. For years they had combed each other's hair like this. Of course she would be here.

For months, Ngọc Lan and the other refugees passed their time on the island without any rescue. Reliant on one another for support, a community of survivors bloomed. They gathered together, ate together, cleaned together, celebrated birth together, mourned death together, and more or less subsisted off the land together.

Ngọc Lan's newfound friendship kept her away from Chị Mậu while simultaneously allowing her to contribute by bringing back fruits and vegetables she and Thảo gathered while exploring.

Then one day, a large helicopter swooshed overhead. Dangling beneath the loud blades was a large wooden crate. It fell to the ground, cracking open with a thud. The box had canned food (but no opener), new clothing, and hygiene products. Despite what seemed like imminent rescue, several more months passed before a humanitarian ship docked near the island. They were told the boat would take them to America. But first, they would stop in Hong Kong, then head to Guam.

As groups of refugees piled into inflated motorboats, Ngọc Lan wondered if this was not another ploy to drag them out to sea to drown them. The motorboats shuttled one group, then two, before Bác Nga convinced Ngọc Lan to join the line.

Once they were aboard, the engine rumbled to life. Ngọc Lan's hands trembled. She gripped the metal railing on deck for support. Then something unexpected happened. As the tiny island receded, her heart tightened. She had no affinity for the place, but she was tethered to it because her sister was there.

"Her body is there, but her soul is gone," Bác Nga said, resting her palm on Ngọc Lan's back. Ngọc Lan nodded. She appreciated Bác Nga's attempt to comfort her. The ship's vibrations intensified as it reached full speed. Over the intercom someone announced their departure from "Kuku Island."

"Ku ku, ku ku," Ngọc Lan repeated to herself. "Ku ku, ku ku, ku ku . . ." She clasped her hand around the hem of her pants, clinging to the only thing she had left of home: her mother's jade pendant and gold necklace.

CHAPTER 24[22]

PAUL

I awake to the echoing chatter of Bà Ngoại and Anh Sáu. They're talking about fish sauce. I rub my groggy eyes before getting up. In the kitchen, I find bánh cuốn, steamed rice-flour rolls filled with ground pork and minced mushrooms—my favorite. *Lucky guess or something else Cậu Hòa told her about me?* Small dishes beside the rolls include a sweetened fish sauce, dried shredded pork, Vietnamese pork sausage, and pickled daikon and carrots. I greet my grandmother the way Mợ Bích taught me. "Dear Bà Ngoại, I just woke up."

"Giỏi," she says, acknowledging my greeting. She's dressed in a bright pink gown with a sequined cape that looks like a mixture between a ball gown and a traditional Vietnamese áo dài. It's fancier than anything I've ever seen. "Both of you eat. Bà needs to shower and change before we go."

"When we have time, will Bà Hang show me how to make your nước mắm?" Anh Sáu asks.

---

22 *This is getting a little ridiculous. I can't avoid four forever. Plus, I haven't heard any superstitions about the number twenty-four. Maybe the two cancels out the bad luck. Yeah, let's go with that.*

Bà Ngoại laughs. "Bà would need months to show you. It's been a long time since I've made it."

I side-eye Anh Sáu's morning ass-kissing. He ignores me. I scarf down breakfast like it's nobody's business. Partly, I'm hungry; mostly, the food tastes super fresh. It's calling me to eat it right away.

"Did you know Bà Hang used to make her own fish sauce? It was popular. Sold out at the market every time until the Communists took over and confiscated her lot to 'share among the people.'"

"Isn't that like really stinky?" I ask.

"During that time, it must have been the aroma of gold. Anh doesn't know anyone who makes their own nước mắm these days," Anh Sáu says.

"Probably because it's not worth the effort. Did she not say it takes a month?"

"I'm drooling just thinking about it," he muses. I think maybe he's having a conversation with himself.

I shake my head. Don't get me wrong, I love fish sauce, but to drool over it? I'll admit most Vietnamese dishes don't taste right without it, but the sauce itself is a seasoning, so it'd be like me saying I'm drooling over mustard. Anh Sáu is an odd duck. But I gotta admit, his ability to hang with both of my grandmas is impressive. It doesn't even seem like he's trying that hard.

I finish eating and do the dishes. Apparently, Anh Sáu adheres to the "men don't do dishes" mantra, so I clean his plate as well. When I finish, he slaps me on the shoulder. "Ey, let's get out of here so Bà Hang can sleep. She just got home two hours ago. She must be exhausted."

Guilt socks me in the stomach. I assumed my grandma went to

bed when we did, but it makes sense that most of her work happens at night. In our house, no one sleeps in later than my dad. Typically, I'm an early riser too. Paranoia kept me up later than normal. Plus, I'm not only dining with the enemy, I'm starting to kind of, like, respect(?) her.

"There is no time for sleep. Let's go," Bà Ngoại says, coming down the steps. She has changed into simple black pants. Her white, long-sleeved silk blouse with gold buttons has small ruffles that bounce as she moves.

We get into the car. It's still unreal to me that I'm here. That I'm sleeping in the house of a grandparent I didn't even know existed and she's unlike anything I could've imagined. I wonder if my dad kept me from her because of what she does or because her authority challenges his. I wish Jane were here even though I know that if she had come, *I* wouldn't be here. We drive for a long time in silence. Conversation with Vietnamese adults doesn't come as naturally to me as it does to Anh Sáu.

I assumed that a grandparent who doesn't bother to connect with her grandkids and raises a daughter who abandons her children is a bad person. But it's obvious that's not true. She has photos of me. She kept tabs. She knows what I like to eat.

Bà Ngoại's head leans against the window as she naps.

"Ey, you remember when I jumped into the ocean? Did you see the ghost that tried to pull me under?" I ask Anh Sáu.

"No, but I only needed to see the look on your face to know what happened."

"So you believe me when I say I saw a ghost?"

"Of course." The way Anh Sáu says it suggests that I'm an idiot for denying fact. "There are many drowned people in the water. When your soul is weak, they can drag you under. Spirits have to replace themselves with new spirits in order to cross over."

"What makes my soul weak?"

"Well, you're American, for starters." I should've seen that coming. "But you also don't have a strong self. Your insides are confused. You don't know who you are."

"And *you* do?" My defenses rise.

To my surprise, he doesn't point out his superiority. "No." He pauses for a moment, then adds, "That's why I control my temper. I don't dive into oceans I know nothing about, like an idiot." I spoke too soon.

Bà Ngoại's head shakes. Her eyes open so suddenly, she startles us both. I wasn't expecting that. Covering her yawn with a hand, she says, "Spirits seek those who are marred by tragedy. Sadness makes the soul weak." Well, that's creepy. I thought she was knocked out.

"See that?" Anh Sáu looks all kinds of smug. If I didn't know he was here to extort Bà Ngoại, I'd say he was a convert. I bet if she started a book club, he'd be the first to sign up. I stare at the scroll Anh Sáu bought from the soothsayer, which is attached to his belt loop. I wonder how protected he feels.

"So . . . ," I start. Anh Sáu and Bà Ngoại turn to me. "Does everyone believe the soothsayer? If she knows all these things, wouldn't she be famous?"

"She *is* famous. People come from all around the world hoping for auspicious fortunes. That said, we trust about ninety percent. There is nothing that can be one hundred percent certain." Bà Ngoại says this so matter-of-factly that it's like she's criticizing the question.

"When Dì Diễm died, how old was she?"

"Sixteen."

My age. The hairs on my arms rise.

"In what method did she become dead?" I fumble. I've never asked this question before, and my Vietnamese falters.

"Dì Diễm and your mother were very close. At that time, Bà Ngoại was extremely poor." Her eyes water. I expect her to stop. To not answer my question. This is what adults do when they become emotional.

"A family that separates is never as strong. Bà Ngoại didn't want to send both girls separately, but Bà Ngoại didn't have enough money to send them together. I sent Ngọc Lan first, then a few days later, I found a church group willing to take Diễm. Dì Diễm should have been right behind Ngọc Lan, but she drowned when her boat sank off the coast of Indonesia."

Anh Sáu hisses at me. "Are you stupid? Why are you bringing up people who have passed away?"

"Because she's haunting me. Plus, how are we supposed to learn about our history if no one ever talks about it?" I mean, it's not like I can call and ask Bà Ngoại these questions whenever I feel like it. If my dad has anything to say about it, I'll probably never see her again.

"If you have questions, just ask them," Bà Ngoại says. Her demeanor is calm, but I'm skeptical. The adults in my life don't tend to be very open or candid about the things that matter. Anh Sáu cracks his window open. Fresh sea air spills into the car. The breeze lends me courage.

"What happened to my mother?"

Bà Ngoại nods as though she knew this would be my next question. "Your mom focused on rationing her rice instead of gathering toppings to fill her bowl."

"I don't understand," I say. Mợ Bích taught me a few proverbs. This one is unfamiliar.

"In every person's life we are given one bowl of rice. When you're rich, you can supplement the rice with fish, meat, vegetables, things like this. But when you're poor you eat one grain at a time to stave off total starvation. Your mom, after Dì Diễm died, she wasn't the same. She didn't have a taste for life—Bà Ngoại thinks maybe she craved the feeling of hunger."

I'm stunned. That's the most honest answer anyone has given me.

"What about Cậu Hòa?" I ask. Why doesn't he feel this guilt? Why is he around when she is not?

"Before the war ended, Cậu Hòa was drafted. I had no idea where he was until I received a letter from America in 1983, eight years after the North Vietnamese officially took over. Cậu Hòa never told me what happened to him, but Bà knows he suffered in the reeducation camps." She pauses and takes a deep breath. A few tears sit at the bottom of her eyes, just waiting for her to blink so they can drop. "To tell you the truth, I wonder about my choices every day. When Ngọc Lan wrote to me more than four years after their departure, it broke my heart to hear that Diễm had drowned at sea." Grandma's voice is shaky as she dabs away tears. "I knew the risks, but there are no words to describe the pain of knowing your child is dead. What's more, her body was buried far from everyone in a mass grave in Indonesia. So my daughter died alone, on foreign land."

Damn. I'm not gonna lie, my heart kinda hurts. I've been angry with my mom for as long as I can remember, so I kinda thought I'd feel vindicated if I heard that she'd had a bad life. In my mind this moment is where I'd get to be like, *See? Shouldn't have left us if you didn't want to end up so miserable.* But it's not like that. It's not like that at all.

Same goes for my grandma. When I first judged Bà Ngoại's wealthy appearance, I assumed that she ditched her kids. I see now that actually, she lost them.

Anh Sáu hands her a tissue, which he somehow stealthily swiped from the driver. She wipes her face. After a deep breath her business-like tone returns. "Are we almost there?" she asks the driver. I'm not surprised by her abrupt ability to go from sad to normal. Jane does it all the time.

"We shall arrive in five minutes," the driver says.

Short beaches, tin homes, and restaurants flash by outside. Nearly every awning and sign has faded with time except for the occasional Coca-Cola canopy, which pops out of the scenery like a whale on land. There's something so different about the buildings here. What is it?

It's the doors. Before, I saw the lack of them as something missing, but actually *not* having them makes the space communal, like family picnics where everyone is meant to eat together. Inside the shops, the handmade crafts are artisanal. Not in that crafty hot-glue-gun, boxed-junk kind of way. Things in Vietnam are made by the owners. The man selling coffee also built the store, printed the sign, and gathered all the tables and chairs—I know this because it's the same way my dad does things. He's not a sign maker, but he made our sign; he's not a contractor, but when someone smashed our window, my dad replaced it. He's not a builder, but we have an extra tin shed attached to the store that resembles these same storefronts.

We pass under a sign that welcomes us into the province of Phan Thiết. A few minutes later we drive onto a dirt parking lot. Chú Phương opens the door. From the trunk he hands us each a drawstring bag.

"Cảm ơn, Chú Phương," I say, bowing in thanks. He nods back with a smile. Anh Sáu does the same.

Bà Ngoại tells us to kick off our shoes, then leads us to a shallow stream. The water is murky even though it's only ankle-deep. I'm hoping she's not about to go in it. So, of course, the first thing she does is glide right in. This moment is so damn Vietnamese that I almost start laughing. Don't want to eat something? It'll be the main dish on the menu. Afraid of heights? A sky-high bridge will suddenly appear. Not a fan of murky water? Here's a cloudy stream.

Giving in to my fate, I sink my toes into the slowly moving river, only to find that actually, I was wrong. From a distance, the water *looks* muddy and murky. Up close I can see my toes clearly. The stream winds through a narrow canyon. On my right is a bright orange rock cliff. On my left, dark green fruit trees.

"Is that pineapple?" I ask. At the base, I notice that the roots are spidery, like the famous banyan tree Jane is always droning on and on about. She thinks the banyan tree is like the Mother of Vietnam.

"This is a pandan tree," Bà Ngoại says.

"Ohh cây lá dứa," I say, repeating the name in Vietnamese. This tree is to Mợ Bích what the banyan tree is to Jane—a symbol of Vietnam, the homeland. At least Mợ Bích's love makes sense, because she uses pandan to make delicious desserts.

"You know this plant?" Bà Ngoại seems impressed, which fills me with pride.

"Mợ Bích uses it to make rau câu." This Vietnamese Jell-O is my favorite because it's not super sweet, and it usually comes in cool animal or floral shapes.

Bà Ngoại laughs. "You are surely Vietnamese. But did you know this leaf has many other uses? We can wrap it around our joints for pain, and it helps regulate blood sugar. You can even suck on it for bad breath or chew on it to stop bleeding gums."

"Is Bà Ngoại saying that eating rau câu is healthy?"

"Correct! If you eat it raw."

Eww. I make a face.

"Don't worry, no grandchild of mine will have to chew on raw leaves. I put pandan candies in your bags."

I bristle a little at her use of *grandchild* but try to hide it.

"Whaaaat?!" Anh Sáu peels the strap off his back, takes out a candy, and pops it in his mouth. "Uhmm," he hums. "I feel like my blood sugar is regulating nicely."

I eat one too. Bà Ngoại laughs. I see so much of Cậu Hòa in her now. He's a serious guy, but when he does laugh, his shoulders bounce as his body sways in a circle from the waist up, just like Bà Ngoại's does now.

We continue on the serene path, turning where it bends, until we come upon small rapids cresting over basketball-sized boulders. I'm mesmerized.

"Ey, look up," Anh Sáu says, smacking my arm.

Bright orange-and-white rock formations fill the landscape. The deeper I venture, the taller the mountains become. Wow, I've entered another world. I guess because we mostly visit with family instead of sightsee, I didn't think of Vietnam as a place that had nature like this. I snap a photo of the waterfall with my phone.

"This place is called the Fairy Stream. Pay attention to your feet. Do you feel that?"

A warmth passes over my ankles. Instinctively, I lift my foot because the temperature rises so quickly that I'm afraid it could turn scalding. "Where is the hot water coming from?"

"No one knows." From her bag, Bà Ngoại takes out a Ziploc filled with tiny rice-paper cranes. When she dumps them near our feet, they float for mere seconds before dissolving. "Through water flows the spirit of the Vietnamese people. Every time you feel the heat, that is a spirit. Bà Cố[23] used to say 'From dust we came, to dust we will return.' When I stand here amid this flesh-colored sand, I am closest to all the generations that have come before us." She bends down, scooping a handful of the vibrant orange sand into her palm. "See how it sparkles? Those are the fairies. Those are your ancestors."

Bà Ngoại looks at me. "This is where I want Diễm's ashes scattered."

"You want me to bring Dì Diễm's ashes back?"

"No. This business is not for you. Bà Ngoại brought you here because I want you to know your ancestry. When you feel lost throughout your life, I want you to return here. You live in America,

---

23 *my great-grandmother*

but your blood is Vietnamese. Bà Ngoại knows you feel the pulling at your feet."

Great. I was hoping the finger strokes in the water were just my imagination. But she's telling me they're spirits.

"Don't be afraid. Ghosts can push you, but they can also protect you."

Her words *sound* reassuring, but they don't *feel* reassuring.

"Bà Ngoại knows that my mother abandoned us, right?" I ask. I assume she knows, since my mom is her kid. If Cậu Hòa doesn't, though, maybe she doesn't either.

"I do." Or she does.

"Does Bà Ngoại know why?"

Grandma looks at me strangely. Her eyes squint; then she casts her gaze away before admitting, "Yes. She left because Bà Ngoại told her to leave."

CHAPTER 25

NGỌC LAN

"I think you got the timeline wrong with Cô Thảo. She didn't get here until like 1987."

"How do you know?"

"Because I asked her."

"You've met *her? I thought you said you didn't remember anything about Mom."*

"I lied," Jane says, as though that should've been obvious. "Like a dumbass, I asked her how a Mexican person could speak Vietnamese so well." Oh, that's bad. It explains the guilty look because Cô Thảo is half Black, not Mexican.

"That's messed up, Jane." I laugh, because c'mon, how is that not hilarious?

"Anyway, the point is, Mom didn't meet her till later," Jane says, still staring at her feet. Guilt is Jane's Achilles' heel.

I consider this for a moment. Jane's info jacks up my storyline, and I don't know how to fix it. "Well, in my story, she came in 1977 with Mom. You can fix it when you write the novel of our family history."

"Why would I do that? You're the one who's obsessed with digging into the past."

"Well, then it can die with us. Do you want to know why Mom left us or not?"

Jane says nothing for a moment, then stares me dead in the eyes. "Well, what are you waiting for?"

I smile. It's a tedious process, but those walls are crumbling.

The skyline in Hong Kong looked nothing like the tropical oasis of Vung Tau. Even the uninhabited Kuku Island felt more alive than this densely populated area covered in concrete and steel. Ngọc Lan was homesick. She heard birds but saw none flying. In her search for comfort, she found only change. Even the water appeared darkened and barren. It was impossible for her to see Hong Kong as anything other than another place far from where she wanted to be.

When Ngọc Lan boarded the ship with the Lê family, she thought Thảo's family would be there too.

At dinner, she and the Lê family sat at picnic benches with food that tasted strange on their tongues. Ngọc Lan craned her neck in search of her friend.

"Eat," Bác Nga urged.

"Stop looking so pathetic. I'm sure your friend is around here somewhere," Chị Mậu admonished.

Ngọc Lan sat down. "You'll find her. Thảo is somewhere on

this ship," Anh Luân offered. Ngọc Lan nodded. She didn't like the food, but she ate every last bite.

She didn't find Thảo that day or the next. But the boat was so large; she could easily imagine Thảo searching in earnest for Ngọc Lan and the girls just missing each other as they turned the many corners on the vessel. Ngọc Lan was so hopeful, in fact, that she spent the entire trip to Hong Kong walking the perimeter of the boat in search of her friend, but she wasn't there. Ngọc Lan gave up when they docked. Like her father, brother, and sister, one day Thảo was in her life, and the next she was gone.

After only a brief stop where more Vietnamese refugees boarded, the large American military cargo ship pushed back from the Hong Kong port and set sail again—this time for Guam. Ngọc Lan sat on the top deck with her legs draped over a walkway below. The boat picked up speed, and her stomach twisted into knots. Then, just before the nausea-induced vomit, a sparkling shimmer of blue and gold appeared.

Like a mermaid painted with undefined brushstrokes, Chị Diễm slithered and swirled beside the boat. Ngọc Lan knew it was her sister the same way she knew that the faint white glow hidden behind thick clouds was the moon.

Below her dangling feet was a teen about her age walking funnily. He stood straight, bent down on one knee, then stood up. Placing his hands on his hips, he repeated the motion. Slowly his body marched forward in this deliberate albeit painful manner. She had seen men who'd lost their legs move about in surprising ways. She wondered if he too had been wounded.

The guy didn't notice her for the longest time. Then, when he finally looked up, his gaze was intense, dark, and focused on something beyond her. She swiveled her head around. No one was there. She tried to meet his gaze once again, but he was staring at something beneath her.

"Stop kicking!" he shouted. Ngọc Lan's heel hit the boat one last time before she realized he was talking to her. She froze. Embarrassed, she pulled her legs into her chest, then locked them with her arms. The knocking was a nervous reflex. She hadn't even realized she was doing it.

Ngọc Lan opened her mouth to apologize, but an American soldier approached him. The two began conversing. After a while, the teen began his routine again. This time, the American soldier corrected his posture. Once the soldier was satisfied, the two began performing proper lunges across the deck together.

Ngọc Lan covered her mouth in a giggle because their movements looked ridiculous. But then something strange happened. Others joined them. Soon there was a line of men and women, both Americans and Vietnamese, keeping fit together.

The spontaneous event made the guy a quasi celebrity on the ship because it was the first time the two cultures melded with one another. Everyone realized then that they could interact despite the language barrier. At dinner, Anh Minh and Anh Luân recounted the event to their parents. It was here that Ngọc Lan met Phúc for the first time. As the youngest girl, it was her job to serve everyone at the table. She did so silently, listening to the boys make fun of each other for their lack of stamina or general weaknesses.

Chị Mậu, who only spoke to Ngọc Lan when correcting something she did wrong, suddenly became very interested in Ngọc Lan and Phúc's similarities. Why? Ngọc Lan had no idea. Perhaps she disliked the attention Phúc was getting also. For her part, Ngọc Lan tried to stay out of Chị Mậu's way. She never borrowed Chị Mậu's things or sat in her direct line of sight at dinner. As a rule, she also avoided eye contact.

"Ngọc Lan is traveling without her parents, like Phúc. You two probably have lots of stories you could share with each other," Chị Mậu said.

Ngọc Lan stopped midscoop. She had been refilling Bác Hiếu's bowl. What she wanted to respond with was "At least they're not dead," but she couldn't bring herself to be that cruel. Chị Mậu's parents had died when she was young.

"No offense to Ngọc Lan, but Anh doesn't like to dwell on things of the past. Furthermore, our stories could not possibly be the same," Phúc said, handing Ngọc Lan his empty bowl. His condescending tone was not all that unusual for a Vietnamese man, so that didn't bother her. What did bother her was the way he gave her his bowl—with one hand, like he would a servant. Ngọc Lan kept her face impassive but was far from happy. She especially hated the smirk on Chị Mậu's face. Ngọc Lan knew that look. Chị Mậu thought Phúc's treatment of Ngọc Lan was fitting. In her eyes, Ngọc Lan needed someone who would keep her in her place.

After filling Phúc's bowl, Ngọc Lan noticed Anh Luân's empty one. "Let me scoop you more rice," she said.

Anh Luân bowed his head in gratitude. *He* properly handed her the bowl with *two* hands. "Cảm ơn." He bowed, thanking her despite Chị Mậu's glare. He didn't particularly like his sister-in-law either.

Thankfully, Phúc's popularity meant he dined with a different family nearly every night. Without someone around to treat Ngọc Lan like a servant, Chị Mậu returned to ignoring her.

In the early morning, the calisthenic exercises continued with more and more people joining, eager to stretch their joints. A camaraderie between the two groups formed as they made their way across the ocean.

The dining hall, a large open area on the second floor below the deck, became the central gathering point. Folding tables and chairs filled the room in perfect rows of six. Each night after everyone finished eating, a few soldiers would reset the whole room into perfect order. But on one lazy evening, after dinner, the American sailors moved all the dining tables to the side. Out came several long jump ropes.

The Americans had a team of jumpers who hopped adeptly over the weaving snake on the floor. They jumped in and out, past each other, traded places, and never stepped on the slithering rope. The moves were most impressive when the boat hit an occasional swell, which made even Ngọc Lan, who sat cross-legged on the floor, have to grab her feet for balance. When the Americans offered to teach the Vietnamese to jump, Ngọc Lan felt herself rise from her seat. The game looked fun. Plus, she wanted to feel the joy etched on the Americans' faces.

As she approached, the Americans clapped. They waved her forward. The ropes began wriggling as Ngọc Lan's legs shook with anticipation. From a distance, the game looked straightforward. As she stood before it, suddenly, it became impossible. A man stepped in front of her. Without touching Ngọc Lan, he faced her. He showed her how to jump in before hopping from one foot to the other. She watched his feet move in a mesmerized trance. Then, nodding to the beat of music she didn't understand the lyrics to, she jumped.

The initial leap surprised her. Her legs were unsteady. She stumbled. Catching herself, she kept her eyes focused on its weaving pattern. Her confidence grew with each successful leap. Then her stomach dropped. The boat hit a wave. She stepped on the rope.

"Awww." The audience collectively sighed.

Ngọc Lan laughed, doubling over to catch her breath. She hadn't realized how weak her limbs had become in the last few months. Her legs, which had once felt firm and muscular, trembled from the exercise.

"Hi, I'm Colin. You did great," the American said, giving her a polite wave and a thumbs-up. Ngọc Lan returned to where the Lê family sat, unable to hide her smile.

"What fun. Prancing around like a woman with no value," Chị Mậu mocked.

"What is Chị Mậu implying?" Ngọc Lan asked. Her eyes shouted what her mouth couldn't say.

"Watch your mouth."

"Devil," Ngọc Lan muttered under her breath.

"Speak louder," Chị Mậu dared her. When she swallowed her words, Chị Mậu glared smugly. "You should practice shutting your mouth more."

"That's enough," Bác Hiếu interjected firmly.

Ngọc Lan knew that Bác Hiếu and Bác Nga wanted to get along with their daughter-in-law. Still, she couldn't understand why they allowed her to act this way. In those days, it wasn't uncommon for the groom's family, any member, to beat their daughter-in-law. If there was anyone with a slappable attitude, it was Chị Mậu. But Ngọc Lan had grown up around the couple. They weren't the type to resort to hitting. For his part, Bác Hiếu had a way of expressing disappointment that made Ngọc Lan never want to upset him, yet his daughter-in-law appeared immune. As for Bác Nga, she loved her son too much to wedge herself into his marriage.

Chị Mậu made it abundantly clear to Ngọc Lan that she wasn't a welcome addition to their family. Unlike Thảo's adoptive parents, who treated her as their own, Ngọc Lan knew that her time with the Lê family was limited. Being around them often made her lonelier.

Every nautical mile they traveled expanded the physical distance between Ngọc Lan and Vietnam. Isolation had become her closest companion. So she kept an eye on Chị Diễm's sparkle in the water, vowing never to let her go.

On the lowest open deck, Ngọc Lan let her feet dangle over. White bubbles crashed against the deep navy surface of the ocean. She thought of the countless times she'd watched this same salty water crash against her feet at home. Without notice, the ship's rumbling engine slowed to a crawl. The deep blue turned clear, docile, and calm. Schools of yellow-and-black-dotted fish danced beneath her legs. Mesmerized by the hypnotic color, Ngọc Lan leaned through the railing. She stared into the rippling turquoise as it called forth a friendly invitation. *Come, come join us in the deep,* it beckoned. Like a siren calling beneath the water, Chị Diễm's enchanted summoning was as beautiful as it was sinister, urging Ngọc Lan to dive into the underworld.

"Careful. If you lean any farther, we'll end up drowning this time," Anh Luân said, yanking her from the trance.

Ngọc Lan looked up, momentarily forgetting where she was. Recovering quickly, she smiled at his joke but said nothing as she returned her gaze to the now darkened waters.

When the boat docked in Guam, Ngọc Lan and the Lê family were among the first to be airlifted to Orange County, California. Ngọc Lan's father resided there, which gave them top-priority status. Having a destination address in America made it easier to get the proper paperwork to enter the country. Ngọc Lan didn't know it then, but her father's address fast-tracked the whole Lê family's entrance. Once she landed, Ngọc Lan focused on the one positive thing to come from fleeing. She was about to be reunited with her father.

CHAPTER 26
PAUL

I feel as though I've been sucker-punched. Anger burns in my stomach, but I cannot find the words to express my fury—not in English, definitely not in Vietnamese. Crouching down, I scoop a handful of sand—my pathetic attempt at crushing my rage. To hell with this river. Why? Why would someone who regrets sending her kids to America then tell my mom to abandon us? My mom was not fleeing a war. She had a choice. She *made* a choice.

"Let it go," Anh Sáu says, gently resting his palm on my forearm. Where did he come from? I open my hand. The river washes it clean within seconds. If only it were that easy.

Bà Ngoại stands tall, gazing directly at me. There doesn't seem to be a flicker of sorrow or regret. "Your mom was like sunshine, so bright with joy and hopeful despite our circumstances. I knew if she crossed paths with the wrong person, they'd snuff her out. Bà Ngoại doesn't mean to say ugly things about the father of Quốc. Everyone has obstacles in life they must overcome. But Phúc is like a bird with broken wings who will bite the wings of another bird to keep from being lonely." She takes a heavy breath, like it's painful to cop to what she says next. "Your dad wasn't the only reason. Your mom and your dad were not compatible, but Bà Ngoại has to commend your father for taking care of you and your sister when most men would have abandoned you too."

"Took care of us? He used us for free child labor, beat us whenever he felt like it, and—"

She cuts me off. "A father hitting his kids is normal. When your mother and father were small, they worked from the time they could walk. Go out into the street, turn over the hands of any child you see. You will find calluses."

Oh, *hell* no. "So what if my mother and father suffered? Parents are supposed to protect their kids, not push them into equal situations of suffering." My dad, my aunt and uncle, and even, to a certain extent, Jane, all excuse abusive behavior by pointing out my dad's hardships. That's a bullshit excuse. My dad's anger has nothing to do with discipline and everything to do with himself. When he needed a punching bag, we were the bags. "A rough childhood is not an excuse for beating someone," I bark. I didn't accept this excuse from Jane, I'm not accepting it now.

Anh Sáu flinches like he expects a slap across his face. I'm not surprised; punishment in Vietnamese households is a communal affair. One kid acts out and every kid gets whipped. The ten-year age gap between Jane and me made me an exception. But his reaction shows how Vietnamese Anh Sáu is versus how Americanized I am. I do not recoil. I am *not* apologetic.

"I want to know what happened. Not hear excuses," I say.

My grandma doesn't get mad like I expect her to. "Bà Ngoại

will not tell you about things she doesn't know. Only the things that Bà did."

Still mad, I do my best to keep my face impassive because I want the answers. "In 1994, Bà Ngoại had been a madame for quite a few years." She pauses and looks at me. I don't react. She expects to shock me. I refuse to give her that satisfaction. She doesn't mention how she came to be a madame and I don't ask. Anh Sáu, on the other hand, cannot keep his cool.

"My mom told me, at that time, men hitting women was common. Bà Hang was not afraid?" Anh Sáu asks.

"Of course I was, but I needed work. My family was gone. What did I have to lose?"

I remain stoic, staring vacantly into the water flowing around my ankles. From the corner of my eye, I can see Bà Ngoại searching me for signs of comprehension. I consider stopping. I need time alone. Time to think. My body doesn't listen. One foot in front of the other, I'm drawn obediently forward. An uncomfortable silence hangs in the air for a long while, until she finally begins speaking again.

"You need to know that your mom loved Việt Nam. She never wanted to leave. You complain about work, but your mom loved working. Every day, she and Diễm caught clams together. Then they helped me sell them at the market. After the war, everyone was poor. American money had kept businesses running in the South. When the Americans left, the economy stagnated. There wasn't enough food to eat. Diễm became ill. She almost died and I knew my children needed to leave Việt Nam. I regret that she survived tuberculosis only to die in the ocean."

Something soft tickles my ankle. I look down. A small goldfish brushes my skin.

"What happened after my mom left Việt Nam?" I ask. What I mean to ask is, was my mother depressed, but I don't have the right words.

"To be honest, I don't know. I think, to protect me, she carried her sadness alone. But I know Diễm's death haunted her."

Grandma tells me that after Cậu Hòa was drafted, Dì Diễm and my mom clung to each other. Dì Diễm dropped out of school when they could no longer afford to send Ngọc Lan. "They went everywhere together. Had I not lied to her, Ngọc Lan never would have left Việt Nam without telling her sister."

This guts me. I don't know what I'd do if Jane died.

"Dì Diễm dying caused her sadness?" I ask.

"That was one thing of many. Your grandfather left on an American helicopter without us."

"Are you saying my mom abandoned us because Ông Ngoại did the same thing? That's not an excuse. If anything, it's even more of a reason why she should've stayed."

"If you want to understand, open your ears and listen. If you want to be stubborn, that is your own sin." The harshness of her words makes my ears burn.

Then I get angry.

Is she serious right now? Who is the person who sought her out? Me. Who is asking for the truth? Me.

Listen? You want me to listen to who? You?

I have every. single. right. to be angry.

I'm still deciding which insult to hurl first when Bà Ngoại continues with her story.

"During the war, I sold nước mắm, fish and clams, whatever we caught in the morning. There was a man, Anh Duy, who would come every month to buy a bottle for his wife, Chị Chau. He was a businessman with ties to the Việt Cộng, or maybe he was Việt Cộng. I never asked unnecessary questions. A few months after I sent my children to cross over, he returned with Chị Chau. She was the first madame I'd ever met. For many years, this was how I survived.

"Then around 1996, I was fifty years old when money began flowing into Việt Nam. Chị Chau, a clever entrepreneur, began building her businesses. We would have afternoon tea in expensive places. At first, I didn't understand why she was showing me such kindness, but then I looked around and realized that many of the men I served were also there, dining with their families. Chị Chau was cunning. By bringing me into the light, she was subtly showing the men that her bars held many secrets. You see, the men's indiscretions were of little importance. What she had was information. Multimillion-dollar deals were being struck in her spaces. And our girls had very keen ears."

"She used you," Anh Sáu says.

Where has *he* been? I turn around. He's been walking just behind us.

Grandma shakes her head at Anh Sáu. "No. She brought me, a poor country girl, into the social circles of Việt Nam's wealthiest and most influential individuals. She showed me how to dress, act, and move between people like air—unseen."

"What does this have to do with my mom?" I ask.

"The thing I'm really good at, what's made me valuable in my work, is reading people. Your mother was careful with how she talked about your dad, but I could tell that with every passing day, she withered more and more. She called once to say that it was her fault that Diễm was lost at sea. I told her no; it was not her fault. It was an accident, but then she told me Diễm was calling to her in the water; that the two sisters had reunited in a bath upstream. I knew that couldn't be true. I had many letters from other acquaintances who fled, expressing their grief for my loss, and all of them wrote that Diễm drowned before reaching Ngọc Lan. Diễm never made it to Kuku Island. From that moment, I knew your mother was falling apart."

"I don't understand. Is Bà Ngoại saying my mom went crazy?" The question comes out of my mouth so fast that I have no time to consider who I'm talking to.

"No," she replies sternly, her tone chastising and angry. "Open your ears and listen if you want to understand."

I shut my mouth. Twice she's said this now. I'm confused, I don't know what she sees, but my ears *are* stretched open. I'm listening to everything. I'm trying to make sense of it. It's a lot.

"Once a bird stops chirping, its days are limited. Over thirty years, I listened to her voice get softer, more quiet. When Bà Ngoại finally saw her in person, she was but a whisper. For this reason, Bà Ngoại condoned her departure."

"What about *us*?" I catch her eye, defiant. She meets my gaze with such intense sadness that I cannot look away even though I want to.

"Sometimes, when a person is sinking, it is better to let go than to pull everyone down with you. You were young. You still had enough energy to swim."

I get it. Still stings, though.

Bà Ngoại exits the stream. "Come."

"Did you know your mother witnessed her sister die?" Anh Sáu asks, coming up beside me.

"What? No. How do you know that?"

"Bà Hang just said. Weren't you listening?"

"Umm, yes, asshole, I was listening. She said they were on separate boats, and my mom feels responsible for Dì Diễm's death but that her sister never even made it to the island."

"You need to learn to listen better. Pay attention to what is *not* being said. Quốc's Dì Diễm must have drowned when her group crossed over or was kidnapped by Thai pirates, or got lost in the Malaysian jungle. The point is: She felt her die. I've heard of that happening to people."

"Which one?"

"All of them. Different people. Viêt Nam has a lot of dead people around the world." After a while, he adds, "I've heard Americans call Viêt Nam dirty. It's *not*."

I'm about to answer when I feel a tug at my ankles, like instead of my foot sinking naturally into the sandy bottom, it's being pulled by an invisible force that doesn't want to let go. I'm in up to my knees now, except I haven't moved. It's as if I fell into a hole while standing still. That same enchanting music from the ghost in the ocean plays in my ears. Alluring and melancholic, it's comforting and familiar, like being in a womb. How could I know what that feels like? I can't—*but I do.*

Hm, hm, hm, hm, hm, hm, hm-hmmmm . . .

Hmmmmm, hm, hm, hm, hm, hm, hm, hm-hmmmm . . .

Water splashes my face. "Go away!" Anh Sáu shouts. He yells toward me but not at me. Can he see the siren? I snap out of my trance. "Weak Việt Kiều," he mutters.

Yanking hard, I pull my leg free, accidentally kicking water onto Bà Ngoại. Hadn't she kept walking when I paused? How is she in front of me now? She must have stopped when I did. Time feels missing from my memory.

Grandma turns around and faces me. I start apologizing for getting her wet when I see that she's completely dry.

"It's a place that only shows its magic to those who are worthy." Anh Sáu finishes the sentence he started before . . . before what? Before the ghost started luring me? Freaked out, I stumble from the water, checking behind me for signs of a divot or dip, but there's nothing unusual. It's all in my head.

Then something else occurs to me. "You saved me back there. I'm growing on you. You're starting to like me," I say to Anh Sáu.

"Don't flatter yourself," he says.

His acknowledgment means two things:

1. *Anh Sáu saw the ghost.*
2. *The ghost is real.*

I make a mental note to add these to my journal.

On the drive back to Bà Ngoại's house, I imagine my mom as a young girl living here. The few memories I have of her suddenly feel tangible. Like wiping the dust off an old photo album. I blame Jane for keeping the memories of my mom hidden. Except I was angry too. *I* kept whatever memories I had of her stashed away like dirty underwear. I thought I had forgotten. But I'm finding pieces. Like that melody I've heard twice now. I swear I've heard it before. But is it familiar because it's something I remember or because being here is making it seem familiar?

I picture my mother. Thin and lanky, her long, twisted hair chasing behind her as she swims brazenly out toward the horizon. She is utterly unafraid of where the tide might pull her. I imagine my mother squeezing her feet into the sand. Her toes gripping the grains the way I used to. Sand between my toes was always my favorite part of oceanside visits. But is this connection real?

I used to compare my mom to Joe's mom. I wondered what made his mother stay while mine took off. For a while, there was mad jealousy as I measured myself against Joe in every way. Looks, grades, achievements, it was like I was trying to beat him to prove that I deserved to be loved too. I didn't even know I was doing it. One day, while Mai and I swayed in the backyard hammock, I said, "I can't believe Joe only got an eighty-two on that math test. It was easy. It's like he's dumb or something."

Mai glared at me. "That's really messed up, Paul. He puts up with your BS because your dad's a jerk and your mom left. But I'm not listening to you put him down. If that's what you think friends do, count me out."

Embarrassed, I tried to play it off like I was kidding. But Mai wasn't about to let that slide as a bad joke. She pressed me to answer, "Well?" and her tone was downright scary.

"I don't know," I said honestly.

"I'm going inside. When you figure it out, come find me." Then she straight-up left me.

Alone, I became angry at Mai *and* Joe. I had defensive thoughts and justifications galore. *It isn't my fault Joe is dumb. We're friends. I'm not his mom. So why should I have to help him raise his grades? He has a mother, and she does everything for him. She cooks. She does his laundry. All kinds of shit.* Then it hit me.

"I'm jealous," I said as soon as Mai opened her patio door.

"No shit, Sherlock."

"Does Joe know?"

"Yes."

Joe knew. He let me throw punches at him anyway. I never apologized. To this day, Joe hasn't ever brought it up. He's a damn good friend for forgiving me without an outright apology. I let out a long breath, as that lesson rolls into this one. If Joe could let me off the hook without forcing me to grovel, maybe I can do the same for my mom and grandma. I just gotta know one more thing.

"It's been thirteen years since my mom left. Why hasn't anyone from the family reached out to us? How could you have no desire to get in touch with your grandchildren for more than a decade?"

Bà Ngoại looks at me. "Do you really think Cậu Hòa and Mợ Bích just appeared at your door out of nowhere?"

CHAPTER 27

NGỌC LAN

"Wait, wait, wait. Go back to Mom and Dad. That's not what happened. I told you what happened," Jane says, sitting up straighter, as though her posture could change my story.

"That's what Mom told me. She said they met on the boat going to Guam, but he treated her like a little sister, and that was it until they met again outside the Asian Garden Mall."

"That doesn't make sense."

"Who told you your *version?" I ask, already knowing the answer.*

"Thi."

"Humm . . . ," I say, feigning deep thought. "Mom, who was there, versus our cousin, Thi, who was not *there," I say, making a weighing motion with my hands.*

"Smartass," Jane says. I take that as my cue to continue.

Ngọc Lan stood on the sidewalk staring at the building for a long time. America was completely different from Vietnam, Indonesia, and what she had seen of Hong Kong. Bác Nga hadn't let Ngọc Lan leave the ship in Hong Kong for fear that they wouldn't allow them back on. In the United States, where the air was dry, cars drove fast, and land felt vast, Ngọc Lan waited. She waited for the Lê family to settle into an apartment before asking Bác Nga to locate her dad.

Now, here she was. Slung across her shoulder was a small satchel containing everything she owned. Inside a large warehouse, she had been allowed to pick through colossal cardboard boxes full of brand-new clothes and shoes. A small tear on the inside of the bag kept hidden her mother's jade pendant and necklace—her only family mementos.

The two-story apartment complex on Oak Street was beige with dark brown trim. It looked like a dirty barn she'd seen in Western television programs. To the left, a large tree with sprouting roots cracked the gray asphalt driveway. From it hung a wooden swing. Finally, moving beyond the patchy lawn, she walked up the stairs. She straightened the white polo shirt and flower-printed skirt she wore courtesy of a group called the Salvation Army. After a breath, she knocked on the door.

No answer.

She stepped back, wondering what to do. Ngọc Lan hadn't considered that her father might not be home. He knew she was coming, albeit not precisely when, but he had signed the paperwork for her arrival, so he had to know she would be showing up. Scanning the doorframe, she searched for a note or sign indicating that she was at the right place. Down below, a group of Vietnamese kids, from toddlers to teens, emerged from the apartments. They started playing—it was almost like home. A boy her age taped some old clothes to the swing seat, and tested it with his own weight. Once satisfied, he put a little girl, presumably his sister, onto the plank. As he pushed her, she kicked higher and higher.

"Who's there?" the boy asked. She hadn't realized she'd been staring.

"My name is Ngọc Lan. I am looking for my dad, Vinh Ha. Is it right that he lives here?"

"Chú Vinh, that's correct." With a big push, he left the girl swinging and joined Ngọc Lan. Without hesitation, he knocked loudly on the door. "Chú Vinh! It's me, Bì. Open your door."

To their surprise, the door opened. "What do you need—" He stopped short when he saw Ngọc Lan. "My daughter."

"Ba—" Ngọc Lan choked, taken aback by her own emotion. Two years had passed since she'd last seen him. Without any news, she'd often wondered if he was even alive. His face, round and full, actually appeared younger.

A portly woman appeared beside him, wearing a linen pantsuit. Around her neck was a sparkling gold pendant with a large inset jade jewel. So similar to her own. On her wrist dangled three jade bracelets in varying shades of light to dark green. Her hair was short, her eyes suspicious and steely—she did not like seeing Ngọc Lan.

"Come in," the woman said, though her tone was far from welcoming. She left them in the sparse living room, which had a couch wrapped tightly in brown sheets, either to preserve what was beneath or hide it. Ngọc Lan's father gestured for her to sit on the couch. Two armchairs, one a deep magenta, the other a faded orange brown, sat across from her. He settled into the brown one. When the woman returned with a red McDonald's tray and three cups of tea, she served Ngọc Lan and Ba. Then, picking up the last cup for herself, she took her seat.

Despite the aged furniture, the way they posed themselves, upright and regal, made Ngọc Lan feel as though she were meeting with nobility. Her father, she realized, hadn't even embraced her when he saw her. He also never introduced the woman, who Ngọc Lan sensed was his new wife. She didn't ask. If this woman was to replace her mother, Ngọc Lan wasn't ready to acknowledge her.

"It's only been two years, but you have already grown so much," Ba said.

Only two years? He spoke as though he hadn't missed her, as though they were acquaintances meeting for afternoon tea. More astute in her observations, the woman noticed the bag of Ngọc Lan's belongings at her feet.

"How lucky you were to know the two Bács. What were their names again? My memory has lost them," she said, glancing at Ngọc Lan's father.

"Bác Hiếu and Bác Nga. How are they doing? Why didn't they come with you?" Ba said, looking at Ngọc Lan.

Everything about this conversation was wrong. Why were they talking like this? Like she hadn't crossed an entire ocean, lived in squalor, and nearly drowned trying to get here? "They're busy applying for work," Ngọc Lan answered. Then she studied the woman. Had this person put a curse on her father? She couldn't make sense of what was happening.

It was a Saturday at home, yet she wore full makeup, with her short hair perfectly combed and curled. Even her toenails were manicured—the color a deep green that matched her suit. "This circumstance is normal. So many of us have had to overcome difficulty here," the woman said.

"I'm sorry, Bác, I don't know what to call you," Ngọc Lan said in her most neutral tone.

The woman shot her a warning glare. She saw the insult for what it was. "Con can call me Cô Hoài."

Sensing the friction between the two, Ba barked at his daughter, "What did you come here for?"

Her father's curt tone caused a lump to form in Ngọc Lan's throat. This simple question told her everything she needed to know. Still, she couldn't believe it. "What? A daughter cannot come halfway across the world to see her father?" Ngọc Lan asked with exaggerated innocence.

"I signed the papers for you. What more do you want?"

"You signed papers?" Ngọc Lan asked with annoyance. Was her father acting as though the stroke of a pen was such a hardship? Was he so oblivious that he couldn't see her struggles from how thin and broken she appeared? Question after question ran rampant in the back of her mind. How could a father be this cold to his own child? How could twelve years of being a family so quickly be erased by one witch? Was her spell powerful or was her father weak? The person sitting before her looked like her father, but he was not her father—he was no one, a ghost. For a fleeting moment, she thought, *I'm glad Chị Diễm is dead, so she doesn't have to see what he has become.*

Adopted was the only word Ngọc Lan heard amid the burning fury crackling in her head. She willed herself to come back to the room. To focus on what her dad was saying. Who was adopted? *Herself?* She looked down at the body that no longer felt like hers.

"Leaving you behind was very hard . . ."

"Your mother didn't understand . . ."

"Ba needs you to empathize . . ."

"There is no space . . ."

"Ba goes to work sixteen hours a day."

"Living with Bác Hiếu will be more suitable for you. Bác Nga loves you like a daughter."

These fragments of his explanation floated across her mind as the weight of his words collected into a pit at the bottom of her stomach. She scanned the small apartment they didn't offer her a tour of. The living room was small, but there was a hallway with two closed doors. Spatially, his home was probably the same size as their own in Vung Tau. Yet the two of them could find no room for her.

"It is with such luck that two people who need each other can find one another," Cô Hoài added.

Ngọc Lan stared at her, then moved her gaze to her father. She said nothing. Inside, her mind was screaming, begging, pleading with him not to do this, but her exterior remained quiet, stoic, and unemotional. She returned her attention to the woman, wondering if she herself had been charmed just now, but no, Ngọc Lan didn't feel taken over. Instead, what she felt was tired. Too tired to make an enemy out of a woman as cunning as Cô Hoài. Living with this woman who was not her mother would not be easy.

"Ba remembers you used to love eating cookies with tea. When you were little, you would hold the cracker ever so delicately between your fingers and take the smallest of bites." He smiled at the memory. "Ah, that reminds me. Em, get the gift we wanted to send back with Ngọc Lan for the Lê family."

Ngọc Lan didn't know for whose benefit he was rewriting history, hers or his new wife's. They'd never had cookies with tea; even if they had, Ngọc Lan would never have eaten like that. The person who would eat like this was Chị Diễm, and she was dead.

Cô Hoài disappeared into the kitchen. She retrieved a red tin box with Chinese lettering and a picture of beautiful golden cookie rolls.

"Cảm ơn," Ngọc Lan said, finding her voice again, though she was hardly grateful. Seeing such delicate, beautiful desserts caused a swell of mixed emotions to surge within her. She didn't know if it was the fact that she hadn't had anything so sweet in more than two years or if her mind was finally catching up with reality. She stood abruptly to leave.

Bowing to them as she had been taught to genuflect to all adults, she formally excused herself from their home. "Dear Father and Cô Hoài, I am going home."

Her father nodded at her as though this was the appropriate response. Easy lies continued to slither out of Cô Hoài's mouth. "Oh, you're going so soon. Come back to visit us, okay? Good girl."

The door closed as soon as she stepped past the threshold of their apartment. They hadn't even bothered offering to accompany her to the bus stop.

On the sidewalk in front of the building, Ngọc Lan surveyed apartment 202's window, hoping to see her father's contrite face. There was no one. Bì, the kid from earlier, stared at her as though understanding everything that had transpired inside. He shook his head sadly but continued pushing his gleefully unaware sister on the swing. Ngọc Lan walked away.

The box of cookies sat on her lap as she rode the bus. It was too big to fit into her bag of things. She tapped her white-and-purple high-top sneakers against the bus floor as it traveled through town.

At a transfer stop, she let several of the buses she was supposed to get on pass by her. The sunlight felt good on her face. She was in no rush to return to the cramped apartment. Instead, she observed the cars whooshing by, the beautiful concrete sidewalks, and the green manicured lawns. Suddenly, her throat erupted in laughter. Uncontrollable, loud, wicked, and sad—the hilarious culmination of her journey. Once she started, she couldn't stop. Tears filled her eyes, her belly ached, the laughter continued.

America had been described as a promised land. Challenging obstacles would need to be overcome to reach it. Upon arrival, though, opportunity awaited. The reunion with her father was supposed to usher in a life of belonging; instead, she was nothing more than crumpled garbage—the butt of a cruel joke.

Still clutching the tin of cookies, she tore it open. Then, roll after roll after roll, she smashed them into her mouth. She ate past the point of being full. She ate carelessly, letting the crumbs fall to the ground in a small pile of yellow flakes. She never would have dared let something so precious go to waste in Vietnam, but she wasn't in Vietnam anymore. Tilting the tin upward, she shook the crumbs toward her mouth, letting the contents spill across her shoulders and shirt. When nothing else was left, she stood up and threw the tin into the trash. After brushing yellow buttery bits off her clothes, Ngọc Lan did the only thing she could. She sat back down and waited for the bus.

CHAPTER 28

PAUL

Cậu Hòa is a spy! I think this, but I do not say it aloud because, for once, I know how ridiculous it sounds. Damn, though. I feel like I'm in a movie where the villain just reveals she's been looking out for the main character the whole time, and she is actually *not* a villain but a hero. This really jacks up the story I've been telling myself my whole life.

The sun is high above the horizon when Chú Phương drops us off at the bottom of a hill. Sprouting from the top is a giant marble Jesus.

"Aren't you Buddhist?" I ask Bà Ngoại.

"I don't follow either. I listen to both. I take the parts that fit my life. For the person I want to be. You shouldn't ever follow one religion or group so blindly. You should always think for yourself," she responds.

The pathway is covered in flowers. It smells like spring, despite being hot and humid. At Jesus's feet, we walk through a door. I follow Bà Ngoại up a narrow spiral staircase where my stretched arms can touch the walls—it's that tight and dizzying. When I see sunlight again, I'm standing on Christ's shoulder.

"Anh ơi, take one photo for me," Bà Ngoại calls to a man behind us.

The guy holds a large camera. He squeezes past us to climb out on Christ's right forearm, which is essentially a marble ledge about a foot wide. On either side of this ledge is NOTHING; if he twists two inches the wrong way, he's a dead man splattered on concrete.

Anh Sáu digs his hand into my arm, squeezing it like he's afraid I might push him over. The photographer snaps our photo. When he's done, I turn to Anh Sáu to make fun of him. "That guy is the one risking his life to take our picture. Why are you over here giving my arm the death squeeze?"

"Don't kid yourself," he says, playing it so relaxed I almost believe him. He's exactly like my dad, unable to admit when he's afraid. If my dad were here and I called him a chicken for being scared of heights, he'd climb up on the ledge like the photographer. He'd risk his life just to prove he has no fear. Maybe this is something all Vietnamese kids are taught in school.

Grandma pays the man. He hands her a handwritten slip with a number on it. One thing I've noticed about my grandmother is that she never haggles. My dad doesn't either, but I always felt he overpaid because of his pride. Like he wanted everyone to know that he left Vietnam for a better life. With Bà Ngoại, though, I'm pretty sure it's purely about generosity. I've never heard her say "Keep the change." Or "I don't need change." She simply hands them the money and says "Thank you," with finality in her inflection. They don't offer change; she doesn't ask for it, and that's that.

In front of us, the bright blue ocean sparkles with white waves. Behind are lush green hills. A scattering of colorful wooden boats idle in the bay. "Is it right that those are the boats people crossed over on?" I ask.

Bà Ngoại shakes her head. "Those are too small. It's possible some people tried. They probably drowned."

"How can you say that so casually?" *Especially when your own daughter died this way,* I add in my head.

My grandma studies me for a moment. "Because it's the only way to not have the pain swallow you whole. Mothers, fathers, aunts, cousins . . . they left this world in explosions. If I allow myself to sink into the sorrow, I would suffocate under the emotion."

"That's why I'll never swim in thc occan," Anh Sáu says, giving me side eye.

It would've been nice if he let me in on this *before* pushing me to dive off his basket boat. "Umm, hello? What about the basket fishing?"

"Did you ever see me swim in the water? No. I stay safely in my boat."

"I can't believe you let me jump in," I lament.

"I can't control your stupidity," he says matter-of-factly.

How is it possible to work on a basket boat every day and *not* end up in the water every once in a while? I wonder. "What about falling in? Like on accident?"

"That doesn't happen," Anh Sáu says. He's dead serious too.

"But it could," I say, goading him.

"No." I guess Anh Sáu is a perfect human.

That night my grandma leaves us alone again. We borrow her spare motorbike to get to the market square. As we roam around looking for souvenirs for me to bring home—a wallet made of silk for Mai, a miniature xích lô[24] bike for Jane, a Vietnamese áo dài for Joe, medicinal herbs for my aunt and uncle—I mentally parse out the information I've been given.

"Do your parents talk about the war?" I ask Anh Sáu.

"What for?"

"For knowledge?" I say. Does wanting information require an explanation?

"No."

"Then how do you know so much about the dead people, the ghosts?"

"Use your imagination," Anh Sáu says. He must sense that I'm not satisfied with this answer because he adds, "You need to ask less and listen more."

"I have been listening!" I shout. I lower my voice when I notice people looking at me. "You told me to talk less and open my ears. But how can I learn forty years of history from what is *not* being said?"

"Good," he says. With that, he walks away. I'm pretty sure he purposely didn't answer my question. I try a different tactic. He told me to listen to my grandma. He never said I couldn't ask *him* questions. "Does Anh ever get hit?"

---

24 *rickshaw*

Anh Sáu laughs at this. "Are you joking?"

"No." Who jokes about this? Oh, that's right, Vietnamese people do.

"In Việt Nam, it's not just your parents who can beat you. Your teachers have the right to hit you with a stick. Getting hit is an ordinary thing."

"And Anh Sáu never asked why elders need to hit kids?"

He shrugs. "Sometimes I deserve it. Sometimes they need to let their demons out."

"How can Anh accept getting hit without knowing what those demons are? What if there are no demons and all the adults are just assholes? What then?"

"This question you ask shows that you're dumber than a cow."

Well, that's harsh.

"Are your feelings hurt?" he asks.

"No," I lie.

The look on his face says *Cry me a river, you wimp.* "I think you say you want to know, but you aren't listening with a careful ear. Didn't you hear Bà Hang's story? Did you hear her talk about her own sorrow and loss?"

"General loss, yes. Her personal loss, no."

"Exactly. You have to extract information from what's left unsaid. Those blanks you so badly want details about? Those are most likely her most painful memories."

"I hear you, but I need more information, more details, to understand." Logically, what he's saying makes zero sense.

He shakes his head. "You can't come back here for one summer and think you will understand your Bà Ngoại's whole life."

"I know that. But I can't learn, either, if everyone dances around what happened." Why isn't this obvious?

"You want a story. I'll tell you one. When I was little, my Bà Ngoại passed away. You know the body stays in the house for three nights, right?"

I didn't know that. Scary.

He registers my shock and smiles, pleased with himself. "One night, I came out of my room to get some water and found my mom rubbing lotion on my grandma's feet."

"If you're trying to give me nightmares, it's working," I say.

Anh Sáu ignores me. "I could tell she was sad, so I went to sit in her lap while she did this. I even dipped my finger in the lotion and rubbed a little on too."

Gotta respect that. That's brave.

"My mom ran my hand along all the white cracks on the bottoms of my grandma's heel. 'Every line is a sorrow that Bà Ngoại endured for you to have a better life. Today, Mẹ smooths the cracks so that Grandma may walk in peace,' she told me."

"Were you close to your Bà Ngoại?"

"Yes." The fact that he doesn't say more tells me I've hit a nerve. *Ohhhh, so that's what he means by listening for what's not said.* His grandma's cracked feet are the physical embodiment of her love.

I can tell that recounting the memory is emotional for him, and I want to be sympathetic. I just don't know how. I gamble on a joke. "I'm sorry. But, dude, there is no way in hell I'm touching anybody's dead feet," I say.

To my relief, Anh Sáu howls with laughter. "This is why you don't understand anything. Your feet are too soft."

"Maybe her ghost presses down on you because she was trying to rest, and you tickled her feet," I say, pretending to look frightened.

"That is probably the truth. Anyway, after that, I try to not be so naughty."

"I don't know about that. You stole a motorbike and nearly let a Việt Kiều crash it."

He laughs again. "I said I don't do naughty things. I didn't say I stay away from danger. There's a difference."

Sure, dude.

A little girl wearing two fishtail braids skips past me, waving a paper fan. I wonder if this is what my mother was like as a child. I wonder if she wandered these same stalls, ate candy with her siblings at the beach, or biked along the hundreds of dirt paths that connected the beach to the market. I wonder how often she saw food she couldn't afford and new clothes she'd never get to wear. I wonder if, despite the poverty, she felt loved in a way that she never did in America.

It's the middle of the night. Anh Sáu is snoring so loud I can feel the walls vibrating. No wonder he feels ghost pressings all the time. If I were a ghost, I'd press on him too, to get him to stop. I roll over to turn on the light, thinking that might wake him up. He's quiet for a moment, but then his trumpet nostrils open wide and flubbery gurgles fill the room. If I weren't complete chickenshit, I'd move myself to the living room so he could sleep. Given all the ghost talk of late, though, I'm not moving from this bed until the sun is up. Picking up my journal from the nightstand, I write:

Facts:

- *My ~~mom~~ mother had a sister who died as a refugee.*
- *Cau Hoa was in a reeducation camp. Also, he tells Grandma things.*
- *Grandma. Feels okay calling her that.*
- *Mom . . . is too familiar. Mother sounds strange, but will have to work.*
- *Check Grandma's feet for cracks.*
- *Anh Sau snores if he drinks beer.*
- *Not all banh mi stands are created equal.*
- *" " applies to pho shops.*

Then I add:

- *Ghosts are not real. Ghosts are not real. Ghosts are not real. Ghosts are not real. Ghosts are not real. Ghosts are not real. Ghosts are not real. Ghosts are not real. Ghosts are not real. Ghosts are not real. Ghosts are not real. Ghosts are not real. Ghosts are not real. Ghosts are not real. Ghosts are not real. Ghosts are not real. Ghosts are not real.*

I stop as soon as the repetition freaks me out even more. My notebook reminds me of horror movies where nasty phrases are scrawled across mirrors or bathroom walls or whatever. I scoot closer to Anh Sáu. Snoring McGee, next to me, lies splayed out without a care in the world. I nudge him. Nothing.

I grab my cell phone. The battery life is at 12 percent. I should check in with Jane.

From: Paul
I'm alive.

From: Jane
Why are you texting me at 3am?

From: Paul
Isn't it like afternoon there?

From: Jane
Yes. You should be asleep. What are you doing?

I start to text her about the ghost but stop myself. That's the kind of shit Jane will only make worse. She'll start talking about paranormal activity just to scare me.

From: Paul
Did you know that Ba Ngoai sent Cau Hoa and Mo Bich to live by us?

From: Jane

Um, no. Dad asked around when I was leaving for college for someone to come help out, and they needed work. It was purely coincidental.

From: Paul

Grandma told me she set it up.

A minute passes without a response, then another. After five, I wonder if maybe Jane got pulled into a meeting or something. I'm about to close the phone when a message pops up.

From: Jane

I couldn't get ahold of Dad. I think you should leave. This woman is obviously toxic.

From: Paul

She says that Mom was like a wounded bird. That Dad clipped her wings to keep from being alone.

From: Jane

Dad's coming to get you tomorrow.

I read the text twice. It's like we're having two different conversations.

From: Paul

Are you getting my texts? I think maybe it's time we look for Mom.

From: Jane

Abso-fucking-lutely not. You know where I stand when it comes to Mom. You can add this lady to that list. Actually, let me be clear about something. If you reach out to Mom, I'm out. I was done the day she left. I do not need her drama in my life.

From: Paul

What do you mean you're out?

From: Jane

I mean what I said.

From: Paul

You're saying, if I reach out to Mom you'll never speak to me again?

From: Jane
Your choice.

Wow, Jane has said a lot of crazy shit over the years, but this is extreme even for her. I mean, it's so close to absurd that I think she might be joking, except Jane's not funny.

Grandma, Anh Sáu, and I sit solemnly on the beach, waiting for my dad. He's supposed to be here sometime around now. A woman pushing a metal cart walks by selling fresh coconuts. Grandma buys three. The woman chops them open right in front of us—one swing per coconut, like a fruit-chopping superhero. Curiosity has me looking down at the woman's sandaled feet. They are crusted in calluses.

Bringing the coconut to my mouth, I gulp. Damn, fresh coconut is nothing like the canned stuff. It's warm and thick but refreshing.

"Let's go." I jump to my feet, startled by the sound of my dad's voice despite expecting him. Behind my dad is my *other* grandma, Bà Nội.

"Chào Cô Tâm," Bà Ngoại says, using the title of deference to greet my dad's mom. Not gonna lie. It's odd to see my two grandmothers side by side.

"Cô Hang is well?" Bà Nội responds curtly. Is it just me, or is she being borderline rude?

My dad looks uncomfortable. "Sorry, Mẹ, but we are beyond late. We need to catch our flight in two hours."

Bà Ngoại ushers us toward the house. We load my and Anh Sáu's two bags into a waiting taxi. The usual pleasantries of sharing tea and making small talk are apparently not happening today. In a rushed goodbye, I give my grandma an awkward hug. Mid-embrace it dawns on me that this is the first time we've been this physically close. She is stiff at first, then softens and does that breathing in of my scent that my other grandma does—still not used to it.

As we leave, Bà Ngoại presses an envelope into my hand. Then, as suddenly as I arrived, I'm watching my grandma's figure shrink into the distance. I open the envelope. It's the photo of her, Anh Sáu, and me on Christ's shoulder.

"Photos of three are bad luck," Bà Nội says, looking over my shoulder.

Anh Sáu smacks his forehead. "Ay! I forgot that. This Việt Kiều is always causing me trouble."

My dad looks at the portrait but says nothing.

I do a double take. At the front of the photo, Anh Sáu stands with both hands at his sides. Bà Ngoại is at the back with both arms also at her sides. *Who squeezed my arm?* I bring the photo closer to my face. No matter which way I look, no human is touching me. Holy hell.

CHAPTER 29
NGỌC LAN

"I don't know much of what happened in these years. Mom said she was not clearheaded. That her body moved but her mind doesn't remember. I think it's called depression, but I'm not sure. We're alive, so she wasn't just sitting there doing nothing, but much of this stretch of time is lost.

"Here's what I do know. She went to school, but she wasn't good at it. Kids made fun of her clothes and accent. She had a hard time learning English. The Lê family shared their apartment with another family, the Hoàng family. Get this, have you ever noticed that Mợ Bích never talks smack about Mom?"

"Some people don't care for gossip. So what?" Jane says.

"It's because she knows *her! Mợ Bích's maiden name is Hoàng. She was one of the daughters of the other family. Small world, right?"*

"Why didn't Mợ Bích ever tell us?" Jane asks. If I'm not mistaken, she sounds kinda angry.

"She says it wasn't her place. They lived together years before she ever met Cậu Hòa." Crap, I hope I didn't just add Mợ Bích to Jane's shit list. I quickly continue so Jane can't dwell on this too

long. I love Mợ Bích, and if Jane "Jackies" her out of our lives, I don't know what I'm gonna do.

To this day I still don't know what happened between Jane and Jackie, who were BFFs since before I was born. What I do *know is Jackie is AWOL due to "two roads diverging."* Weak.

I'm not certain Jane has this kind of power over Mợ Bích, given my aunt's superior adult and family status; however, one should never underestimate Jane.

"Anyway, in those early days, everyone was just trying to figure out how to get to the next chapter, the next generation. Us."

For the first year, the Lê family and Ngọc Lan shared a two-bedroom apartment with the Hoàng family. The Hoàng family had two daughters, Chị Bích and Chị Đào. The sisters, who knew they were lucky to have each other, tried to include Ngọc Lan in their activities and the games they played. Ngọc Lan sat with them as they made popcorn necklaces while trying to follow the plots of the English-language movies they rented. But Ngọc Lan couldn't build a friendship despite their kind attempts. The sisters were a constant reminder of what she'd lost. Why did both of these sisters make it to America while her sister was dead?

Since arriving in California, Ngọc Lan found it difficult to stay connected to Chị Diễm. When she could—with a house of ten sharing a single bathroom, it wasn't often—Ngọc Lan would draw a bath, drop her feet into the scalding water, and slowly immerse herself. Once her head was underwater, she'd hear Chị Diễm's voice.

"What took you so long?"

"You know how the family is about saving water," Ngọc Lan replied.

"I've been bored to tears."

"Me too."

"This place is rotten. Take me home," Chị Diễm said.

Ngọc Lan sighed.

Since arriving in America, there was no talk of going home. Ngọc Lan started school, where the kids made knock-knock jokes that somehow made her feel more alone despite being surrounded by classmates. Then Mẹ cut her off.

Don't look back with regret. Look forward to the future, her mother had said. Believing that her daughter needed to forget the past in order to find her future, she severed direct communication. It broke her mom's heart to do it, but Mẹ wanted Ngọc Lan to succeed, no matter the cost to herself. Letting go of her would force Ngọc Lan to seek happiness elsewhere. It was sacrificial love.

Huuuuh! Ngọc Lan gasped, coming up for air. She was constantly pushing the boundaries of her lungs. Her legs reflexively kicked the tub, pushing her to the surface.

Ngọc Lan never told anyone about the encounters with Chị Diễm. They wouldn't understand. No one understood. When one classmate told her to "go back to your country," she asked her librarians and her teachers to show her how. They told her the opposite. They told her America was her home now. Without any real family, kinship, or community, Ngọc Lan retreated inward.

Then the Hoàng family moved away. Despite not having known them long—and being purposely avoidant—when they found a new home, her void grew wider. Her depression spiraled deeper.

Ngọc Lan only cared for the connection to her sister, and her sister's spirit was tired of waiting. Chị Diễm's presence diminished.

Time passed like the turning pages of a blank book. Ngọc Lan went to school. She slowly learned English. Sometimes, she walked to a park to sit and swing, to feel a breeze. She made no friends. Work or school consumed the lives of everyone else in the Lê family. Even Chị Mậu had gotten a job cleaning hospitals at night. Undeterred by menial labor and low wages, they forged a future while Ngọc Lan wasted away. She didn't blame the family. They tried to encourage her, but they were starting anew. No one had either the time or the energy to carry her along. Ngọc Lan's purpose was supposed to be school. Except she hated school. Yet another reason Chị Diễm belonged in this life instead of her. Still, she tried to focus, to store away what knowledge she could for a future she couldn't see.

Then one day, Ngọc Lan heard a familiar tune call out to her.

Tình mẹ bao la như biển khơi xa
Như dòng nước ngọt chảy mãi trong ta

Mẹ bước trên con đường gập ghềnh, sáng ngời
Để bảo vệ bước chân con trong đêm tối.[25]

The hypnotic melody danced in her ears, luring her out of the building. In the neighboring apartment complex, the sound grew louder. Ngọc Lan gasped. There in the middle of a concrete area, she found a swimming pool.

Never had she seen a tub of water so large or so blue. The gate was unlocked. She walked in. Reflected on the aqua surface was the sky. A bird flew past, then perched itself on nearby electrical wires. At the pool's edge, she put her hand in. The movement caused a ripple. Ngọc Lan instinctively jerked her arm away. The bird flew off. She looked at the water. She looked at her hand. Then, palm open wide, she smacked the surface hard. Tiny waves rolled into the wall at the other end of the pool.

Surrounded by concrete and metal, the landlocked basin appeared majestic—perhaps it was. Ngọc Lan had never seen water so clear or a bottom so smooth. She was drawn to it despite its funny smell. Lying flat against the pool's edge, she let her arm dangle in. Ngọc Lan peered at her reflection. Loneliness and solitude stared right back. She had no one. No father, no sister, no brother, and a mother who no longer answered her letters.

A familiar warmth wrapped itself around her arm. Chị Diễm's fingers entwined in hers, the way they had in the lake on

---

25 *A mother's love stretches ocean wide*
Like sweet water flowing endlessly inside
She walks a broken path, calm and bright
To protect her child's steps in the night.

Kuku Island. This connection, however tenuous, combined with the promise of bringing her sister home, was one of only a few reasons keeping Ngọc Lan alive.

"Chị Diễm, I don't want to be here anymore," Ngọc Lan whispered. Chị Diễm tightened her grip. Tears cascaded into the pool.

"Stand up," Chị Diễm demanded. "What kind of person lies on the ground like this?"

"I'm too tired."

"Get up," Chị Diễm commanded. Trembling, Ngọc Lan got to her feet. "Look at yourself."

Ngọc Lan didn't want to. She couldn't stand the sight of herself. To avoid facing her own reflection, she plunged into it—shattering her own image. The chlorine hit her nostrils with a flare. The shock of it caused her to swallow more. Ngọc Lan hadn't been in a body of water deep enough to swim in since the lake in Indonesia. She hadn't forgotten how to swim, but this water was airy and tasted like poison. Luckily the pool wasn't deep. As soon as her shoes touched the bottom, she stood up.

"Hueiigh," Ngọc Lan breathed. She could've gotten out, but her body wanted to glide. She reached one arm above her head. Then the other. With each stroke, she felt herself come alive again. From one end to the other, she swam, even as her arms ached and her thighs burned.

Ngọc Lan's fingers stretched forward as her back arched in preparation for the flip. She spun herself like a bullet piercing through water. Wisps of blue-and-gold ribbon twisted with her. She wasn't alone. Ngọc Lan tumbled. She kicked off her shoes.

Transparent green-and-purple fish scales appeared along her legs. Faster and faster she darted, until her beige skin disappeared into the golden sparkle of two glittering fins.

Ngọc Lan chased her sister's tail until the sun faded and the water turned a sinister blue. Chị Diễm wasn't here to play. She was here to remind Ngọc Lan of her duty and promise.

A year passed like this.

Then another.

Suddenly she was seventeen.

Ngọc Lan was about to become an adult.

"You're lazy," Chị Diễm chastised.

"I'm trying," Ngọc Lan said in a lackluster tone. She was used to the barrage of insults.

She knew her sister was right. Since arriving, Ngọc Lan had done little to assimilate. Worse still was the lack of progress she'd made on her plan to return home. Unlike Bác Nga, whose hands ached from sewing ten hours a day, Ngọc Lan had scraped together barely enough credits to graduate high school.

"You're selfish," Chị Diễm continued.

Ngọc Lan said nothing. She had run out of excuses long ago.

"You've forgotten all about me," Chị Diễm admonished. The pool turned ice cold. Ngọc Lan hadn't forgotten her sister, but she had no way to fulfill her promise of returning to her sister. In geography class, when they studied the world, Ngọc Lan found Vietnam. She found Indonesia. But Kuku Island wasn't listed anywhere. Every time she passed a map or saw a globe, she searched. How could a place where she'd lived for months not exist? Hope dwindled.

"I'm sorry," Ngọc Lan said, begging. But her sister's presence, once warm like tea, turned tepid. "Chị ơi, come back."

Ngọc Lan shivered; Chị Diễm was gone. Resting her head on the concrete ledge, she sobbed. "Trade places with me," Ngọc Lan whispered to no one. Chị Diễm should have been the one to live. Her sister would have made more of the life she was given. She would not be the disappointment that Ngọc Lan had let herself become. The more the tears fell, the more Ngọc Lan hated herself. She let them keep coming.

CHAPTER 30

PAUL

The airport in Ho Chi Minh City is busy. We shuttle between two ticket counters before I register that we're sending Anh Sáu home on a separate flight. I'm not prepared for the abrupt goodbye when we drop him off in front of the domestic departures.

"Cảm ơn, Anh Sáu. For, you know, everything," I say. He reaches out to shake my hand as I move in for a hug. My chest awkwardly bumps into his pointed fingers. We laugh. I take his cue. We shake.

"Return home safely," he says. He bows to my grandma and dad. "Chào Bà Tâm. Chào Chú Phúc." There's no "I'll miss you" or "Keep in touch."

Dad pulls at my arm. "Đi, we late." I don't move. I'm forgetting something, I just don't know what. I'm about to follow my dad when two things dawn on me: (1) Anh Sáu never actually extorted my grandma. (2) I owe him more than just a lame *thank you*.

"Wait!" I shout. Anh Sáu doesn't turn around. "Anh Sáu! Come back," I yell. He doesn't hear me. I sprint toward him. "Hey!" I pull his arm. He bursts with laughter.

"You run slow as a turtle," he chuckles. He heard me and kept walking so I'd have to chase him.

"You asshole!" I manage to say while catching my breath. "Here." I hand him the cell phone. "Wait to sell it. When I get home, I'll text you."

He looks at me with genuine gratitude, which makes me feel all weird inside. "Cảm ơn, Quốc." He unhooks the scroll (the one he bought from the soothsayer to protect him from my ghost) from his belt loop to give to me. "Now that you're leaving, I won't need it," he says, smirking.

"Yeah, yeah. Okay, I have to go now. Bye!" I race after my dad. Partly because I know he's in a hurry. I'm not over here trying to get in trouble. But also because I think I'm really going to miss this guy. Halfway to my dad, I turn around and see Anh Sáu waving the phone at me with a big stupid grin on his face.

We reach our gate just before the doors start to close. The plane takes off, and we're thirty thousand feet in the air before I realize I have no idea where we're going.

"Are we flying home?" I ask my dad. He's sitting in the middle seat, fussing over the screen that Bà Nội won't stop messing with. I honestly can't tell if she's curious or wants to break it. My dad nods at my question, so I clarify, "To San Jose?"

"Uh-huh," he says, pointing at the buttons on the remote control to show Grandma how to change the channels.

"Don't scrunch your face," Bà Nội scolds Dad. She uses a phrase I've only heard adults say to kids. But I mean, I guess he *is* her kid. "You made me leave my home so I can look at your scrunched-up face all day? Take me home then. I don't need to go to America."

"Bà Hang helped us push your papers through. Why prolong the move? It's not that you're leaving forever. Your things will be here when you return to visit."

"That lady, she *helped* me as payback for her daughter. A mother always blames the other mother," Bà Nội mutters. This is a Vietnamese thing. The family unit operates as one, so if one person does something bad, it reflects on everyone else. The way she says "helped" suggests the opposite, but that doesn't ring true to me. If I'm understanding the situation correctly, and that's a *big* if, my mom's mom used her connections to help clear my dad's mom for immigration to America.

To an outsider, this might not make sense because my uncle is in the Communist Party, so why couldn't *he* help my grandma, right? According to Jane and Mợ Bích, my uncle's allegiance is to the party first, so of course, it wouldn't look good if he was trying to send his mother to the United States. A true patriot would want his mother to stay in Vietnam, at home. That's where my Bà Ngoại's connections probably helped. All I know for sure is it's all really complicated. My Bà Ngoại is a lot of things, but she doesn't seem vindictive. Plus, why would Bà Ngoại blame Bà Nội for what my dad did? Sounds to me like my mother was dealing with a whole lot more than just my dad.

"Bà Nội is old. If Bà Nội doesn't come live with Quốc, how can I be close to her before she passes away?" I joke.

Grandma reaches past my dad and knuckles my head. "I told you already. When I die, I will come to visit you all the time."

"No thanks," I say in English with a laugh.

"Rude," my dad snaps, pushing my head into the airplane window with too much force. He's angry because Bà Nội doesn't want to move to America, but how is that *my* fault? No wonder my mother left him. On a plane filled with mostly Vietnamese passengers, no one says a word. Not even a glare of distaste for causing a scene.

"What are you hitting him for? You want to hit someone, hit me," Bà Nội says sharply. Ohhhh, shit. I look downward, forcing the smile on my lips into a quivering pucker. I can practically feel the steaming rage emanating from my dad's seat. He doesn't dare say anything back. Instead, he folds his arms into himself. To ignore us, he clicks through the shows on his screen. I wonder if he regrets sponsoring my grandmother's immigration now.

Seeing how much my Bà Nội doesn't want to vacate Vietnam adds to my growing certainty that my mother never wanted to leave either. Bà Ngoại mentioned that my mom blamed herself for Dì Diễm's death. That's heavy. I could see how she might think her sister would be alive if they hadn't fled Vietnam. How could it be my mom's fault, though, if it wasn't her choice to escape? I'm not excusing my mother for leaving us. Jane and I didn't deserve to grow up without a mom. But my mom didn't deserve anything that happened to her either. And there's still so much more we don't know.

It's mind-blowing how eighteen days away can feel like an eternity. Sleeping in my bed after being gone for so long feels weird. It's chilly. For a fleeting moment, I imagined a ghost sleeping in it while I was gone. The frigid spirit moving about the house, leaving cold spots wherever it went. I shiver, then push the thought away. It's possible that I got used to the thick humidity of Vietnam, but that's not really why the house feels chilly. It's an unoccupied sort of emptiness.

The last time I remember feeling this way was when Jane left for college. I expected Vietnam to feel lonely in the same way, but it was the opposite. I was never alone. I had my grandmas or Anh Sáu with me 24/7. I guess I got used to the company. Anh Sáu isn't Jane. He's similarly annoying, though. In another life, we'd be brothers. He'd fit right into all the times Jane and I did stupid stuff together. Like making tents out of blankets so we could camp out in the living room while watching movies. Or making s'mores on the gas stove, nearly causing a fire. I assumed Bà Nội would live with us, but my aunt, O Uyên, whisked her away as soon as we exited customs in San Francisco.

The quiet I feel as I stare up at the ceiling is so icy it's making my ears burn. I scoot closer to the wall and pull the blankets up to my chin. No matter what I do, I cannot fall asleep. A light pressure on my arm gently turns me away from the wall. Maybe it's jet lag. Maybe it's Dì Diễm. Unlike with the pressing I felt on the airplane, though, I'm not immobilized. *This* time I am paralyzed by my own fear. I don't want to move. My body has other plans.

"Hu-ah!" I shout, bolting upright. Possessed by a mind of its own, my leg lifts and kicks the blanket to the foot of my bed. Great, now I don't even have a blanket for protection.

"What the hell?" Jane asks. She's standing in the doorway.

My heart throbs with adrenaline. "I—why did you sneak up on me?" I'm not about to explain to Jane that it was my way of trying to show this ghost I'm not afraid of her.

"I didn't. I said 'Hellooooo' from downstairs. Get up. It's three p.m., you can't be sleeping."

"I'm fighting jet lag."

"Fight it over lunch. I'm hungry. Let's go."

We walk next door, where Mợ Bích has made bún riêu.[26] "What happened? Couldn't eat in Việt Nam? Why are you so skinny?" my aunt asks. Jane grabs utensils from the drawer. We all sit down to eat.

"I ate a lot!" I say, patting my stomach.

"So, tell me about Vietnam?" Jane asks. What she means is *What did that evil lady, who is our grandparent in title only, do or say to you?*

"Not much. It was uneventful," I say. Jane made her stance clear. Plus, I'm not about to start a fight in front of Mợ Bích.

Jane doesn't let it go. "How much money did you give her?"

Something about the way she asks pisses me off. I unleash on her. "I didn't give her anything. She's rich. She doesn't need your money."

Jane huffs like she doesn't believe that for a second. I remember how Anh Sáu got mad at me when I made fun of his sandals. "Don't be dumb, Paul. She's obviously trying to manipulate you," Jane says.

Mợ Bích slurps her food, pretending not to understand us, but I've always suspected that she understands more English than she admits.

"Have you ever considered that maybe you don't know what you're talking about?"

"No," Jane says flatly. I stare at her.

"I'm not a kid anymore. You can't just bully me into doing what you want. I've been thinking a lot lately about how *you* decided we couldn't find Mom. *You* decided she was evil. *You* decided that I didn't need a mom. But what about what *I* want?"

---

26 *crab noodle soup*

Jane shakes her head and stands up. "Damn, Paul. That's pretty disappointing. After all the shit I've done for you." Her bowl is still full, but she dumps the broth in the sink. The rest goes into the trash can. That's a big freaking no-no in a refugee family. We do not throw away food. Jane never would have done that if my dad were here. She knows Mợ Bích is too nice to reprimand her.

To Mợ Bích she says, "I have to go back to work." A lie no one believes. Jane exits.

Without addressing anything that just happened, Mợ Bích takes some extra pork and shrimp clusters from her bowl. She drops them in mine. "Eat," she says simply. I'm not hungry anymore, but I'm not about to be as rude as Jane.

Mợ Bích has been around me and Jane fighting before, so it's not all that awkward. But it gets me thinking, Jane might actually be serious about cutting me off.

"Give her time to cool down. She'll come around," Mợ Bích says.

I don't answer. Jane might come around, but here's the thing: I'm different. This summer changed me. I'm over ignoring problems because answers make my family uncomfortable. It's like that kids' book about going on a bear hunt; the only way forward is through. So, for the first time in my life, I really don't care what Jane thinks.

A surge of energy rushes through me—I know what I need to do. In my room, I power up the desktop computer Jane set up last summer. I sign on to the internet. A chat box pops up on the screen as soon as I'm logged on.

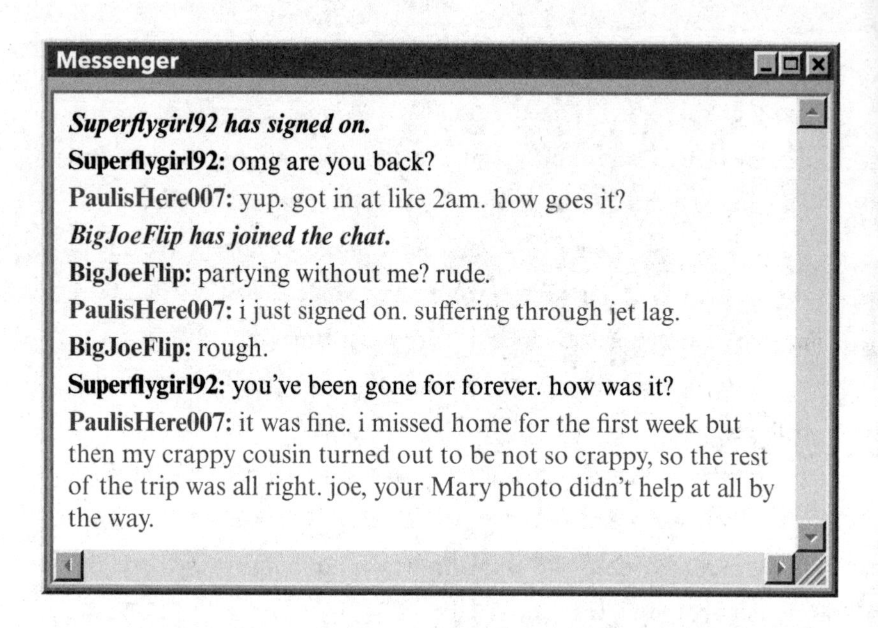

My fingers are getting antsy. Like they know I'm supposed to be doing something and they're waiting for my brain to catch up.

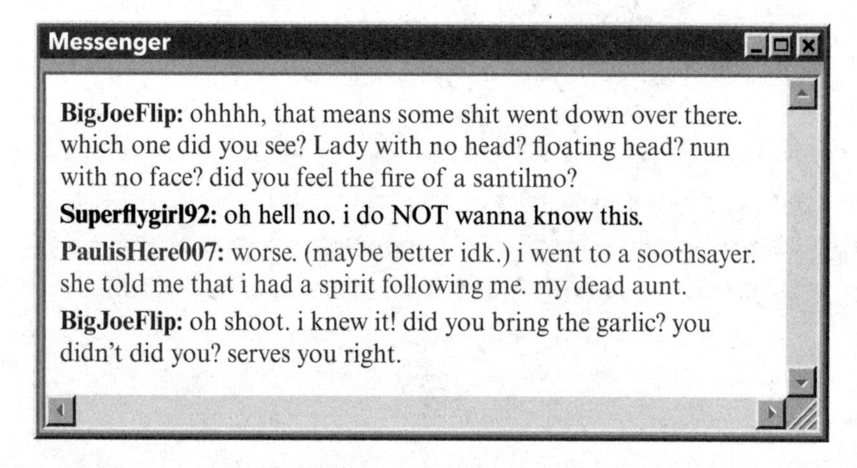

I can practically hear Joe laughing and smacking his leg like he's just watched a cat try to leap over a toilet only to fall in instead.

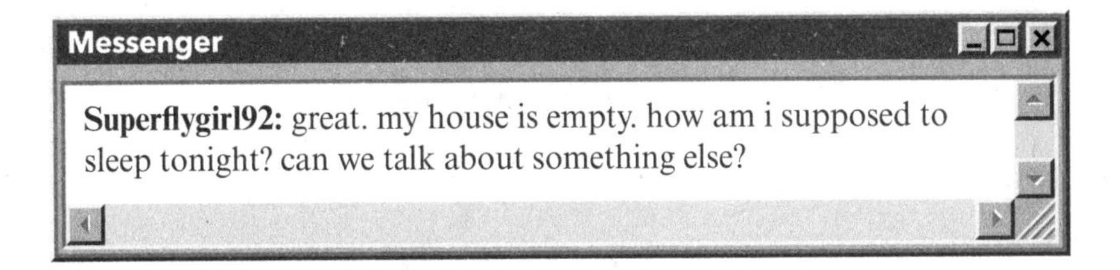

My fingers twitch. I spill the news.

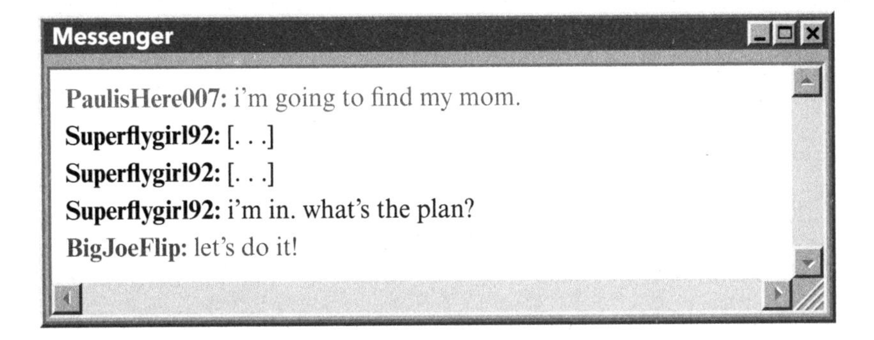

CHAPTER 31

NGỌC LAN

Ngọc Lan knew it wasn't proper to hang on to her sister's soul. However, she was also fairly sure that the rituals families performed to get their loved ones to cross over didn't work. Why else would there be so many lost and wandering souls? Why would people who had prayers said for them night and day still haunt the earth? Despite her skepticism, she knew it was her duty to assist, and she wasn't. In fact, she was doing the opposite.

When Tết, the Vietnamese New Year, came around, Ngọc Lan made preparations. She collected things Chị Diễm would love: a whistle covered in gemstones, a butterfly hair clip, fancy chopsticks, a teacup, the comb from Kuku Island, the jade pendant and necklace. Tết was the one time a year when Ngọc Lan dug up the jewelry. She hid it in a tin mint box, which she buried under a large rock near the back of the apartment. These were things she knew would lure Chị Diễm to visit. As the superstition goes, what one does on New Year's Day, they will be doing all year long. So in 1980, the year of the monkey, Ngọc Lan carried her collection to the pool.

When she arrived, panic set in. All the water had been drained from the basin.

"What happen?" she asked the pool workers.

"There's a crack we need to seal. The association didn't send you a memo? Pool is closed today. Tomorrow too," a man in dirty gray jeans and a polo shirt with a wave insignia on the lapel said.

Ngọc Lan raced home. She scrambled for the bathroom, where she turned on the faucet to fill the tub.

Knock knock.

Ngọc Lan ignored the tapping.

Knock knock.

"Ngọc Lan, there's no time for a bath. Get yourself ready, we need to leave soon," Bác Nga coaxed through the door.

Ngọc Lan's heart raced as she stared at the flowing water. The universe wanted her to let go. She wasn't ready. She reached into the tub. "Ah!" she shrieked, jerking her hand out. The water was scalding hot despite the knob being turned to warm. Steam, which had not been there before, rose from the bath. Chị Diễm's anger was present in the moisture.

"Don't be mad," Ngọc Lan pleaded.

Chị Diễm didn't respond.

"Hurry up. I need to use the restroom," Chị Mậu chastised. Ngọc Lan opened the door, releasing the steam. Chị Mậu skittered backward, wiping at her pink shirt as though water touching it might ruin the satin. "What were you doing using such hot water?" she scolded.

Ngọc Lan stepped past, smiling to herself. Her sister might

be angry with her, but she still had a sense of humor. Ngọc Lan resolved to draw a bath at the end of the night. A visit on Tết was crucial. True, Chị Diễm appeared to be distancing herself, but missing a visit today would be the ultimate betrayal.

Ngọc Lan dressed in her newest outfit, a red áo dài with gold beads along the wrists and hem. Then she went outside to wait.

"You clean up nice," Anh Luân said, stepping out to join her. He wore a gold áo dài.

Embarrassed by his kindness, Ngọc Lan dusted off her already clean dress and shrugged. She saw how other girls made themselves up, but Bác Nga was too tired to teach her how to curl her hair or wear makeup and Chị Mậu wasn't about to offer her tips. So instead of acknowledging Anh Luân's flattery, she deflected. "Chị Mậu rushed me from the bathroom. I didn't even have a chance to wash my face."

"Chị Mậu needs the makeup to soften the scowl her eyebrows make. You have natural beauty," Anh Luân replied. Ngọc Lan turned beet red. No one had ever given her such a brazen compliment.

Thankfully, Bác Nga emerged from the house in a bright yellow áo dài and immediately cut the tension. "Okay, let's gather together for photos."

For two people who lived in the same apartment, Ngọc Lan and Anh Luân didn't interact much. He was gone early and home late, studying for long hours at the library to earn two degrees at once, in what, Ngọc Lan had no idea. For her part, Ngọc Lan did her best to make herself small in a space where she felt like an intruder. She attended school, cleaned the house, and helped make food that Bác Nga sold to coworkers for extra money. Occasionally, though, like today, Anh Luân would say things that made her wonder if he liked her.

The rest of the family emerged. They stood together as Ngọc Lan took family photos, using a disposable Kodak camera that another Vietnamese man had taught Bác Hiếu to use. Moments like this reminded Ngọc Lan of her place in the home. As an outsider, she was the person best suited for standing far enough away in order to capture a really great family portrait.

Ngọc Lan peered through the lens. Then froze. The neighbors' sprinklers had turned on, creating a fan of water behind the Lês. Among the spray of droplets, blue and gold danced. In the viewfinder Chị Diễm was clear as day. She stood beside Bác Nga with her chin out and her head turned at a slight angle. Her sister wore a beautiful bloodred áo dài, displaying for Ngọc Lan what belonging looked like. Chị Diễm wasn't standing there to be next to Bác Nga; she was standing where a girlfriend might stand in the arms of Anh Luân.

Ngọc Lan snapped the photo and dropped the camera from her face.

"Where are you staring? Look at us when you take the photo," Chị Mậu snarled. Ngọc Lan couldn't be sure, but in that moment, she swore she saw Chị Mậu's body shudder despite it being eighty-two degrees outside.

On the forty-minute bus ride to the festival celebrating the Lunar New Year, Ngọc Lan peered out at the city and thought about the photo. Was her sister showing her where she wanted Ngọc Lan to stand, or was she placing herself where she would want to be if she were still alive? *What does it matter anyway?* Ngọc Lan thought to herself. *You're dead and I'm not staying here.*

In just a few months she would graduate from high school, get a job, buy a plane ticket, and go home. Already she could smell the aroma of fish sauce. She could feel steam roll off the boiling pot of phở she planned to surprise her mother with. In every letter to Bác Nga, her mom reiterated her wishes for Ngọc Lan to look forward, to make a new life. Mẹ would be disappointed to see her, but Ngọc Lan would work hard and prove useful.

Lights danced in the distance. The festival was ablaze. The small Tết Nguyên Đán[27] celebration was held at the corner of Westminster and Bolsa. On any other day, this intersection was nothing but an empty dirt patch off the main stretch of road. From a mile away, Ngọc Lan could hear the popping sound of red-tubed firecrackers ripping through the air. Floating red lanterns amid an array of traditional offerings like fish sauce and pandan marked the beginning of something new. Something that would later become the Asian Garden Mall. For Ngọc Lan, seeing the pageantry and vestiges of home reinforced her notion that they never should have left in the first place.

Ngọc Lan wandered through the stalls organized by elderly women. They sold moon cakes, egg rolls, phở, glistening duck, fried

---

27 *Festival of the First Morning of the New Year*

rice, and red envelopes, among an array of toys. She stopped in front of a stall selling bánh tét (southern) and bánh chưng (northern) cakes. Both savory desserts were made of glutinous rice, sweet mung bean, and pork; same ingredients, different shapes. Picking up the round one (southern) in her left hand and the square one (northern) in her right, she weighed their differences.

"The round one is tastier than the square," a voice said beside her. *Where had she heard that voice before?* Looking up, she saw that it was Phúc. Ngọc Lan was surprised to see him again. She hadn't seen him since they disembarked at the port in Guam. He looked older with the stubble of a few unshaven days. Dressed in a blue suit with bell-bottom pants, he looked handsome. There was something lighter about him too, something less brooding and broken.

"Ah, Anh Phúc!" she exclaimed. "Is Anh well?"

"I'm well, I'm well." Phúc smiled.

"But the square one is heavier, and they're both the same price. That means the square one is definitely a better value for the money," Ngọc Lan said, returning to the sticky rice cakes.

"It's not a better deal if it doesn't taste better."

"But the ingredients are the same."

"Correct. Yet somehow, the round one tastes better," he said.

She knew what he meant. For him the southern version, the one he grew up with, was sweeter on his tongue. But Ngọc Lan didn't see it this way. Similar to how governments arbitrarily divided Vietnam into North and South, the different shapes of this same cake felt unimportant. What mattered was the inside. The fact that they were made of the same ingredients meant that deep down they were the same. Just as all Vietnamese people, at their core, were Vietnamese. Knowing that a woman was not meant to be disagreeable, though, she kept this idea to herself.

Phúc picked up one of each and handed them to the saleslady to bag. He paid and gave the bag to Ngọc Lan. "A gift from anh to em," he said. Ngọc Lan immediately protested; gifts were meant for courting. He couldn't possibly be courting her. She knew she shouldn't accept, but her hands, which craved this cake she hadn't had in years, reached out to take it. She bowed slightly and thanked him with both hands. "Cảm ơn, Anh Phúc."

"Phúc! Many days, many days. Are you well?" Anh Luân said, appearing out of nowhere. He and Phúc shook hands in a greeting that appeared friendly but felt stiff.

"Do you live near here?" Ngọc Lan asked Phúc as the three of them walked around the courtyard.

"No. I live in San Jose. I just came down for the festival."

Ngọc Lan's eyes went wide. "How many hours is that? The bus must have taken a long time."

"It wasn't long, only six hours because I have my own car."

"That's fortunate that you had someone to teach you to drive," Anh Luân said.

"Yes, who taught you?" Ngọc Lan asked. Phúc, like her, had come to America with no family, so she was genuinely surprised to hear about his easy immersion in American culture.

"I taught myself. In America, you can learn anything if you want to," Phúc replied. His bravado and confidence were alluring.

Ngọc Lan wondered if she had misinterpreted the sharpness he displayed on the boat. After checking the time, Phúc said, "I need to start driving back so I can make it to work on time tomorrow. Do you have a phone number I can reach you at?"

Ngọc Lan gave him the number for the landline they had at the apartment. Then Phúc left.

At dinner, Ngọc Lan presented the family with the savory rice cakes. They smiled wide with acceptance. In her most deferential tone, she said, "I wish for your family good health, great wealth, and lasting beauty."

"Bác Hiếu wishes for the sadness to wash away from you so that your flowers may bloom," Bác Hiếu returned. This was the bluntest he had ever been with her. Ngọc Lan felt ashamed at his obvious disappointment in her.

The eldest son went next. "Anh Minh wishes for em good health and a successful family." Since Ngọc Lan didn't have family here, she thought this odd. But it was a common Tết greeting, so she dismissed it as him not knowing what else to say to her.

"Chị Mậu wishes for em to start a family as soon as possible." Her wishes made Anh Minh's seem even more sinister. It was not uncommon for people to wish single ladies good fortune in seeking husbands. Ngọc Lan just knew that anything Chị Mậu sent her way came laced with venom.

Ngọc Lan was accustomed to Chị Mậu being mean. This time, though, the mention of family cut her in a way she didn't expect. She tilted her head, hoping her hair might obscure her tears.

Noticing the hot exchange, Anh Luân swooped in with a joke. "Anh Luân wishes em a full stomach, fat cheeks, and the winning lotto ticket."

Everyone but Chị Mậu laughed.

"If you let me win, what good fortunes will be left for you?" Ngọc Lan replied, regaining her composure.

He pretended to think about it for a moment. Then he added, "I will allow you to win this year. Next year I will keep the winning ticket for myself."

Not missing a beat, Bác Hiếu jumped in. "I don't care which of you wins. As long as I get a nice plot of land on the beach with a boat. And none of you are living under my roof, eating all my food." He kept his face impassive for a few seconds before breaking into laughter. Everyone joined. Ngọc Lan hadn't seen the family laugh like this since before they left home.

"Bác Ngà wishes for you a fresh start and a calm heart."

Ngọc Lan accepted the Lê family's good wishes—both the good and the bad. At least they thought of her. Unlike her father, who couldn't be bothered to even call since shooing her away from his new life.

Ngọc Lan awoke in the middle of the night with a jolt. After the long day of festivities, she had lazily skipped her bath.

"No, no, no, no," she muttered. She raced to the tub to fill it. Shaking with anxiety, she didn't wait for the tub to warm. Her foot hit the icy water. Goose bumps raced up her legs. She put her hand under the spigot. She waited, and waited, and waited. No hot water.

Shivering by the time the tub was full enough to immerse herself, Ngọc Lan held her breath and slid under. Nothing.

Short on luck, Ngọc Lan found it fitting that this year—the year of the monkey—life would play such a cruel joke on her. Still, she persisted. She tried again the next day. And the next. And the next.

For a year Ngọc Lan chased her sister, who appeared with heartbreaking irregularity. When trust was broken with a ghost, it was difficult to earn it back.

CHAPTER 32

PAUL

Once Jane makes up her mind about something, she doesn't turn back. Jane's best friend (ex–best friend) Jackie is proof of that. They were friends since like kindergarten or something. Out of nowhere, the summer before college Jane just straight-up drop-kicked Jackie. Her reasoning? "We're different people." But that's stupid. Mai and Joe and I are different people. We're going to be best friends till our hair turns gray and we forget who we are. Hell, I didn't even like Anh Sáu when I first met him and look at us now.

I saw Jackie two years ago. She looked completely different. She had choppy blue hair, wore a plain white T-shirt with combat boots and high-waisted jeans. The biggest changes, though, were the nickel-sized gauges in her ears. I don't know how else to describe it other than she became cool. When she saw me, a huge grin spread across her face. She came right over. She was nice, even offered to stretch my ears (jokingly). When the topic of Jane came up, I felt Jackie's old self come back.

"How is your sister?" Jackie asked me.

"She's good. She's a lawyer now. Works in the city."

Jackie nodded. "When you see her, tell her I miss her."

That was crushing to hear. I called Jane immediately, thinking they'd make up after seven years of not talking. Jane shocked me when all she said was "Humm. Okay."

"Are you gonna call her?" I asked.

"No." Jane was stone.

Whatever Jackie did was unforgivable, kinda like what I'm about to do.

Last night I came up with logical reasons for why Jane shouldn't be allowed to cut me out.

1. *I'm her brother.*
2. *I'm not doing this to her.*
3. *I would always, of course, choose Jane over Mom. (Need answer for when Jane says, "Oh yeah? Like right now, right?")*
4. *It's not fair that Jane gets to decide for both of us. I should get a say too.*
5. *I'm being haunted.*
6. *I'm being haunted (needs to be said twice).*
7. *I deserve to know.*

Number seven is probably my strongest argument. Ultimately, it doesn't matter. Jane's going to react however she wants to regardless of my reasons.

I pull out the scroll from Anh Sáu. Since my fight with Jane, Dì Diễm has left me alone. Maybe she sees the rift she's creating.

Once I told Jane I left the phone with Anh Sáu, she cut off the service. So wrong. She blames him for leading me to our grandma. Truth.

Part of me hopes that if we meet, I'll hate my mom just as much as Jane does. I'm pretty sure Jane could forgive a slipup. It might even make her happy. Jane loves being right.

If I don't hate my mother, though, I will lose Jane. I'm surprised my dad hasn't yelled at me for going behind his back to find my grandma. I wonder if he's scared of her. *Actually,* I bet he's scared of Dì Diễm.

I've gone my whole life without knowing my mother. The choice here is easy. And yet knowing my mom is out there, knowing she's alive and maybe not as horrible as my family has portrayed her to be, is . . . it's like having a rash and being told not to scratch it. Maybe this is why my dad is always saying I have itchy feet; I can't leave things alone. Anyway, my itchy feet best get moving; I start work again in two days.

"Don't be chickenshit. Just do it," Mai says while licking her fingers clean of the red Flamin' Hot Cheetos powder. She tilts her head back, dumping the crumbs into her mouth as she chews loudly. She never remembers to chew with her mouth closed. I called Mai and Joe as soon as I swiped my mom's number from Mợ Bích's address book. It took me a while to locate it because there's no order to the names. To be clear, this isn't an actual address book, it's just a small spiral-bound notebook about the size of my palm. The names probably went in in the order she collected them, starting in like 1979 when she arrived in America. Each name and number is written in large alphanumerics and inked over several times.

"It's like ripping off a Band-Aid. You just gotta do it quick," Joe adds. He and Mai are both sitting with their feet propped up on the extra patio chairs in our backyard. I'm sitting on the stoop, rolling a rock around beneath my bare foot.

"What if Jane's right and she's an asshole?" I ask.

"She's not going to be an asshole because Jane isn't right about everything. She doesn't even know your mom," Mai says. In case it isn't obvious, Mai doesn't like Jane.

"What if she's, like, really hot?" Joe says, snickering.

"Gross." I gag.

"Why would you even say that?" Mai laughs.

"What? You don't know her. What if you're attracted to her? It happens, you know," Joe says seriously.

"Dammit, Joe. For the last time, reality TV is rotting your brain," Mai says.

"It's the greatest human experiment!" Joe counters.

I snap my fingers at them. "Stop. Focus, people!"

Mai turns to me. "Just call her. She might not even answer."

"Exactly," I say. "Then what? Do I leave a message? Oh hey, uh, person? Mom? Do I call her Mom? This is your long-lost son, you know, the one you abandoned?"

"Duuude, what if you're not the only kids she's left? What if you have a bunch of half siblings?" Joe wonders.

"Not helping," I say, throwing my own crumpled-up Cheeto bag at him.

"Hey, pick that up before it blows away," Mai says. Mai is the litter police. "If she doesn't answer, hang up. This is not the kind of thing you leave a message about."

That seems easy enough. My mom probably won't answer, and if she doesn't, I can just hang up. Hanging up is easy. "Okay," I say, more to myself than them.

Using my old cell phone, I scroll to the number I've saved under Ngọc Lan Mom Ha. After I typed it, I saw how the universe laughed at me. My mother's last name is Ha, as in *haha*, so funny. I press the green call button before I lose my nerve.

Ring.

"Hello?"

I bolt up. "Hello?" My hands have suddenly become sweaty. I fumble the phone but catch it. Mai and Joe freeze.

"Hi, who is this?"

"This is uh, um, this is Paul. I—" I don't know how else to describe myself, but I don't want to use the word *son* because it seems so aggressive.

"Paul!" she exclaims. "Mẹ wait a long time to talk to you."

"Me too," I say, though I'm unsure if it's true. "I, um—" Shit, what do I want? I look at Mai and Joe, who both shrug. Useless! They mime talking to urge me to keep speaking. *Dammit, Mai, I told you I needed topics,* I say with a glare. "Mom khỏe không?" *How are you?* must be a reflex in both Vietnamese and English.

"Khỏe, khỏe! You speak Vietnamese so well," she remarks.

"Mợ Bích taught me," I say, continuing the conversation in Vietnamese. From the corner of my eye, I see Mai translating everything I'm saying to Joe, who nods in understanding.

"This is so great. Listen, Mẹ is thinking of coming to San Jose next week. Are you free?"

No one has ever asked me this before. Am I free? Technically, I have no plans, but the real question is *Will Dad let me go?* Mai nods at me vigorously, so I say, "Yes."

"Okay, Mẹ will make plans and call you? This is your phone number, right?"

"Dạ." I nod, then realize that she can't see me.

"Good, good. Okay, Mẹ will make plans and call you, huh?" she repeats.

"Yes," I say.

"Yes. Good. Okay, bye, con," she says.

"Bye," I say. I wait for her to hang up. She doesn't, so I take the phone away from my ear and shut it off.

"So, what did she say?" Mai says.

"She's coming next week." I stare at the phone in shock. I'm going to see my mother next week. What. The. Fuck.

"Holy shit . . . ," Mai says.

"How are you gonna tell your dad?" Joe asks. I look at him. Good question.

"What? No, you're not telling your dad. Why would you do that? Just sneak out," Mai says.

Oh. Good idea. Of course Mai is right. Whatever the consequences, I'm going. "Oh, shoot. One sec. I forgot your gifts." I run inside and retrieve the wallet and áo dài for Mai and Joe.

"This is so pretty. Thank you," Mai says, admiring the soft silk.

"Dude, I've always wanted one of these! I hope it fits me," Joe laughs, holding up the Vietnamese dress shirt.

From my belt loop I unhook the scroll Anh Sáu gave me. I hand it to Joe. "This is for you too. I'm sorry I wasn't always as good a friend to you as you've been to me. Thanks for always having my back, Joe."

Joe's eyes widen into saucers. "Is that what I think it is?"

"A real talisman." I nod.

"Come here, bro," Joe says, wrapping me in his famous bear hug. I look at Mai, whose expression reads: *Took you long enough.*

CHAPTER 33
NGỌC LAN

Donning a maroon cap and gown Bác Nga borrowed from a friend's son who graduated the year before, Ngọc Lan sat in the middle of the amphitheater as one of the unremarkable students in a sea of robed graduates. When her name, "Knock Lan Ha," burst through the speakers, she heard a light sprinkling of claps from the Lê and Hoàng families. She quickly shuffled across the stage. Afterward, the Lê and Hoàng families huddled around her in celebration. For a microsecond she thought her dad might also be present. He wasn't.

"She may be the smallest in her class, but she walks the fastest." Bác Nga laughed.

Bác Hiếu rattled his clasped hands across each of his shoulders. "Chúc Mừng. Chúc Mừng!"[28] He smiled while congratulating her. His enthusiasm radiated through a huge grin. Ngọc Lan smiled despite feeling that her accomplishment was pathetic.

"Chúc mừng em!" Chị Đào said. Ngọc Lan nodded with

---

28 *"Congratulations. Congratulations!"*

gratitude, but she felt embarrassed that they had even been invited to attend. They weren't close. They weren't family.

"Chúc mừng em!" Chị Bích added with sincere enthusiasm.

Ngọc Lan stepped away from a hug, noticing Chị Bích's belly. "Chị Bích is pregnant!" Ngọc Lan exclaimed. She couldn't believe Chị Bích could be married and carrying a child already—time was passing her by.

"Let's go home to eat before the food gets cold," Bác Nga said, herding everyone toward their cars.

"Where are your friends? Don't you have any friends?" Chị Mậu asked. She pretended to look around.

"They're all busy with their families," Ngọc Lan lied.

At the apartment, photographs of Ngọc Lan in her graduation attire were taken with the same disposable camera from New Year's. Chị Bích and Chị Đào were in charge of taking the pictures. As the honoree, Ngọc Lan took turns posing with each family—all the while wondering if they wished they could cut her out of what would otherwise be a beautiful family portrait. Because Ngọc Lan felt as though she didn't belong, she assumed everyone else thought it too.

Picnic tables were set up on the lawn. Everyone had sat down to eat when a brown two-door coupe Ngọc Lan didn't recognize parked in front of the complex. Ngọc Lan's face went pale. Stepping out of the car was a man who looked exactly like Anh Hòa. She blinked, certain her mind was playing tricks on her. When she opened her eyes, she saw that it was in fact her brother.

"Anh Hòa?" she shouted. Ngọc Lan ran to the car with tears in her eyes. "Is it really you? When did you get here? How did you find me? Finally, the universe has listened to my begging. I've missed you so much."

"Ah-Anh," Anh Hòa stammered. Ngọc Lan wrapped her arms around him, not noticing how he didn't return her embrace. He stood for a moment gently patting her. Then, using his palm, he separated her from himself.

"I can't believe it's you," Ngọc Lan said. She reached up to grab at his face, but he stepped away.

At the disappointment on Ngọc Lan's face, her brother tried to deflect. "You and I have so much to talk about, so many stories to tell. But today is your graduation. Let us celebrate and we'll talk later." Suddenly, Chị Bích was beside Anh Hòa. She took his hand as Anh Hòa explained to his wife that this was his sister, Ngọc Lan.

"Ngọc Lan is your biological sister?" Chị Bích exclaimed. "I can't believe I lived under the same roof as your younger sister and didn't know."

A dark realization hit Ngọc Lan all at once. Her brother hadn't found her. He hadn't even been looking for her. He came to America, fell in love, started a family, and his new life only accidentally collided with hers. Her brother was just like their father.

Ngọc Lan stared in disbelief. "Does Mẹ know you're alive?"

Anh Hòa shook his head. Sensing the barrage of questions Ngọc Lan was about to unleash, he said, "Tomorrow, Anh Hòa will tell you everything. Please, everyone is waiting for you. Let's sit down to eat."

"Chúc mừng em that today you not only graduated, you found your older brother too," Chị Bích said warmly. "Today is a truly historic day."

Ngọc Lan nodded. She did her best to push aside feelings of betrayal by telling herself that she didn't know the whole story. This was her brother. Anh Hòa had always looked out for her and Chị Diễm—surely, he hadn't intentionally forgotten about her? Most importantly, he was alive, her brother was alive. And for that, she reminded herself, she needed to be grateful.

Feeling hot, Ngọc Lan peeled off the maroon gown. Beneath her graduation regalia, she wore a simple blue áo dài with yellow birds perched on thin branches. This áo dài—a graduation gift from the Lê family—was the most luxurious thing she had ever owned.

Chị Đào gasped with glee as she came over to admire the beautiful dress. "So pretty. Let me look. Oh, wow, the sewing is exquisite. Who made this?" she asked.

Bác Nga answered. "That's the masterful work of Bác Hồ. You won't believe that she didn't *even* accept payment. She said sewing reminded her hands of home. *She* thanked *me* for letting her do it!"

This overgenerous way of speaking was so utterly Vietnamese that Ngọc Lan felt herself tugging at the hem. She wished that wearing it would transport her home.

Bác Nga had barely finished setting the table when a sky-blue 1963 Buick GS pulled up to the curb in front. Phúc stepped out. Ngọc Lan looked at him in surprise. She hadn't spoken to him since the Tết festival months ago. Why was he here? Even stranger, why was he carrying a tray covered in a red cloth with gold tassels—the universal offering for engagements?

Chị Mậu stifled a giggle as Bác Hiếu and Bác Nga stood up to accept Phúc's sad display of offerings to them. Typically, a fiancé would arrive with an entourage of people. He'd also have seven or nine trays containing betel leaves, areca nuts, marriage cakes, wine, tea, a whole roasted pig, fruits, and tobaccos or rice flake cakes. Not one. Unlike Chị Mậu, Ngọc Lan didn't judge him for the sad display. What she saw was a reflection of her own value.

"I'm sorry, this isn't a proper engagement display," Phúc said.

Before Ngọc Lan could answer, Chị Mậu rushed over. "Phúc, oh, Phúc, how lucky you arrived on such a celebratory day. Today is Ngọc Lan's graduation."

Phúc nodded hesitantly at Chị Mậu before warmly greeting Bác Hiếu and Bác Nga. Later that evening, Ngọc Lan understood why.

As she was carrying the last remnants of dishes from outside to the kitchen, she overheard Chị Mậu whispering to Chị Đào.

"Can you believe my shock when I picked up the phone and Phúc was asking for Ngọc Lan?" Chị Mậu snickered. "When I realized he was interested, I told him that Ngọc Lan wouldn't stop talking about his heroism and bravery on the boat." She laughed.

"Why did you lie?" Chị Đào asked.

Chị Mậu shrugged. "I was having fun. I mean, what a

gentleman he would be to sacrifice himself at the altar of marriage to someone as pathetic as Ngọc Lan, right? I keep telling my mother not to worry about that girl. Now she doesn't have to."

Ngọc Lan didn't need to see the smirk to know it was there. This explained the extravagant dress Bác Nga had purchased for her graduation. Her surrogate mother had known about the proposal.

Ngọc Lan didn't want an engagement. Not because she disliked Phúc but because in her mind she already had different plans. Marriage had been the farthest thing from her mind as she struggled to complete the required courses and maintain her 2.7 GPA to graduate. The few times she considered it, she imagined being married to Anh Luân. He was familiar, whereas Phúc was a stranger. When she looked toward Anh Luân, he avoided her. She knew then that he had thought the same thing.

Thanks to Chị Mậu, that possibility was gone. If Anh Luân spoke up now, it would appear as though he was trying to steal another man's wife.

Bác Nga, misconstruing Ngọc Lan's sadness as shyness, smiled broadly as she ushered the festivities onward. "Wait one minute. I have a gift for you," Bác Nga said. She disappeared into the apartment, then returned with a Reebok shoebox. Inside was a khăn đóng, a beautiful halo made of the same fabric as Ngọc Lan's dress. She pinned the turban to Ngọc Lan's hair. "Today is your special day," Bác Nga said. "Bác doesn't have much to give you, but this outfit will make you the brightest bride in America."

"That's prettier than the one I had at my wedding." Chị Mậu was seething.

Ngọc Lan ignored the comment and bowed low in thanks. "Cảm ơn, Bác Nga."

"Given the circumstances of our new arrival in America, our families being split across the world, Bác Nga and I stand here representing Ngọc Lan's father and mother, who could not be in attendance. They have both joyfully blessed this union. With unbelievable luck, though, today we have in attendance Ngọc Lan's older brother. Hòa, we'll ask you to join us for the ceremonial tea."

Ngọc Lan's father blessed the union? This was news to her. Her mother, she knew, had given Bác Nga permission to mother her as needed. Therefore, Bác Nga's approval was, by extension, her mother's approval.

"Dạ." Phúc bowed to Ngọc Lan's surrogate parents and Anh Hòa. "I am humbly here with not enough offerings or people to carry the gifts because of our current circumstances. Please forgive me. My family wishes they could be here. They send their greetings. They wish for Ngọc Lan and me to build a family that may be rooted in this new land here." Taking the teapot prepared by Bác Nga, Phúc poured cups for Bác Hiếu, Bác Nga, Anh Hòa, Ngọc Lan, and himself. Then he raised his cup of tea to them and together they drank.

The very next weekend, Ngọc Lan was married.

She was powerless to stop it. Ngọc Lan begged Anh Hòa

to intercede, to halt the wedding. She explained her need to go home. Her need to bury their sister.

"You cannot return to Việt Nam. You cannot return to Kuku Island," Anh Hòa explained. This was true. At the time, international law did not protect refugees who returned to Vietnam from being detained. As for Kuku Island, most of the world had no idea it existed, let alone where it was. Travel agents had never heard of it, and no airlines flew there. Her more immediate obstacles, though, were things that would take Ngọc Lan many attempts to obtain—US citizenship and an American passport.

Fighting in the war and his time in reeducation camps had dulled Anh Hòa's sensitivity to emotions. He wasn't bothered by his sister's disappointment. His only real regret was that someone had not told her sooner. "Marriage is the most logical next step," Anh Hòa said. There was no convincing him otherwise.

The ceremony washed over her in a blur.

All Ngọc Lan remembered was brushing her fingers over her mother's gold necklace and jade pendant. They were safety-pinned to the inside of her pants. Cold at first, the jewelry slowly warmed to the temperature of her body. Heeding her mother's advice, she never let anyone know she had it. Not even her brother. Now that she was about to start her own family, she felt its significance multiply. Ngọc Lan hadn't chosen the marriage or the groom. With her future unknown, this dowry was the only safety net she had.

Bác Nga tried her best to make miến gà—Ngọc Lan's favorite dish—like the noodle lady back home. It wasn't the same. The lack of fish sauce and use of macaroni noodles felt emblematic of the erasure Ngọc Lan had begun to feel. Could miến gà really be called miến gà when it lacked the very essential miến noodle?

Once the steaming bowl was placed in front of her, her hand reached for the chopsticks but stopped. Remembering her manners, she invited each person seated to eat first. When she got to Anh Hòa, her words were laced with resentment.

"Mời em," Anh Hòa said quickly, raising his hands toward the couple. He appeared to be genuinely happy for them. "Mời em Phúc."

Phúc, who had not spoken a word to Ngọc Lan the entire time, turned to her with a spoonful of noodles and said, "Let Anh Phúc feed my new wife." The table erupted in laughter and cheers. A horrified but subservient Ngọc Lan opened her mouth to receive the food.

"Ah!" Ngọc Lan gasped, waving her hands frantically as her mouth burned. Not knowing what to do, she swallowed. The heat scorched her throat.

"What's wrong?" Phúc asked, seemingly unaffected by the spoonful of hot noodles he fed himself.

"It's no problem," Ngọc Lan replied. Despite knowing she wouldn't taste the rest of her meal, she brought the noodles to her lips and slurped the broth. What was warm to her lips, scalded her throat—odd. Soft, slender fingers pressed against the nape of her neck. Ngọc Lan reached up to thank Bác Nga, who sometimes gently squeezed her in the same spot, the way a mother might soothe a child when they were nervous. But Bác Nga wasn't there. *Chị Diễm?* The more she ate, the harder the hands pressed. By the end of the meal, she was certain her sister had come. Spoonful after spoonful, Ngọc Lan swallowed the burning broth because in bite after bite, she found comfort.

After marrying, Ngọc Lan moved from the two-bedroom apartment she shared with the Lê family to a two-bedroom apartment shared among four young couples. Each bedroom was partitioned in half using paper folding screens. Since each resident was either working two jobs or working while also attending school, the place was never fully occupied.

For a year, Ngọc Lan worked in fast-food restaurants, eventually getting a second night shift job at the Del Taco next door. Meanwhile, Phúc finished his degree and started a job at a mechanic shop. Ngọc Lan made breakfast, the only meal they shared. She also packed both of their lunches and dinners. Subsisting on a frugal diet of rice, canned tuna, and eggs with scallion, they eventually saved enough money to move into their own apartment. Just in time, too, because Ngọc Lan was pregnant. To celebrate, Ngọc Lan splurged on buttered baguettes with sugar.

That first year of marriage was the hardest for Ngọc Lan. True to the Tết legend, missed encounters with her sister would happen all year; Chị Diễm became as elusive as a seahorse. At her new residence, Ngọc Lan had no access to a pool. And neither of the apartments in San Jose had a tub, only showers. Occasionally, when she made a cup of hot tea, she could feel her sister in the cascading warmth that filled her mouth and throat.

But the days of gliding together through shimmering water were over. She looked for her sister on the two occasions when Ngọc Lan and Phúc visited a cold northern California beach, though. Chị Diễm never appeared.

Then she had you.

"Wait, are you telling me I was conceived in that unwelcoming dark apartment? How did they even do it with other people sleeping nearby?"

I stare at her with what I hope is a look of pure disgust.

"Oh, ew!" She shrieks and throws a pillow at me. "Shit, that's gross. She didn't tell you that, did she?"

Now it's my turn to throw the pillow back at her. Jane's laughter is out of control. "Way to ruin a good moment," I say.

Jane rolls her eyes. "Oh, please, like my birth mattered to her."

Her laughter stops. I watch as she registers her own words. She really believes them. I don't think I realized how much our mom leaving affected Jane. It's so obvious now.

CHAPTER 34[29]

PAUL

I recognize her the moment I see the turtle-green Honda Accord rental car pull into the parking lot. It's not so much that I see myself in her as that I feel a gravitational pull toward her. She has long jet-black hair, eyes the shape of pearls, and a flat round nose like Jane's. The green jumpsuit she's wearing makes her look like a fashion drawing, where the legs are disproportionately longer than the torso. Still, she moves comfortably in what can only be described as ankle-breaking shoes.

Whereas my sister is monotone, my mother looks vibrant. Her face is a palette of colors I've never seen on Jane. Pink and purple eye shadows with an unmistakable bright red lipstick—she's . . . *loud.* The closer she gets, the smaller she becomes. By the time she's standing in front of me, she has to reach up to touch my face.

"Paul," she says, cupping my cheeks in her soft hands.

We're not an affectionate family. Rather than hug her, I rest my hands on hers and eke out a "Mẹ." I don't know why I used the

---

29 *Keeping it. New motto: Be steadfast. Show no fear.*

Vietnamese form of *Mom*. It oddly feels more intimate than the English *Mom*. I cringe. She may be my biological mother, but she has hardly been a mom to me.

She nods vigorously and breaks out into a wide grin, confirming that I should've used the English word. *Mẹ* carries weight; it's not like when Americans say, "Hey, Ma, can I get blah blah blah?" *Mẹ* in Vietnamese has that dot below the *ẹ*. When spoken, the inflection is heavy—immovable, like a rock. Anyway, it's a term that represents a bond we don't have.

"Con trai của mẹ lớn quá!" my mother exclaims, looking me up and down as though she can't believe my height.

"Maybe big for an Asian kid," I say in English. It's an attempt to get back on better footing, but it comes out wrong.

A flicker of disappointment crosses her face, but she covers it with a smile. "You are so grown-up," she tries again, in English.

"I understand you. I just prefer English." This exchange is quickly becoming uncomfortable. Part of me wants to run.

"Không sao. Sit, sit." She takes my hand. Holding it, she leads me to an empty bench She doesn't let go. "Mom really miss you," she says, fresh tears forming.

"Me too," I say, though I'm not sure I mean it. Can you miss someone you don't really remember?

"Are you hungry yet? Con thích ăn gì? We can find phở or hambuh-guh?"

Her accented *hamburger* makes me laugh. Then I mentally smack myself. Anh Sáu is in my head calling me judgmental. Now I feel bad. "I'm not hungry," I lie. "Are you?"

"Maybe later," she says. She pulls out two boxes from her purse, a modest brown faux-leather bag. "I have something for you. One for you and one for Jane." I take the boxes but don't open mine. I'll look later.

"Oh, Jane, she—"

But my mom cuts me off. "I know she's mad at Mom. You try to give it to her, okay?"

"How do you know that?" I ask.

"After she in college, Mom try to call her, but she hangs up on me."

This knowledge both surprises me and pisses me off. Jane never told me our mom reached out, but also, why did she only reach out to Jane and not me? "Why did you leave us?" I blurt.

Her face drops, but a smile covers it just as quickly. "Con trai của Mẹ," she laments. The phrase nearly breaks me. The words *My son,* spoken in Vietnamese, wrap me in a warmth that quickly turns to suffocation. How can this woman I barely know feel so close? How can such simple words be biting? I stiffen my jaw. Straightening her posture, she smiles. "Mom knows you will ask many questions, and I will answer them in time. But today, let's not talk about sad things. Come, let's go find something to eat."

I want to say no. To tell her that I came here for answers that she owes me. I want to throw the tantrums I never got to throw when I was a child because the punishment for acting up was so severe. I want to know how she could leave us with a man she knew would beat us. Why didn't she protect us? I want, I want . . . and yet what comes out of my mouth astonishes even me. "My bike. I have to take it home."

Without missing a beat, she says, "No problem. We'll put it in the trunk."

I look at her Accord. "It's not going to fit."

"It will." The words spill out with such conviction that I believe her despite seeing what is logically impossible.

I walk my bike to her car as she rushes to unlock it. Inside, she pulls a cord and the rear seats drop. To my surprise, they fold completely down. For a moment, it appears that my bike might actually fit—it does not. I'm about to give up when I watch my mother push her seat as far forward as possible, creating enough space for the bike to fall in.

"How are you going to drive like that?" I ask.

"Get in, get in." She laughs, victorious.

I slide into the passenger seat and watch as she kicks off her heels before sliding into the driver's side. Actually, she fits quite comfortably—who says there aren't perks to being short? She starts the engine. We take off.

"Where are we going?" I ask.

She shrugs. "We drive until we find something."

She can do that because San Jose, California, has the third-largest population of Vietnamese people in the United States. When we drive through certain neighborhoods, Vietnamese shops and restaurants make it so that I swear even white people say English street names with a Vietnamese accent. Okay, that's not true, but maybe with enough time, it will be.

My mother pulls into an indoor shopping plaza. People know it's Asian because flanking the entrance doors are two huge guardian lions. They know it's Vietnamese because it's called Little Saigon Plaza.

"Okay?" my mom asks while scanning the rows for a parking spot.

"Sure," I say. "How long are you here for?"

"Only today. I fly home tomorrow."

Home. She has a different home. Hearing this bothers me. I'm not sure why. I obviously knew she had a place and that it wasn't the same as mine. Yet it feels like she's rubbing it in. "Are you going to tell me why you left?" I ask.

My mom parks, looks up at me, and smiles. "How did you end up such a delicate calm boy?" Okay, she doesn't say *delicate* or *calm;* she says *hiền,* which is impossible to translate into English. It means delicate and calm in Vietnamese but is more complex than those two simple words. In any case, they're not exactly qualities I want to be known for. "Your grandmother told me to be wary of you. She warned me about getting too close."

What the hell kind of statement is that? I thought Grandma was on my side. Maybe Jane was right. This was a bad idea. "I don't need anything from you. You don't know this because you haven't been around, but Jane is a big-time lawyer. She makes lots of money."

My mother smiles at this. "Mom knows." I think she means for this to be reassuring. I find it anything but. How could she know? She doesn't know anything about us.

I open my door. This was such a mistake. Now that I think about it, she probably has been waiting to ask Jane for money. Maybe she already has. Oh god.

"You don't understand Mom," she protests gently. I head to the entrance and she follows me. "There's a lot you don't understand."

"I'm aware. I'm the one who found you, remember? Also, it's kind of hard to understand someone who is never around," I shoot back.

She takes the hit. "It's not that your grandmother doesn't love you. It's not her fault that your mother has a weak mind. Bà Ngoại remembers when I lost my mind. I didn't take care of myself enough when you two came along, so that when you were born, I had nothing left. She worries that your anger will shatter me."

My anger? So . . . what? I'm not allowed to be angry? I'm supposed to let her reenter my life after more than a decade of being gone without any resentment? Maybe something is being lost in translation. I reconsider what she said. Only it makes me angrier. Is she saying that our births drained her of . . . what? Happiness? We never asked to be born. If she had nothing to give, she shouldn't have had us. "Mom is right. I don't understand. Can I get my bike, please?" I'd rather bike a hundred miles than spend another minute with her. Jane was right, everything is about protecting my mother's feelings—because my mother is selfish.

We return to the car without speaking. I pull my bike from her trunk and drop it so hard on the concrete that the wheels bounce. The pedal scrapes my shin. Ignoring the cut, I hop on. I race home as fast as I can, slowing only when I see her car pass me. She turns up ahead. I relax, knowing she doesn't plan to chase me.

Twenty minutes later, sweat drips down my forehead as I bike up our driveway at home. Her car is parked in front of Mợ Bịch and Cậu Hòa's house. Only after I've gone inside and cooled down in the shower do I realize I never gave her my address.

CHAPTER 35
NGỌC LAN

When you were born, Mom fell in love with you immediately. Her days became filled with purpose, and every time you laughed or smiled, she felt like she was home.

Jane glares at me.

"That's what she said."

"Mom said she fell in love with me? She actually used the word love*?"*

"Okay, it's not exactly what she said, but it's the essence—it's the truth."

Jane goes quiet. I don't know how to ask her how she feels. Talking about emotion is not something we do. I try being clever.

"You completely missed the transition when I switched from Ngọc Lan to Mom."

"I didn't miss it. I ignored it."

I take the hint and back off. "Okay, well, I'm going back to using her name. You're making this weird with your judgy faces."

Jane says nothing. With caution, I forge on.

Ngọc Lan thought that new life could replace old life, but she was wrong. Jane's bubbly face and squishy cheeks opened up a part of Ngọc Lan's heart that she hadn't known existed. However, the gaping hole of loss was there also. She never stopped missing Chị Diễm. After giving birth, Ngọc Lan had to quit her job. This meant she spent day and night in the apartment with only herself and an infant. She tried her best to fill their time with activities, like walking to the nearby park or around the neighborhood. Often, they sat at home in front of the TV while Ngọc Lan practiced her English by copying the weather lady's daily monologue. After Jane's birth, Ngọc Lan was determined to speak better English. She didn't want her daughter to be dumb like her.

The highlights of her weeks were short exchanges she had with the person working the register at the grocery store. Nine times out of ten they'd ask a variation of the same question: *Hi, how are you doing today?*

Ngọc Lan relished replying, "Hello. I'm fine. Thank you. Today is a beautiful sunny day."

With Jane strapped to her chest, Ngọc Lan systematically walked down every aisle in the store. For a short time Ngọc Lan considered that maybe, if she could learn to love the food, she could learn to love America. So she tried everything (when it was on sale, obviously).

Cereal, peanut butter, sweet jams, canned fruit, cookies, ketchup, mustard, barbecue sauce; the list was infinite. As was customary with Vietnamese dishes, Ngọc Lan put everything over a bed of rice—most tasted awful, but sometimes she would find new flavors that felt like sunshine on her tongue. Ketchup added a tangy flavor to chicken and rice that she liked, whereas mustard on pretty much anything was terrible.

When she didn't know what something was, she'd ask a stranger. She asked. She learned. And she discovered that ketchup and mustard were meant to be eaten on meat tubes called hot dogs. Ngọc Lan hadn't ever been a fan of dog meat, but everyone in America seemed to love it, so she bought a pack with matching bread buns. To her surprise, the meat was tender and juicy. She learned the hard way that adding relish, chili, and shredded cheese gave her a stomachache. With every bite she took, she forced herself to digest her new life.

When Jane started kindergarten, Ngọc Lan began looking for a job. Because they only had one car, she still hadn't learned how to drive. She walked from business to business seeing if anyone needed help. As she roamed, a bright pink paper fan caught her attention. She peered into a small shop she must've passed a hundred times without noticing. The swinging door, covered in advertisements, made it hard to see what type of store it was. Past the threshold,

Ngọc Lan found a small local grocer that stocked mainly Asian products. When she looked behind the counter, she was surprised to find that the woman there was Asian, though not Vietnamese. She wore a short Hawaiian dress that fell beneath her knees and had lips stained so red they reminded Ngọc Lan of the fire station.

Ngọc Lan browsed, finding lemongrass, rice paddy herbs, and fresh mint stems. All herbs she hadn't been able to get in American grocery stores.

"How do you have this one?" Ngọc Lan asked, bringing the herbs to her nose to inhale their fresh scent.

"I grow it all myself," the woman said, not at all irked by Ngọc Lan touching her clean produce.

"Can I see? Maybe you sell me a root?" Ngọc Lan asked.

"I could, but then who would buy mine?" The woman laughed.

Ngọc Lan immediately apologized. "I'm sorry. I don't compete with you. I just want for my home. I miss this smells."

The clerk smiled. "I understand. I'm from Laos. Where are you from?"

"Việt Nam."

Nodding, the lady put one of each herb in a bag. She handed the bag to Ngọc Lan. "For you." When Ngọc Lan hesitated, she added, "Take it, really, before I close the shop and there is none left."

"You closing forever?" Ngọc Lan couldn't believe her bad luck. She had finally found a store that sold products she wanted, only to have it go out of business.

The woman tilted her head to the side. "You want to buy? I'll sell to you for a good price," she said.

"No money." Ngọc Lan smiled wistfully.

"Never enough money, right?" the lady commiserated. "Well, I'm selling cheap. The landlord is what you have to worry about. Rent here is only getting more expensive."

"How much is it?"

"The business? I am asking for fifteen thousand dollars, but I would consider less. The lease is good for another two years. After that, you will have to negotiate with the owner, but now I pay eight hundred dollars a month."

Eight hundred dollars was more than twice what they paid in rent. "Is the business profitable? Are you moving because you cannot afford rent?"

"Oh no. I make plenty to cover rent. My father is ill. I cannot keep this place open and take good care of him. If you apply for a liquor license, you could make double, maybe three times more money."

Ngọc Lan considered this. She thought the woman could be lying, but her gut said she wasn't.

At dinner, Phúc praised her bánh xèo. The yellow rice crepe filled with bean sprouts, shrimp, pork, and green onions had actually turned out quite well because of the ingredients Ngọc Lan had found in the Laotian store.

"I found a local store today that sells these herbs. I hadn't realized how much I missed them," Ngọc Lan said.

Phúc plucked a few leaves, breathing in the familiar aroma

as though the smell alone could transport them back home. "Was it expensive? Did you bargain?"

"Actually, she gave it to me for free," Ngọc Lan replied. She took a deep breath, then added, "Because she's closing the shop."

"Too bad," Phúc replied, with real disappointment.

Seizing the opportunity, Ngọc Lan blurted, "I think we should buy it."

Phúc laughed. "With what money?"

Knowing this would be his response, Ngọc Lan excitedly laid out her ideas—the ones she had crafted while making the meal. "We could take the money I made from before. Plus what you've saved. I talked to her. It's very profitable. Plus, if we get a liquor license she says we could make three times more."

"No."

The word was sharp and final. Ngọc Lan closed her mouth. There would be no further discussion.

Despite Phúc's refusal to even consider buying the business, Ngọc Lan found herself walking in the direction of the shop the next day.

Go home. Phúc told you no already.

Remember how bad you were at making sales at the market?

What do you know about running a business?

Most people can't even understand your English.

You barely passed high school, how can you be a boss?

Doubts raced across her mind; and yet something about the

smell of those herbs, the smell of home, lured her through the swinging glass door.

"You're back! Come, I have plants I want to give you." The woman smiled, waving her over. "By the way, what's your name?"

"Ngọc Lan."

"Ngoak Lan?" she repeated. She led Ngọc Lan to the stock room. "I'm Evette."

"Ev-wet," Ngọc Lan practiced.

"Yes!" Evette said brightly. Bending down to pick up two potted plants, she gestured for Ngọc Lan to take the next two.

"For me? Free?" Ngọc Lan asked. Hopefully, the woman remembered that Ngọc Lan didn't have any money.

"Yes, free." Evette smiled. "Where's your car? I hope you have trunk space."

"I have no car," Ngọc Lan replied. "I walk."

"You need a cart or something. These are way too heavy to carry even two blocks. How far are you?"

"Not far. Twenty-minute walk."

"Twenty minutes?" Evette exclaimed. With a hand on her hip, she pointed to the eight plants on the ground. Then she walked to the back of the store. She returned with an old two-wheel folding cart. "This is old, but it should work."

"Okay." Ngọc Lan bowed in thanks. "I can go now and come back. Four times today, no problem."

"No, no!" Evette said. "Come back tomorrow, no rush. I will keep them alive."

Ngọc Lan broke out into a wide grin. She bowed deeply. "So happy. Thank you."

The sun beat down on Ngọc Lan's head and shoulders as she walked home. The leaves of her new plants brushed against her arms. She imagined owning the shop. She saw herself waking up early, tending to a small garden, unlocking the store doors, even managing the inventory. There would be lots to clean and organize, but she was confident she could do the work. Maybe she wasn't the best seller in Vietnam, but she was older now. With Jane in school, Ngọc Lan could walk her there in the morning, close at lunch to pick her up, and bring her back until closing. The more she thought about it, the more sense it made.

At dinner, Ngọc Lan prepared Phúc's favorite meal, braised pork belly with quail eggs. Nervously, she waited to bring up the shop for a second time.

"Ba, look at my gold stars." Jane beamed, showing him a piece of paper with the days of the week and a star in each box.

"Good job," Phúc said, not looking at the paper. For a five-year-old, Jane was clever. She knew the stars would make her dad happy. She also knew that the vocabulary matching test with too many red marks would anger him. She hid that one beneath the sweater in her backpack.

"What did you do to earn the stars?" Ngọc Lan asked.

"Atten-dance," Jane said.

"What does that mean?"

"When the teacher calls my name, I am at my desk, ready to learn." Jane smiled.

Phúc scoffed. "You get a star for just showing up? American schools are too easy. In Vietnam, you come one second late and the teacher will beat you silly."

Jane looked down, no longer proud of her achievement. As they ate, she slid the paper from the table and hid it beneath her thigh.

Watching Phúc deflate Jane's ego so swiftly caused something akin to anger to swell up inside Ngọc Lan. Out spilled "I will buy the grocery store. I will take only the money I made and ask Evette to pay off the rest over time."

Phúc calmly continued eating. In fact, he didn't speak for so long that Ngọc Lan wondered if she had spoken aloud at all.

When he finally did say something, it was with a hint of laughter. "Your part-time money is only six thousand dollars. You think she will loan you nine thousand dollars for free?" His condescension underscored what he believed was Ngọc Lan's idiocy.

But Ngọc Lan had come prepared. "With interest."

"And for how long? You think she can wait thirty years for you to pay her back?"

"I will pay her back in five years."

Phúc laughed. He had recently been promoted to manager. This meant he now wore a crisp white button-down with his name stitched elegantly above the left breast pocket. On the right was the Goodyear company logo. His new uniform came with added ego. "You don't know anything. Most businesses take two years to even make a profit. Where do you think you'll come up with your monthly debt payments from?"

"I will figure it out."

"Do you think I work every day like a water buffalo so you

can burn money trying to act like you are better than everyone? Don't be so uppity."

"This is not just for me. It's a business for the whole family."

"Can you not hear? I said no."

Ngọc Lan didn't argue. This was already far more fighting than they had experienced in the entirety of their marriage. She knew there was no changing his mind. So instead, she sat quietly plotting how she would go to the bank, extract the money, and buy it behind her husband's back.

CHAPTER 36

PAUL

Jeez, what a way to wake up. We live in separate town homes, but we share a wall, which my aunt and uncle have obviously forgotten because it's 9 a.m. and they're screaming at my mom. Well, my uncle and mom yell while Mợ Bích referees. I would *not* want to be her. Things must have been brewing overnight for it to erupt like this.

They started out arguing about me. Cậu Hòa asked, "What kind of mother shows up after the kids are grown? You're exactly like Dad. You only think about yourself."

"What does Anh Hòa know about Ba? Has Anh ever called him?" she retorts.

"Anh has no need to call that man," Cậu Hòa claps back.

"*That man?* Disrespectful. That man is still your father. Don't you remember when he used to swing us around at the beach? Or dive for crabs with us?"

"That man never did those things."

"Yes, he did. You used to tell me about it all the time. Don't you remember?"

"I lied!" Cậu Hòa booms. "You were just a kid and you kept

crying for him, so I told you those stories. He never did those things. *I* did. My father died long ago."

"But I remember!" my mom begs. I can hear how much she wants to be right—it's sad.

Their argument feels private, personal, painful; yet I cannot stop eavesdropping. I've never heard about my grandfather. It didn't occur to me to think about him because my mother was gone. Even though I've lived next to Cậu Hòa for more than eight years, I forget that he's my mom's brother. Probably because this is the first time I've seen—uh, heard—them together.

"There was fighting. Anh Hòa doesn't remember?"

"Remember? Anh sat in prison for two years. Em is the person who doesn't understand that time," Cậu Hòa says. "Did you work in the labor camps with the Việt Cộng? No. Then mute your mouth." In Vietnamese, *Mute your mouth* has more bite—it's probably better translated as "Shut the fuck up," even though it sounds benign. I didn't know my uncle worked in the labor camps. He's never mentioned it before. No one talks about that time like I'm hearing it now.

"Correct. Anh Hòa went to prison. Anh Hòa knows the dirty business of the Việt Cộng," my mother says. "Because of this, Anh Hòa must understand Ba's situation. Ba could not possibly have stayed in Việt Nam." Is she saying that my grandfather is still alive? I assumed he was dead.

"The old man came to America, found a new wife, and forgot about his family at home," my uncle scoffs. "And em did the same thing."

I bite my fist, expecting my mom to explode in anger. That was mean. *True,* but mean. Also, why am I defending her when I'm mad at her? A long silence follows . . . too long, an eternity, really. I press my ear closer, wondering what happened. Did she faint? No, there'd be even more commotion. Maybe she started whispering because they realized I was here. Instinctively, I step away from the wall, even though, obviously, none of them can see me. But I can't help myself. I lean forward again, pressing my ear to the wall.

When my mom finally speaks, her voice has an eerie calm, more broken than angry. "Anh didn't live with me. From the day the war ended, I suffered loss after loss. Ba, Chị Diếm, Anh Hòa." She pauses for a long time. "Anh Hòa cannot possibly understand how a person can try to fix their mind but fail to protect their children. Anh Hòa doesn't know how much my heart hurt."

"Em—" my uncle begins, but pauses.

"Forget it," Mợ Bích chimes in. "These stories have passed. Let's not talk about it anymore."

"Anh—" Cậu Hòa starts.

Mợ Bích stops him again. "Stop, don't speak more." Mợ Bích's tone is firm but soft. She's not very confrontational, but everyone listens when she takes this tone, even my dad. Maybe because she doesn't use it often? I don't know, but she's always had more control than my uncle or even my dad in this way. They boss her around and make her do all the things "men" don't do. She does them, but Mợ Bích ain't no wallflower.

Their voices go quiet. Even using a glass cup, which I've seen people do on TV, I can't hear their conversation anymore. Of course, it could also be because they're no longer speaking, but I can only assume since I don't have X-ray vision.

The doorbell rings.

That's odd. No one ever rings the doorbell. I honestly can't remember the last time I heard it ding-dong.

Through the peephole, I see my mother. Thankfully, my dad's already at the liquor store. I'd like to *never* cross that bridge if it's possible. I open the door. For a second, I don't know if I should let her in. So I just stand there, waiting for her to say something.

"Son, have you eaten breakfast yet?"

"Cereal," I say in English because there is no Vietnamese word for it.

"Today, are you busy?"

"Today, I work from ten until six at night," I say.

She looks at her watch. "Đi, Mom will take you."

"I still need to shower," I say.

"Đi, Đi, hurry up," she says, shooing me to the bath. "Mom will wait."

I feel weird leaving her alone in the house because—I don't know why. It just feels funny. "Does Mom want something to drink?"

"Go shower. If Mom is thirsty, she will find water."

While I scrub shampoo into my scalp, it dawns on me that she's probably curious about where we live. I bet she's snooping around. Too bad there's nothing interesting.

From my bedroom I can hear the low humming of a song. At the top of the stairs, I stop:

Hm, hm, hm, hm, hm, hm, hm-hmmmm . . .
Hm, hm, hm, hm, hm, hm, hm-hmmmm . . .

Mẹ bước trên con đường gập ghềnh, sáng ngời
Để bảo vệ bước chân con trong đêm tối.[30]

She's sitting upright on the sofa with her legs crossed, swaying to the music in her head. She hums some parts like she doesn't quite remember the lyrics.

I clear my throat. "I'm done," I say, feeling the need to announce my arrival.

Something is off in the room, but I can't pinpoint what it is . . .

"So fast!" she quips. "Đi, Đi," she says, ushering me toward the door. She exits first. I follow, glancing around the living room one last time before closing and locking the door. That's when I see it—the missing photo of me, Jane, and Dad, at Disneyland. We don't have many pictures displayed in our place, but Becky and Vicky made us a copy of the image they took of us at Disneyland many years ago. Becky and Jane have been BFFs since Jane ousted Jackie. I haven't seen Vicky in years, after she moved to Philly for college. Technically we're not related, but they have cousin status because of how close my dad was to their dad. It's the only real family photo we have, and I *know* Jane will be pissed if she finds out Mom swiped it. I make a mental note to think up an excuse later.

We drive to the liquor store in semiawkward silence. Yesterday's meeting hangs between us, and inside I'm a jumbled mess. I don't know

30 *She walks a broken path, calm and bright*
To protect her child's steps in the night.

where to put my hands. Crossed over my chest seems too aggressive, at my sides is awkward, and folded in my lap makes me feel like a kid. I opt for aggressive. I want her to know I haven't forgiven her. My mother still hums the song from earlier.

Humm, hum, hummm, hum, humm, hummm, humm, humm . . .

"What song is that?"

Instead of explaining, she sings the lyrics, and suddenly it clicks. This is the song I heard when I almost drowned in Vietnam. And again, when the spirit tugged at my ankles in the orange Fairy Stream.

"Do you remember it?" my mother asks.

A chill races down my spine. How could she know that this is the song I've been hearing? For a second I wonder if Dì Diễm has taken over her body. If, sitting next to me, it's actually my aunt controlling my mother.

"When you were little, you cried in the middle of the night a lot. This was the only song that soothed you."

The trees outside are still; yet I feel like a tumbleweed blowing in a windstorm. Is this why the song initially pulled me in? Because somewhere locked away in my brain, this tune had once calmed my nerves?

"Do you remember it?" she asks again. The desperation in her voice is painful. I don't want to forgive her so easily, but it's hard to hate someone who clearly wants me to feel her love.

"I remember," I say. I cough to cover the crack in my voice.

My mother turns into the parking lot of the liquor store. For the first time in my life I'm grateful that I have to go to work.

"Do you want to come inside?" I ask. *Why did I ask?* I *do not* want her to come inside.

"No, Mom has business she needs to attend to." I breathe, relieved.

I step out of the car. This part doesn't seem to get less awkward. "Bye, Mom." *Mom* slips from my tongue accidentally, but unlike the first time, it doesn't feel wrong.

"Okay." She smiles, waving me off.

Inside, I head to the register and sit dumbly. I've sat here a million times before. I know every inch of this ridiculously small cashier's area. I am comfortable here, except I'm not. Suddenly I feel this urgency to be somewhere else, not with my mother, or anyone really, just . . . on my own. Making my own choices, like my mom did. Like Jane did, when she left for college. Suddenly, I see these walls as the cage they are, and I want freedom.

Dad walks in with Mợ Bích. "Who car is that?" he asks.

I hesitate. Should I lie? If my mom is staying next door, maybe my aunt has already told him. Surely it would be better if the news came from her. The problem is my dad is exceptionally attuned to lying. Or is it that he's made me very afraid of lying? Either way, I've paused for too long. The only option now is the truth. "Mom."

No reaction. Literal stone face. "Okay."

I know I was scared before, so this doesn't make sense, but now I'm mad. *OKAY?* Seriously? That's all he's got for the woman who walked out on him and his kids thirteen years ago?

He goes outside to smoke a cigarette. I'm left with Mợ Bích.

"You know it was your mom's idea to buy this liquor store. If she hadn't defied him and bought it behind his back, your dad would still be a mechanic," Mợ Bích says.

"What do you mean defied?"

"She took the money from their account and bought it. Your mom didn't even know what she was doing. Lucky for us, the Lao woman who owned it was honest. She helped your mom set it up correctly."

"Why would the Lao woman help a stranger?"

Mợ Bích shrugs. "Sometimes people remember what it is like to struggle and they help us."

"If Mợ Bích knew my mom was around, why didn't you tell us?"

"The business of your house is not my business," my aunt says simply. This is shorthand for *That's all I'll say about your mom out of respect for your dad*. Frustrating.

I go online.

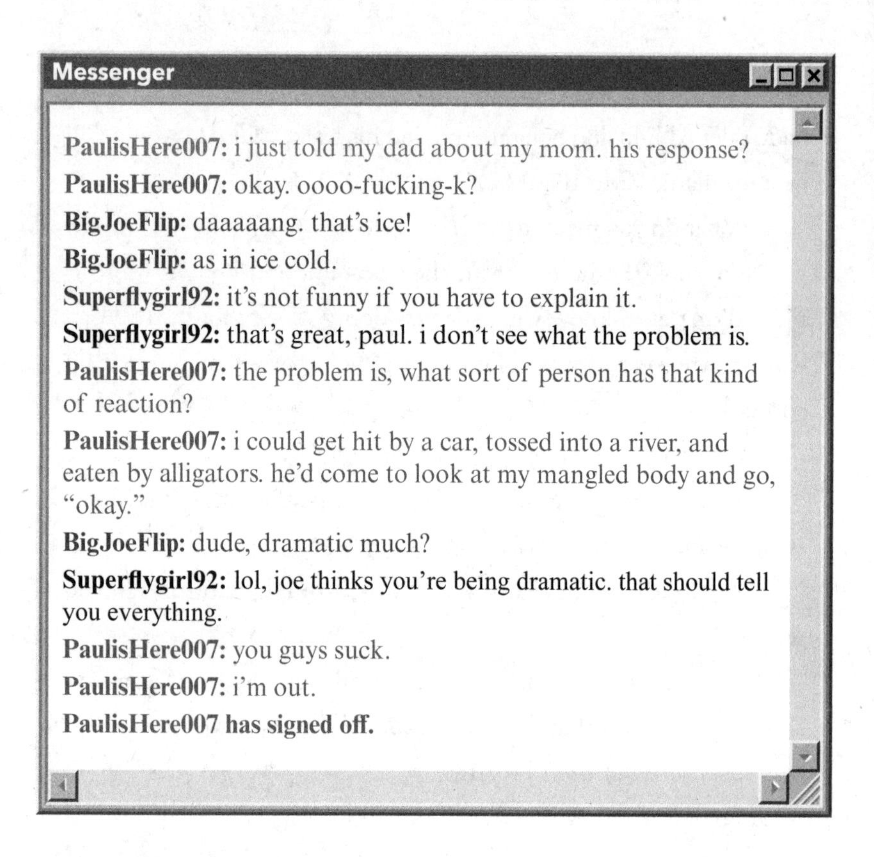

After I close the chat, the significance of what I've done really sinks in. My mom is back, my dad knows, and Jane's about to find out. Whatever happens, I did this to myself.

CHAPTER 37
NGỌC LAN

The afternoon Phúc realized what Ngọc Lan had done was a Friday. He picked up his check from the stack of envelopes on Mr. Khan's desk; then he walked four blocks to Bank of America. Sliding in his ATM card, he deposited the check and waited for his receipt to print. The balance stunned him. He knew what had happened without needing to ask. Forced to return to work to finish his shift, he felt his fury mounting over the next four hours until, finally, he couldn't take it anymore. Phúc left his job thirty minutes early to deal with his wife.

Ngọc Lan braced herself for Phúc's backlash. She knew he'd be angry but assumed the yelling would happen at home—in private. This was why, after she picked Jane up from school, the two of them were strolling carelessly to the Lao Market.

Phúc's car pulled up beside them. "Let's go," he barked. His tone indicated that she had underestimated his ire.

Ngọc Lan did not want to get in the car. His direction wasn't a question; he hardly ever asked her questions. Springing from the vehicle, he grabbed Jane. He tossed her into the booster seat so hard that her chin clapped against her chest. She began screaming. This was the first time Ngọc Lan saw Phúc's anger manifest physically. It scared her. Quickly, Ngọc Lan hopped into the back seat to buckle in her daughter. Jane, a child as bull-headed as Phúc, kicked the seat in front.

"Stop!" Ngọc Lan shouted at Jane, though it was a plea in her mind.

Before Ngọc Lan could get either of them buckled in, Phúc sped toward the highway. In the rearview mirror, Ngọc Lan saw fire fill Phúc's eyes.

"Slow down," Ngọc Lan suggested meekly. The last thing she wanted to do was make the situation worse.

The white of his knuckles turned nearly translucent as the rage from his foot moved to his mouth. He lifted his foot from the gas and shouted, "What a cruel joke that the universe married me to such a stupid, stupid wife!"

They drove and drove until tall redwood trees engulfed the tiny car. The narrow one-lane road made Phúc's erratic steering all the more treacherous. Deeper and deeper into the dense foliage they went, until Phúc abruptly veered into an empty parking lot. With the engine still idling he barked, "Get out."

Ngọc Lan unbuckled Jane, folded her into an embrace, and lifted her out into the cool, damp air.

"Close the door," Phúc growled.

She pushed the door shut. The red brake lights went dim. Then he was gone.

Ngọc Lan looked to the heavens. Flecks of light danced

among the leaves. Dressed in a cotton floral dress, blue cardigan, and plastic flip-flops, Ngọc Lan clutched Jane's hand and began walking. Phúc had gone right. She knew better than to follow him. She went left—back the way they'd come.

The distance between one parking lot and the next was long. Ngọc Lan passed three lots before she began to sweat. Moisture pooled at her feet, causing them to slide across her cheap plastic sandals. Blisters formed. They stopped. Setting Jane on the seat of a bench, she slid her yellow thongs from her feet and rubbed them dry on her dress.

Tired, Jane crawled into her mother's lap to rest. Ngọc Lan nudged Jane's head with her shoulder. "I need you to walk."

Jane shook her head and nuzzled deeper. "Stand up," Ngọc Lan gently cajoled. "It's almost dark. You'll miss all the beautiful scenery."

Jane lazily sat up. "I'm hungry."

Ngọc Lan reached into the pocket of her cardigan, grateful for the breakfast bar she always carried in case Jane wanted a snack after school. As her daughter ate, she looked around at the forest, which at once felt otherworldly and utterly familiar. She leaned her ear toward the trees. Relief. There it was, the unmistakable sound of trickling water.

"Come." She waved to Jane as she followed a dirt path into the dense foliage.

Jane stood defiant for only a second before sprinting to take her mom's hand. Together they walked a short distance to a small stream. Clear water cascaded over moss-covered rocks. Ngọc Lan reached in to drink from her hands.

Pink, purple, green, and red streaks shot forward like glistening eels. Ngọc Lan's eyes went wide. *Chị Diễm?*

Kicking her useless sandals to the side, she stepped into a shallow pool. Then Ngọc Lan sat down. Warm, colorful swirls swarmed around her hands and ankles.

"Whoa!" Jane exclaimed.

Ngọc Lan's eyes shot toward her daughter. "You can see it too?"

"It's so pretty," Jane answered, stepping in beside her mother.

Pink and purple sparkling ribbons raced around them, but before Ngọc Lan could introduce Jane to her elders, Jane's tiny hand hit the water.

Smack! Like schools of fish swimming in formation, the glitter dispersed before retaking its shape.

Jane giggled. "This water is warm." Kicking her foot in a circular motion, she asked, "Why is it so warm?"

More colors appeared—red, orange, green, and yellow. Ngọc Lan stretched her leg into the stream, hoping to feel the familiar finger-tickling wiggle that Chị Diễm used to wake her up with every morning as a child. She looked and looked, but her sister's signature blue and gold never appeared. The blast of color was filled with aunts and uncles, grandparents, cousins, and more. Every generation before had come to meet Jane. Everyone but Jane's aunt—Dì Diễm.

"You were born in America, but the warmth you feel comes from your ancestors. Viết Năm is far away from this place, but water is the one natural element that connects the whole world. No matter where you end up, if you can find a stream, river, or ocean, it will always connect you back to your family. When you feel this heat and see these colors, that's how you know your ancestors are here," Ngọc Lan explained to Jane—the same way Mẹ had once explained it to her.

Jane listened intently, wiggling her toes in a manner that suggested she felt her family's touch too. "Momma, does this mean I can jump in polar bear water and not get cold?"

Ngọc Lan started to say no. She started to tell her daughter about the dangers of freezing water. But when she considered her daughter's understanding of the message, she found no better explanation. "Yes."

Jane stood up. She twirled in the water, then bowed to the spirits. "Thank you, ông, and bà, and chú, and bác, and everyone."

"And Dì," Ngọc Lan whispered.

"And who?" Jane asked.

"Your aunt. She's mad at Mom."

"Bác Nguyệt?"

"Yes," Ngọc Lan lied. One day she would tell Jane about her aunt, but she was too hurt at the moment to bring her up. Chị Diễm had every right to be mad at Ngọc Lan. More than a decade had passed while her sister's body still lay buried in a shallow grave on Kuku Island. After failing her citizenship test three times, she had put it off. No citizenship meant no passport. When a travel agent explained that the area was haunted due to the large numbers of reported suicides or accidental drownings, her hope further diminished. *I am trying, though, Chị Diễm,* Ngọc Lan thought. And she was.

Unbeknownst to Ngọc Lan, in 1980, after the last refugees

were relocated, the area had returned to its uninhabited state. This was why she couldn't find it on a map.

Despite her plea, the vibrant shimmers faded to dust. The water changed from warm to lukewarm, then turned cold again. Jane shivered. It was time to go. Reaching for her daughter's hand, Ngọc Lan said, "Come."

They wrung out their clothes, twisting whatever water they could off the fabric, then returned to the main road. This time, Ngọc Lan walked barefoot, pressing her feet into the cool black asphalt. With every step she took, she became more and more driven.

Whether Phúc liked it or not, they owned this shop now, and Ngọc Lan was determined to make it profitable.

He can leave if he wants to, Ngọc Lan thought. She would build the market the way her mother and Bác Nga taught her in Vietnam—one customer at a time.

Intent on walking a new path—her own path—she moved with stalwart resolve.

"Momma! Slow down," Jane said, growing tired.

"Slow? You rested for half the day already. Move faster," Ngọc Lan chided. Jane skipped along. Jane didn't know why her mother was so happy or why they were walking barefoot on the shoulder of the road through a redwood forest. All she knew was that her mother was giddy. Jane loved it when her mom was this way.

"Oh, so now you're going to tell me how I felt at the time?" Jane interjects, glaring at me.

"No, but you haven't exactly been forthcoming with stories about you and Mom, so this is what you get," I say. I also wanted to make sure Jane was still listening, because halfway through the river story, her mind seemed to drift elsewhere. I keep that part to myself.

"I remember the forest. I remember the colors too and the hot spot in the middle of the stream. That wasn't the only time we went, though."

Now it's my turn to confess. "I know. I've never told you this, but I have these fragments of memories, like, there was one time . . . they were fighting, and you were holding me in the back. You told me the story—"

"Of the Three Little Bears," she finishes.

"But wrong?"

"Yeah," Jane laughs. And then she goes quiet. I give her a moment. Then I continue.

They walked and walked, passing more giant trees with no end in sight; before very long, Jane's legs grew tired. She pleaded to be carried. "Just walk a little more," Ngọc Lan prodded. "You're a big girl already. You should practice walking."

"I know how to walk, but I'm tired. Let's call Dad to pick us up!" Jane suggested, proud of her ingenious idea. Between her discoveries and adventures, she had clearly forgotten how they got here in the first place.

Ngọc Lan's lips pursed. "You want to go home to your dad?"

"Dạ." Jane nodded with the exaggerated exuberance that always made her dad smile. She lived to make her dad laugh. Her affable singsongy attitude could sometimes draw from Phúc a rare, atmosphere-changing belly roar. A mother should never be jealous of her daughter, but at this moment, that was exactly what Ngọc Lan felt—angry envy.

"What a dumb child," Ngọc Lan muttered, erasing the smile from Jane's face. This was not the first time Ngọc Lan criticized her daughter, but it was the first time a new look flashed across Jane's face—hatred.

Ngọc Lan returned her daughter's glare with a glare of her own. "I feed you, I clothe you, I take care of all your needs day and night. What does your dad do for you?"

"Ba makes money," Jane said, not understanding the rhetorical question.

"Money." Ngọc Lan seethed. "You're just like your father."

"Money is the thing that buys the food and clothes you put on me," Jane continued, recalling a phrase her dad used often.

"Shut your mouth!" Ngọc Lan roared. She remembered how her mother would work from sunrise to sunset while her dad was gone for months at a time. She remembered the reverence they were taught to give him for being the breadwinner. For bringing home money. She also remembered how easily he had abandoned them—her—for his own selfish needs. It angered her that her own daughter, her flesh and blood, could be as stupid as she once was.

Jane obediently fell silent, then whimpered, "Mẹ, can you carry me?" She didn't know why her mother was so mad. Or why everything she said and did was cause for rebuke. Even though her mother had never been affectionate, Jane craved closeness.

Ngọc Lan ignored her daughter. When Jane started crying, Ngọc Lan let go of her hand and continued walking. Even as she heard the cries fade behind her, knowing that Jane had stopped to throw a fit, Ngọc Lan didn't look back. Guilt tugged at her, of course it did, but rage overrode her conscience. She didn't stop.

Jane's cry turned into a wail; then the pitter-patter of running footsteps came up from behind. Ngọc Lan felt relief for her daughter's safe return, but something else emerged too. Sadness. With startling clarity, she realized that no matter how much love she gave, she would never be enough.

Relenting, Ngọc Lan stopped, took off her wraparound cardigan, and put it on backward, creating a makeshift carrier. Jane's head rested against her mom's shoulder, her small sobs slowly returning to normal breaths. Ngọc Lan in turn rested her chin against Jane's neck and, together, they continued toward home. No words were spoken, no apology issued, just her mother's gentle circular strokes warming her back.

When Ngọc Lan found a ranger station, she told them she was lost. She asked for the bus route. The two men were so stricken by the state of her bare feet that one of them, Andrew, offered to give them a ride home instead.

"Home sweet home," Andrew said, putting the car in

park when they arrived. He hopped out to open the door. Despite the chafing between her toes, made by obvious blisters, Ngọc Lan slid off the leather seat, pretending they were perfectly fine.

"Thank you," she said, bowing slightly.

"No problem. Y'all have a good day now," he said with a salute, and off he drove.

For years after that day, Ngọc Lan would wonder what might possess a man to be that kind, to drive them nearly an hour out of his way with no expectation of anything in return.

When Phúc finally arrived at the apartment, his face registered surprise only momentarily before he said, "Where's the food? I'm hungry."

Dinner was already on the table. A fact that he could see as plainly as the stoic silence plastered across Ngọc Lan's face. He sat down. She served him a hot bowl of steaming rice, the same as she had every day for the past six years.

Ngọc Lan did her wifely duties, but what had already begun to break inside her cracked deeper when Phúc came home and pretended nothing at all had transpired—as though he had not abandoned his wife and daughter in the forest. Ngọc Lan thought of the jade pendant and necklace her mother gave the girls before they left. Her mom had kept this jewelry secret from their dad for their entire marriage. Now she understood why. When Phúc showed how callous he could be that day, Ngọc Lan resolved to collect a "dowry" for the future.

It was obvious to Evette, when Ngọc Lan showed up with a cashier's check for $6,000, that Ngọc Lan needed help. Evette immediately closed the shop and took Ngọc Lan to a bank, where they prepared the proper paperwork for transferring the title. She did more than sell the business to Ngọc Lan, though—Evette guided her through every part of the process, working side by side with Ngọc Lan for weeks while the sale moved through escrow. Beyond the logistics of business, Evette taught her practical skills too. She taught Ngọc Lan where to stash cash so they wouldn't lose everything if someone tried to rob them. And while Ngọc Lan concealed money from thieves, she took the liberty of hiding a little from her husband too.

Her intention wasn't ever to leave. She didn't know what she was saving for, she was simply compelled to do it.

Ngọc Lan's intuition about Evette was right: she was good people. She recognized in Ngọc Lan a kinship born of pain. Evette's ex-husband had been her high school sweetheart, a big Filipino man whose embrace felt like a blanket, secure and warm. But he went to Vietnam and came back a different person. Evette never needed to meet Phúc to know that his demand for control was a by-product of having none during the war.

A few days before closing—when the keys would officially be handed over to Ngọc Lan—Evette finally got to the part Ngọc Lan wanted to learn most, farming the crops. Ready to work hard and get dirty, Ngọc Lan arrived wearing tattered jeans and an old T-shirt. She found Evette at the back, Saran-wrapping packets of fresh jalapeños. The shop was closed on Tuesdays, so the two locked up and walked to Evette's rental plot in a nearby co-op garden. There, the two women tended to the soil, planted seeds, and laughed about how milkshakes gave them stomachaches but they drank them anyway.

As she learned each new skill, Ngọc Lan grew more confident in her ability to make this small business turn a profit.

And it did.

Within six months, the shop made more money than Phúc's mechanic shop paycheck brought home. One day, without notice, he quit and came to work at the store. He simply showed up in the morning and began fixing wobbly tables, clearing vents, and telling Ngọc Lan how to better to organize the merchandise. To his credit, he had a good eye for shelving, and by the end of three days, the little store rivaled other American-owned minimarts. Another change he insisted upon was that she keep meticulous books, a useful carryover from his previous job.

Weeks later, at a backyard barbecue at Phúc's friend Bác Luy's house, Ngọc Lan heard Phúc tell his friends about what Ngọc Lan had done. How she stole the money and bought the liquor store behind his back. He even admitted that if it had been up to him, they would never have done it.

"You're lucky," Bác Luy said. "That you married someone smarter than you." Everyone laughed as Ngọc Lan winced. She knew better than to laugh at a wounded man's ego. To her surprise, though, Phúc laughed along. The store's success seemed to ease a lot of stress.

Then the liquor license arrived.

When Evette bought the place, it had been a liquor store, and instead of getting a new sign, she simply flipped the sign inside out and wrote LAO MARKET in black paint. Ngọc Lan, seeing the wisdom in this, took the sign down once again. She scrubbed LAO MARKET away using baking soda, vinegar, and boiling-hot water. Then she flipped it back. The old banner matched the new store, and so it was that the liquor store was returned to its former glory.

And then the prodigal son was born. Me.

CHAPTER 38
PAUL

I'm sitting in my aunt and uncle's house, as I have a million times, except my mom is in the kitchen, cooking a giant rice cracker sheet over blue flames on the stove. Somehow, she belongs here, and *I'm* the guest.

"Cậu Hòa tells Mom that Paul is very smart. You get that from your Ông Ngoại. Ông was a man with an education. He designed buildings for the Americans."

"For real?" I say in English, and then rephrase in Vietnamese. "Are you telling the truth?"

"You shouldn't speak like a gangster," my mom says.

I laugh. "How does Mom know what a gangster sounds like?"

"Mom works in a casino. Mom sees everything," she says sternly. It dawns on me that she's actually chastising me. I'm not sure how I feel about that. On the one hand, who is *she* to be lecturing me? On the other hand, it's motherly, which *is* what she is. Mợ Bích shoots me a cautioning look. I let it go.

It's strange how sitting down to dinner together can feel so normal and completely wack. My mom and Cậu Hòa are nothing like

Jane and me. Mom is friendly and deferential in the way that Vietnamese women are. She serves my uncle his rice first; she hands him his beer with two hands. Even though I'm almost legally an adult, everyone treats me like a child. My uncle debones the catfish before putting a large piece into my bowl. No complaints here; deboning is a pain in the ass. I pour some sugared fish sauce over the catfish before cutting into it with my chopsticks.

"Here, make sure you get some of this fried pâté. I picked it up this morning. It's the best in town," my mom says to her brother.

He nods and takes a piece. You'd never know the two of them were screaming at each other yesterday morning. I get it, though. Jane is annoying as hell sometimes. We've had fighting matches that involved breaking things, only to return to normal a few hours later.

Suddenly, my mom's eyes go wide. "Is that—?"

She walks around the table to a small wooden elephant sitting on the ledge of a cuckoo clock. This ornately carved cabin cuckoo clock has been there for as long as I can remember. I never put it together that an elephant makes no sense next to a water wheel and barn.

My mom picks up the elephant, turning it over in her hand. "I can't believe you kept it all this time." To me she says, "Dì Diễm and Mom gave this to Cậu Hòa for his eighteenth birthday."

"Like back in Vietnam?" I ask. She nods. "Wow." In this moment, I've learned more about my uncle than in the entire eight years I've lived next to him. The fact that he kept this memento, this tiny wooden elephant, through battle, across an ocean, clear through his life in America, means my mother and her sister must have meant a whole freaking lot to him.

My mom's face tells me that she recognizes it too.

I slurp the rest of my food as my mom says, "Come, we have business."

I lazily drink a Coke, thinking they're about to go at it again, when I realize she's talking to me. "Business? What business do we have?"

She doesn't respond as she continues out the door. I drop my chopsticks over my empty bowl and follow.

My mom doesn't tell me where we're going. We drive north on the 680 freeway for twenty minutes until she pulls into a large driveway with colossal iron gates, CEDAR LAWN CEMETERY.

This is not good.

Mom walks about halfway up a hill. Sunlight beats down on my shoulders and a heat creeps up my neck. Cemeteries have always unnerved me. Hanging branches sway and flutter. Leaves flutter all around me, but I cannot feel the breeze. She stops at a grave marker with the name Diễm Hà and the dates July 19, 1961—April 1977. A chill runs down my spine. This is her—my ghost—my aunt.

"You've never been here. Cậu Hòa doesn't like to talk about his younger sister."

I swallow a pool of my own saliva. It singes my throat. Dì Diễm is here, all right. Mom is silent for a long time. I don't say anything in case she's praying. Eventually, she sighs loudly and says, "It's possible that remembering her hurts his heart, but Mom cannot fathom forgetting Chị Diễm."

My mom is being serious, but I can't stop thinking about the dead bodies under my feet. Vietnamese people don't put their feet on pillows—I can't imagine how they must feel about being stepped on. I move to the side. The headstones are placed so close together, though, that there's no way the bodies aren't overlapping underneath. Standing between the markers is still probably standing on someone. Even so, it's the best I can do. When I gaze at Mom, she seems hurt. She thinks I want to get away from my aunt.

"I don't like to stand on dead people," I say. To my relief, she laughs.

Still smiling, she winks at me deviously, then jumps up and down on the grave. My horrified expression makes her more hysterical. *My mother has lost it . . . or has always been lost,* I think. When she finally stops, she has tears in her eyes. I don't know if they are tears of joy or tears of anger—maybe both. "In this entire cemetery, this is probably the only burial place that does not have a body. Son, don't worry. Dì Diễm is not here."

"I don't understand," I say.

"Dì Diễm died at sea and is buried on Kuku Island. That is why there is no day of death here. Mom doesn't know when she died. So here," she says, pointing to the area she jumped all over, "for sure, there is no body. But that spot?" she adds, gesturing to my feet. "Mom doesn't know about."

I quickly move so that I'm standing next to her.

"If Dì Diễm is not here, why did you put this marker on the ground?"

"In Việt Nam, landowners were considered rich. Dì Diễm wanted nothing more than to own land. This plot isn't much, but it is a piece of earth she now owns."

That weirdly makes sense to me. I'm not real sentimental or anything, but I can see how much this means to my mom. To give my aunt something she always wanted. A cold, damp draft lingers at the base of my skull. I touch my aunt by grasping my neck. This time, though, it's to comfort my aunt. Dì Diễm is to my mom what Jane is to me. I get it.

Jane is like the backbone of my life. I can't imagine not having her around. Yes, she's a bossy know-it-all, but I know she made a lot of sacrifices to be at home with me when I was too young to take care of myself. Now that I'm the same age she was when she was taking care of me and thinking about leaving for college, I can see all the things she missed out on. Jane never went to any dances or parties. She never had friends over. Before college, I'm not sure Jane had ever set foot in a movie theater. If Jane complained about this, it was never to me. I always had clean clothes, and even though her cooking was horrible, I'm alive, so it was at least nourishing. She always found time to help me with my homework. Even when she left for college, she'd sit on the phone with me for hours while I learned to solve fractions (which, by the way, are the worst kind of math).

After Jane left, there was a void in the house. An empty chill that replaced her presence. I can't imagine how it would've felt if instead of leaving for school, she were dead. I feel for my mom. Losing her sister must have been hard.

"When you were still small, Mom remembers your big sister worrying about you. Jane is exactly like Dì Diễm—never thinking about herself. Mom knows leaving her children isn't right, but Mom knew your sister would watch over you."

The skeptical part of me wonders if she's making excuses for herself. Yes, Jane did step up, but Jane wasn't the one who had me. It wasn't her job to be my mother. The way my mom says this, it's almost as though she's saying she knew I would be okay because Jane was so much like her sister—a caretaker.

"Mom has been selfish."

Well, that's an understatement, I think. I'm thinking about how great it is that she's finally acknowledging her mistakes when she says, "Mom knows that Chị Diễm would want to be buried in Việt Nam, close to the ocean and by our mother, but Mom's life in America has been so lonely. I could not let go of her hand." And I realize she isn't talking about us. A conversation for another time. "Next month, I will fly to Kuku Island and bring her ashes back to Việt Nam."

"Why does Bà Ngoại think she's here? When I stayed with Grandma, she said Dì Diễm's soul was not at rest because you brought her to America instead of home."

"Mom didn't want Bà Ngoại to worry or see the sad place where we lived as refugees. So Mom lied to Bà Ngoại."

No wonder my aunt's spirit is restless. Her body is stuck on some random island far from family. I'd be pissed too and haunting the shit outta everyone.

"Mom is telling you this because even though you never knew her, Mom wants you to say goodbye."

I grapple with telling her that I *do* kind of know her. She's been haunting me. And not to be rude, but I would greatly appreciate her crossing over. "Chào Chị Diễm—"

"Xin chào Dì Diễm," my mom corrects. Right. *Chị* is older sister and *Dì* means aunt—the two are interchangeable for my mom, but she is Dì to me.

"Xin chào Dì Diễm. Về quê hương Việt Nam bình yên," I say. I really do hope she finds peace, not just for my sake but because thirty-something years seems like a long time to be wandering unhappily.

My mother nods. She bends down to touch the headstone marker, even though we both know her sister's not hanging out underneath it. "Em will return Chị Diễm home to be near Mẹ. Mẹ has really missed you. Does Chị know that? From now on, Mẹ will care for and look after you." It's weird for me to hear my mother call her own mom Mẹ, probably because I know my grandma and I know my mom, but I don't know them together.

I expect my mother to cry hysterically, to throw herself at the marker in a frenzy, but she doesn't. Instead, she says this in a tone as calm and breezy as Mai might say, "I'm going to grab my coat. I'll see you at the mall." That's when I notice how clean this grave is compared to the ones around it. Along the perimeter of the gravestone is a clear glass moat housing freshwater lilies.

"Has Cậu or Mợ ever taken you clamming?"

"No." What an odd thing to ask.

"When Mom was small, Cậu Hòa, Dì Diễm, and Mom used to catch clams every day. Bà Ngoại shared a stall at the market with a family from the community. Later Mom escaped with them. Come, let's go catch clams."

"Since Bà Ngoại sent you with another family, did they become your family?"

My mom nods. "In a way, yes. They live in Florida. Bác Hiếu and Bác Nga were always generous with what they had, even when they had little. They taught Mom how to do business when I was a small girl."

"Do you still talk to them?"

"Not much. People have their own lives. Everyone in America is so busy." The way she says "busy" sounds like she doesn't think it's a good thing.

We drive more than an hour to Half Moon Bay. Mom, with her hands clutched tightly on the wheel. Me, thinking about all the things I don't know. As we cruise along the coast, I think about Anh Sáu. He always thought I was judging him. I thought he had his head up his butt. He's wasn't totally off base, though. I'm so used to noticing all the ways that our Vietnamese-ness doesn't fit in, in America, that I judged his sandals because here in America *I* would be embarrassed to be seen wearing them. I've never considered that from his perspective my embarrassment was a reflection of him. When I do, it is pretty messed up.

Once we arrive, my mom nudges me out of my thoughts. "Leave your shoes in the car," she says. I kick my checkered Vans sneakers onto the car floor, peel off my socks, and leave them on the front seat. I can't remember the last time I walked around barefoot outside—it's nice. We head toward the ocean, passing a trash can, where my mom pulls two large Big Gulps out from the top. Each has a little soda still left in it, and one has bright pink lipstick caked onto the straw. I wish I could say this surprises me, but it barely registers until I see some girls my age gawking at us. The twisted, disgusted look of pity is nothing new to me, but I shift my eyes to the sand. If I don't look at them, they don't exist, and maybe the same will be true in reverse.

Việt Kiều thinks he's better than his mom? Dammit, Anh Sáu, get out of my head. That's not what I think. I'm just . . . I mean, she's pulling stuff from the *trash*. That's ghett—

I stop, glancing at my mom. She hasn't noticed my shame. Taking the lids off, she dumps the liquid before poking around to see if there might be another cup. When she doesn't spot anything, she says, "Better than nothing," in English.

The girls are already splayed out to bake in the sun.

My mom hits my arm. "Don't chase after girls like that."

She thinks I'm checking them out. "I'm not," I say in English.

She clicks her tongue against her teeth, unbelieving. "Those girls have no loyalty. You need to find a girl who is gentle and sincere."

"How does Mom know they have no loyalty?" I laugh.

"Mom just needs to look, and she knows." When she says this, she sounds so much like Bà Ngoại. My mom left Vietnam when she was twelve; it's been more than three decades of separation; yet this similarity is undeniable. Is this what it means to be family? To share the same blood?

"Okay, Mom," I say in English. What's hilarious is that if she knew what I was thinking, we wouldn't even be having this conversation. I change the subject. "What are the cups for?"

"To hold the clams."

Duh. See, most people would think to themselves *I want to go clamming.* Then they'd go to Walmart or Big 5 and buy supplies for the activity. They'd get a cooler or net or shovel or whatever—not my family. My family knows anything they need can be found in a trash can, so here we are. I suppose the upside is in a recycling competition, we'd win with our eyes closed.

At the shoreline, she rolls her pant legs up to her thighs. I'm wearing jeans, which makes this more complicated, but I follow suit. I'm able to get them above my knees. Then she stares, peering daggers at the sand. We walk for about a hundred yards, far enough away from the tanning girls that my ears have stopped burning—the sea breeze also helps.

"How does Mom know where to look?" I ask.

"Find seaweed first, then spot the places with little bubbles in the sand, like here." She points to an area that, to me, is identical to everywhere. I peer closer. Oh! There are pin-sized holes in the sand. I guess that's what she means by bubbles. She digs carefully with her hands. Within seconds she pulls up a clam.

"Easy." She smiles.

I shove my hands into the sand, immediately slicing my finger. "Ow!"

She laughs, because of course this is funny to her. The cut isn't deep. "Wash it in the beach water," she instructs. I do as she says. The gash stops bleeding pretty quick. Actually, it doesn't even sting anymore. *That's cool.* "Put your hand in the sand slowly. Feel for the clams. They're not deep."

I try again, cautiously this time. The tip of my finger hits something hard. But before I can get my grip around it, it's gone.

"You have to scoop from the bottom," she says, showing me that she's not grabbing like a claw clamp. She's sliding her fingers into the sand, then pushing sideways to scoop the clam into her palm.

I try again. "Yeah!" I shout, showing her my catch.

"Too small," she says. "Put it back."

"Oh," I reply, disappointed.

I go a little deeper. More small ones. Then finally I pull a three-inch clam. "Good, put it here." She hands me a Big Gulp containing a mixture of sand and water. For my one, she's already added what looks like ten or fifteen.

It doesn't take long to fill the cups. Done, we find a place to sit in the sand.

Looking out at the vast ocean, I hate to admit it, but this is the first time I've actually pictured myself setting off toward a horizon of nothing. So okay, maybe Jane was right in saying that we'll never know everything about our parents. It's one thing to know that they were refugees, it's a whole other thing to consider what that actually means.

"I want to know what happened to you. How you got here. Why you left us." Uncomfortable as it is, I stare directly at my mother. I'm not going away without an answer.

She doesn't speak for a long time, but when she does, she says, "I don't know if I have all the answers you want, but I will tell you my story." Her hands tremble, and her jaw shakes. "When I left you and your sister, I didn't think I'd be gone longer than a week. One week, a month, three years, now thirteen. Mom was really naive, extremely naive." The words tumble out, sounding defeated. "I thought once I decided to bring my sister home, I just had to do it. But because I fled Vietnam, no one, not the Americans, not the Vietnamese, would make it easy to return. Please try to understand. I had no passport, no papers, not enough money, many different problems."

Remembering the lessons from Bà Ngoại and Anh Sáu, I do my best not to sound accusatory. "When a week turned into a month, why didn't you come back?"

She nods. "The truth is I don't know. One part was fear. I was afraid that if I turned around, I wouldn't ever find the courage to try again. Another was I knew I was not a good mother. I'm sure Jane told you I nearly drowned you?" I shake my head and make a mental note to confirm this with Jane later. "Sometimes the only way is forward and when you make the mistakes I did, that means moving away." Her answers feel like disconnected thoughts, but I can tell she's trying. Her head drops. She swallows hard, shaking her head—at what? I'm not sure. Then she says, "I did the unforgivable, and then I forced myself to accept it."

"How? How could you be okay with leaving us?" I press.

"Before I left Việt Nam, the war broke my house. After I fled, it crumbled more. By the time you were born, I was used to surrendering to loss. I shouldn't have, a stronger mom wouldn't have, but I did."

Her words drip with shame. So many thoughts race through my mind, but time is the one that stands out. I've been blaming her for how much time has passed without acknowledging that before this summer it wouldn't have mattered if she returned. I never would have listened. "It's okay, Mom," I say. "We are here now. I'm ready to listen."

As she tells me about her childhood, about Vietnam during the war and after, the sun falls below the horizon. Stars begin to dot the sky when she recounts the Malaysian Navy sinking boats, and living on the uninhabited Kuku Island. Aching from the stillness of sitting too long, we stand to walk along the moonlit shore.

After Dì Diễm's body washed ashore in Indonesia, my mom

explains, her mind was constantly playing tricks on her. "I hugged her tight on that sand. I held her hand. My mind knew I had lost her. But my heart could not believe it."

The air is chilly, but the water is warm. As she recounts the loneliest parts of her history, I see a shimmer of blue and gold criss-cross around our ankles.

My mom stops.

I press my palm into the water beside my mom. I feel it too—the warm presence of my aunt. Neither of us speaks.

To anyone else, the faraway expression on my mom's face probably looks odd—like another personality or ghost has taken over—but I know what she's seeing. I see Dì Diễm too. She is here, bidding me farewell because she knows my mom will take her home soon.

"I don't want to let you go," my mom whispers. Her words are intimate, not meant for me to hear. I wish I could step back, except my feet are locked, ankle-deep, in the wet earth. So instead, I cover my mom's fingers with my own. Her hand trembles as she takes hold of mine. I squeeze firmly until the haze lifts and my mother returns.

Suddenly, the blue-and-gold specks turn fiery red. I look up to see ambulance lights in the distance. Coincidence? I'm not sure. The wave recedes, and with it, the colors drift with the tide. Together we watch as a shimmering aqua-yellow fishtail vanishes into the deep.

"Đi, let us go," Mom says. It's time to go home.

CHAPTER 39

NGỌC LAN

My birth set in motion a cascade of joy and fanfare. Finally, Ngọc Lan had given birth to a son.

Jane rolls her eyes but smiles in spite of herself. This is good because I don't think she will like what I'm going to tell her next.

When Paul was three, Ngọc Lan decided to teach him how to swim. She found an ad for the local YMCA, which hosted a free public use day once a month. A few other kids splashed around, but for the most part they had the pool to themselves.

Jane had learned how to swim from her friend Jackie, and she prided herself on being able to hold her breath and dive to the bottom, collecting plastic treasures Ngọc Lan tossed throughout. Kids always forgot toys at the park, and Ngọc Lan had amassed a shoebox of random plastic animals, rings, bracelets, doll accessories, toy cars, and Jane's favorite, a pink-and-purple seahorse, for this very occasion. She tried to mimic the treasures she and Chị Diễm used to find along the seabed back in Vietnam. Even though the waters were completely different, she could tell from Jane's agile movements that her daughter would gravitate to the natural wonders of the sea.

Unlike his sister, Paul did not like the water. When Ngọc Lan dipped his toes in, he shrieked as though covered in hot lava. But it was time. At the shallow end of the pool, Ngọc Lan gently rocked Paul in her arms until he stopped crying. Slowly, she peeled his body away from hers until he was at arm's length. He kicked like a horse underwater. She let him.

"Can I add more toys?" Jane asked from across the pool.

Ngọc Lan nodded while avoiding the splashes from Paul's flailing arms. Jane dumped the entire box into the pool. Most everything sank to the bottom immediately. The seahorse bobbed at the surface for a moment before drifting toward the deep end. Eventually, the seahorse also sank.

Exhausted, Paul reached for Ngọc Lan's neck. He clung to her for safety. Ever diligent, she gave him a tight squeeze before pushing him back onto his tummy.

"Gentle. Kick your feet like a duck. One up, one down. Move the water, don't hit it."

Paul slapped the water, kicking with revived energy. When he saw his mother stretch away from his splashes, he giggled. Ngọc Lan let him splash about, using his feet in a manner more akin to stomping than swimming. Finally, he was having fun. Her gaze moved to Jane.

In a single breath, Jane dove for the grouping of toys, gathering them all in her arms. She hesitated, deciding between the surface and the seahorse. Then, with steely determination, she swam toward the sparkling trinket. Bubbles floated along her braided hair—*had her hair been braided before?* Ngọc Lan wondered. Jane reached the seahorse and turned to Ngọc Lan, smiling. Only it wasn't her smile; it was Chị Diễm's. In a millisecond, Chị Diễm's grin turned grim.

Frozen in place, Ngọc Lan looked on as her daughter glided to the surface, leaving a trail of blue and gold in her wake. Within seconds, Jane stood before her.

"Mom! What are you doing?" Jane screamed.

Ngọc Lan looked down at Paul, who actually, at the moment, appeared quite serene beneath the water. She remembered he couldn't swim and immediately lifted his body up. Gulping for air, he wailed in fear. Jane pulled Paul from her in a protective embrace.

"He's fine," Ngọc Lan said, playing off her mistake. "This is how he learns to swim."

"By drowning him? Are you crazy? No." Jane moved away from Ngọc Lan. Ngọc Lan didn't follow. She stood fixed in place, watching as Chị Diễm's blue-and-gold fishtail disappeared from around Jane's legs.

Turning her gaze to the pile of toys Jane had dropped in the deep end, Ngọc Lan dove for the seahorse. As she picked up the jumble of things, she felt the familiar circular warmth of her sister dance around her. Above her, at the edge of the pool, she watched Jane comfort her brother. She knew then that her inability to let go of Chị Diễm was harming her children. Today it was nearly letting Paul drown, tomorrow it would be something worse. It was then that she knew it was time to go.

Ngọc Lan left her children behind in 1995, the first year since the end of the war that US-Vietnamese relations were friendly. This meant Vietnamese refugees in America could apply for visas to return to Vietnam. A gateway to Kuku Island had opened—it was time. Ngọc Lan planned to be gone for a week. But returning was not simple. One week turned into three months, then became three years, which turned into now.

For more than a decade, Ngọc Lan planned. But it wasn't until this year, 2008, that she was able to set foot in the place where Chị Diễm was buried. Fulfilling a promise long overdue, Ngọc Lan collected Chị Diễm's remains and carried her sister home.

"The end."

I finish awkwardly. It's awkward because even though this is the end of my story, it doesn't feel like the end. It feels like the unraveling of a beginning.

Jane sits still, calmly peeling away at some dry skin at the edge of her thumb. Then she turns to look at me. I think she's about to drop all kinds of feeling-bombs. That we're going to finally talk about our history and experiences so we can get on with our lives. Instead, she says, "You know, I've often felt like there was someone else jumping in, inside me."

Jane turns her head robotically and looks at me. I swear the blacks of her eyes have zero light. I stare in disbelief. "Uh . . . uh-hh," I stammer.

"I remember that day she tried to drown you. I was so pissed at her," Jane says. I was wrong, the stoicism is not Jane being apathetic, it's Jane trying to hide her emotions. Before this summer, Jane has told me she loves me maybe once in my life, but I've never needed to hear it. It's so clearly plastered all over her face; she loves the shit out of me. I wish she would talk to me, though. I wish I weren't so afraid that my forgiveness for my mom might drive her away.

"I d-don't remember it," I stammer. A stupid thing to say, because of course I have no recollection, I was only three at the time. But emotion makes me weird.

Jane ignores my bumbling response. "She didn't leave that day, though. It was months after."

I thought she might have an issue with that part. Before I can explain, she throws the blanket off her legs and asks, "Is that it?"

"Yeah," I say.

Jane stands up, folds the blanket (a neurotic tell that indicates my sister has not been taken over by a spirit), and declares, "I'm hungry. Let's go eat."

I follow her into the kitchen, thinking we're going to make ramen. Jane has other plans. She grabs her purse and drives us to a diner. Callahan's is inside a brown building with a pointy roof, making the restaurant seem like it might have been a church in its past life. I've never been here. We breeze inside. Jane swipes a menu from the empty hostess desk, ignoring the sign that reads PLEASE WAIT TO BE SEATED. *She takes up residence in a booth by the window. I slide in across from her.*

A waitress approaches with coffee for Jane and water for me. "The usual?" she asks.

"Yes. No, I'll have steak and eggs this time. And whatever he wants."

The woman looks at me as I quickly scan the menu. All the items blur together.

"It's a diner. Eggs, bacon, pancakes, French toast, waffles . . . ," Jane offers.

"Eggs, scrambled, with French toast . . . and bacon," I say, stumbling over my order.

"You got it," the woman says, without writing anything. She walks away.

"Dad took me here the morning after Mom left. I started coming back a few years ago. It's comforting." She takes a deep breath. Then looks me straight in the eye. "You can tell her to come in now."

I look out the window and see our mom's green Honda parked across the way. Mom knew I was telling Jane her story today. She must have followed us here.

"How—" I start, but Jane just stares at me. I hate it when she does this: acts like she's in control, even when she isn't. I open my phone, but Mom is already walking toward the entrance.

Nerves grip my shoulders as I wait for an explosion of angry yelling to disrupt the quiet of the diner. I move over so Mom can sit beside me. I decide I'll hold her hand, even though I don't want to take sides. On the real, though, Jane is no-joke scary when she's mad.

Mom nods at me but slides in next to Jane. I ready myself for an avalanche of questions, heated, angry, and full of resentment. But Mom's bold move appears to rattle Jane.

"Mẹ xin lỗi con," Mom apologizes.

And Jane, the strong, fierce, "get out of my way or I will crush you" boulder that is my sister, completely shatters. Tears cascade down her face. I'm pretty sure those four words, an apology without excuses, spoken sincerely by the person Jane wanted to feel loved by—but hasn't—held in them everything Jane had wanted to hear for over a decade.

I slide Jane's box across the table. This thing has been burning a hole in my pocket ever since I started telling her our mom's story. She opens it.

Inside the box, she unzips a small silk pouch, two things fall into Jane's palm: a circular jade pendant with a simple gold clasp and a gold bar with a dog. Jane was born in the year of the dog. My own box also had one, except with a monkey. "Is this from Bà Ngoại?" Jane asks, holding up the pendant.

Mom nods. "I carried that pendant with me from Việt Nam. It goes with the necklace around Paul's neck."

My hand shoots to the gold chain I've been wearing all summer. "Huh?"

"I hid it in a metal pipe by the register." Yup. That's where I found it. This necklace, an heirloom, was with Dì Diễm when she drowned. Knowing this makes the chain carry a certain weight it

didn't before. Where once I would've found the necklace chilling, now I find it comforting. I haven't felt Dì Diễm's presence since we met at the beach. I'm glad she's crossing over, for both her own peace and my mom's. There's a part of me, though, that wishes I'd actually gotten to know her. To know this aunt who affected my mother so deeply.

That's the thing about waiting so long to seek answers. Sometimes, by the time we're ready to listen, the memories have faded, or the person is no longer here.

I listen while Mom and Jane tumble toward a connection; it's stilted and uneasy, just as my own first meeting with Mom had been. Then suddenly, Jane turns to me with tears still in her eyes and laughs. "I love how you thought I wouldn't know Mom was here. I knew she was nearby the second you started telling her story."

I smile because this time I'm prepared for the L bomb. *"I love you too, Jane."*

CHARACTERS

MAIN CHARACTERS (IN ORDER OF APPEARANCE)

Paul Quốc Vũ—Ngọc Lan and Phúc's son. Jane's brother.

Jane Vũ—Paul's older sister. Daughter of Ngọc Lan and Phúc.

Ngọc Lan Hà / Mẹ—Paul and Jane's mother. Bà Ngoại's daughter.

Chị Diễm / Dì Diễm—Ngọc Lan's older sister. Paul and Jane's aunt. Anh Hòa's younger sister.

Cậu Hòa Hà / Anh Hòa—Paul and Jane's maternal uncle. Ngọc Lan's brother. He is married to Mợ Bích and lives next door.

Mợ Bích Hoàng / Chị Bích—Paul and Jane's aunt who lives next door. Cậu Hòa's wife. Ngọc Lan's sister-in-law. Cô Đào's sister.

Lê family—Bác Hiếu, Bác Nga, Anh Minh, Chị Mậu (daughter-in-law), Anh Luân.

Phúc Vũ / Chú Phúc / Ba—Paul and Jane's dad.

Anh Sáu—Paul's second cousin. Son of Mỹ Khanh, who is the daughter of Bà Kính, the eldest sister of Bà Tâm (Paul's grandmother).

Mẹ / Bà Ngoại / Grandma / Hang Ngô—Ngọc Lan's mom (women don't change their last names). Paul and Jane's maternal grandmother. Bà Ngoại means maternal grandmother. Ngọc Lan would call her mom Mẹ, whereas Paul will refer to her as Bà Ngoại. It's a Vietnamese thing.

Ba / Ông Ngoại / Vinh Hà—Ngọc Lan's dad. Paul and Jane's maternal grandfather. Ông Ngoại means maternal grandfather.

Ngọc Lan and her siblings call him Ba, for father, whereas Paul, the grandson refers to him as Ông Ngoại.

Bà Nội / Grandma / Bà Tâm—Phúc's mother. Paul and Jane's paternal grandmother. Anh Sáu's great-aunt.

Ông Nội / Ngọc Thái Vũ—Paul and Jane's deceased paternal grandfather. Bà Nội's husband. Phúc's father.

OTHER CHARACTERS (IN ALPHABETICAL ORDER)

Becky—Bác Luy and Bác Nguyệt's daughter. Vicky's sister. The sisters made the photo that Ngọc Lan steals at Paul's house. Paul and Jane's pseudo-cousin.

Bì—Teenage boy who lives in the same apartment complex as Ngọc Lan's dad, in America.

Bé Bình—Neighborhood boy whose body washes ashore.

Bác Cào—Chị Tuyết's father.

Chị Chau—Đại Tá Duy Thái's wife. First madame to help Bà Ngoại / Mẹ when she was starting out.

Anh Chim—Paul's motorbike driver in Vietnam.

Chó—Dog. Ông Nội and Bà Nội's dog in Vietnam.

Bác Chuyên—Deacon, largely featured in *My Father, the Panda Killer.*

Colin—US Navy man who jumps rope with Ngọc Lan on the boat to Guam.

Chị Đào / Cô Đào—Mợ Bích's sister. She lived with the Lê family in their first apartment.

Đạo—Anh Minh's friend who loses his father to a Malaysian sniper.

Bác Dạy—Ngọc Lan's most militant uncle, who dies in the war.

Đại Tá Duy Thái—North Vietnamese businessman/member of the party. Frequent buyer of Mẹ's fish sauce during and after the war.

Evette—Laotian store owner who sells the present-day liquor store to Ngọc Lan.

Anh Hiệp—Anh Sáu's motorbike driver in Vietnam.

Bác Hiếu Lê—Patriarch of the Lê family who flees Vietnam with Ngọc Lan. Husband of Bác Nga. Father of Anh Minh and Anh Luân.

Bác Hồ—Seamstress who makes Ngọc Lan's engagement áo dài.

Cô Hoài—Ngọc Lan's stepmother. Ba / Ông Ngoại's second wife.

Jackie—Jane's former best friend.

Jacob—Filipino soldier who helps Ba / Ông Ngoại flee Vietnam via helicopter.

Joe—Paul's best friend, along with Mai.

Mr. Khan—Mechanic shop owner. Phúc's boss.

Chị Kim—Bà Ngoại's soothsayer at the Buddhist temple.

Bà Kính—Anh Sáu's maternal grandma. Bà Nội's older sister.

Bác Loan—Family maid in Vietnam.

Bác Long—Paul and Jane's paternal uncle. Phúc's brother.

Anh Luân—Bác Hiếu and Bác Nga's son. The man Ngọc Lan wanted to marry. Anh Minh's younger brother.

Bác Luy—Phúc's best friend. Husband of Bác Nguyệt. Father of Vicky and Becky. Largely featured in *My Father, the Panda Killer.*

Mai—Paul's best friend, along with Joe.

Anh Minh—Bác Hiếu and Bác Ngà's oldest son. Husband of Chị Mậu. Older brother of Anh Luân.

Mỹ Khánh—Anh Sáu's mother.

Mỹ Linh—Half-Black friend whom Ngọc Lan meets in Indonesia.

Bác Nga Lê—Matriarch of the Lê family Ngọc Lan flees Vietnam with. Bác Hiếu's wife. Mother of Anh Minh and Anh Luân.

Bác Nguyệt—Bác Luy's wife. Mother of Vicky and Becky. Largely featured in *My Father, the Panda Killer.*

Chị Oanh—Neighborhood girl whose fiancé died in the war. According to Chị Diễm, his ghost keeps trying to tell her he's dead.

Chú Phương—Bà Ngoại's chauffeur.

Chị Quyên—Chị Diễm's childhood friend who disappeared, then later found Chị Diễm's body.

Ông Sơn—Horticulturalist who makes Ngọc Lan a comb in Indonesia.

Chị Tuyết—Ghost. Teen whom Ngọc Lan encounters when looking for Chị Diễm at the burning market. Bà Ngoại says she has been dead for a long time.

O Uyên—Paul's aunt. Phúc's younger sister. Bà Nội will live with her in America.

Cô Văn—Chị Diễm's boss. Owner of a fabric and sewing stall at the market. She burns her own business when the Communists try to loot it.

Vicky—Becky's sister. Bác Luy and Bác Nguyệt's daughter. Paul and Jane's pseudo-cousin.

HONORIFICS

Mẹ—Mother

Ba—Father

Ông Nội—Paternal grandfather

Ông Ngoại—Maternal grandfather

Bà Nội (Mệ)—Paternal grandmother

Bà Ngoại (Mệ)—Maternal grandmother

Ông—Refers to any male of grandparents' age

Bà—Refers to any female of grandparents' age

Anh—Older brother or a polite term to use toward an unfamiliar male regardless of their age in reference to the person addressing

Chị—Older sister or a polite term to use toward an unfamiliar female regardless of their age in reference to the person addressing

Em—Younger sibling or refers to someone younger

Bác—Aunt or uncle who is older than the parents of the person addressing. Also a polite term to use toward anyone older, of an age comparable to one's parents, not related to the person addressing

Chú—Younger uncle on father's side

Cậu—Older uncle on mother's side

Cô—Younger aunt

O—Aunt on father's side

Dì—Older aunt on mother's side

Thím—Younger aunt-in-law

RESOURCES

If you or someone you care about is going through a tough time with abuse at home or mental health struggles, there are people and resources ready to support you.

Asking for help is hard, I know. If this book resonated with you, then "breaking the cycle" begins with you. Remember to be gentle and kind with your healing self. You have been through a lot.

The following organizations provide confidential services to support teens in exploring safety plans and understanding their legal rights and options.

If you are experiencing an immediate crisis, call or text 988.

FOR ABUSE

National Domestic Violence Hotline

Call 1-800-799-SAFE (1-800-799-7233)

or text START to 88788

thehotline.org

Crisis Text Line

Text HOME to 741741

(Available 24/7)

National Runaway Safeline

Call or text 1-800-RUNAWAY (1-800-786-2929)

1800runaway.org

FOR MENTAL HEALTH

National Alliance on Mental Illness

Call 1-800-950-6264

or text HELPLINE to 62640

or email helpline@nami.org to connect with the teen and young adult helpline

SAMHSA's National Helpline

Call 1-800-662-HELP (1-800-662-4357) for help locating the right services for you or your loved one

AUTHOR'S NOTE

Mother-daughter relationships are beautiful, nourishing, and complex. A Vietnamese reader will not be surprised to hear that my mother never said "I love you." In fact, if you're anything like me, you're probably tired of the trope of the Asian parent who does not show affection through dialogue.

My mother loves me. I don't need verbal confirmation to know that she does, but throughout my life, she made choices that were not in service of protecting me or my siblings. Those choices led to the feelings of abandonment that fill the pages of this book.

In my story, Paul lacks answers because Ngọc Lan was not physically present. For me, I lacked answers because my mother is emotionally inaccessible. Both are the result of unprocessed trauma. When I first heard the antanaclasis "Hurt people hurt people," I did not yet have the language skills to interpret the phrase. When I figured out that it meant unprocessed trauma lends itself to abuse, I spent years learning how to balance forgiveness *without* acceptance. This was key. To accept was to repeat. My goal was to break the cycle.

In order to do this, I had to realize that the language barriers—both verbal and emotional—were *not* a lack of love but rather an inability to express that love. This leads me to my next topic: word choice. Throughout this book, readers are likely to find insensitive terms. I kept these phrases in part because this story takes place in 2008 but also because even in 2025 conscious word choice is still a work in progress; my work reflects my reality. That said, I hope readers have circled the words (yes, I write in books), made a note, and debated my usage with one another. Then email me about it. Really! Let's talk.

I am a writer on a journey of understanding and healing. The work is as daunting as it is often lonely, so I sincerely thank you for walking alongside me as I explore an ocean of emotions.

ACKNOWLEDGMENTS

I have been fortunate in my life to be surrounded by so many strong women. This book is dedicated to you: Mệ, Mom, Dì Van, Kimberly, and Lillyan. I could fill ten books with the lessons/gifts my grandmother, mother, aunt, and sisters have given me, but for the sake of time, I'll say this: I would not be the person I am without your influence. Together, we have fought—both against and alongside one another—for better. It is not easy to change the status quo, but we have. Of course, I am also grateful to my dad, Richard Hoang, and brother, Andrew Quoc-Viet Hoang, who have long been outnumbered.

A great many thanks to:

My editor, Phoebe Yeh, who not only shaped and refined the story but continues to fight for my work to get into the hands of teen readers everywhere. I am lucky to have you in my corner. And to everyone at Random House Children's Books, who worked tirelessly behind the scenes, especially Joey Ho, Daniela Cortes, Adrienne Waintraub, Natalie Capogrossi, Michelle Campbell, Trisha Previte, Megan Shortt, Tisha Paul, Patricia Callahan, Debra DeFord Minerva, and Alison Kolani. Stars of gratitude must also go to Marcos Chin. Your work sparks joy; thank you for lending such a careful hand to the creation of Paul's and Jane's images. You are magic.

Jennifer Weltz and the whole JVNLA team, you were the first agency to give me a chance. I am grateful for the guidance and opportunities you've given me.

My extended family. My in-laws, aunts, and cousins, whose stories have filled my belly with literal food and figurative joy. Especially Shirley Stimac and Ed Eslinger, Lynneara Hoang, Kym Oanh Solancho, Mai Dinh, Linh Nguyen, Nguyet Reilly, Khannie Bueno, Kim Nguyen, Bao Nguyen, Dang Khoa Nguyen, Kristine Hoang, Gimy Nguyen, and Kevin Nguyen.

Those who answer my phone calls and texts at odd hours without exasperation or judgment: Mai Nguyen Ha, Jessica Ng, Stephanie Tang, Indigo Wilmann, Chi Thuy Rhee and Dr. Ed Rhee, Sara Taylor, Khanh Thai, Eric Gee, Mikey Ngo, Adam Vaun, Nicole Noonan-Miller, Lina Wood, Shawn Muttreja, and Ellen Burns.

My husband, Ryan Eslinger, who is my first reader, final critic, and tireless cheerleader. Not only do you make the latte that jumpstarts my creativity every morning, you carry mc through the slumps and remind me to enjoy the wins. Also, let it be immortalized here that currently, Tash thinks you're hilarious.

Taschen, you are the future every generation before you made sacrifices for. No pressure. I kid, I kid! Our only hope for you is that you find joy in whatever you decide to pursue. I promise that my vise grip on your shoulder is really just a steady hand of support.

YOU, the reader. Thank you for riding these emotional waves with me. Every page you turn is another swell we crest, and I don't know about you, but I could use some Dramamine.